Deborah Wright's first novel, *Olivia's Bliss*, was a best-seller in 2000. It won the *Ireland on Sunday* 'Write a Bestseller' competition and was chosen for the WH Smith Fresh Talent award. She divides her time between London and Manchester and enjoys fencing, writing songs and transcendental meditation.

Deborah loves to hear from her readers, so you can e-mail her: deborah@deborahwright.co.uk or visit her website, www.deborahwright.co.uk

The Rebel Fairy

Deborah Wright

TIME WARNER PAPERBACKS

A *Time Warner* Paperback

First published in Great Britain in 2002 by
Time Warner Paperbacks

Copyright © Deborah Wright 2002

A CIP catalogue record for this book
is available from the British Library.

ISBN 0 7515 3204 5

Typeset in Plantin by M Rules
Printed and bound in Great Britain by
Clays Ltd, St Ives plc

Time Warner Paperbacks
An imprint of
Time Warner Books UK
Brettenham House
Lancaster Place
London WC2E 7EN

www.TimeWarnerBooks.co.uk

★

This book is for
S.L.K.
With all my love

Acknowledgements for Humans

Lots of thanks, hugs, kisses and love to everyone. To my family – especially my mother for giving me a newspaper article on my birthday in '97 which first sparked the idea for the book; to Popsicle, Jules and Candida.

My friends: special thanks to the wonderful Alexander Hewitt for spending hours taking me around Primrose Hill, showing me the sights. To Paul Stanley for supplying a quiet house, to John and Nicky Collins, and David W. To Alex Hankey for his warm friendship and support (love to Geoffrey and all at No. six too!), Ray, Gary Robertshaw, Sarah Plaitt. Thanks to mrx for passionate inspiration. To Dylan Evans and Scarlett Thomas for advice and friendship. Thanks to people who agreed to look at early versions of the book and give comments, especially Lewis and Victoria Connelly. Thanks to Felicity, Eric and all at Badingham for providing such a lovely, welcoming place to rest and recuperate and revive my creative energies. And thanks to the friends I made there who supplied amusing anecdotes (you know who you are!).

A big thank you to my editor, Tara Lawrence, for her warm friendship, enthusiasm and meticulous editing, and for her stream of e-mails and phone calls of support during the frantic rewriting periods! To my excellent agent, Simon Trewin, for saving me from bankruptcy, and for his helpful advice and great sense of humour, and also to his lovely assistant, Sarah. Thanks too to Tom Bromley for sparky copy and Jo Coen for her splendid editing. To the formidable Ursula Mackenzie, and everyone else at Little, Brown and Company.

Above all, thanks to S.L.K., for everything. Your invisible watermark is stamped on each page of this book – every word is inspired by my love for you.

Acknowledgements for Fairies and Other Supernatural Creatures

I will admit that this book is not entirely a product of my imagination. Many real fairies assisted me in my task. In order to protect them, I have changed the names of all the fairies except for Puck, who made a personal request that I use his real name.

Thank you to Charlie, Fairy of the Tiger Lily, for telling me about the history of fairylore with such wit and zest, and for reading through the final copy of this manuscript to check for magical errors. During the writing of this novel (1997–2001), I frequently visited Primrose Hill where the London Fairy Circle resides. However, I have been asked to remind readers that if, after reading this book, they decide to visit the tree in Primrose Hill where the fairies live, to please keep quiet during the daytime when the fairies are asleep.

Thank you to Puck for coping so well with my brief and embarrassing crush. (I mean, I've never been a woman who worried about size but when the man in question is only 10 inches tall, well, fairies and humans, I concede, are just not meant to be together.)

Thank you to all the fairies who volunteered to be photographed for my website. Thanks too for teaching me spells to enable me to ensnare the man of my dreams. Not to mention cursing my enemies (so if anyone reads this book and writes a bad review – remember, I have friends in high places).

The
Rebel Fairy

1

Jack

Jack sat in The Goat pub that Sunday night with no idea that his destiny was about to change. In truth, Jack didn't believe in destiny and he didn't care much about the future. Unlike most of his friends, he didn't concern himself with pensions, mortgages or marriage certificates, or anything of permanence, anything requiring a signature, anything binding.

Eight years ago, after scraping through University College, London, with a third-class degree that he felt ought to have been for 'Getting Pissed In The Student Bar', with an Honours in 'Having To Be Carried To Bed at Two In The Morning' rather than English Literature, Jack had drifted through the '90s travelling, temping, travelling, having flings, having fun.

He never stayed anywhere for too long, with little idea of what he would do next. Currently he was back in his home city, London, in a small flat in Camden. He'd got the flat on his return from three months in Thailand, arriving as brown as an acorn, his dark hair streaked blond like a tiger's coat, shivering in the grey English drizzle as though it was the Arctic, a shock after the warm kisses of the rosy Eastern sun. He'd wanted to jump on a plane and go right back, but his wallet was empty and his credit cards bursting. So instead he'd responded to an ad in *Loot* for a 'comfortable one-bedroomed flat with kitchen and pleasant view'. It had turned out to be a pretty dire one-bedroomed box with a fridge and a view of some dustbins, but it was cheap and near to his old university friends, so he'd taken it.

He'd been there six months – his longest lease so far. He'd even acquired a dog – a large, brown-eyed, chocolate-coloured mongrel, who at that moment in time was lying in her newspaper-filled basket, thumping her tail, watching TV (Jack was always forgetting to turn it off), barking at John Cleese and Mark Lamarr, waiting for her master to return.

No, the only pressing worry on Jack's mind was how he was going to afford his next pint. He'd had four tonight. He was just slipping into a mild hazy state where the edges of his brain were brown and pleasantly foggy. The pub had taken on a kind of cosy, ye olde glow and the shouting din had somehow muted.

There was one other slight annoyance at present, however.

And that was the girl by his side.

'Shall I get us a drink?' she asked tightly, inadvertently solving his first problem.

'Er . . . yeah, great.' Jack looked relieved. She smiled too, rummaging in her shiny black handbag, catching a long, hard, frosty nail as she clicked open her purse.

'A Guinness, thanks.'

'Fine.' She leaned over and he paused awkwardly. Oh wonderful, she was going to buy him a drink and now she wanted a kiss! For one awful moment he felt like shoving her away and barking, 'Look, it was just a *one-night stand*.

4

A last tango in Camden. And that's it. And I'm really sorry but it is what we agreed, OK? Why can't you just fuck off and leave me *alone*?' Instead he swallowed it all back, compromised and gave her a light kiss on the cheek.

Jack watched her go. His friends did too. Her bottom sashayed in her tight PVC trousers, her bra straps peeped tantalisingly through her silky pink shirt, her ankles slender in her black high-heels. He watched her nails tapping impatiently on the bar counter. The same nails that had left scratch marks on his back last night, the little pinky scars still visible, like initials etched possessively on to a tree.

'She's nice.' Steve nodded appraisingly.

Jack nodded glumly.

Nice. Yes, last night she'd seemed nice, when he'd spotted her in that wine bar in Soho. He'd gone along with Henry, a friend from his university days. Jack and Henry were complete opposites – Jack had been brought up on a council estate in London, Henry had been educated at Harrow. Jack looked rough and laddish; Henry was tall and slender with floppy Hugh Grant hair and a faint stutter when he was nervous. Jack never got nervous. But though he couldn't resist taking the piss out of Henry a lot of the time, he had huge affection for him, as though he was his brother. So when Henry had asked him to the wine bar, he'd said sure, why not?

The wine bar had been very posh and filled with women. Beautiful, rich women everywhere, like birds of paradise – a menagerie of suits and jewels, perfumed hair and champagne laughter. Jack's eyes had been on stalks. He'd felt weak. After a string of disastrous love affairs he'd promised himself not to pull tonight but he'd felt like an ex-alcoholic staring at a pint of foamy beer.

5

Most of the women had been looking at Jack too. He had exchanged his usual Levis and T-shirt for chinos and a blue shirt, borrowed from Henry. He looked like a preppy City lawyer. He'd felt awkward and clumsy, like a dressed-up little boy who was allowed to look but not touch.

He'd met Dominique when he'd accidentally walked into the Ladies loos (the modern circled symbols on the doors had been ambiguously androgynous).

'Hi,' he'd laughed. 'Oops!'

Dominique had looked at him and thought, *God, this guy is gorgeous, I want to marry him.*

Jack had looked at her and thought, *Oh God, please can I go home with her tonight?*

And so he had. They'd left at eleven in a taxi, after Jack had said a sheepish goodbye to Henry, having spent the evening ignoring him. He and Dominique had knocked back cocktails, their body language sizzling with suspense, their eyes undressing each other, hands brushing as Jack had tucked a little cocktail umbrella behind her ear, her breath tickling his ear as she'd bent over to shout above the loud music. In the back of the taxi Jack had cuddled her against him, looked up at the white moon bobbing above London, impaled on a spire like the head on a jester's stick, and felt happiness explode inside him. Overwhelmed and on a high, he'd turned and kissed her and whispered drunkenly in her ear, 'I love you!'

Big mistake. The next morning he had slowly peeled open his eyes, feeling his hangover not only in his head but all over his body, as though his limbs had been ripped apart and clumsily sewn back together.

He'd done a double-take. UrghohGodwhowasthis girl lying beside him? Awake, watching him sleeping, with a soft, gooey smile on her face?

'I love you,' she'd whispered tenderly.

Jack had felt bile rising in his throat, leaped from the bed and only just made it to the bathroom in time.

After that, he'd done all he could to make it clear it was just a one-night stand. He'd told her he had to go to the dentist.

'On a Sunday?' she'd frowned.

Good point. Jack had turned away, cursing his stupidity while pulling on his socks. That also cut out excuses about having to dash off for a crucial doctor's/chiropodist's/optician's appointment or a phantom job with an angry boss who would kill him if he wasn't there by nine on the dot. Shit, shit, shit . . .

'Sorry – my Mum.'

'What?' she'd replied as she came out of the kitchen carrying two mugs of tea.

'My Mum. She's sick, I have to visit her.'

'I'll come too.'

'You can't. She's . . . senile. Ga-ga. Goes mad if anyone new comes along. She might get violent – she throws sugar bowls about.'

'Well, I'll just wait outside.'

Oh God. Jack had realised that he had a challenge on his hands. A limpet woman. And he was too hungover to be a real bastard and just tell her to go away. He didn't have the energy.

So he'd let her follow him back to his flat, hoping that the mess would shock her and put her off for life. But apart from her initial cries of, 'Oh, you've been burgled!' and then embarrassment at the realisation that the magazine-strewn, underwear-splattered carpet, dirty mugs piled high on the table and boxer-shorts-hanging-off-TV-aerial effect was a normal state of affairs, she hadn't blinked. Not even when his dog, Dido, had bounded about maniacally, barking as if to cry, 'Why haven't you taken me for a walk? Who is this girl? Introduce me, Jack!' before slobbering over Dominique with her tongue as if she wished she was human and could say hello. Even when they'd taken Dido for a walk and the dog had fouled the pavement, she'd merely smiled. When they'd wandered vaguely past the closed shops and cafés and she'd paused outside a jeweller's, Jack had nearly fainted, convinced she was picking out engagement rings.

She'd stayed throughout the afternoon, even though he'd put on the football (a video, too, not even live) and ignored everything she'd said, wincing if she got up past the TV to go to the loo. She'd offered to cook tea but he'd snarled, 'I'll do it,' and gone off to make her a Pot Noodle. If there was one way to put a girl off, Jack had figured, it was to make her something that required the least amount of effort possible. It was the reverse of offering someone your last Rolo. She'd have to hate him, he'd thought, pouring on hot water and watching the noodles puff into yellow and red sluggish shapes. But no. She'd merely eyed it up, cried, 'Yummy – how sweet of you to cook!' and then delicately eaten it as though it was a pot of caviar. Incredible.

Jack had retreated to the loo and sat with his head in his hands. He'd come out fifteen minutes later to find her looking a little put-out.

'Your mum called,' she'd said a little icily. 'She said she'd just won a game of Scrabble with your younger sister. I didn't catch the crash of flying sugar bowls.'

She'd come along with him to the pub, despite his protests that his friends would hate her. By now Jack was starting to go mad – he'd been nice, he'd been a gent, but couldn't she take a hint? What was she made of, Velcro? It was a Sunday night – normally his quiet night, when he and his friends drank and recalled the weekend – tales of pints and scores, football and cricket debates, card games and snooker matches. He'd seen all his friends' raised eyebrows and *nudge-nudge-wink-wink* looks when he'd had to stand there and introduce her to them all: 'Dominique – meet Steve. David. Frog – don't ask how he got that name. Phil. Mark. Pem.' He could see they were all thinking, *Wow, Jack's finally done it, found a girl he actually likes.* Only he hadn't. He felt tired and drained; he wanted to be alone.

And, worst of all, he could feel the time coming when he would have to say out loud: 'Dominique, you can't come back tonight, or any night. It's over.' How would she react? Tears, no doubt. Insults. It was going to be awful; he had a headache thinking about it.

As Dominique returned with the drinks, Jack hastily picked up a *Sunday Mirror* that was strewn on the table, moodily shutting her and the group out with a wall of newspaper.

Anyway, Jack carried on, justifying it to himself fiercely, *I'm crap at relationships.* It was better to end it all now rather than in a few weeks when she would be even more attached. He knew there was no point in dating; it would just be his usual three-month cycle.

It always followed the same pattern. At first there was euphoria. Wonderful sex. Three-hour telephone conversations, where they seemed to have everything in common and there were constant exclamations of, 'Oh wow, I've always felt that way too!' and 'Is *The Godfather* really your all-time favourite film? You're kidding because that's *my favourite* too!' Life seemed perfect; he found himself grinning all the time, as though he belonged in a musical with Julie Andrews.

And then he would start to notice things. Annoying things. Tiny things about his girlfriend, who had seemed so perfect, began to niggle him. Like the way she sneezed, or her knobbly knees, or the fact that she had no ear lobes.

And soon enough that seven-week itch would be creeping up on him. He would find Friday nights cuddled up watching a video boring compared to all the fun his friends were having. Instead of feeling butterflies when she called, he spent most of the conversation doodling on the phone pad. And then, because he always felt guilty, he would try to push them into dumping him. Only that never worked either – it generally led to a barrage of nervous questions: 'Are you all right? . . . You seem quiet . . . You seem *funny* tonight . . . Was it something I said?'

Every time this happened, Jack grew increasingly exasperated with himself. He didn't know what the matter was. He couldn't settle down with anyone, just as after spending a few months in a foreign city he had the urge to pack up, pick up his passport and move on to explore virgin territory once more.

So he'd decided to leave off relationships and just have flings, to avoid the heartbreak and misery. Which was all rather ironic, considering how Dominique was behaving in the pub tonight.

'What are you reading?' Dominique peeled down the corner of his newspaper.

Jack rolled his eyes huffily as though he was a passenger on the Tube and a stranger was reading over his shoulder.

'Oh, wow. Stars!' Dominique cried. 'What star sign are you?'

'Don't know.' Jack fixed his eyes on an article with an outrageous headline: WOMAN SPOTS UFO OVER HOUSES OF PARLIAMENT.

'Don't know! How can you not know what star sign you are?' Dominique looked appalled. 'You're a Scorpio, I bet – sexy and stinging.'

'No, I'm not a Scorpio.' Jack carried on reading. *Ms Martha Matthews, aged 48, has claimed to have spotted a UFO in the sky on her way home from work. Ms Matthews, who works for the Inns of Court School of Law . . .*

'But how—'

'Will you listen to this?' Jack appealed to his table and they all perked up, grinning – Jack was going to start on one of his monologues and it was bound to be funny. 'According to the *Sunday Mirror*, a 48-year-old Ms Matthews has seen a UFO above the Houses of Parliament.'

'UFO!' Steve snorted. 'More like Gail Porter – didn't they flash her picture up on Parliament?'

'Must have been a flying breast!' Jack said and they glanced at each other and exploded into laughter.

'Oh, I think it could be real!' Dominique looked upset. 'The other day, my grandma was telling me about a group of scientists who had discovered some dead rabbits, their insides dissected using alien surgical techniques – as if aliens had done it to find out more about humans! My grandma says we're being observed.'

'Your grandma probably needs to go to an OAPs home,' Jack muttered into his beer.

'Really.' Dominique looked flushed. 'The unexplained has to be real. There are people all over the place who have had out-of-body experiences and they have all said the same thing, even people who don't believe in them. It's the same with ghosts – and hey, what about crop circles? Nobody can explain them. It can't all be people making it up or going mad.'

'Oh bullshit.' Jack, who loved arguments, could feel

his anger revving up. They were using the story as a front now – a way to insult each other under the guise of a 'debate', words clashing and interrupting like swords. 'It's all psychological.' Jack's voice rose. 'What happens if you see a scary movie, like *The Shining*? You spend the night rigid in bed, thinking every noise is a ghost. And some people are naturally nervous; they hear a few creaky doors – which would be solved by a bit of oil – and their imagination goes bonkers. The next thing you know, they're living in a haunted house. Ghosts are just names we give to our own fears. OBEs – just weird dreams when you've eaten a particularly painful curry. As for crop circles – what is so amazing about them? It's just a natural phenomenon. Unusual, I admit, but nature is full of unusual things. Earthquakes are unusual, if you think about it. So are typhoons, but we don't make up silly explanations for them. It's all in our heads.'

'Maybe it's a government conspiracy to distract us from the Railtrack fiasco.' Steve tried to lighten things up.

'I'd put money on it,' Jack told them. 'A hundred quid that in two weeks there will be another article with the headline WOMAN SEES UFO AND IS COMMITTED!'

'But the photos—' Dominique began.

'Photos are easily touched up. I read men's magazines so I'm an expert,' Jack said, prompting more laughter. 'They're always removing moles and eyebrows or whatever on models these days. This photo –' he jabbed the *Mirror* '– is just like the Cottingley fairy hoax. For years people believed fairies existed from those photos – and then what? We find out they were just cardboard cut-outs on sticks.'

'Yeah, Jack,' Pem blew out cigarette smoke, 'but Ms Martha Matthews or whatever this woman's called could hardly have got her friends to sit on the top of the Houses of Parliament with a flashlight, could she?'

12

'Yes, she could hardly have got her friends to sit on the top of the Houses of Parliament with a flashlight, could she?' Dominique repeated stutteringly.

'Could she?' Jack mimicked sarcastically. 'I don't know. The white light could have been a firework. Anything.'

'It could have been a falling dolphin covered with fluorescent paint,' Steve suggested, who was rather a fan of *The Hitchhikers' Guide to the Galaxy*.

'Have you been drinking again?' Jack put on a Northern accent, an old banter they shared when Steve got wacky. 'No, it's all rubbish – ghosts, fairies, UFOs, the lot. Crap. A human invention to try to make the dullness of life that bit more interesting.' He took a sip from his pint.

'Amen,' Dominique finished sulkily. She was looking put-out; she was obviously getting the message now.

A brief silence descended over the table. Jack picked up his paper again, self-conscious. Out of the corner of his eye he could see Dominique biting her lip, blinking hard, taking a thick sip of her Baileys. She looked as if she wanted to cry. Jack pictured her going home that night, after he'd told her to get lost. He pictured her being like his younger sister, Kelly, who was twenty-four and on the look-out for Mr Right but always finding Mr Commitment-Phobic instead and ending up getting dumped. Afterwards, Kelly would curl up in her duvet with a Chocolate Orange and call her girlfriends for hours, crying and unpicking every thread of the tapestry of their break-up. Often Jack would barge in and try to cheer her up with a pillow fight or a big hug, declaring the ex was a bastard he'd like to beat up.

Suddenly he felt a wave of sympathy for Dominique and had to stop himself from reaching out and stroking the back of her hand. He loathed himself for a moment. God, if he was a girl he'd hate to go out with someone like him; why did women love bastards so much? Maybe he could take her number, they could make amends and be friends, have the odd pizza, offer each other advice on failed romances. Or maybe not.

'Fancy a game of snooker?' Steve asked.

'Sure.' Jack jumped up in relief.

Three hours later, Jack turned up at Katie's house in Princess Road, Primrose Hill. His fingers trembled as he pushed the doorbell. Down by his side, Dido barked and Jack put a fierce finger to his lips.

Shit, Katie, come on, you've got to be in, he prayed. He rolled his tongue around his mouth, tasting the sick from earlier, and he shuddered, drumming his fingers on the wall.

Finally, the door opened. Katie was standing there, plump in jogging bottoms and an apple green T-shirt. Her long blonde hair was tied back in an old tartan scrunchy that spewed elastic like wires from a plug. She smiled at him – one of her big, shiny, dimple-cheeked smiles. Jack was so relieved he enveloped her in a hug, nearly knocking her over.

'Whoa – Jack – you OK?' She pulled back. 'Hey – what's up?'

Jack swallowed, took a sheepish step backwards. He watched Katie's eyes travel over his belongings.

'Jack, what's happened? Why's all your stuff here . . . and not . . . at your place?'

Jack opened his mouth to make excuses . . . like his landlord had turfed him out. Or the arsonist drug-addicts living in the flat above his had set fire to the building. Or he was going travelling and needed a quick place to stay.

But then he looked up at Katie. She was his best friend. She could always tell if he was lying. And Katie was so sweet, she'd forgive him . . . wouldn't she?

'I . . . I . . . just lost my flat – oh fuck, Katie,' he hurried on, seeing her eyes moon in shock. 'I was down the pub, having a quiet drink, and then I got into this game of snooker and everything just went out of control . . .'

2
Charlie

We didn't mean to ruin Jack's life. I swear it was a mistake. As Puck said, it turned into a bit of a *Macbeth* situation. You know – one small sin leads to a bigger sin and before you know it the whole thing has snowballed into a tragedy of mammoth proportions. The thing is, with Jack it all started out as a joke. We happened to be flying around The Goat pub that evening and one thing led to another . . .

I'm sorry. I'm not making any sense, am I? I'm scampering too far ahead and you don't even know who I am.

My name's Charlie and I'm a fairy.

Not a homosexual, you understand. Or a bloke, for that matter. I'm a girl and my real name is Charlize, but I felt it had too much of a Hollywood-and-beauty-parlours ring to it. So Puck started calling me Charlie, and the name stuck.

No, I'm a fairy fairy. A real, honest-to-goodness, silver-winged sprite. I know you probably don't believe in me. Right now you're thinking, 'Hmm, I'm sure my ten-year-old niece would love this charming little book, I'll put it under her pillow along with twenty pence for her tooth.'

Or else you're picturing me as a clichéd, white-gossamer, two-inch tall wisp of a fairy – like those dreadful decorations you stick on your Christmas trees, with inane smiles on their faces, one arm stuck out at a right angle, grasping a curling wand. Well, believe me, I wish I did look like that – it would save me having to try out so many diets. In truth I am seven inches tall, but I also have wild red hair and I'm . . . well, people are too polite to call me fat. Instead, they mumble, 'Well, I'm not saying Charlie's fat, she's just *big*.' Or 'cuddly'. Or 'jolly', if they're being really kind. I've tried Fairy Slimming (our equivalent of Weight Watchers) but all I was allowed to eat every day was one piece of bark with a tiny portion of moss on top. After a week I was howling with hunger, ready to eat my own wings. So I gave up, and remained a fairy size fourteen.

Or maybe you never believed in us at all. Maybe in your mind we have always been just a few fanciful wisps who tinkle about in the movies you watch at Christmas if there's nothing else on. Urgh. I hate those Walt Disney adaptations. Puck and I went to see one recently and threw popcorn at the screen until two poor yobbos got chucked out by the usherette. The government has made a mess out of the education system as it is, without the kids of Great Britain growing up so misinformed about the spirit world. Of course, the only reason New Labour got in was 'cos Puck tampered with the ballot papers, but I'm not supposed to talk about that . . . Anyway, we fairies are not the only ones: ghosts, UFOs and angels are all equally misunderstood. Personally, I blame the media, Hollywood, but most of all, *The* bloody *X-Files*.

So before I tell my story, maybe I should just dispel a few illusions for you about the fairy myths which have been flying about over the past few centuries. Let's be blunt, ninety per cent of it is bullshit.

Some people, for example, claim that the word 'fairy' comes from the Latin 'fata' and refers to the supernatural women who turned up when babies were born to predict their future. Well, sorry, but we're really not into that New Age kind of rubbish. Then there are tales of fairies stealing babies and replacing them with changelings, or being blamed for the sudden death of cattle. I can assure you that you're making a perfectly good job of that one on your own with BSE, not to mention foot-and-mouth disease. Nor are we ghosts or fallen angels condemned to wander about on earth because the gates of heaven are closed to us. We are entirely different from elves, who are spirits of the earth, or nyriads, who are spirits of water, or daemons who are spirits of fire – fairies are spirits of air. So that clears a few things up right from the start.

One of the reasons I'm selling my story to you (apart from the fact that it'll make me rich and famous) is that I feel the public deserves to know the truth. Because things have been hotting up lately, and people are starting to show interest in us again . . .

We've been around for thousands of years. Hundreds of thousands. We were all here long before you. Our stories have been passed down from one great-grandmother to the next . . .

We trembled in the bowels of the earth as dinosaurs thundered above us. We saw the apes climb down from the trees and learn to walk on their feet and to say a little more than 'Ooger'. We saw Jesus feed the five thousand (well, to be accurate, I'm told it was more like five hundred, but still, it's a pretty impressive spell). We've seen it all. Wars, famines, plagues, coronations.

Now, there have been times when fairies were the next big thing. In the Victorian era, for example, we were the equivalent of the Spice Girls. The Victorians loved us – and because they believed in us, we flourished in abundance.

Often fairies were invited to great banquets where, in return for a delicious meal, we would provide after-dinner entertainment with a dance, a song, a spell or a parable. You know those paintings by Doyle and Dulac? Well, they weren't figments of the imagination, they weren't art – we actually posed for them. We got paid a lot – fairies back then could boast, 'Well, I don't *get out of bed* for at least ten thousand petals a day . . .' And the highlight of our social calendar was when Queen Victoria invited us for afternoon tea on Christmas Day and we could drop a few titbits of advice on how to improve the running of the country.

But recently – well, times are hard. Adults stopped believing in us. Slowly, our only fans became children. And now even they've lost their faith. All they want are machines, blood, guts and gore. All they want are those beepy-shrieky Nintendo toys. Lara Croft is no friend of ours, I can tell you – she's considered our worst enemy, her name is a swearword in fairy circles. I mean, you'd only have to bring your six-year-old kid home from school and ask them:

'Now, darling, would you like to watch *Mary Poppins* or *Fairytayle*?'

'I don't wanna watch boring old Walt Disney!' I heard one kid yowl, 'I wanna watch Arnold Swarrssnegger! Bang, bang, bang! I wanna see that bit where he rips the guy's head off!'

See?

*

Because times are so tough, we have to stick together in protective groups. We hang around in small numbers – there were only twenty of us left in London at the turn of the Millennium. We live in Primrose Hill. You might recognise our tree – the large oak in a 'V' of green grass overlooking the aviary cages at London Zoo. For a while our group had a nomadic existence, hitching lifts with unsuspecting humans, nervously hanging about in Glasgow, Birmingham and finally Wimbledon Common. We could have happily settled there if the bloody Wombles hadn't told us to clear off. Puck did all he could to protest, to talk them round. But Puck's a bit of a lad and his diplomatic skills weren't aided by him cheekily singing, '*The wankers of Wimbledon, common are we . . .*' At which point they retorted, 'Look – who's been on TV – us or you? Now bugger off.' And that was that.

We live tucked away in the oak tree. Through the leaves we can observe kids playing on bright plastic swings, girls jogging in the misty mornings, guys walking their dogs. We shiver in the rain, wince at the slime and the mud puddles, remembering better days, better days . . . There's a sense of vulnerability about us now, like butter-flies or flowers; a feeling that something so fragile, so beautiful can't survive much longer in this crazy, grime-and-crime infested city. We're a race in decline, soon to die out . . .

Occasionally Puck and I do break the rules and make a little mischief. We have been known to hang about on the London Underground, whispering words in people's ears to make them shake and wonder if schizophrenia is setting in. Or undoing a bloke's flies at the wrong moment. The funniest and meanest joke to play on a male human is to splash the tap when he's rinsing his hands in the Gents, so he comes out looking as though he's wet himself – usually just as the woman he fancies is walking past.

That was how it was supposed to be with Jack. It all started out as a joke on one Sunday evening . . .

3
Jack

Katie couldn't believe that Jack had turned up on her doorstep homeless and destitute. Jack regularly came by on Sunday nights after the pub. Normally she cooked him some chips or pizza in case he was hungry – being a human dustbin, he usually was. They'd crash out on the sofa, munching happily, watching videos. Jack was a real soap addict – he adored everything from *Home and Away* to *EastEnders* – and Katie had recorded about a hundred episodes while he'd been in Thailand, so they still had some left to watch.

And then, normally around midnight, they'd be falling asleep over some black-and-white movie when Jack would struggle to his feet and say a sleepy, happy goodnight. And Katie would surreptitiously stand by the window, watching him fondly, gazing at his lovely loping stride, his funny tufty hair as he walked back to his place in Camden.

Now Katie was standing in the kitchen, looking into the teapot at the tea she'd brewed for Jack earlier on. It was cold, the leaves a slimy black mush at the bottom, so she emptied it out, sprinkled in new ones, and switched on the kettle. She just couldn't believe it. All day she'd been working so hard and her evening with Jack had been like a light at the end of the tunnel, when *she'd* finally get to have some fun and unwind. How could an ordinary Sunday night have come to this? And how had she agreed to let Jack stay? It wasn't even her house. It was Leila's. Who, unfortunately, hated Jack. What the hell will Leila say? Katie fretted, rummaging in the drawer for a spoon. *Oh God, I ought to have known better than to invite Jack DeAntiquus into my house . . .*

Jack couldn't believe it, either.

He was slumped on the sofa, nursing the cup of tea Katie had pressed into his hands, circling his fingers around the Mr Happy boinging across the side of the cup. The TV was on quietly in the corner and he stared at it, stunned, not taking in a word of the tacky late-night sci-fi film on Channel 5, just seeing the scene in the pub over and over again . . .

It all started when he and Steve went over for a game of snooker, Dominique watching forlornly from the table.

'Twenty?' Steve grinned; he and Jack always liked a small bet on the game, it made it all the more fun.

'Why not?' Jack laughed. 'You're going to be a dead man, Steve.'

Steve gave him a play-kick, but his shrug was already one of happy defeat. Jack was brilliant at sports. At school he'd scored all the winning goals or tries in football and rugby. He'd been a genius at tennis, annoying his opponents by slamming aces down the court, then distracting them by tossing jibes over the net with the cocky swagger of Andre Agassi. During his university years he'd joined the rowing team and even run the London marathon. But during his mid-twenties he'd lost his fitness. Too much drink and too many cigarettes had corroded his hard, clean body, softened him and slowed him down; now he mostly lived out his passion by watching Michael Owen or Eddie Irvine on TV. But he still enjoyed darts, cards and snooker – sports which allowed him to indulge his competitive streak but didn't require him to rise at 6 a.m. for a jog or be forced to eat muesli on some ghastly fitness diet.

Jack was especially good at snooker. He tended to go to the pub five or six times a week; he always squashed in two games a night. He'd never been beaten once. Well, so Jack claimed.

'See, told you!' Jack grinned as Steve opened his wallet, peeling out a twenty.

'Yeah, well, you can buy me a commiseration drink,' said Steve. 'God, how d'you do it?' What had made the game even more annoying was that Jack played with such languid grace, alternately slouching by the table and sipping his beer, then picking up his cue and slipping balls into pockets without even aiming.

'Talent.' Jack took a mock bow, then hit Steve playfully. 'Sure, I'll buy a round,' he added. Jack was generous with his money and never resented spending it on other people; it slipped through his pockets and fingers like sand.

He went up to the bar and ordered five more beers and another Baileys for Dominique. Mick, drinking a pint of Guinness, nodded at the snooker table.

'Fancy a game?'

'Er . . .' Jack blinked, pocketing his change. 'Uh . . . well . . . why not?'

Beside him, Steve, who was just swinging off to the Gents, turned and gave Jack a slightly wide-eyed, raised-eyebrows glance. Jack hovered uneasily. Steve was right to warn him; after all, Mick was seriously dodgy. In his thirties, with a shorn head and a sharp tongue, he was a good laugh but always dealing in shady stuff – whether it was skunk or coke, cheap hi-fis or reduced Spice Girls CDs. The one time Jack had made the mistake of agreeing to buy a TV off Mick instead of going down to Currys, he'd discovered it was the very one stolen from his grandma's the Saturday before. It had been such an awful coincidence it was almost funny, though Jack had been much less amused when Mick had brushed him off and failed to offer a refund. Jack, seeing Mick was twice the size of him, hadn't pushed it, but he'd always bristled with a slight indignation and underlying dislike for Mick ever since. He'd felt a prat for being ripped off; perhaps a snooker match might be a good chance for revenge . . .

'Tell you what,' Mick grinned, 'I'll bet you. Money.'

'OK,' said Jack warily. 'Fifty pence?'

'I was thinking of a bit more than that.'

The casual but barbed tone of his voice made Jack feel oddly uneasy and yet excited. Was this a set-up? What was Mick up to?

'How much?'

'Three thousand.'

'Three thousand!' Jack spluttered. 'Come on!'

'Afraid you'll lose?'

'Look, I haven't lost a game this year – I'm wondering if you've got three thousand.' Jack frowned at him quizzically. Mick was always telling jokes with a deadpan face; it was impossible to tell if he was serious.

'I've got it.'

'Well, I don't.' Jack shrugged, feeling strangely relieved to have an excuse to wriggle out.

'Well, you can bet something else,' Mick suggested as Jack turned away.

'Uh?' Jack turned back, two pints in his hands, beer slipping and dripping over his fingers and on to his trainers.

'Your car, your flat.' Mick shrugged.

'I don't have a flat. I have a hovel, which I rent.'

'Car!' Steve had returned from the Gents and was doing up his flies. 'Have you *seen* Jack's car?'

'Shut up!' Jack put his pints down with an offended thump. 'Michelle is a very sexy car, thank you very much, Steve.'

'What car is it?' Mick asked.

'A Fiat.'

'Well, at least it's not a Lada,' said Mick.

'Well, at least it has wheels,' Steve added wryly.

'No, my car is brilliant!' Jack declared.

'OK, your car and your flat,' Mick said. 'You move out and you pay my rent for a year, which will be roughly three thousand. You pay me in cash, at the start. It sounds as though your car's about to die anyway, so you won't miss it. Fair?'

Jack paused. His mind was buzzing, his stomach tingling with a delicious glow of *am-I-really-going-to-do-this* excitement. It was crazy, it was nutty . . . but three thousand pounds. Steve was right; his car wouldn't fetch fifty quid if he tried to sell it. It was only fit for being crunched in the metal teeth of a bulldozer at a wrecker's yard. Three thousand pounds. He'd seen Mick lose snooker games before. He'd seen Steve beat Mick, and if Jack could beat Steve then . . . three thousand pounds would be his. Three thousand pounds.

'OK,' said Jack. 'You're on.'

And so Jack found himself standing in front of the green table, surrounded by a dozen or so thrilled onlookers who were hardly able to believe that this was happening in their habitually dull local, where the most exciting event normally was someone sticking a Kylie Minogue record on the jukebox. There was Steve, shaking his head but with his face creased in a pleased, slightly proud smile, certain that Jack was about to win. ('You can take us all on holiday to Thailand!' he'd joked.) He was being a sweet gentleman and holding hands with Dominique, to comfort her. She was looking very pale, her fingers nervously looping and relooping a button in her pink shirt. Dominique had hissed at Jack that he was completely mad. Now Jack, fraught with nerves, felt a sudden spark of anger towards her for voicing his own fears, corroding his confidence. If it went wrong, it would be half her fault for putting him off.

'Are we going to stand here till next year?' Mick finally cut the silence and Jack blushed as everyone tittered. Sod them. Part of him was holding back, knowing that when he made the first stroke, he'd set the whole farcical thing in motion. But there were a few seconds left to change his mind. His eyes flitted to Dominique. He could back out now, couldn't he?

Whack! As if acting with a will of its own, his hand picked up the cue and sent the white schlocking into the red balls, sending the static table into a chaos of coloured energy. Balls knocked balls. Nothing was potted. Jack stepped back and let Mick take his shot.

Mick missed the red, lining up an easy shot. Jack leaned over and missed.

There were a series of groans and Dominique's lips thinned to a pink pencil line. Jack shrugged, chewed his lip, picked up his pint from the side and took a sip, hiding a nervous smile. This was the plan – to lull Mick into a false sense of security, make him relax and get sloppy; then Jack would jump in with his killer instinct.

27

As Mick potted the first ball of the game, he jumped up and raised his cue as if it was a trophy, evoking cheers from the crowds.

See? Jack thought, forcing a gracious smile. False security.

What would I do with the money? Jack wondered, watching Mick dreamily. He'd be able to repaint his car, Michelle. Pay off his debts . . . Jack shrank away from that – it was ridiculous to have so much lovely money and then hand it over to someone else. No, he'd buy his mum a new car. And a washing machine – hers was always flooding. It was worth taking the risk just for her.

Bang! Mick pocketed the pink, turning to the red.

Mick: seven points; Jack: nil.

And after this, somewhere along the way, it started to get a bit scary. Maybe the false security thing had been a mistake, a trap Jack had laid and then inadvertently stepped into.

For Mick, adrenalised, carried on hitting the balls. A red, a blue. Jack's turn: a red, a miss. Mick: a red, a brown. A red, a black. Jack's turn: a red, a yellow. A red. Jack was already losing. Still, there were plenty of balls left on the table. Ten points down. Phew. *I can win, I can. I. Am. Going. To. Win.* He suddenly remembered sports day at school – stupid event, where mums came and cheered at the finish line. And though the only prize for running the 100 metres had been a tacky silver medal, Jack had treated it as though he was running in the Olympics. As he'd bent down on his knees, heard the starter gun grenade in his ear, felt the rush of adrenalin pumping through his veins, the same mantra had ticked over and over in his mind: *I am going to win. I am going to win.* And somehow, like a spell, it had worked. For a moment his body had become liquid, superhuman, as he'd found himself edging past taller guys, stronger guys, bursting through the white tape. He'd lain panting in a heap, gasping in the cold air, his body screaming with joy and pain, his mind still singing, like an echo, *I am going to win, I am going to win . . .*

Jack pocketed the red. He was narrowing the points gap. *I am going to win.* He leaned over the snooker table. He'd set up a beautiful opening: all he had to do was knock the black in and that'd be another eight points.

Jack knocked the white gently. It rolled a few centimetres, then, as if with a will of its own, circled to the left, just missing the black. There were a few groans. Jack glanced up at Steve, who was starting to look worried. Jack couldn't believe it. It had been the easiest shot in the book. An idiot could have hit that. *Dominique* could have got that in. What the hell was happening?

He was starting to wish he'd stayed in tonight. Why had he come to the pub? He ached to turn back the clock, to be sitting at home on the sofa, with Dido's head in his lap, her tail giving the cushions a *thump!* every time Jack leaned over to pick up the remote control or to call someone. He could have called his mum, he could have been listening to her with affectionate exasperation as she peppered him with questions: *Are you eating enough, Jack? Are you OK for money? How's Jackie? What d'you mean, you're not with Jackie any more, you were going out with her a few days ago?*

Even being forced to stay in and have sex with Dominique again would have been better than this – watching Mick zoom around the table, popping in balls, and seeing the looks on people's faces, the nudges, the whispers: '*What's wrong with Jack?*'

What was wrong? He went for the red, lunging in and knocking the white ball the wrong way. A miss. Unbelievable. Jack blinked at his stick. Was Mick tampering with it, was this all some set-up? On his next go, he spent a painstaking two minutes lining the ball up so he couldn't fail.

Again, he missed. Now he was trying too hard.

'Thinking of saying goodbye to your car?' Mick rubbed his hands like a pantomime villain.

Jack thought of his car, Michelle – messy, with doors rusting and ready to fall off. The car that had been with him for six years, looked after by friends when he was away. The car that'd put up with all kinds of abuse – love-making on the backseats, puking on heavy nights, being forced to shoot 90mph down the M25 – but yet had carried on dragging itself through MOTs, as if quietly supportive of Jack.

He thought of the time he and his friends had driven up to Box Hill a few years back. Jack had been drinking – just one pint – and the rest of them had been stoned, the car filled with greeny smoke, throbbing with *Bohemian Rhapsody*. A car had suddenly come zooming towards them and Jack had sworn later that he felt the steering wheel swing away from him, that no matter how hard he twisted it to the left, invisible hands seemed to be taking it to the right, sending them spinning round and round on to the bank and into hospital for six weeks. Jack had suffered a broken leg; Michelle was barely dented.

Mick potted another red.

That had been an odd night, the night he'd crashed. As if he'd been doomed. First of all, Michelle had obstinately refused to start, coughing uneasily into life after half an hour of revs. Then he'd had to change the tyre. Later, he hadn't thought of these things as omens . . . and yet the night had been coloured, as if by a dark cloud, as if everything had been destined to go wrong. The gods had not been on his side . . .

30

Like tonight. Jack just knew. He realised even as he leaned over the table and finally managed to pot something, desperately repeating over and over, *I'm going to win, I'm going to win*, that he was going to lose. Don't be silly, you're not jinxed, he kept shouting at himself. But deep down he knew. He felt sick. I'm going to lose my flat and my car, he thought blankly. Everyone was still watching open-mouthed, hardly able to believe that Jack was about to be beaten for the first time. The only one who realised was Dominique, and she was glaring at him with terrified eyes. In his panic, all the worries that had been swimming about in his subconscious rose to the surface. It was easier to think of Dominique than his fate, slamming down on him like a guillotine. *Why can't I commit?* he wondered, staring at her in horror. *She's a lovely girl. Where does this bored, empty feeling come from, that six hours after being with a girl I just want to throw her away? Is that why I agreed to this stupid bet? And, oh shit, where the hell am I going to get three thousand pounds? And where am I going to live?*

Unable to face his friends' surprise or sympathy, Jack walked off in a forced careless stroll to the Gents. He splashed his face, gazing into the mirror as water slithered and dripped over his bushy dark eyebrows and stubble, and thought, *You stupid, stupid bastard.*

Steve came in, smiling cheerfully, to take a piss. Jack swallowed and casually asked if he could kip at his place.

'Come on,' Steve said, doing up his zip. 'Mick won't really hold you to it. Maybe just your car, but not the flat and the money. Anyway, I'm getting married in six weeks, remember? And Mandy would go mad – we're having our honeymoon at home what with the mortgage and everything. Mick isn't serious.'

Unfortunately, back in the pub, they discovered that Mick was serious.

Deadly.

After joking failed, Jack tried to barter. But Mick just kept repeating, 'We. Had. A. Deal,' while staring at him with his brown, psychotic eyes. Then several of Mick's friends started getting loud, calling Jack a coward, until even Steve whispered, 'OK – maybe he is serious. You're fucked, Jack.' Jack kept thinking, *I can't believe Mick is making me do this. The bastard.*

They hung around the pub, Jack's side silent and awkward, Mick's group rowdy and jubilant. Jack sipped a pint blankly, vaguely aware of Dominique crawling across him like a vine, showering him with little consoling kisses.

Pushing her gently off him, he said he needed to be alone for a minute. Outside the pub, he leaned over the curb and threw up in the gutter, sick spilling out over the russet autumn leaves. He held his head in his hands, listening to the gurgle of the water in the drains. The wind whipped up the leaves; one scratched his face. Then he heard Dominique behind him, crying 'Oh God!' in such a tone of disgust that Jack realised, with a bitter-sweet smile, that he'd finally succeeded in turning her off him.

He tried to be cool and calm about everything. Steve was a good mate; he went with Jack to his flat to help him pack up his stuff.

'Oh well, don't worry about Michelle. Rumour has it she was two-timing you with a Ford Fiesta anyway.' Steve kept cracking sympathetic jokes but Jack remained sullenly quiet, just wanting to move ultra-fast, not wanting to prolong the pain.

Jack hardly had any boxes so most of his belongings

were stuffed into carrier bags. Luckily he travelled light and there wasn't much. His photographic equipment. A few books – Jack Kerouac's *On the Road*, Robert Pirsig's *Zen & The Art of Motorcycle Maintenance*, and Nick Hornby's *About a Boy*. He left *War and Peace* as he'd never got past page twenty-five. Not that Mick would manage even a page, he grimaced. He took down his posters from the walls – the one of Marilyn Monroe with her skirt lifting up and the one from *LA Confidential*. He wondered what Mick would put up instead. Though Jack was naturally messy, he kept having nightmarish images of Mick smoking and dropping ash over the sofa, or having friends over and leaving beer cans scrumpled on the floor. He pictured Mick in his bed, his greasy, spotty body between the covers. He pictured Mick peeing in his toilet. He felt like being sick again. He took Dido, put on her lead, and they left.

At least he knew Katie would help him. Katie: his best friend. He ached for her sympathy, to pour out the whole story, for her to hug him and say everything would be fine.

And Katie had been sweet to him. She'd hugged him, made him tea, said she'd do her best to persuade Leila to let him stay. And yet he could see the same look on her face that Dominique had had. A look that quite plainly said, *Jack, I can't believe what a stupid wanker you are.*

Even worse, he hadn't even mentioned the three thousand he owed Mick. He didn't want to worry her and he knew she'd flip.

Jack took another sad sip of cold tea. He just couldn't understand it. He was always doing crazy things like this – like the time he'd lost his passport in Prague and somehow sweet-talked the customs officer into letting him travel anyway. He'd always got by by the skin of his teeth. Tonight his luck just seemed to have run dry. He felt a flash of irrational paranoia – the world was against him, everything was conspiring to bring him down . . .

4
Charlie

If I'm going to tell my side of the story, I think I must introduce you to Puck.

Puck is my best friend, my partner in crime, as close as a brother. How can I describe him? Well, the first thing that springs to mind is that he is incredibly handsome. Only, boy, does he know it. So don't tell him I said this, because he's far too head-over-wings in love with himself as it is, as are most of the other flower fairies.

And – look, I admit it – yes, I've always been a little bit in love with Puck too. But I'd never tell him; Puck is a real fairyiser, and he'd only seduce me, sleep with me and then spit me out like chewing-gum when the flavour has gone.

He is quite tall for a male fairy at about ten inches, and the plant he represents is the thistle. He wears a thong made of thistle leaves and sharp thorns around his waist. He has long dark hair that flows down to his chin and a strong face that other fairies always look twice at. He has a snub nose, aristocratic cheekbones, a very full, sulky mouth, fierce hawk's eyebrows and black eyes that just gleam with wickedness.

Like me, Puck is a fairy who was born to rebel. If you belong to a Fairy Circle, you're supposed to stay inside the perimeters of the fairy camp. But Puck and I love taking illicit trips out, though they are highly dangerous – the equivalent of you humans taking a stroll in the middle of an Iraqi war zone.

Often Puck and I spend evenings floating about Camden or Primrose Hill, watching the web of Londoners work, sleep, play, lie, break friendships, begin affairs, give birth to illicit babies, all caught in the wheel of life. It's better than any soap opera – even *EastEnders*. How can I describe it? Well, it's a bit like having your own *Big Brother*, twenty-four hours a day – your own private web-cam, where you can creep into people's houses, and be, literally, a fly or a winged creature on the wall. We are hooked.

There is Mr Thomas at number 17, for example, who is a born-again Christian but conveniently forgets the 'thou shalt not commit adultery' commandment when he visits Mrs Kay at number 23. Then there is Leila Clare – Ms Career Girl – a tough literary agent who barks orders all day at work and cries in her bed at night, showing us a vulnerable side her workers never see. She is seeing three different men, all of whom are foolishly convinced that she is (ahem) deeply, madly and passionately in love with them.

The trouble is, we can do more than just watch people. We *feel* people. We can stand by a person and hear their thoughts, their inner voice. Call me a psychic, but it's natural. No man is an island – we're all in a sea of consciousness. How often have you switched on the radio and heard the very song you were humming? Or thought of a friend and find they call you that very moment? Or been with a partner and both caught yourselves saying the same thing at the same time? Even when you meet people, you don't just take in how they look, or what they say, you get a sense of them. That private vibe or feeling, an intuition. After all, Einstein estimated that you humans are all only using ten per cent of your brains. You have no idea of the powers you could cultivate if only you knew how . . .

But all the same, after my big speeches about human thought, it has to be said that humans don't really think very interesting things.

God, sometimes it's like watching a goldfish going round a tank.

'What shall I get tonight at Tesco's? . . . Bugger, I've forgotten the list again . . . What was it I was supposed to remember? Pink toilet roll . . . and that extra turkey, they're coming over this weekend . . .

'God, my boss is a loser . . . why do I do this job? . . . oh well . . . 4:34 p.m. . . . nearly five, then I can escape this stupid office prison . . . wonder if anyone would notice if I went to the loo and had a wank? . . .'

And yes, *Cosmo* and the other magazines are right. Men really do think of sex every six minutes.

The night we first met Jack at The Goat, where this nightmare all started, was just like any other evening.

We decided to take a trip to one of our favourite haunts: a quiet little run-down graveyard in south Camden, linked to St Mary's Church.

Arriving at St Mary's, Puck was as hyperactive as ever. While he flitted about, I crashed out on a gravestone, gazing up at the sky. Occasionally the drifting white clouds cleared, allowing the moon to fill the graveyard with her beautiful silver beams. But after a while the clouds hunched up in a brooding mass and the dark shadows of the night crept in. I kept yawning and trying to twitch myself awake. I was just drifting off when a voice cut through my dreamy haze.

'Hey, Charlie, come over here and see what I've found!'

'What?' I blinked.

It was Puck.

'Over here!' His voice echoed in the distance. 'Come and see!'

I staggered to my feet, squinting in the gloom. All I could see were spidery nettles and the dark humps of tombstones leaning into the grass.

I walked forward into the blackness, arms outstretched, until my hands fumbled something warm and hairy. I realised I was stroking Puck's chest and I stumbled back hurriedly. Then my eyes grew accustomed to the gloom and I caught the glint of his white teeth as he smiled evilly, brandishing a puffclock.

Do you know what it's like to do something you realise is completely wrong, and yet you still find yourself doing it anyway? To think, 'This is a sin,' but find your body acting as though it has a will of its own, as though you're possessed?

Well, this is exactly how I felt as Puck and I stood there, sniffing up the puffclock seeds. Blow – sniff – spin – light – spin – blow – sniff. *Whooppee!* yelled Puck, getting an instant high. *I think I inhaled too much*, I tried to say, my nose quivering as though a thousand tiny red-hot needles were pricking every cell. I turned in a giddy circle. Puck laughed and spun me round and then cried out to have some more.

Within ten minutes, we had snorted so much that Puck was lying on the grass, panting and whispering hoarsely, 'More, give me some more!' He held out his brown hands in an impression of Oliver Twist. 'Please sir, let me have some more. One last blow. C'mon Charlie.'

'No, you most certainly cannot,' I said, doing an impression of Tulip's high, prim voice. Tulip is one of the strictest and most elderly of the Fairy Council. 'Two puff-clocks is quite enough for any growing lad.'

'Oh, give me more, you bitch!' he cried, catching my ankle and sending me toppling over him. We untangled ourselves, giggling hysterically.

'Hey, will you look at that?' Puck exclaimed, gazing wide-eyed up at the clouds. 'Look, look, it's just like a unicorn. A splendid white unicorn with a horn of ivory galloping across the sky. Hey, Charlie, maybe it's an auspicious omen,' he teased, clutching my shoulder. I've often forced poor Puck to take a detour of thirty yards to avoid walking under a ladder and I wear a chain of preserved forget-me-nots around my neck (a twenty-first birthday present from Puck) for good luck.

Well, I couldn't see such a cloud at all, but it was nice to just lie there, as the puff took effect and drew me down into a dazed, sleepy sort of trance where it seemed anything might happen but it wouldn't matter very much if it did. Then my body convulsed once or twice and I saw flashes exploding behind my eyes like light bulbs smashing. This was a sign that the poison was now buzzing through my bloodstream. It would be another eight hours before my system had purified the toxins and put itself back to normal. So I lay very still, waiting for my body to adjust, to surrender to such abuse, while Puck, who was much stronger, got up and started dancing around and pretending to blow through a cigarette stub as though it was a hunting horn.

'Tally-ho, Charlie! Come, my love, come and play. The night is young . . . but the hours are running . . . still time to have fun, if we are hurrying.' Puck giggled and clutched himself. 'Hey, I'm a poet and I didn't know it. A dreadful one, but still. Ba ba!'

Well, while the puff was unleashing Puck's poetic genius, my body was still refusing to give up without a fight and now I was willing my stomach not to throw up my dinner all over the grave. I tried to sit up but my limbs felt alien and heavy.

Puck, however, continued to dance about impatiently and eventually ended up strewing daisy petals and stems over my face.

'Come on, Charlie,' he insisted. 'It's all in the mind. If you get up now and have a walk about, you'll feel so much better. And there's loads to explore. I want to go inside the church.'

Churches have always been my favourite places. I know humans don't like them much any more but to my mind they are the oasis in every city. Especially those old ones with their stained-glass windows and crumbling roofs; the silence feels so thick, it's as if the grey stone walls sigh with serenity.

One of the cool things about puff is that it gives you supersenses. Ironic, because when it does wear off it leads to fuzzy sight, poor hearing, premature ageing. It's no wonder that even Goblins are forced to put small print on their packets of the stuff: 'Sniffing puff can seriously damage your aura'.

I found my sense of hearing becoming so fine-tuned that I could detect the scratch of the church mice rattling beneath the floorboards, the haunting lament of an owl screeching for its cuckoo-killed young. The occasional drip of holy water was like a silver bell. Then I started to hear the groan of the stone walls shifting in their foundations.

40

I even discerned the faint tap of a tree root many feet below, trying to push its way back up through the stone vault. I heard the building whisper its secrets from the past, saw visions of medieval worshippers, witch hunts, a wife in love with the vicar, recriminations and regrets, confessions . . .

By now this was all starting to freak me out. For some time I simply gazed at the way the shaking trees formed patterns of dark and light on a marble grave cut into the stone floor . . . a hooked thumb . . . a lady's profile . . .

'Hey, space cadet,' Puck called over at last. 'Let's go and party! Let's visit some humans. A public house. Come on, I want to have some fun.'

'Oh, but Puck, can't we stay here . . . I'm totally spaced out . . . I'm having fun . . .'

'Charlie, don't be such a *bore*. Come on.'

I knew it spelled trouble. I could feel it in the pit of my stomach.

Puck led the way as we flew to the pub. I dawdled behind him, watching the sharp, excited flick of his wings. The trouble with Puck on puff is that he loses all sense of boundaries. It's this aspect of his personality that is so refreshing when sober, yet so alarming when not. Fortunately, even if I do go off my head, I still have some sense of moral judgement. But Puck is liable to do anything from changing the time on parking ticket machines to unlocking brake handles and watching cars go smashing into lampposts. Beforehand, he always pleads with me to keep an eye on him and stop him from going too far. The trouble is that once he gets into one of these moods, the last thing he's interested in is being told what to do . . .

Puck spotted the pub. I can't remember much about it

now, except that it was grimy-walled and grotty and called The Goat. The windows shook with the sound of music and shouted conversation, and a group of green dragons wearing short shiny skirts and bright pink lipstick came spilling out of the door. Suddenly they metamorphosed into a group of girls. *Girls*, not dragons. I shook myself and realised the puff was still taking effect.

We were hovering in mid-air. I looked at Puck and swallowed hard. One last try, I thought.

'I'm not going in, Puck,' I said. 'I'll l-l-leave you and I'll go off home on my-my-my-my own.'

God, I couldn't even speak properly. My voice was slipping and slurring all over the place like a drunk on an ice rink.

'OK, fine.'

'I'll just stay out here. I'll be left out in the cold,' I pleaded weakly, but with a whisp of wind, Puck had already flown in.

Bastard.

I hated being alone in the human world. I felt a bit like a female human in a lonely bus shelter at night, nervously shoving her hands in her pockets, convinced that every man who walks past is a rapist. I shook myself and muttered firmly, '*Sober up*, Charlie, *sober up!*'

I debated whether to go back and leave Puck or not, but that meant flying over Regent's Park, and there was a particularly pervy badger who lived there who always shouted obscenities at me.

Sighing, I flew in after him.

Inside, the noise hit my delicate ears like a thunderstorm. I'd flown in right by the jukebox and Daruda's 'Sandstorm' was playing, the *thump-thump* hitting me as though a baseball bat was being slammed into my spine. Then Puck burst into roars of laughter as, in my panicky bid to avoid going deaf, I flew away without looking – straight into a girl blowing out a stream of cigarette smoke. I coughed, wheeled about, and felt a warm hand on my shoulder as Puck guided me to a corner.

'All right?' He kept slapping my back as I choked. 'God, you look a state,' he smiled affectionately.

'Urgh,' I spluttered. This is what happens if you're a fairy and you fly through cigarette smoke. One puff can turn your human lungs to black tar – so you can imagine what it does to us. I was covered with a thin layer of black grime, as though I'd spent all day travelling on the Underground. Yuk.

We hovered around the pub for a while, flitting here and there, catching snatches of gossip and human thought. *Shall I have another beer? . . . I wish I was at home watching* The Vicar of Dibley *. . . If he finds out I'm pregnant, he'll kill me . . .* buzzed through my mind like conflicting radio waves.

One group of people drew us to them like a magnet – though at first sight there was nothing special about them. Just a large group of lads, maybe five or six, sitting and drinking pints. There was one guy who stood out at once: he was called Jack. He had the air of a leader and the good looks that made my wings tingle pleasurably, causing Puck to turn and give me a teasing smile. I poked my tongue at him and quickly swung my attention to the only girl sitting in the group. She was blonde and, despite the smile pasted on her face, was emanating vibes of such sadness that I rested by her ear, feeling my heart ache to comfort her, and listened to her thoughts.

Why am I here? Why am I sitting here with a smile on my face? Why can I hear my voice saying all these sweet, nice things to Jack when it's obvious he's behaving like a total BASTARD!

43

I was starting to get weak. This is the paradox of being a fairy – by listening to people's thoughts, by trying to help them, you start to absorb their emotions. We're so sensitive, so transparent, that we become like sponges, sucking away the pain and the stress. Have you ever been in a really foul mood and suddenly felt your emotions swing upwards, so you shrug to yourself and think, 'Hey, no, it's going to be OK, why worry?' Well, more often than not it's because a fairy has given you a helping hand, sat on your shoulder like an invisible councillor, heard your rants and blown a bubble of bliss your way . . .

Trouble is, it's exhausting. We're left soiled with your pains. My body felt drained, swollen with Dominique's worries.

'Puck, can we go?'

And we were just about to, when Jack uttered those fatal words.

'. . . *just like the Cottingley fairy hoax. For years people believed fairies existed from those photos – and then what? We find out they were just cardboard cut-outs on sticks.*'

Looking back, I can see those were the words that changed everything. I could sense Jack was putting on a bravado act, playing Devil's Advocate. He wanted to make his friends laugh and put Dominique down. But Puck's face slowly darkened with rage.

'Er, maybe we'd better go,' I said hastily, sensing trouble. When Puck loses his temper, he really does go mad.

'No,' said Puck tightly. 'Let's hear what Socrates here has to say about our existence.'

And, oh God, you'll never guess what Jack said next.

'*No, it's all rubbish – ghosts, fairies, UFOs, the lot. Crap. A human invention to try to make the dullness of life that bit more interesting.*'

44

'You bastard!' Puck swore, dancing in front of his face. As Jack picked up his pint, Puck very nearly fell into the beer. I yanked him away just in the nick of time.

'Puck, leave it alone.'

'I can't believe it! The bastard!' Puck cried. 'The bloody bastard!'

'Puck, calm down!' I replied. 'Come on, what's the big deal, nobody believes in us.'

'How the hell would he, bloody Jack, feel if I said to him, Well, actually, how can you prove humans exist? What's to say you're not just a figment of imagination, a dream in a fairy's mind! Ha!'

Puck put his hands on his hips, watching Jack with narrowed eyes as Jack stood up and grabbed a snooker cue.

'Right,' said Puck. 'Humans versus the fairies. This is war.'

5
Katie

On Monday morning Katie woke up from an uneasy dream to the sound of violent yapping, as if an animal was being choked to death, and a female voice squawking, 'Just what is that *thing* doing in my kitchen?' She heard Jack reply gruffly, 'Katie said it would be OK. Hey, don't hit her! D'you want me to call the RSPCA?'

Shit. Katie hurriedly dragged on her dressing gown, her slippers flip-flopping down the stairs as she rushed into the kitchen. She skidded slightly on the glistening floor, where Jack was kneeling down and mopping up a small pool of urine with that morning's *Daily Telegraph*. Leila, who was dressed for work in a smart, sexy charcoal suit, her hair wound into a golden coil, was looking furious. Leila was a woman who liked her routine. She liked to rise at 6 a.m., shower, have her quiet cup of coffee and be in the office by 7:30.

'Just what is going on?' Leila snarled at Katie. 'I come downstairs and nearly break my ankle tripping over boxes of stuff everywhere – his stuff, I suppose.'

To add to the commotion, Katie's daughter, Susie, sensing an interesting argument, came into the room half dressed for school. She was wearing tartan pyjamas but her feet were encased in white school socks and shiny black patent shoes.

'Is Uncle Jack coming to stay?' she cried eagerly, bouncing up and down.

'Go back upstairs and get dressed, Susie!' Katie ordered firmly.

'Is he?' Leila asked acidly. 'It would have been nice if one of you could have asked me first, but no, it is only my house.' She threw open a drawer, rummaged amongst a pile of spoons, forks and knives, then slammed it shut without taking anything out.

'I'm sorry – it was past midnight last night when Jack came over, and, look, I was going to tell you this morning.' Katie tried to smooth things over.

'Tell me? Don't you mean *ask* me?'

Oh shit. This really wasn't going as desired. Katie had planned to visit Leila during her lunch break at work and quietly plead a case for Jack like a defending lawyer. Not have a row in the kitchen over the tantivy of a barking mongrel.

Jack, who was sullenly fiddling with the fridge magnets, suddenly said in a sharp voice, 'Look, I'm sorry, Leila, I'm in the middle of a crisis at the moment and I need a place to stay, just for a few weeks, OK?'

Leila folded her arms, narrowing her eyes at him. Katie sighed. For God's sake, Jack could at least sound contrite, instead of roughly addressing Leila as though she was the inept manager of a hotel.

They were interrupted by the shrieking of Leila's mobile. As Leila stalked into the hallway and began nattering in the background, Katie glared at Jack and mouthed: 'Be nice.' Jack merely looked sulky, but when Leila came back in and muttered, 'OK, maybe you can stay,' he went up to her and threw his arms around her, showering her with Italianiate kisses.

For God's sake, thought Katie again. She knew Jack liked manipulating women by flirting but this was a little over the top. Leila disentangled herself, blushing slightly; she wasn't a tactile person. Katie noticed she always seized up whenever she tried to hug her.

'But, look, if you're going to stay, it's only for a few weeks. Maximum, OK?' Leila said, pulling on her black jacket. 'I don't want any loud music. I have no wish to be woken at 11 o'clock at night by Robbie Williams at full blast.'

'Robbie Williams?' Jack looked insulted.

'OK – The Manic Street Preachers. Whatever.'

'The Manics are made to be played at top volume,' Jack said earnestly. There was nothing he loved more than turning up his stereo and crashing out on his bed, feeling the guitar notes sweep through his body and twang his nerve-ends.

'Well, not any more. And you'll have to get rid of that dog. No – Jack – don't even try arguing. I won't have it. I have a cat, Candida, and I have no wish to come home to find a mauled cat body.'

'Cat soup is a delicacy in some countries,' Jack tried to joke, inwardly crumpling. Dido was his best friend – after Katie.

'Well, Jack soup is going to be a delicacy in this house. Look, d'you want to stay here or not, Jack, because I don't appreciate you winding me up like this.'

'OK, it's fine,' Katie intervened. 'Right, Jack?'

Thankfully, before Jack could argue any further, Leila's mobile rang again and without even saying goodbye, she stormed out. Jack mouthed 'Bitch' at her back. Katie

48

sighed; this didn't bode well. After all, Jack and Leila had never been the best of friends . . .

The first time Katie and Leila had met Jack was in 1993. Eight years ago. They had both been twenty-one years old. He'd been taking his clothes off.

'God, will you look at that!' Leila nearly choked on her Baileys.

Katie, collecting her change from the barman, dropped a few coppers as she turned.

There he was – a crazy guy on the dance floor, jigging about wildly and laughing his head off, doing a mock striptease. As he danced down the steps, swinging off his shirt, the nightclub lights streaked him mauve, scarlet and green like a Zulu warrior. Guys closed in around him, cheering and jeering; girls screamed as if Beatlemania had returned. He was just dropping his trousers when the bouncers came up and tapped him on the shoulder. He had given an apologetic shrug and pulled on his shirt once more.

Just at that point, as though his womanising antennae had picked up beeping signals, he looked over at the two girls standing by the bar.

'He's staring at you!' Katie nudged her friend in delight.

'Poser,' said Leila, in such an icy tone that Katie knew at once Leila fancied him.

He approached them, still doing up the buttons on his shirt. Though his eyes were fixed on Leila, Katie felt her knees go weak. He might be behaving like a complete idiot, but he did have such lovely Johnny Depp cheekbones and melted-chocolate eyes, and a sort of boyish air, as if he didn't really mean any harm, he just wanted to have some fun.

49

'D'you want to buy me a drink?' he asked.

Leila and Katie looked at each other, blinking. Katie started to giggle.

'Er, haven't you got that a bit wrong?' Leila demanded. 'Like, you're supposed to be offering to buy *us* a drink?'

'Well, if you could lend me a tenner, I will,' he said cheerfully. 'It's just that as I was getting some money out of the cash machine, an alien spaceship landed crash in the middle of the road. In order to return to the planet Zob, they needed twenty pounds to buy some green petrol for their wrecked machine. So, being the kind of man I am, I gave my last twenty to them . . . And I'm, er, broke.'

'Oh, yeah, yeah, yeah. That is quite simply the most pathetic story I've ever heard,' Leila said, rolling her eyes. But, to Katie's amazement, she clipped open her handbag and pulled out her purse. Normally Leila, who attracted guys like bees to honey, used men as banks ('The Male Bank of Testosterone,' she joked in girly chats) to buy her dinner, rings, clothes . . . And now Leila was handing over a crisp ten-pound note; she must be smitten.

Jack returned with the drinks – a Guinness for himself, a Bacardi and Coke for Leila, a half-pint for Katie.

They all sat down on tall stools. Katie fidgeted uneasily, feeling her large thighs squashed unbecomingly against the sucky plastic.

'So, what d'you do?' Jack asked Leila. He had such a nice voice – deep and gruff.

'Oh, I'm a Personal Assistant,' Leila rattled off.

Katie stared at her reflection, concave and bloated grotesquely in the curve of her glass. Her red cheeks looked chubbier than ever, her double chin quadrupled. Urgh.

People often wondered why Katie and Leila were friends. They were such an odd pair. They were both the same age, but there the similarities ended. Everyone noticed Leila – her swinging vanilla hair, her blue, cat-shaped eyes, her long, long legs, highlighted by her short business skirts and confident stride. Katie was five-foot-six and a size sixteen. She had long blonde hair, but it wasn't silky like Leila's; it hung in messy greasy curls down her back and she never knew what to do with it but tie it back in a scrunchy.

But Leila and Katie had been friends since high school. Katie had been shy, Leila the new girl (she'd already been to five schools before she met Katie, due to her parents' changing jobs) and their loneliness had gelled them together.

Katie felt that friendships started in school were often the strongest. They were formed before you became an adult, before you found an identity and an image, before the layers of pretension and superficiality had encrusted themselves. Teenage friendships had a kind of innocence and intimacy; she and Leila had shared everything from comparing notes on their first kiss to their parents' divorces. Despite the fact that Katie seemed to be trapped in Leila's shadow, Leila, funnily enough, was the more clingy of the two. She'd chosen the same subjects as Katie for GCSE and A-level; she'd followed her to the same temping firm; they'd ended up sharing a flat together in Battersea.

But one area in which Leila did lead the way was men. Whenever Leila and Katie went out clubbing together, the blokes (also hunting in pairs) fought to chat up Leila. They'd all sit at a table, both the men plying Leila with drinks while Katie got shoved into a corner, nodding and smiling and pretending she was involved in the conversation. Until finally, the less good-looking one would turn away in defeat to Katie, as if she was the booby prize.

So Katie was always left with the odd bloke – the bloke with the squiffy mouth or the bald German doctor. She got the leftovers. Men who, because she was fat, assumed she must be just as desperate as them.

Katie had never forgotten the time one bloke had been kissing her, slobering over her neck and then thrusting his hand up her top, burrowing like a ferret. She'd kept pushing him gently away; the ferret had carried on. Finally, she'd shoved him back.

'What the hell?' he'd cried. 'You can't reject me! You're a fat girl.'

Katie had slapped him and burst into tears.

'So, what d'you do?'

Katie jumped; she was back in the nightclub, playing gooseberry again.

'What d'you do?' Jack repeated. Katie blushed, not just because Leila was poking her and laughing, making a comment about her being a dreamer, but because Jack was looking at her with such an intense, laser stare. As if he was genuinely interested in what she had to say.

'I'm just a secretary,' said Katie.

'So.' Jack paused to light up his Silk Cut. 'Are you sleeping with your boss?'

'No!' Katie nearly spat into her beer.

'Why not? The pros and cons of being a secretary – too many paperclips, but free sex with the boss,' Jack said with a deadpan face.

'Jack, you are incorrigible,' said Leila. 'So what—'

'If you knew my boss, you'd believe me,' Katie barged in enthusiastically. She paused, aware she'd interrupted rudely, that Leila was twisting her rings in annoyance, then carried on regardless. 'He's always wanking up against the photocopier under the guise of "fixing the mechanisms".'

'Oh my good God!' Jack roared with laughter, causing several passing teenagers in hot pants to turn and stare. Katie wondered if Jack ever felt like a creature in a zoo.

There was a moment's silence. Katie, desperate to fill it before Leila got there first, blurted out the first thing that came to mind.

'If – if – you could compare us to animals, what would we be?'

An even longer silence. Oh God, she'd just said something really silly – but she'd been so keen to remain part of the conversation.

'Katie!' Sure enough, Leila was sniggering.

'No,' Jack said kindly, giving Katie an encouraging grin. 'That's a good question. Now, Leila . . .' He ran his eyes over her and Leila, squirming, uncrossed her legs. 'I'd say you were a gazelle – elegant and graceful.'

'And you, Jack, you're a grizzly bear,' Leila smiled.

Katie privately disagreed. Jack had more cunning than that. No, he was like a tiger. Or was that too fierce? Perhaps like a tiger cub – sweet but dangerous, playful but deadly.

As the spotlight turned on her, Katie cringed. She watched for the inevitable 'elephant' comparisons.

'I think you're a panda,' said Leila. 'Soft and cuddly and black-eyed – your mascara's always running.'

'No,' said Jack. 'I think you're like a tom cat. You're friendly and cuddly but strong.'

A tom cat! Charming! So she was fat and ginger and peed everywhere. Katie wasn't pleased. But then she looked up and caught Jack gazing at her with smiley eyes, and she felt herself grow warm, as if she'd just come into a cosy, fire-lit pub on an icy winter day. God, he was lovely.

'So what do you do?' Leila tossed her hair impatiently, irritably.

'Oh, I'm a photographer.'

'What d'you photograph?'

'Girls. Page Three girls,' said Jack. 'My daily motto is "spread them a little bit wider, darling".'

For a moment Katie and Leila looked at each other in horror. Then Jack burst out laughing again.

'Ha, you should have seen your faces!' He roared again, and they all giggled, on a high. 'No, no, I just do bits of photography as a hobby – I'm not that good. I'm flying to Prague tomorrow actually, to do some shots and have some fun.' He bit his lip, looking a bit sheepish at their disappointed faces. 'Still, there's always tonight.'

It was as if Jack had picked up an hour-glass and tipped it upside down. Leila started going in for the hard kill, bombarding Jack with questions about his travels. Katie shut up, aware of Leila's irritation. *I'm not a tom cat, I'm a snail*, she thought, slowly retreating into her shell, leaning away from the bar, allowing Leila to take centre stage.

Jack had always had a certain effect on her, Katie reflected. He was always prompting her to do the wildest things, suddenly pulling her out of her usual mould as Ms Kind and Ms Sensible, breaking the boundaries of her behaviour. Looking back, she felt sure it was he who was to blame for everything that had followed.

As she sat there on her bar stool, watching Jack and Leila slow-smoochy-dancing in the white mist like a couple at the end of a Hollywood movie, she felt envy stab into her heart. And when, a few minutes later, a tall, slim man with round-eyed glasses approached her, in that desperate hour when all the left-overs stuck their tongues down each other's throats in an attempt to prove they were attractive to the opposite sex, Katie had agreed to his offer of a drink. He introduced himself as Keith; she introduced herself as Louise, infused by Jack's lies. She naughtily told him she was a large model; he told her he worked for an environmental charity.

'D'you want to dance?' she asked, toying a strand of hair around her finger. She felt almost beautiful – radiant and bold. She kept flirting and laughing, yet found herself swivelling slightly to look for Leila, as if hoping Jack might be watching her . . .

The four of them shared a taxi back home. She and Keith were wedged in one corner, Jack and Leila in the other. Keith had clamped a stiff arm around her as though they were posing for a photograph as a Victorian couple. Katie's eyes flicked nervously over Leila and Jack, who were kissing with delicate voraciousness. Jack's hands travelled down Leila's back, over her buttocks. His fingers teased the edge of her shiny skirt, then crept up her thighs – lovely, sexy, feely fingers, brushing the black lines of her suspenders. Then Jack's eyes flicked open and he caught her staring. He smiled and Katie jumped and turned away, blushing like an embarrassed schoolgirl caught with a porn mag, feeling an odd pulse throbbing between her legs.

When the taxi stopped outside Keith's house, Katie felt that wild, un-Katie-like impetus catch hold of her again. When Keith hopped out and held out his hand, instead of politely declining, she found herself grabbing his thin, spindly fingers. Leila and Jack looked out at them, Leila slightly surprised.

'OK?' Leila kept asking. 'You're sure you'll be OK? Shall I lend you some money for the taxi back? You've got my mobile number, haven't you?'

She's just putting on a concerned sisterly act for Jack, Katie thought coldly, then she turned away – what was the matter with her tonight, where were all these horrible thoughts coming from?

The taxi chugged away in the rain, leaving wet saliva lines, like giant snail tracks, in the empty road. They were somewhere in Camden, looking up at a peeling house. As Keith took her arm, Katie shivered uneasily, firmly reassuring herself that she was a modern woman, in control, that she could leave whenever she liked.

Katie came home three hours later feeling seriously depressed. She couldn't believe what she'd done. She cried all the way back, the tears forming itchy streaks on her face. Outside her flat, she fumbled in her bag for her keys. Normally Katie always had her keys ready; she was a girl who walked the streets at night with edgy fear, pounding up the steps to get into her flat, convinced rapists were lying in wait in the dark corners of the staircase. Tonight, she didn't care. Didn't care if she lived or died. She finally found the keys wrapped up in a dirty tissue, then winced at the torn, shiny purple square. Seeing the condom wrapper brought such a shiver of revulsion that she felt more tears pierce the numbness.

She went into the dark hallway and nearly tripped over the shoes – a pair of dark DMs, and Leila's brown kinky knee-length boots. Giving them a savage kick, Katie carried on into the kitchen.

A cup of coffee would only keep her awake and she wanted the inky comfort of sleep, to blot out the pain . . . So she made herself a cup of peppermint tea and sat on the sofa, warming her hands on the mug, feeling cleansed by the hot liquid. Outside the window, the dawn looked as if someone had dipped a finger in a pot of pink paint and run an outline over the silhouette of London. A few birds peeped; from the bedroom there was silence – or did she catch the odd creak, a sigh, a muffled laugh?

Suddenly there was a sluicing noise. The splash of

water on tiles. Katie pictured them wrapped together in the shower, kissing under the spray, and quickly took another sharp sip of tea.

Seeing the bedroom door creak open, she jumped, spilling a few drops of tea on her knees. Jack emerged from the bedroom. His dark hair was all mussed up, his sideburns were squiffy and he was wearing a pair of boxer shorts.

'Oh!' he started, seeing Katie.

'Sorry, I'll go.' Katie hastily got up, all shaky and with her heart hammering.

'Don't be silly, it's your flat. Leila's having a shower. I just came out to get my fags.'

'Well, there they are. On the table.' Katie kept trying hard not to look at him but she couldn't help it. His skin was the colour of whisky and he had layers of dark, fine hair over his thighs and arms, thickening on his chest and tapering to a V at his bellybutton.

Jack picked up his (or, more likely, Leila's) Marlboro packet and slumped down in an armchair. As he lit up his cigarette, orange flames orbed in his eyes and, with the moonlight falling on his chiselled face and spiky hair, he suddenly looked like a wicked elf – like Shakespeare's Puck, Katie fancied.

'So, did you have a nice night?'

'Mmm.'

Nice! thought Katie. She remembered with a shudder walking into Keith's room in the grey gloom, trying to flick on the lamp that wouldn't work, the mounds of grimy clothing on the carpet.

'Come on, give me the juicy details. You can tell Uncle Jack. Did you have sex?'

'No!' Katie cried.

'Oh, come on. What did you do then, discuss how Proust can change your life? I bet you did. You have a glow about you, as if you've just been taken to heaven and back several times.'

'Actually, it was horrible,' she said in a tight, high voice.

'Really?' Jack looked interested. 'What? Did he have a peanut-sized penis?'

'No!' Katie gave a gasp of shocked laughter. She wasn't used to talking about stuff like this with men.

'What then? Peanut-flavoured penis?'

'More like mint-flavoured penis,' Katie blurted out, then blushed. 'I mean, he had to go down to the local garage for some condoms and that was the only flavour they had,' she mumbled in embarrassment. 'Mint!'

'Oh, that is classic!' Jack slapped his knee. 'Imagine giving someone a blow job with that on. You might get muddled up and absent-mindedly think you were cleaning your teeth. Painful!' He was laughing so hard now that he started to choke on his cigarette and he coughed, flapping the smoke away. 'Carry on . . .'

Katie opened her mouth to speak. Suddenly her laughter trickled away. She had a fleeting vision of Jack going back into Leila's bedroom and repeating all of this to her, and both of them laughing smugly, knowing that with their good looks and radiance bad sex was just out of the question. Not like silly Katie, fat Katie, Katie the Clown. And she felt tears rushing up inside her throat.

'So which condom did you have for dessert? Curry-flavoured?' Jack carried on, not noticing. Then suddenly a sob cut through the air. 'Katie?'

Katie quickly bent forwards and tried to shield her face. Jack put his cigarette down and came across to the sofa. As he put his arm around her, she tensed.

'Katie?' He kept rubbing her back. 'I'm sorry, I didn't mean to be rude. I just have this foul sense of humour.'

58

'Really, I'm fine . . .' she sobbed.

'You're clearly not fine, darling. Come on, what is it? Did I upset you?'

'No, it's not your fault, it's not you.'

'Keith. He didn't . . . did he?'

'No! No, I . . . nothing like that.' Katie couldn't look at him. 'I'm fine.'

'Sure?' Jack lifted a curtain of hair away from her face.

'No – just too much to drink, I guess.'

'You alkie. Come here and have a cuddle, you poor thing.' He spread open his arms and she tentatively laid her head against his chest. He cuddled her, stroking her hair and back of her neck with the nub of his thumb, muttering soothing noises. Katie felt herself turn to liquid against him. She could hear his heart beating in her ear, feel the soft fuzz of his chest hair against her cheek, smell the slightly sweaty scent of his body. She thought her heart would break.

How could she say it to him? Her night with Keith had been horrible, worse than her worst nightmares. But it wasn't that Keith had taken advantage of her. She could have said no at any point. She'd just found herself swept along like a zombie. Wanting to prove that she was having a good time, that she was a woman.

But when it had come to the sex, it had been dreadful. Wet kisses and no foreplay, and as he had thrust inside her, she'd felt all the emotions that had been coiled up tight in her heart ever since Jack had asked Leila to dance start to unravel. Tears had pricked her eyes. Keith had moved above her, his eyes scrunched up, his mouth tight. Behind him, the night had been as black as tar. She'd pictured Jack and Leila together, writhing deliciously on silky sheets. A tear had eeked out of the corner of her eye. She'd felt as though her mind was separate from everything

59

else, a bubble filled with unrequited love and pain, and Keith was making love to some body, some thing attached to her. As he'd climaxed, she'd cried out with pain. As he'd sunk his head back down into the pillow, she'd sobbed, staring up at the sky, thinking, *What am I doing here? Why did I do this? Does Jack really care where I am? As if . . .*

Winners and losers. That's what Leila was always saying. Life was filled with winners and losers. Well, what if she was going to be a loser in love, only able to attract men like Keith? She was always picturing a time in the future when everything would be better, when she would be thinner, blonder, happier. What if it never came? What if she never ever met another Jack and only got Keiths? Her mum was always reassuring her that as men matured they started to care more about personality than looks but – come on. Men were men.

She had quietly detached herself from Keith, dressed and walked out of the flat and into the night.

But Jack's hug made her feel better. A little better.

'You OK now?'

'Mmm.' She didn't want him to stop holding her. But . . .

'What about you and Leila?' she suddenly burst out.

'Well, I'm going to Prague this morning, so . . .' Jack shrugged vaguely.

Katie lifted her head. Their faces were only inches apart. He smiled, a little sheepish, a little awkward. Suddenly she felt anger flare up inside. Perversely enough, she would have liked him more if he had stuck with Leila. Why did people like Jack, people who found love easily, always treat it like a toy, something to play with and then throw away?

'You don't realise how lucky you are,' she said sourly.

Jack frowned.

'You're really sweet, you know that? Why don't we go out for a drink sometime?' he said, ignoring her remark.

'Jack!' Leila suddenly burst into the room, her silky white dressing gown clinging to her body. Katie and Jack quickly disentangled themselves. Jack went off to get dressed; Leila gave Katie a possessive glare and disappeared into the kitchen to make some coffee. Katie sat on the sofa, feeling tired and very confused. It had been a long night.

It was three months later when they bumped into each other again, quite by chance. Katie was in the supermarket on a Sunday. She was suffering one of those horrible embarrassments – she'd absent-mindedly slung a few tins and a loaf of bread into her basket, got to the checkout, realised she'd spent her last ten pounds at the cinema the night before, and was now counting out £4.85 in twenty, ten and five pence pieces, plus coppers, into the hand of a very bored assistant. Katie felt a blush sweeping over her face like a rash as the queue behind her multiplied impatiently. And then a wonderfully familiar voice cried out, 'Katie!'

Jack.

'Here.' Jack passed over a ten-pound note to the relieved assistant. 'Come on – coming for a drink? Catch up on some gossip?'

Katie could barely take it in. As they walked to the nearest pub, Jack chatting happily, she just wanted to stop in the street and stare at him. God – he was *gorgeous*. And it was more than his looks – it was just the allure around him. In the pub, while she perched nervously on the edge of her seat, he sat back and sprawled out his legs. He was so cool, so happy, so relaxed, as if life was one big party and he belonged in a beach hut in Malibu drinking cocktails for ever.

At first Katie felt like a jelly on steroids. But gradually she started to relax. There was only one really embarrassing moment when Katie (God knows why) pretended she smoked and accepted a Marlboro from him. She ended up almost coughing her lungs up. But Jack was very sweet; he gave her a gentle pat on the back, retrieved the cigarette and said, 'I'm sure you don't want that. I'm sure you've given up,' he winked.

'Erm, yes,' said Katie, touched. He could have taken the piss, teased her to death, but he hadn't. He was so lovely.

Jack asked after Leila; Katie explained that Leila had moved to the US to pursue a job in publishing. To Katie's relief, Jack didn't seem to care the slightest. He told her wild tales of his holiday romances and, to make him jealous, she told him that she was now dating Keith.

'Keith!' Jack made puking noises. 'What – that loser from the club? You're kidding!' He shrank back as Katie hit him playfully.

They carried on talking till closing time. Jack, being a gentleman, walked her home and gave her a gentle kiss on the cheek goodnight. Once inside, she couldn't stop whooping and laughing. She danced and spun and cartwheeled her way across the front room, until she landed in a heap on the sofa. *Nothing's going to happen*, she told herself, *he's just a friend. Nothing, nothing, nothing . . .*

Yet one butterfly of hope still fluttered inside her.

Nothing did happen, of course. Not the next Saturday, when Jack invited himself over for dinner. They had a glorious meal, a water-fight washing up and then slouched contentedly on the sofa with a tartan blanket and Leila's cat on their knees (Katie had been drafted in to look after it while Leila was in the US). They watched hours of TV, till 3 a.m., so their eyes were burning and their voices were happily hoarse from so much conversation.

But the night planted a seed of friendship deep in both their hearts which slowly blossomed over the years. At first it was sporadic – odd drinks out, nights in, movie trips, Pizza Express outings, where Jack always had a meaty Pizza and Katie, who was veggie, had the Fiorentina. They both adored films and TV, though their tastes differed, and every time they sat down to watch television it was prologued by a playful fight over *Have I Got News For You* (Jack) versus *Friends* (Katie) or *The League of Gentlemen* (Katie) versus *Frasier* (Jack). When Jack travelled abroad, he became more and more accustomed to arriving back in the UK, tanned and woozy from jet-lag and too much sex, and calling her up, hearing her lovely plump voice promising hugs and a sympathetic ear and hot buttered toast and the creaky sofa and *Friends*.

Over the next eight years, as they approached their thirties, their friendship put down roots and deepened, remaining stable despite the uneven changes in their lives. Life changed a lot. While Jack was content to drift lazily through the dating game like a piece of seaweed carried along by the tide, Katie put down roots. She got married. Unfortunately, to the wrong man. Though she only realised this, with perfect timing, just after their baby, Susie, was born after a year of marriage.

Much to Jack's amazement, Katie ended up marrying Keith.

The knot of their friendship loosened during her marriage; to say Keith was the jealous type was an understatement – he once gave her a black eye for talking to a pizza-delivery boy. But Katie's divorce had tightened the knot again. Jack had been wonderfully supportive throughout, helping Katie to pluck up the courage to leave, finding her places to stay, playing bodyguard, changing her locks and fending off her irate ex-husband when he called twenty times a day to make threats about court and custody battles.

Leila, too, had got married in America, to some high-flying publisher, a man almost twice her age, called Ray King. Five years later, they had divorced.

At school, Katie and Leila had always joked that their lives ran in parallel, that the same things happened to them at the same time. Their divorces coincided and when Leila moved back to England, she bought a huge house in Princess Road, Primrose Hill, and allowed Katie and Susie to move in. Leila had received an enormous settlement from her divorce and she charged Katie a ridiculously low rent.

Katie had been staying there for three years now and she liked it. She and Leila didn't even see each other that often – Leila worked long hours as a literary agent and often they only bumped into one another coming in or out of the bath-room, either early in the morning or late at night. Leila seemed to prefer it that way. She kept herself to herself.

Leila wasn't easy to live with. She was fastidiously tidy, so Katie was always having to keep Susie's overflowing toys under control and wipe the crumbs from the kitchen table. Leila was also very sensitive to noise, which meant having to keep Susie's kids' TV very quiet and ensure that the doors were kept shut.

Even though Katie was relieved that Leila had finally let Jack stay, she realised that Jack wasn't going to fit in very well. He was a complete slob. Now, seeing Jack sitting at the kitchen table, leafing lazily through a dog-eared copy of *Marie Claire* and chuckling at an article entitled 'I Had a Threesome with my Boyfriend and His Sister', Katie decided he was going to need training.

'Come on, you need to get into tidy habits,' she said firmly, ignoring him pretending to ignore her. 'Let's clear these carrier bags out of the hallway while we're here.'

They shunted them up to the bedroom on the second floor. At one time it had been Susie's nursery and playroom; the walls were painted pink, and yellow plastic stars glistened on the ceiling.

'Phew.' Jack crashed out on the bed when they had finally heaved everything up. As he flicked his hair back from his face, he left a dusty smudge on his forehead. 'I'm knackered.'

'Well, you ought to jolly well go and look for a job,' Katie said.

Jack gave a faint smile. Oh well – there wasn't time to nag him any more. She was in a rush.

The rest of the day was a whirlwind. She'd been so preoccupied with Jack that she'd forgotten to give Susie a packed lunch so she had to dash out, buy some brown bread, whip up some cream cheese and cucumber sandwiches, drop them off at school, then hurry to GLENCO for the afternoon, the local environmental charity she worked for.

In the evening, after she'd put Susie to bed and Jack had read Susie a story, they crashed out in the living room, slumped on the big stuffy red couch. They put on *The Life of Brian*, but as they'd already seen the film twenty times, started chatting over the top.

'Phew, it's SO nice to relax,' Katie said, tipping her head back and swinging her feet on to the coffee table. 'I love Susie to death but when she's in bed – God, it's heaven.'

'We could relax even more if we had some wine,' Jack said, going over and unlocking Leila's oak drinks cabinet.

'No – don't! Leila will kill you. Seriously Jack – she gets very sensitive about people "borrowing" food, drink, towels or clothes.'

'What a shame. I was dying to steal that skirt she had on this morning but maybe I'll keep out of her wardrobe,' Jack joked with a wry smile, delving into the back of the cabinet and pulling out a bottle.

'*Jack!*'

'Actually, this one is ours. D'you remember?' Jack's eyes gleamed as he held it up to the light. The bottle was green, the liquid deep plum, the label scrawled with a black-ink sketch of a leaf and black calligraphy, now blurred with water spots.

'Oh God,' Katie groaned. 'Don't tell me, it's Henry's home-made concoction?'

Jack's friend Henry had gone through a phase of making his own wine a few months ago when his acting work dried up and he'd had nothing to fill his days. It hadn't been a hugely successful hobby. Jack found two small crystal sherry glasses in the cabinet – he was too lazy to bother going six feet down the hall and into the kitchen for wine glasses. As he poured the wine out, it glugged with the consistency of thick syrup, the occasional piece of pulp and chunks of fuck-knows-what tumbling out too. As Jack handed her a glass, Katie took a sniff and pulled a face. It actually smelt quite nice, like winter punch, but she was still dubious. It was Susie's parents' evening tomorrow and she had no wish to spend the evening puking in the toilets and smelling like an alcoholic.

'You go first.' She nudged Jack with a grin.

'You.'

66

'Gentlemen first, darling.'

'OK.' Jack took a tiny sip. 'It's lovely,' he said in surprise.

'OK.' Katie, surprised too, took a large gulp. Her expression tightened. Her face turned purple. She rolled the wine around her mouth like a poisonous marble, flapping her fingers in front of her taut lips while Jack laughed. Finally, she ran to the window and spat it out on to the grass, slinging the rest of the wine with it. 'You bastard, Jack! It's *nice*. Yeah right.'

Jack picked up the bottle again, shaking his head.

'So,' Katie said, when she'd finally recovered and got herself some slightly flat Coke from the kitchen. Jack, bizzarely, was carrying on with his wine, declaring that it was somehow addictive. Swallowing back a burp, Katie asked, 'How's the job hunt gone today?'

'Shit,' said Jack, pursing his lips and leaning his head boyishly against her shoulder. 'I'm so unemployable. I have only three pounds in my bank account at present and I owe –' he gulped, very nearly saying, 'I owe Mick three thousand pounds' but just catching himself in time '– Barclaycard squillions and squillions. Maybe I should just copy bloody Leila – it's all right for her, she marries some rich American, conveniently divorces him a couple of years later and walks off with five million. Joan Collins, here I come.'

'Now, now, Jack,' said Katie. 'Leila is letting you stay here. She is nice.'

'Yeah, well.' Jack sank further and further down the sofa until his head was nearly resting on the seat cushions. 'What I need is to win the lottery!' He raised his glass in a mock toast. 'To the lottery!'

Katie chinked it, laughing. Katie and Jack did the lottery every Wednesday and Saturday nights. Despite the various winning theories Jack had concocted over the last few years, they'd only ever won ten pounds.

'Mmm, what would you do if you won the lottery?' Jack sighed.

Katie smiled. She loved conversations like this with Jack. They could just talk and talk and talk, for hours and hours, about nothing really, and yet he made her laugh and that made her feel alive.

'Oh – I'd love a house somewhere in the countryside, like the place in Wales I spent my early childhood, away from the mayhem of London, with a farm – just something simple, a few ducks and sheep – and a bedroom with a curving, oak-beamed roof.' For a moment Katie pictured waking up beside Jack, his face all soft and creased with sleep, him smiling at her affectionately, them sharing breakfast in bed. She shook herself. 'What about you?' *Do I play any part in your fantasies?* she wondered silently.

'I'd buy an island. A tropical island with sand so fine it's almost white flour – like the beaches in California. And there'd be an endless supply of food on the island – oh, and a bar with girls in skimpy bikinis serving cocktails and a large hi-fi system playing all the albums by The Manic Street Preachers and Madonna. And there'd be parties all night in the moonlight on the beach, and dancing girls.'

'Yeah, I'll have a few dancing boys on my farm,' Katie added to annoy him. 'To get up early and milk my sheep for me so I can have a lie-in.'

'It's your Welsh roots, Katie,' said Jack. 'You're just a sheep-shagger at heart. It's in your genes. I bet you only have to pull on a wool jumper and –' he tickled his fingers up and down her arm '– you start feeling all sexy and hot and—'

'*Jack!*' Katie was feeling sexy, though certainly not with the thought of sheep. 'You're so foul when you're drunk.'

'This wine actually grows on you.' Jack held it to the light.

He managed to persuade Katie to join him for another glass and although she wasn't sure that it ever quite 'grew' on her, by midnight they had finished the bottle. Both drunk, they started to clean up, yawning now. Katie gave him a hug goodnight – she'd intended it to be just a breezy caress, but swept with affection, he suddenly pulled her into a tight bear hug.

'Thanks for everything,' he whispered, his breath warm on her ear. 'Thanks for helping me out and cheering me up and sorting it all with Leila. God, I don't know what I'd do without you.'

Getting into bed, Katie noticed her 'List For Monday' (Katie loved lists; she made one every day) lying on her cabinet, with tasks such as 'buy bread' or 'clean cooker' lying uncrossed. That was the trouble with Jack – he always sucked her so strongly into his life, his concerns, that he threw her own life out of kilter.

Her love for him went on in an endless loop, like an eel with its tail in its mouth. She'd pack her emotions into a box, slam down the lid, persuade herself that she didn't fancy him any more, that she'd grown out of her stupid crush. But despite her logic, desire still simmered beneath the surface, until finally the lid came off again and she had to face up to the fact that she loved him.

She was starting to wonder if living with him was such a good idea. Normally, when she found her emotions becoming too painfully Mills & Boon, she would (as if Jack was a box of chocolates and she was on a diet) starve herself of his company for a while, claiming she was busy with work and Susie. But now his presence was everywhere. His aftershave in the bathroom, his muddy boots by the back door, his black jumper sprawled across the armchair . . .

Jack, lying in his bed, was also pining.

For his dog.

Usually Dido slept in a warm bundle across his feet. Jack was always being woken up by her getting bored and starting to chew his socks off, or else yapping at 5 a.m. for her food. He'd had to shunt her off to Steve's house, who wasn't exactly ecstatic about taking her in; his wife-to-be didn't like animals. Poor Dido would probably be shut out in a back shed at night, with only a three-foot garden in which to roam. *I have to get a job,* he thought, the wine dragging him into a depression. Despite Katie being so helpful, he didn't feel hugely optimistic.

He sighed, rolled over, and longed for sleep to drown him. When finally he dropped off a few hours later, he slept until midday, as if not wanting to wake up and face a new day.

6
Charlie

Puck and I were in BIG trouble.

We were supposed to have spent the evening doing service for the Fairy Council. Everyone in the Primrose Hill fairy camp has a different responsibility, from making clothes out of dandelion stalks, to sending out leaflets for the RSPCF. It's all very fascist. Puck and I were on (guess what!) litter duty. I mean, who in their right mind wants to spend the night wandering around Regent's Park picking up Mars Bars wrappers and Coke cans.

Even worse, we were on duty with the biggest square in the fairy camp.

Mervin.

Mervin was a thin, grey, fairy-of-the-pine cone. He was so pathetic, he even collected the ring-pulls off the cans and pinned them to his walls, with little labels underneath such as 'Can of Sprite, slightly bent at tip, spotted 22:34, 3.10.00', as if they were rare and precious butterflies.

He was waiting for us when we flew back from the pub.

'Puck! Charlize! Titania and Oberon have asked that you report to them at once.'

Puck and I exchanged nervous glances. Oh shit.

'After all, we've all been wondering where you've been,' he went on gravely. 'We began litter duty at ten o'clock last night. It is now four o'clock in the morning.'

Despite Puck making up a cheeky excuse that we'd spent the last six hours chasing a stray Mars Bar wrapper because, hey, we were so dedicated to our job, Mervin pointed sharply to the Royal burrow. I swallowed. The dark entrance looked like the mouth of a horrible beast, waiting to devour us.

Puck and I had no time to confer, to conjure up excuses, explanations. We were sent straight into the Royal rabbit burrow with beating hearts, stooping as the earthy ceiling curved low, tree roots hanging here and there in grey tendrils.

Sitting in cases along the walls were some snoozing glow-worms who were supposed to be emitting an attractive green glow. As we walked down the tunnel, Puck played his usual trick of prodding them and whispering, 'It's all right, Dawn's here.'

Glow-worms are incredibly lazy and very slow at passing on messages to each other. If ever Mary, the Royal attendant, has to pass a message down the line that she'd like the hall lit for the arrival of a VIP elf next Thursday, you can guarantee that, come Thursday, they'll all feign total surprise and cry, 'What, I never heard nothing about any elf!' On this occasion, however, the message 'We're off' rippled through the line like lightning. Within a few seconds they were all sighing and saying, 'God, that seemed short for a change, Dawn's obviously decided to get her bloody act together instead of her usual winter lie-ins.' So that by the time we had reached the end of the tunnel, we were stumbling about in pitch darkness. Then we heard Mary's voice screeching, 'What the hell d'you think you're doing? It's only midnight, you bunch of lazy good-for-nothings!'

'But we were told Dawn was here,' one glow-worm objected pitifully.

'Oh yeah? By whom? Some mysterious voice that came out of nowhere?'

'Yes! Yes!' chorused the glow-worms, letting out wails of dismay as Mary made her way down the corridor prodding them all back on.

'Puck, stop messing about,' I hissed. 'We're in enough trouble as it is. Oh God, Puck, what are we going to say to them?'

But then Puck slipped his hand into mine and I felt relief like a cool fountain. Puck would get us out of the mess somehow; he would know what to say. He was Puck, the Oscar Wilde of the fairy world (who once, on leaving the fairy gates, had drawled, 'I have nothing to declare, except my enormous penis'). He who, having recently been caught in Daphne Daffodil's flower with his shorts around his ankles, had managed to persuade Mrs Geranium of all people that he'd been giving poor Daphne a foot massage and that the notches on his belt kept breaking, and then had even had the gall to get her to spend the next fortnight weaving a new belt for him.

Finally, we came to the doors of the Royal chamber. Scarlet and gold-trimmed rugs had been slung over the earthy floor but it was still bumpy, tree roots protruding here and there like knarled fingers.

Puck was about to knock when we heard the shouting. It really didn't sound very regal.

'Look, we simply can't afford to have the roots removed,' said a gruff male voice.

'I tripped on one yesterday—'

'Darling, you keep having the place redecorated, it's becoming a neurosis. Look how much it cost to have the bedroom ceiling studded with flies' eyes? Two thousand petals!'

'Well, that's because those workmen are terrible! Those beetles! They just sit around twiddling their antennae and nibbling grubs. If you could keep them under control . . .'

'Ahem.' Puck knocked nervously.

There was a long, embarrassed silence. Then: 'COME IN!'

Inside the chambers, King Oberon and Queen Titania were seated on their royal thrones looking tense and flushed. Oberon's throne was made of dark mahogany, covered with thorns and bracken. He had a female attendant waving a bracken leaf by his neck to create a cooling breeze (very necessary in autumn, I'm sure). Titania's throne was made of pale gold and covered with intricate tapestries and sweet-smelling flowers.

Oberon, no doubt in a bad mood from his marital tiff, puffed up his chest as he addressed Puck in a pompous drone.

'So, Puck Nigel, son of the thistle, we hear that you and your accomplice have been breaking every fairy rule in the book, including the following crimes, in ascending order of gravity: Section B, Paragraph six, page ninety-three, for your reference, fairies must not wilfully indulge in contact with humans; Section H, Paragraph fourteen, page one hundred and seven, fairies must not wilfully interfere with human lives . . .'

And so it went on. Puck and I exchanged glances. Even Titania gazed at the ceiling. The girl fairy fanning Oberon was so shocked by such a list of offences that she bashed Oberon on the head with the bracken. She coloured and muttered profuse apologies; he cleared his throat, lifted his chin and carried on. I saw Puck's shoulder shake. For a moment I was overwhelmed with a horrible fear that I might start laughing.

'So, Puck,' Oberon concluded, 'I'd like to hear an explanation for this. Before we decide what punishment to enforce, we want to hear your side of the story.'

Puck began the defence with all the confidence and articulateness of a barrister fresh out of law school.

'Yes,' Titania interrupted, 'I think that before you say any more, Puck, you ought to be aware that a water sprite who lives in the beer barrels of a public house observed you entering and reported back to us.'

'Yes,' Oberon repeated, his male ego prickled. 'Besides, Mrs Tulip said she saw you leave at nine p.m. and you didn't return until five a.m. Rather a long time to spend just dithering about, hey? A whole –' he paused, swallowing, ' – seven h—'

'Eight,' Titania interjected quietly, lips moving little more than a ventriloquist's.

'Eight hours,' Oberon boomed. 'The water sprite also observed that you –' Oberon curled his lips sarcastically, '– were involved in some tampering with a snooker match.'

'Ah, yes,' said Puck. 'Yes. Granted, there is a degree of truth in that. We sat on the edge of the table. We watched.'

'So you did make contact with humans,' said Oberon, swooping on his comment like a hawk.

Puck started to make up some bullshit story about trying to help and do his good deed for the day, but he came to an abrupt halt as Titania pinned her laser stare on him. Even the irreverent Puck respected and feared Titania.

'Look, we're sorry,' I confessed shakily. 'We did interfere. We never intended all of that to happen . . . it just did . . . we're really sorry . . . but maybe it's too late now?'

I gazed at her, willing her. *Please Titania, just give us a light punishment, like collecting human rubbish for a week, or helping out at the school, or polishing the royal ladybirds – anything.*

'I'm not going to punish you,' she said coldly. 'You're not children any more, you're adults. You know the difference between right and wrong. It's time for you to learn to take responsibility for your actions. You have taken apart a human's life, now you have to put it back together. You have to make Jack happy. This is your task.'

'Is that all?' I blurted out in relief, then winced as Puck nudged me. 'But what—'

'Can we go?' Puck asked at the same time, anxious to get out as quickly as possible.

'Yes, Charlize?' Titania asked.

I bit my lip as Puck rolled his eyes at me.

'I was just wondering, you know, what happens if . . . well, it doesn't work out . . . for whatever reason. I mean, if we try our best and do everything we can, and then it still doesn't happen?' I stuttered.

'Well, for the duration of this task – which you will keep secret from the rest of the camp – you have my permission to leave the camp as and when you choose. You have the freedom you've been waiting for. This will only be permitted, however, until the New Year celebrations. Then you will have to announce what you have done.'

Puck's eyes, which had been cloudy with worry, started to shine. He made a low, wolfish noise of repressed glee between his teeth.

'However,' Titania added, with an odd, almost vindictive smile on her face, 'if you don't succeed, then I'm afraid you will no longer be welcome back into the camp. You will be asked to leave. For good.'

7
Leila

Leila pulled down the toilet seat and sat on the cold brim, clicking open her blue handbag, anxiously pulling out a mirror.

How did she look?

Not bad. Thank God. Her mascara was smudged under her eyes in gothic circles, but otherwise not bad. She rolled up a piece of toilet tissue, wet it with her mouth and brushed it under her eyes. The toilet cubicle was so narrow her elbows banged against the wall. There was noise all around – the muted tin-tin of music from the pub, the birdsong flutter of voices, the hiss of hairspray. The Ladies at Odettes consisted of three tiny loos and one sink, where women fought around each other for a bit of mirror – which was why Leila had retreated to a cubicle to apply her make-up.

She kept wanting to hug herself in excitement. It was the perfect evening. She'd met a man, a gorgeous, sexy man, and they were going to go back home and have glorious sex – *yeeessssss!* She felt like a footballer scoring the winning goal.

And she hadn't even intended to pick anyone up tonight.

A friend had dragged her along to the pub, a friend whom she hadn't seen for years, on the pretext that it would be 'good to catch up on gossip'. Then, fifteen minutes into the conversation, the friend had mentioned that she was 'fiddling with a book'.

Leila had repressed an inward groan. She was a successful literary agent and every friend, relative, stranger, in-law and their pet seemed to have a book 'they'd always been meaning to send off to a publisher'. It was normally a memoir, something totally boring like *The Story of My Life: Sixty Years as a Car Park Attendant* which about three people would want to buy. The friend, Shelley, had rattled on about 'flat-sharing twentysomethings addicted to alcohol and cocaine due to relationship angst', which was obviously some sort of *This Life* meets *Cold Feet* meets *Sex And The City* thing that had already been done twenty times over.

'So, what do you think?' Shelley asked excitedly.

'Er – do send it in,' said Leila politely. 'I'll take a look at it.' Bin it more like, she thought.

'Great!' Shelley cried, obviously having visions of huge advances, yachts, cars, long literary lunches, signings in Waterstone's. 'Oh thanks, Leila – have another drink!' She waved her Bacardi Breezer exuberantly. 'On me!'

'No, really,' Leila said. She rarely drank alcohol except on special occasions and it always irritated her when people forced it on her.

Finally she agreed to another mineral water. She sighed, deeply bored, and drummed her long polished nails on the bar. If there was one thing Leila hated it was wasting time. She had a stash of paperwork she could be doing. She kept smiling and *mmm*ing at Shelley, whilst surreptitiously edging back her cardigan sleeve, checking her watch. 9:30 p.m. *OK*, she resolved, *I'll leave by 10 o'clock. At the VERY latest.*

The pub was starting to fill up. Leila ran her eyes over the men. They started to notice her too. Leila was pretty noticeable and she knew it.

None of them impressed her. They were mostly office boys in sweaty shirts and glasses. One did catch her eye – a tall, public school type with floppy hair. He had slight acne on his face, but it was saved by his sculptured, handsome features. His hair, though, was odd – blond, streaked with dark, almost suspiciously . . . *green* . . . highlights. How peculiar.

He looked familiar. Then she clicked. Of course – Henry. A friend of Jack's. She knew him very vaguely. She'd always noted how sexy he was.

She watched him over by the bar, fighting through the hoards of people, waving a fiver in the air. Sensing her gaze, he turned. Leila smiled. He gave a shy grin, a little finger-wave.

'Hi – I'm Richard,' a voice said in her ear.

Leila turned to see two eager City blokes vying for her attention.

She crossed her legs, tossed back her hair. Neither of them were beddable (Leila ruthlessly decided *that* about blokes within seven seconds of meeting them). But she liked to flirt and she enjoyed the thought of Henry watching jealously . . .

Their chat-up lines were dreadful.

One had his own dotcom company that sold condoms – con.com. And as soon as she mentioned she was an agent, Richard started ranting about a book 'he'd been working on for the past three years'. Yawn, yawn, yawn.

Leila looked at Henry again. It was funny, he always seemed so awkward – now he was standing over by the Gents, having to hop aside every few seconds as men went in and out, pinned there by a short blonde who was talking to him animatedly. Leila felt peeved. Then he looked up, caught her eye and almost imperceptibly grimaced. Leila grinned, a burst of liking igniting inside her.

'. . . the book is kind of about this stockbroker, he kind of . . . meets a girl . . . and she's a stockbroker!' Richard was exclaiming. 'It's all very autobiographical . . . they do this stockbroker deal, and then, at the end, the twist is, he turns out to be a vampire!'

Leila noticed the office blonde had gone off to get drinks. Henry was alone.

'Mmm,' said Leila, slipping off her stool, taking her drink with her. 'I need the loo.'

She left the men with Shelley, pushed through the crowds, walked straight up to him and said brashly, 'Henry – hi. How are you? Your hair looks crap, d'you know that?'

To her surprise, he laughed.

'Oh – right. Well, I'm playing Puck in a production of *A Midsummer*, so it was actually meant to have green streaks in.'

Leila lit up. She'd forgotten he was an actor. How glamorous.

An awkward silence.

'It's a good play, *Midsummer*,' Henry went on, spluttering with nerves. 'Shakespeare . . . you know . . . erm . . .'

Leila, who'd been taking a sip of her mineral water, curled her lip angrily around the glass. Being blonde and sexy, she often found people labelling her a bimbo the first time they met her. She always corrected them at once.

'A play for men,' she said sharply.

'Well, it is about fairies playing with the lives of two men and two women and they all—'

'Yes, I know that. But all Shakespeare's comedies follow the same narrative pattern: order, chaos, order. Women upset the social order at the beginning by disobeying men – Titania upsets Oberon, Hermia fights with her father, who is forcing her to marry a man she does not love. The centre of the play, set in the dark woods where chaos and magic go wild, represents the feminine psyche. At the end, order is resolved by women coming firmly back under the control of men – Titania is shamed by Oberon by being made to fall in love with an ass and Hermia marries her father's choice, reaffirming a patriarchal social order. Very sexist.' Leila finished off her speech with a charming smile.

Christ – a feminist *and* an intellectual, thought Henry in alarm. Feminists were scary. He somehow had a feeling he was being told off, though he wasn't quite sure what he'd done wrong.

'Er – do you want to escape?' he asked nervously. 'It's just – it's hot in here. I'm boiling, I need some air.'

This was a bit quick. They'd barely exchanged five sentences. Still, Leila was only interested in a one-night stand too, so . . .

'Sure – I'll just go to the loo and I'll be right with you. I need to say goodbye to my friend so I'll meet you outside.'

Henry was waiting on the pavement, hands in his pockets, shuffling from one foot to the other. Leila shivered and pulled her suit jacket around her. She was about to hail a cab when Henry said, 'Er – d'you mind if we just . . . y'know . . . walk for a bit . . . ?'

'Sure,' said Leila, bewildered. *Oh well, go with the flow*.

So they walked down Regent's Park Road in the warm moonlight, passing by the restaurants, bright with rainbow faces and cosy lighting. Every so often, Henry would accidentally brush against her and apologise. *He's so sweet*. Leila hid a smile.

'So, how's Jack?' Henry asked.

'Er – fine,' said Leila, folding her arms. 'I mean – annoying as ever. He's kipping over for a while.'

'Oh well – Jack, hey,' Henry laughed. 'You either love him or you hate him.'

'Anyway,' Leila changed the subject sharply. 'Seen any good movies lately?'

After that, they couldn't get off the subject. Henry seemed a bit nervous about impressing her at first and kept talking about arty subtitled films Leila had never even heard of (though she nodded confidently as though she had). Then Henry started to relax and they compared their favourite films (Henry: *Last Tango in Paris*/Leila: *Dangerous Liaisons*), their favourite actresses (Henry: Penelope Cruz/Leila: Julia Roberts), actors (Henry: Sean Penn/Leila: John Malkovich), and the movie that Henry should have been cast in, had he been a famous Hollywood star (Henry: Hugh Grant, *Sirens*/Leila: Hugh Grant, *Four Weddings*).

Leila also found herself relaxing. She'd started off the evening in her workaholic mode, in a treadmill state, doing one thing while thinking of the next. Now she was beginning to unwind, to feel more loose and feminine, to sink into the conversation like a warm bath and laugh naturally.

They reached the bridge where the old Primrose Hill tube station used to be. Henry paused.

'Er – what shall we do now?'

'Well,' Leila said. 'Why not go home and have mad, passionate sex?'

Henry looked shocked. He turned away quickly and hailed a cab. For a moment Leila wondered if she'd been too unsubtle. Then again, subtlety was something men never understood.

'Er,' said Henry to the cabbie. 'Chalcott Square, please.'

Impressive address, Leila registered, shivering behind him. She was surprised; as an 'impoverished actor' she'd been expecting him to live in a dingy bedsit in Camden. Though she could vaguely recall Jack saying something about Henry's parents being loaded.

'And – you?' He turned to Leila, looking awkward and confused. 'I mean – your address?'

Leila was too cold and impatient to stand around playing *your place or mine.* Maybe he had a girlfriend, a fiancée, whatever – but who cared?

'OK, let's go back to mine,' she said firmly, leaning in to the cabbie. 'I actually live very close – I'm in Princess Road.'

Henry held open the cab door for her.

Leila got in. Henry got in. But instead of slithering up beside her on the seat, he sat right at the other end, a huge expanse of leather between them.

Leila swallowed laughter. God, he was constrained. Like something out of *Pride and Prejudice.* She felt as though the chugging taxi was really a rollicking coach, the cab driver a horseman with a whip, and her Chloe suit a corseted ballgown.

She stared out of the window, humming lightly under her breath. Out of the corner of her eye she could see Henry gently twiddling with his umbrella, turning it round and round and round. Watching his thin, pianists' fingers curl around the black handle, she felt a shiver of lust dib-dabble over her and savoured a vision of them in bed, clothes strewn, covers rumpled, his thighs hot against hers, their mouths hungrily opening, and those wonderful long fingers tracing every inch of her body from head to toe. Shy, slender men were always the best lovers; big, bulky Gladiators always had too much testosterone, too much confidence. They thought they knew it all, and that pawing their huge hands over you was foreplay, while the word 'clitoris' was a foreign concept. Henry would be a skilled lover once he loosened up; Leila remembered with a rush of joy that she had a bottle of champagne in the fridge for a special occasion. She pictured herself lying back on the bed, Henry dribbling champagne into her mouth, licking sticky rivulets off her body, and shivered.

As the cab circled into Princess Road, the sexual tension between them thickened like a mist. Leila began deliberately manipulating it; she threw Henry a light, shy gaze, then, just as he looked back, she glanced away again. She looked, he looked, she looked away. She stared again and for a brief, exquisite second, Leila saw two high spots of colour on his cheeks, his pupils dilating, his mouth so quivery, so kissable . . .

'That'll be three pounds fifty,' said the cabbie.

They both jumped; neither of them had even noticed that the cab had stopped.

Henry got out, ran around the side and opened the door for her.

'Thanks,' said Leila.

'Well . . .' she said, pausing as the cabbie waited. She clicked open her handbag, pulling out her purse.

'No – I'll pay,' said Henry hastily.

'Well – he's – er – waiting.' Leila nodded sharply at the cabbie.

'Yes – well—'

'Do you want to come in for coffee?' she asked.

'Look – I'd better get back – sorry,' Henry said.

'*What?*' Leila couldn't keep the word from bulleting out of her lips.

'I – just – I don't like coffee.' He smiled desperately.

'Oh.' Leila relaxed. *Calm down*, she told herself, *it's just a game, a little play*. 'Well, I've got tea.'

'Mmm . . . hmmm . . .'

'Earl Grey?' She batted her eyelids.

'PG Tips?'

'Yes.'

'With the little triangular bags?'

'Possibly,' said Leila, knowing full well she'd never keep anything as preposterous as triangular tea bags in her cupboard.

'So have you decided on PG Tips?' the cabbie sighed.

'Sorry, sorry. No – really.' Henry smiled awkwardly. 'I won't come in. I must go. I'll call you, though. It was really lovely meeting you again.'

'Uh . . .' Leila couldn't believe it; he was serious. He was leaning over to kiss her – not even on the lips but on the cheek. She turned her head away petulantly so that his kiss was forced to land on her ear. His lips were deliciously light and dry, but she drew back, wiping her skin as though he had slobbered all over her.

'Night,' said Henry, 'I'll call.'

Leila opened her mouth to tell him to go fuck himself. *Don't show him how much he's hurt you*, she told herself.

'Fine,' she shrugged, but she knew from the terrible look of pity on his face that it looked like a tight, taut shrug. She walked up the path, her heels click-clacking in fury, and twisted the key in the lock.

'Well, we'll have those tea bags next time,' Henry called after her.

Leila ignored him, letting his words fall after her like a dropped bouquet.

Inside, Jack was crouching in the hallway. For some reason, he had removed her vacuum cleaner from the cupboard under the stairs and was performing surgery on it; the metal stomach had been opened up and wires and fluff had spewed everywhere. Leila felt the fury she'd been repressing rise to the surface. It was all Jack's fault, she decided viciously, hanging around, treating the place like a hotel, cramping her style.

'What the fuck are you doing with my vacuum?' she snarled.

'I – well, Katie was doing some hoovering and Susie's toy got sucked up and, erm, I was just trying to get it out – one of those green plasticy things you get in cereal packets.' He grinned, trying to turn it into a joke. 'By the way, I think there's something wrong with the dustbag too. I'll fix it while I'm at it.'

'And since when have you been Bob the Builder?'

'I'm just trying to help, since you're busy at work all day.'

Jack rubbed his cheek boyishly, leaving a smudge. Leila could see what he was doing; attempting to play the new man, to ingratiate himself, to extend an olive branch. But she was in too filthy a temper to do anything except throw the olive branch back at him.

'Yeah, well if you break it, you're paying for a new one.'

As Leila stomped upstairs, she caught sight of him flicking her a surreptitious 'V' sign. She turned and quite deliberately flicked him one back, causing him to drop his screwdriver in shock.

Up on the landing, Leila paused by Katie's bedroom.

Her door was slightly ajar and she could see Katie reading in bed, propped up by pillows, with Susie tucked in beside her. She was so contented, Leila felt a stab of jealousy. It was all right for Katie. She didn't need to worry about men; she had a daughter. As long as you had someone to love and love you, that was enough.

Leila stormed into her bedroom.

Slam! She shut the door.

Thwack! She threw her handbag at the dressing table, sending bottles and creams and potions and lipsticks and eyeliners all rolling and dominoeing and falling to the floor.

She sat down at her dressing table and gazed at her reflection.

She looked stunning. Her hair glistened like honey; weren't gentlemen supposed to prefer blondes? So why the hell hadn't Henry come in? Why?

The act of taking off her make-up was soothing. Leila loved make-up; putting it on and taking it off, the exotic names, the colours – rose burnish, amber twilight, musky peach. She'd worn make-up from a very young age because she enjoyed the mask it provided.

But now, as she put down the cotton wool buds and looked at her face, pale and clean and uninteresting, just like any other girl, she felt a sense of loathing and started to put the make-up on all over again. Deep red lips. Black panda eyes. Cobalt eyeshadow and cerise blusher. There.

Now she looked gorgeous. Like a cover girl. A photographer's dream, a David Bailey creation. Unobtainable, sultry, mysterious. And yet.

It's not as if I'm one of those pathetic girls who cling to men like Velcro, Leila thought, *who cry at Meg Ryan movies, who spend their lives waiting – waiting for men to call, for men to say 'I love you', for men to propose.*

God, no. Leila didn't even want to get married again, not when her career was on the up. She was busy and independent and one-night stands, like the salad sandwiches she bought at Tube stations on the way to work, were delicious, convenient and easily disposed of. It was just the way Henry had *won*. Leila always hated losing any game. And he'd won, won, won, quietly and sneeringly, with those two poisonous little words: *I'll call.* Yeah, yeah, yeah. God, just what was the matter with him? Men *never* rejected her. He was a clitoris-teaser, a vagina-breaker, a bastard, and definitely gay.

Leila got up, undressed and climbed into bed without taking off the make-up.

She cuddled up to Candida. Then she reached out to her bedside cabinet, picked up her wedding ring and slid it on to her finger. She fell asleep with her hands laced tightly together, the ring cold and hard against her knuckles . . .

Leila always responded to any emotional crisis by throwing herself into her work. The next morning she got up at 6:30 and went straight into the office. She drank three cups of coffee one after the other, feeding off the caffeine like a vulture. Then she hammered her slush pile, picking one manuscript out and chucking the remaining fifty-seven on to her 'reject' pile. There.

She paused, went to the little fridge in the corner of her office and took out a Bounty bar. She deserved a treat. She sat back in her chair and gazed out at the view over the Thames, pearly in the morning light. Leila loathed chocolate but adored coconut. Her assistant, Zoe, was a chocoholic, so Leila sliced the chocolate away and left it in the wrapper for her, then nibbled the creamy centre with her sharp, white teeth.

89

Still, she mused, *even if I don't have Henry, I am enjoying my little fling with Mr Winterton. Even if it is a sordid affair and I'm a mistress.* It was something to keep her entertained for the time being.

And then, at 9 a.m., a call came through.

'Leila – it's someone called Henry Badingham,' said Zoe.

What an arrogant bastard. She flared up. *Thinking I'm going to take his call at . . . what . . . 9 o'clock in the morning?* She knew his type. The Womaniser. *God, I bet he shagged some other girl last night and it didn't work out so now he's trying me again.*

'Tell him I'm in a meeting,' Leila said coldly, and slammed down the phone.

8
Henry

In a meeting.

In a meeting.

In a meeting.

Henry had called Leila at nine o'clock, ten-thirty and twelve but he'd had the same reply each time from some cocky Cockney assistant. Fuck.

He breathed in the bittersweet aroma of vanilla, cinnamon and chocolate, feeling it slide down his throat and fizz his stomach in a rumble of hunger. He realised in a daze that he was starving. He'd hardly slept and he'd skipped breakfast. His skin felt dry and his hair greasy. He'd just been so worried about why the hell Leila had gone off in such a huff last night.

The chocolate shop was a welcome relief. It was cool inside with a dark, red-tiled floor. The cases were filled with chocolates, spread out on little metal trays like jewellery, in all shades of brown, beige and black. What gorgeous names were written on the little white cards: Hazelnut Heaven, Rose-Cream Delight, Dark Chocolate Brandy Scoop.

Just what went wrong last night? Henry asked himself for about the thousandth time.

It was a mystery. Though all women were a mystery, in Henry's world.

He wasn't like Jack. Jack somehow had a knack for decoding women. He understood their body language. 'Look, Henry,' Jack always said, 'you need to watch and see if they expose their wrists – an erotic area – by fiddling with their earrings. That's a good sign. Or playing with their hair. Women are just like maps. You can read them easily, as long as you know the symbols.'

The moment he'd seen Leila last night, he'd wanted her. They'd kept glancing at each other. He'd met her a few times before through Jack and thought she was gorgeous, but hadn't had the courage to make a move.

Go and ask her for a drink! he'd kept yelling at himself. *Come on! She's playing with her earrings! And her hair! You're in.*

But he hadn't been able to do it. What if she had an ear infection and was stroking it better? What if she'd been in a rush that evening and hadn't had time to brush her hair? What if her hair simply fell in her eyes and annoyed her? His feet had remained glued to the floor, his elbow stuck to the bar. He'd felt defeated inside, knowing it would end up another night of missed opportunity and regret with him going home alone and dreaming about her. What if he had the guts to go up and ask her out, instead of being such a pathetic wimp and behaving like a thirteen-year-old schoolboy?

But she'd approached him. They'd had a great time. And in the taxi on the way home, he'd mentally tossed a coin, working out whether to sleep with her or not. Heads – she was gorgeous. Tails – she'd think he was a bastard who only wanted to get her into bed. Tails – she was special. Tails – he wanted to show her he cared.

Henry surveyed the display on the counter – the long

black rods of vanilla, a lemon plant sprouting Japanese-style blossom, a coconut halve. That was Leila, he felt, a coconut – tough on the outside, soft inside. He'd sensed a vulnerability beneath her brittleness, a feeling that she wanted a man to cherish her, not use and abuse her for a one-night stand.

So why had she got into such a strop?

He'd decided the only solution was to send her a box of chocolates. His last girlfriend, Alice, had declared, 'If there's one thing in the world ALL women love, it's chocolate. Find me a woman who doesn't and she's an alien. Or else had a sex change.'

'Can I help you?' the assistant asked.

Henry took six chocolates – two hazelnut, two coconut, two mint creams.

A card came with the gift-wrapped box. Back home, Henry took out his calligraphy pen and cursed as a drop of black ink dotted the card like a beauty spot. Now what? He surveyed his bookshelves, cluttered with Rousseau and Saussure and Sartre and other lovingly dog-eared books from his philosophy degree. He picked up his *Oxford Dictionary of Quotations*, looking for gems on love and desire. He found a quote from Coleridge: 'The man's desire is for the woman, but the woman's desire is rarely other than for the desire of the man.' *Oh, no*, he reflected, *that'll make me sound like a pretentious tosser.*

Finally he wrote, *Lovely meeting you, Leila, love Henry.*

He decided to deliver them himself, but after lunch (a quick toasted-cheese sandwich) he lost his nerve. What if she just didn't fancy him, plain and simple? Feeling miserable, he tore open the chocolates and ate them himself, leaving one mint cream. Then he felt sick and angry and fed up. He slumped on the sofa and flicked on Channel 4 to find a hyper presenter interviewing teenagers on the street for yet another plastic-wrapped, tacky, all-girl band.

But what if, what if she does like you? a voice kept asking. He looked down at the last chocolate, all his hopes resting on one little ball of sugar, cream and cocoa. What if?

'What kind of nutter,' Leila asked, looking up at Zoe, 'sends *one* chocolate?'

'A romantic!' Zoe cried. 'He was so sweet and shy, Leila; he just dashed in, left it, ran out. He's a looker too.'

Zoe and Leila stared at the chocolate, sitting like an ebony jewel in the cerise box.

'It probably cost him a million quid,' Zoe giggled, 'Probably had it shipped over from Brazil.'

'You have it,' said Leila, shaking her head.

'Ring him,' Zoe pleaded, her mouth thick with chocolate.

'I suppose I'll have to,' Leila sighed, as though she was being forced to ring a tax inspector. 'Or he'll send one every day, probably.'

'Actually, don't ring him,' Zoe cried.

Leila smiled and picked up the phone.

9
Charlie

Well – there were some advantages to our task of Making Jack Happy. For one thing, it meant avoiding Spirit Night.

Spirit Night happened every Saturday on the Primrose Canal. It was even worse than a high school disco. The trees were draped with fairy lights (which Puck had stolen from Currys), the banks festooned with daisy chains. There was a bar run by two thin water rats who served cocktails such as 'A Long Slow Screw Against A Toadstool' (dandelion juice, deadly nightshade and elderflower). The same band always played – The Beetles (I mean *real* beetles, not the phoney human spin-off band). They sang and played the drums (made from bottle tops) and the violin (courtesy of a cricket who drew his leg against his wings, accompanied by the occasional lascivious wink which sent the female fairies into orgasmic screaming fits).

I hated Spirit Night. I never got to dance with any handsome fairies. I was always the one left out at the end, looking at my nails in a casual hey-my-nails-are-so-fascinating-I-really-don't-want-to-dance way. The only person who ever asked me was a wrinkly, smelly, bogey-green toad called Wilbert who was always trying to pretend he was a frog so he could use his well-worn dodgy chat-up line: 'Hey – if you kiss me, I'll turn into a prince.'

I was also conscious of the fact that ever since we'd been set our task for Jack I'd piled on the pounds. I'd been stuffing myself with chocolate-covered earthworm bars. As a cluster of pretty female fairies turned up, I felt myself tense.

I've never fitted in well with the other girly fairies. The most popular was a girl called Rose who was sickeningly pretty. She always bullied me for being born on Halloween (very inauspicious), saying that I was a witch and the child of a goblin. I reacted by becoming a tomboy and befriending Puck.

Tonight she flew in on a beautiful Cabbage White butterfly. Butterflies were The Next Big Thing in the fairy world – our equivalent of scooters.

'Hey, like your wheels,' Puck called out flirtily.

'Thanks, Puck,' Rose said, tossing back a mane of blonde hair as she put on the brakes by tweaking the butterfly's antennae. 'Hey, Charlie, where's your butterfly? Or maybe,' she added, picking up a twig and twirling it, 'you're just making do with a broomstick.'

Bitch, bitch, bitch, I thought. I'd recently heard that she was interested in Puck because going out with him 'would be good for her image'.

'Hi Rose,' I said, 'like your wings. They're looking very . . . nipped.'

Rose flushed angrily. In fairy circles, small, neat wings are very fashionable and a lot of fairies were getting their wings clipped (our equivalent of plastic surgery) on the black market.

'Well, at least I don't look like Dumbo,' she said sweetly, eyeing up my huge pair.

'Come on, Puck,' I said, desperately. 'We need to go and do our research.'

Puck, who seemed to be enjoying our catfight, looked disappointed.

As we flew across London's spires, Puck kept moaning about how were we supposed to make Jack happy when all humans were experts in suffering? *How am I supposed to make Jack happy when I'm not even happy myself?* I wondered. *Here I am, a fat, paranoid fairy in love with my best friend who I know will never want me.*

Then I turned to look at Puck, who was pausing to adjust the time on Big Ben. His black eyes grinned with wickedness. I felt my heart swell. At least I had Puck as a friend. Dear Puck – just being in his company was like injecting happiness into my bloodstream.

We flew on to Trafalgar Square, stopping outside Waterstone's. We stood on the windowsill, looking in at the dark shadows. Pressing our palms to the glass, we slowly slid through. It was a glorious sensation – like falling through a sheet of cold, crystal water. Then, with a wiggle of our wing-tips in the last Perspex fibres, we were in.

We had decided to research the secret of human happiness by reading their books. Self-help books, philosophy books, psychology books. From John Grey to Freud to Jane Austen; you name it, we read it.

We discovered one basic principle: that human happiness is linked to a chemical in the brain called serotonin.

There were a hundred billion ways to bring about human happiness. But a lot of humans, having chased happiness like a butterfly, seemed to choke on it once they had it.

'Lottery winners, having spent their lives hoping to win, are often more miserable in the long-term because they can't handle the money stress,' I said.

'Oh God. Well, why can't we fix it so that Jack wins the lottery and then a week later we'll rob him and take it all back,' said Puck brightly.

'It says here,' I continued, 'that most people enjoy the *journey* of happiness rather than the goal. Once they get what they want, they desire something else. They like the uncertainty of the path.'

'A long journey full of uncertain hope that never comes to an end,' said Puck, frowning. 'We could always buy him a season ticket on a British train.'

'Puck!' I poked him. 'The thing is, perhaps humans shouldn't be naturally happy. The world isn't a very great place to be in. Maybe sadness is just realism.'

'Ignorance is bliss. I guess we could give him a lobotomy, like some of those footballers seem to have had.'

'High levels of serotonin are also found in chocolate, chickens and cottage cheese,' I continued. 'And from listening to Mozart. And, apparently, from going to raves.'

'Great,' said Puck, looking exhausted. 'So, if we get Jack to go to a rave where they play non-stop 'Eine Kleine Nachtmusik' and serve only hot chocolate, he'll be in heaven.'

We found better answers in the Eastern religions which described feelings of universal joy. We unearthed descriptions from throughout the ages, where poets and thinkers had tasted the liqueur of bliss, had experienced a moment of unlimited, transcendental joy.

'Here,' said Puck, 'what about this? Victor Hugo. "The supreme happiness of life is the conviction that we are loved." Hey – what about Jack's friend? You remember, when we were watching him the other night? Katie? They seemed so right together. He just didn't fancy her. Too fat, I suppose.'

'Typical man,' I blushed, thinking of all the earthworm

98

bars I'd eaten that morning. 'So, you think we should force them to fall in love?'

'If we could do that, we'd have the secret to all human happiness,' said Puck, thoughtfully.

'So now what?'

'I don't know. What do you think?'

'I don't know.'

'Hmm. There must be a way . . . to make Jack fall for Katie . . . somehow.'

10
Jack

'. . . well, Mr DeAntiquus, we'll be in touch,' the man in the black suit said, rising from his chair.

Yeah, right, thought Jack. There were no prizes for guessing whether he'd got the job or not. It had, quite simply, been one of the worst job interviews he'd ever had the misfortune to sit through.

'Well, thanks,' said Jack, shaking hands with the man in the suit, Mr Perkins or whatever his name was. He shook hands with the woman with red frizzy hair and she grimaced goodbye at him.

Jack got into the lift, went down to the ground floor, handed back his pass to the security guard and exited the building with a sigh of relief. Thank God that was over. *It's not as if I ever wanted to work for a company that sells dishwashers anyway*, he sniffed.

Outside it was hot, despite the fact that it was nearly October. White sunlight streamed down, so strong that the pavements were like hot coals. The air was smoggy with exhaust fumes, bitter tar and body odour.

The streets were jostling with tourists; a group of girls in pastel dresses were sitting outside the Holborn Pret A

Manger in the sun. Jack gave them a glance but they didn't look at him. He felt his heart fall again. He'd failed the job interview, nobody fancied him, he owed three thousand pounds to Mick and life sucked.

He passed a pub, all cool and beckoning, and lingered outside, tempted. He could really, really do with a pint right now, to wash away the disappointment. But – he checked his watch – he'd agreed to meet Katie in Safeways to help with her shopping. *My good deed for the day*, he thought with a weary sigh.

On the Tube Jack sat and sweated. He fingered the grey collar of the suit he'd borrowed from Henry; he hated getting dressed up. A refugee passed through the train with a pinched face, holding out a polystyrene cup for change. Like everyone else, Jack ignored her, then felt guilty.

He tried to focus on the 'Poems on the Tube' opposite – something about a talking tortoise intrigued by metaphysical concepts – but all he could think about was the interview. All the embarrassing things he'd said.

Jack wasn't a man who had ever relished work.

He didn't want to join the rat race. He didn't want to work nine-to-five. Anyway, it wasn't nine-to-five now, it was nine-to-nine. He saw friends burning out before they reached thirty, sucked dry by stress, with never any time for fun. Jack had a dreadful vision that if he joined in, he would end up forty years old, at some posh west London party, holding a glass of dry white wine, slightly bald, bags under his eyes, boastfully braying, 'Oh, my son Jeremy's got nine As at GCSE, he has his sights set on Oxbridge'. He saw himself staring wistfully at some young blonde and then quickly looking over at his wife – who would be a magazine editor called Isobel who raised money for charity by selling her old pashminas. No. Jack didn't want to spend his life trying to fit into some middle-class jigsaw, to have to buy a house in an expensive postal district just to prove he'd 'made it'.

He wanted to live life with all sincerity. He wanted it to be a long party, full of sparkling adventures and experiences. He wanted every day to shine with a brand new sheen of excitement.

And it had worked. His early twenties had been a rich tapestry of colourful travels. He'd never needed a proper job. He'd always done bit-jobs. A bit of gardening. A bit of building work. A bit of security work. Anything, just to raise enough cash to leave again.

But now, now that he owed Mick three thousand pounds, bit-work was no good. He needed a big, fat pay cheque. And, for the first time in his life, Jack was being forced to get A Proper Job. And it was terrifying him because he'd always thought to himself, *I'll get a proper job when I'm thirty*. Thirty had seemed far off – a time when he would be old, wise, settled, together. And now he was heading for thirty and he still didn't have his own flat. He still couldn't cook. He still took his washing home every weekend to his mum. And he was realising that he was virtually unemployable. His CV had more holes than a sieve. So what did that mean? Could he carry on like this for ever?

As he approached the supermarket, he saw Katie standing outside in the sun. She was wearing a long white dress; she looked like an angel.

'Hi!' He kissed her. 'You've caught the sun.' He touched her cheek, freckled like a pink duck's egg.

He dreaded that she'd ask him how the interview had gone. But she just chatted away, picking up a metal basket. He noticed she had a slightly sad look on her face.

'What's up?' he asked.

'Oh, well . . . Keith.'

'Ah. Keith.'

Keith was a terrible swearword. He was the Devil, Saddam Hussein and Jeffrey Archer all rolled into one. Jack couldn't understand why Katie even let the stupid wanker get to her. He was a waste of space.

'Hang on, let me check my list,' Katie said, pulling it out from her straw bag. Jack sighed; another list. 'Now, dairy – milk . . . vegetarian cheese . . .'

Jack dutifully put in some semi-skimmed, as instructed.

'Oh wow, this looks nice.' He picked up a packet of frozen chocolate cake.

'Do you know how many E numbers and crap they put in those?' Katie looked appalled.

'OK,' Jack sighed; Katie had such *boring* eating habits. Anything she bought had to have lentils in, and be organic, and have a GM-free label on it, which meant she only ever bought lentils . . . and rice . . . and lentils. 'Anyway – tell me about Keith.'

'Oh, he's looking after Susie today – she's got the day off school, teacher's strike. Anyway, I turn up to drop her off and he makes me a cup of tea. And introduces me to his new girlfriend.'

'So?' Jack surreptitiously slipped a bottle of Nestlé chocolate milk into the basket.

'Well – d'you want to guess how old she is?'

'Er, I don't know.' Jack knew Keith was about thirty-three, so . . . 'Thirty?'

'Lower.'

'Twenty-five?'

'Lower.'

'Five?"

'No! Fucking bloody nineteen! He's a cradle-snatcher! It's disgusting. He's old enough to be her father.'

Jack frowned.

'Actually, he would have to have started *very* young for that, Katie. Would've been illegal.'

'Well, perhaps,' she replied, moving past the frozen aisles. 'No, Jack – don't put pizzas in, they'll only end up stuck in the freezer. We've got plenty of lentils and stuff at home. Anyway – I don't approve. But it was so funny – Susie saw them together and said, "Are you babysitting her too?" Ha! Men. Men!'

'Well, come on, be reasonable—' Jack stopped, seeing Katie's face. 'Look, she's just a bit of fluff. He probably can't cope with a woman who has more than one brain-cell. He's probably obsessed with her breasts.' Not that Jack had (ahem) ever been guilty of such a crime.

'She's not even pretty,' Katie sniffed. 'She had braces. And glasses.'

'Oh, well, that is weird,' said Jack, slipping in a pizza as Katie turned to pick up a packet of Linda McCartney sausages.

'No, it's not weird!' Katie flung them in with an icy bang. 'He's a typical man. Why do men like younger women? – not for their looks but because they can boss them around. Young girls will let themselves be domi-nated, and bullied, and steamrollered over, because they're not old enough to know any better. Keith can manipulate her. And he says I'm bitter – bitter! He's says he won't go out with any women his own age because they are bitter. They stand up to him more like. Why are you looking like that? You think he's right . . . you think I'm bitter.'

'No! No!' Jack protested uncertainly. 'But not all men are crap, Katie. Look at me. A shining example of the male species.'

'Well – yes.' She pinched his cheek. 'You're all right. Just.'

Jack sighed again. As they came to the fruit stall, Katie checked the melons.

'Choose with care,' he said with a grin. 'You know that melons reflect breast size.'

Katie nudged him and he turned. An old woman, who had been about to put two tiny watermelons into her basket, had hastily exchanged them for a larger pair.

As she waddled off, the basket straining in her spindly hand, Katie and Jack laughed out loud.

'How about some Jammy Dodgers?' Katie was saying when she stopped short and clapped her hand over her mouth. 'Oh Jack, I forgot! Your interview! And here I was wondering why you were in a suit! I'm so sorry, I was all churned up about Keith . . .'

'It was crap,' Jack said, suddenly feeling punctured. He sighed. 'They hated me. They said I was unreliable and had never held down a job and had no references. And then I got pissed off and made a joke. Which didn't go down too well.'

'Which joke?'

'The dishwasher one.'

'Uh?'

'What do you do if your dishwasher breaks down?'

'What?'

'Slap the silly bitch.'

Katie looked up from her list, her eyes saucering.

'Well, it was a dishwasher company,' said Jack.

'Oh, that makes everything all right then, doesn't it!' Katie cried in disbelief. 'Jack! Honestly!'

'Well – the woman *was* a bitch. You should have seen the way she was looking at me, as if to say, *You're only fit for selling* The Big Issue.'

Despite her laughter, Jack felt chastised, stupid. Particularly when Katie launched into a lecture. Stuff about being patient and mature, about growing up, taking responsibility. Jack wanted to tell her to shut up. Because he knew she was right, and he hated her for it.

When they joined the queue at the checkout, however, they were saved by Henry, who popped up behind them carrying a basket.

'Hi, how are you?' he asked brightly.

As they loaded their goods on to the conveyor belt, Katie related Jack's offensive slap-the-silly-bitch interview to Henry. Jack tried to smile when Henry burst into fits of laughter but his stomach burned and his eyes wandered sullenly over Henry's chinos, smart cream jumper and polished Hush Puppies. He looked even smarter than Jack did; he looked as though he belonged on a day at the races.

Jack didn't mind Katie laughing at him, but Henry was different. Bloody Henry with his posh voice, who would have breezed through the interview and been offered a five-figure salary.

Thankfully, the conversation turned to the subject of Leila.

'How's it going with the Ice Queen?' said Jack a little competitively, knowing full well it would be a mess. Everyone found Leila hell to go out with; she was like a Rubik cube with all the stickers muddled up, impossible to decipher.

'Not very well,' sighed Henry, offloading his purchases (fresh orange juice, garlic bread and about nine packets of chocolate digestives) on to the counter. 'We've only been out twice now, but she's very . . . well, I just can't tell what she thinks of me.' He looked at Katie enquiringly, as if wondering whether they had exchanged confidences.

'Dump her,' Jack said.

'But I really like her,' said Henry. 'I think she's lovely, a really nice girl.'

'Nice!' Jack snorted, stuffing his pizza into a bag and ignoring Katie's frown and interjection of, 'I thought we weren't buying any pizza, Jack?' 'It just slipped in,' he explained, then turned back to Henry. 'Look, Henry, let me tell you a tale about bulls that I read in a newspaper yesterday. Take a horny bull and put him in a paddock with a sexy female cow – nice black and white patches, swishy tail, whatever bulls go for. Eventually he runs out of mating steam. But bring in a new cow and he goes wild, his testosterone goes through the roof and he mates again. See? Evolution does not support monogamy.' He shot Katie a sidelong glance – would she take the bait?

'Jack – you're such a cynic!' Katie cried.

'You ought to be careful, Jack,' said Henry, scribbling out a Coutts cheque for the cashier. 'Cupid might suddenly strike one day, you know. "Love looks not with the eyes, but with the mind, And Therefore is wing'd Cupid painted blind". You might be surprised who you suddenly end up falling for.'

'Uh?' Jack feigned a blank expression; he was always pretending to be a Philistine around Henry. Despite studying English as a degree, Jack had spent most of his time cribbing from York notes and reading Asterix comics in the college library.

'Shakespeare. *A Midsummer Night's Dream*. Sorry – I've got it on the brain. I'm still learning lines like mad for the part of Puck. I've got to get them done by tonight because I've no free time this weekend, what with Steve's wedding.'

'Oh God, yes,' Katie cried, her eyes flashing. 'You've got an invite too, haven't you, Jack?'

'Oh, Steve and Mandy, yeah,' said Jack. 'All the way up

in Yorkshire, of all places. There's nothing up there except sheep. I bet we'll get there and find a church full of sheep in big flowery hats. I don't fancy it,' he lied, to tease Katie. He was definitely going – Steve was one of his finest drinking partners.

'Yes, you do,' Katie retorted.

'I do?' Jack raised his eyebrows.

'Because we can all go up in a group,' Katie suggested. 'All five of us. That way, Henry, it might be easier, less intense, and Leila might lighten up . . .'

'Maybe,' said Henry, uncertainly.

But by the time they had left the supermarket, Katie had persuaded Henry to agree to the idea. As they strolled home, the setting sun warm on their backs, Jack looked out over the glittering waters of the canal and was suddenly reminded of a trip to the Med, of smoothing down his wetsuit, leaning over a boat into the clear water and seeing shoals of fish – deep scarlet, ochre, kingfisher blue – seething beneath the surface like beautiful corals. A tingle travelled down his spine and he suddenly longed to book a flight again . . .

Oh well, he thought, *a trip to Yorkshire will have to suffice for now.*

11

Charlie

Fairies sleep during the day and come out at night. My favourite spot in the fairy tree was high up, separate from everyone else, tucked away in a small hollow I'd asked a local woodpecker to drill for me.

But today I couldn't sleep as I was too worried about Jack. I yawned and read a few more pages of a trashy romance called *And Then He Took Her In His Wings*, about (surprise surprise) a tall dark handsome fairy who meets a small pretty fairy and lives happily ever after. It had been written by an earthworm under the pseudonym of Petulia Blossomingham. There was a photo of her on the back, sloped across a couch like a chocolate finger biscuit, her wrinkly brown lips smothered with ghastly pink lipstick.

. . . Oh darling, I can't hold back any longer. I love you!' he cried in a throaty voice, running his hairy fingers along the trembling edges of her wings, which shone like two lacy pomegranates in the sunset . . .

109

I know it sounds sad, but I couldn't help lying back and thinking of Puck, and I was just starting to drift off when I heard:

'*Pssssssst! Charlie! Pssssssst!*'

I frowned and tip-toed along the edge of my branch. Nobody seemed to be about. All I could hear was the faint noise fairies make when they sleep. (This has become the standard for human cartoons, where a 'z' sails from a character's head. If you sound the letter 'z' continuously between your teeth, that is how fairy sleep sounds.)

Oh-so-quietly I flew down, past the branches laden with sleeping fairies, wondering if it was just a magpie playing a joke, when I heard it again: *Pssssssst!*

The noise seemed to be coming from a few trees away.

I saw a half-face, a harlequin, pop around the edge of the trunk. Puck.

I hurried over to him. From the worried expression on his face, I could tell Something Was Up.

Then I noticed that Puck had a small white cloth, which looked suspiciously like a pair of lacy human knickers stolen from a washing-line, wrapped around his loins.

'Puck, what is it?' I asked suspiciously. 'You look as if you're wearing a tea towel—'

'It's not a tea-towel, it's a sarong.'

'Oh? Is this due to some impending sex change? Should I be calling you Penelope from now on?'

'Ssh, keep your voice down!' Puck said in a shrill whisper, casting a nervous glance at the fairy camp. 'Charlie, this isn't funny. I'm really buggered. I just didn't think about what I was doing. I stole the book and then thought, well, why not try it out . . .'

Puck slowly removed his sarong. For a moment I thought he was playing some flasher joke on me. Then I let out a small scream and quickly bit it back.

The bottom half of Puck's body had completely disappeared. Wiped clean away, like half a sentence dusted off a blackboard. A cry choked in my throat. I'd really gone crazy. I squeezed my eyes shut and then opened them. I was hallucinating. I couldn't even see any more. My mind was fragmented like a broken mirror I could not piece back together.

'It went wrong,' Puck said in a quivering voice. 'I tried out a chant – a spell.'

Puck passed me the book. I took it in numb shock. The pages were tatty and the colour of weak tea, and the yellowing cover was held together with spiders' Sellotape. On the front, in faded calligraphy, I read: *The Brahma Book of Spells*.

'Puck, where the hell did you get this from?' I gasped.

'I stole it. I saw it in Titania's chambers when we were being told off . . . I just took it and it worked, Charlie, it worked! This is how we can get Jack to fall in love!' In his excitement, Puck yanked the book back, flipping through the pages so wildly that some of them tore like tissue paper. Then he thrust it back into my hands. At page forty-six.

A SPELL TO BECOME INVISIBLE

The spell to become invisible is recommended for all beginners and is usually the first spell a fairy learns.

The words swam before my eyes like a row of ants. I found myself sinking to the grass on my knees. Puck kept asking nervously if I was all right. I tried to speak but the words got caught in my throat. All I could do was turn and hug him in ecstasy. I couldn't believe it. The magic was real.

I suppose I ought to explain for the benefit of human readers that magic is not taught in schools any more. It was felt by the fairy elders (much to our indignation) that after the disastrous efforts of naughty fairies that resulted in the Second World War, it ought to be laid to rest. We could take part in group spells, but not perform magic on our own. For our generation, magic was just a legend, like the Knights of the Round Table.

So to find out that magic was really possible was a little like you discovering that horoscopes are true. Half of you wants to believe it, that there is *something* more to life than just the everyday mundanity . . . and yet . . .

Doubts were still flitting through my mind like bats in a well, and yet every time I looked at Puck's lower half another nail of belief was hammered into my heart. To Puck's relief, the spell seemed to be wearing off; the faintest outlines of his shapely grey legs were starting to appear, echoes of bones, pale green rivers of veins, the twists of muscle and bone marrow.

'No,' said Puck. 'It's too dangerous to read it here. Let's go somewhere else.'

We flew to Leicester Square. In my euphoria, the world seemed to buzz and fizz with magic. The sound of animals in London Zoo tingled in my ears like incantations; a wizardish man warming conkers on a grill showered sparks like shooting stars against the inky sky; a group of Iranian women, their exotic faces mysterious behind their black head-scarves, seemed like a trio of beautiful witches.

We finally settled beneath a park bench outside the Odeon Cinema. The din of tourists was almost overwhelming, so we rolled up some weeds and stuffed them in our ears as ear-plugs. Then we propped up the book on our knees and drank in every word in awe . . .

Magic is alive everywhere. It is the whispering energy, the divine intelligence, that runs through all things. Take a look at the picture on the opposite page. It looks like an ordinary daisy. It in fact contains the vital ingredients for the invisibility spell; its stems, stalks and petals sparkle with invisible magic.

While this book makes use of flowers, plants, wands and wizardry for spells, beginners should be reminded that these are only required for amateur magic. The kingdom of heaven lies within us all. When a fairy has become a real magician, they will be able to do anything – tame a lion, turn water into wine, blow away the clouds from the sky and tug out the sun – just from the faintest impulse in their heart, the faintest thought in their mind.

Young fairies usually have the arrogant view that magic is about power. Magic is about surrender. Magic is making a wish and letting it drop into silence . . .

What on earth is that supposed to mean? I wondered.

'This is boring,' said Puck impatiently.

'No, it's not!' I cried. 'This is amazing. This is our – our heritage. It's like . . . finding out who we are, what we're really about. You know – we're all like seeds, containing the potential for anything but not allowed to grow, to blossom into plants, forced to be stunted. It isn't fair! It's like a dog not being allowed to bark, or a nightingale who can't sing!' I was surprised to hear the anger in my voice.

'Keep your wings on!' Puck took the book and flicked to the back index. 'Now – 'L' for love . . .'

Under 'L' was a series of fascinating spells:

Legs: make the wooden leg of a cripple grow long.

Lie: how to brew a potion that will make the victim's nose elongate whenever he lies.

Love/lust: how to cause a human to . . .

'A-ha!' said Puck, flipping frantically to the page.

In the past, these were conducted by appeals to Cupid to borrow his bow, which led to endless paperwork and administration. In modern times, the spell can be ministered through the dream, when the mind of a human is weak and malleable, drifting aimlessly through the sea of sleep, easy to catch and tame.

How to conduct a dream spell on a human being to evoke a sensation of love and lust. When you pick your victim, you must choose between conducting a love spell or a lust spell.

The Love Spell

The famous fairy psychologist, Mary Le Fanu-Fairy, conducted this spell on a well-known pair of humans, Arthur Miller and Marilyn Monroe, in 1956. She chose this couple in particular because (a) they were famous and the results of her research would therefore receive national attention, and (b) they were such an unlikely pair that she felt it would prove the possibility for love spells to bind together completely incompatible humans and still achieve results. She noted that the human victims suffered the following symptoms: Viewing the world as if in perpetual dawn – with a rose-tinted glow; continual

114

restlessness and lack of concentration; hours spent staring into space, with a silly smile on the victim's face, and so on.

This spell will require between six weeks and six months to take full effect.

'Six weeks!' Puck broke off from reading. 'This is no good, no good at all.'

'Hmm,' I was still reading on, fascinated.

The Lust Spell, meanwhile, will take effect within twenty-four hours.

'That's more like it!' Puck cried in glee.

'Yeah, but wait till you see the symptoms,' I pointed out, reading aloud. '"Difficulty in sleeping, violent urges, mood swings, obsessive onanism" – oh, what does onanism mean?'

Puck smirked and curled his thumb and forefinger in a jerky motion.

'Oh, uh huh,' I blushed. 'Well. There you go. Since when does lust make anyone happy? It drives people mad. Love makes humans happy. You don't see the world in a rose-tinted glow when you're in lust, do you?'

'More like a semen-tinted glow,' Puck conceded.

'Exactly—'

'Look, Charlie, you're too much of a romantic,' Puck told me brusquely. 'Lust is exactly what we want. Jack already loves Katie. He loves her like a sister, or a mother. He's already her friend, he already trusts her, he already likes her as a person – all the right ingredients are there, except lust. He needs a spark, he needs to get all boiled up and excited and erotic and—'

'OK, OK, calm down, take a cold shower,' I said.

Puck smiled.

'So, the lust spell it is,' he announced.

'Thanks for taking my view into consideration,' I muttered under my breath. Any female would have known that the love spell was a far better choice; it required patience, but it would have been worthwhile. But Puck, like a typical man, had chosen lust. And yet I couldn't help feeling a thrill of excitement. I guess every altruistic action has its roots in selfishness; I couldn't help fantasising that when Jack and Katie got together, Puck might be inspired to look for the love of his life (and hopefully he wouldn't look too far beyond yours truly). That by solving Jack's love life, I would solve my own.

12

Henry

Henry spent most of the journey from London to Yorkshire thinking about going to bed with Leila.

It was going to be their first night together. Henry wouldn't normally have pushed things. But he'd gone out with Jack a few nights before for a drink. Jack had been on his ninth pint, Henry on his second, when Jack had idly asked if Henry found Leila aggressive in bed. When Henry had revealed they hadn't actually . . . quite . . . well . . . got beyond kissing, Jack had looked as if he'd swallowed a bowling ball.

'You're KIDDING!' Jack had thumped down his pint, soaking his beer mat. 'But Leila's not exactly frigid, is she?'

'What?' Henry had snapped. He'd had a beautiful cut-glass image of Leila and now Jack was attacking it with a blunt scalpel. 'Why?'

'Well – I've slept with her. About half of London has slept with her.'

'Don't say that about my girlfriend!'

'Sorry, sorry. But you know, I do have a video of me and Leila together from way back – the night we first met.'

'What d'you mean, a *video*?' Henry had spluttered.

'A video is a small black cartridge which slots into a machine—'

'Shut up, Jack. What's on this *video*? Leila going swimming? Riding a horse? What?'

'Well, what do you think?' Jack had raised his eyebrows. 'We were, ah, making a video on cake-baking together. Not.'

'Jack!' Henry had felt rage flaring up inside him. 'You're so disgusting. Videoing women having sex with you is so sleazy—'

'For fuck's sake, Henry.' Jack had seemed to find the whole thing hilarious. 'I would *never* video a woman. *She* set the video. And then when I didn't call her, which I think totally pissed her off, and she moved to America the following month, I got a brown package in the post. It had a postcard from New York, plus the video and a sneery message saying she'd shown it to all her friends and everyone agreed I had a tiny cock and if I ever visited New York no girl there would ever touch me. Charming.'

'Well, what did you do with it?' Henry had snarled.

'I sold it on the black market. Five quid a go. I made a fortune. Everyone in this pub's seen it.'

'YOU BLOODY WHAT—'

'Henry, I'm *joking*. Sorry, I've gone too far.' Jack had given him a gentle punch. 'I know she's your girlfriend. Anyway – I slept with her years and years ago.'

But Henry had been furious. Leila was a lovely girl; Jack was just being a bastard. Jack was a decent bloke but he was always cruel when it came to women; they brought out the worst in him. At the end of the evening he'd insisted that Jack find the video; Jack had reluctantly passed it over.

118

Henry hadn't watched the damn thing. It had sat on top of his TV for two days, like a bomb waiting to go off. Half of him was desperate to watch it. The other half of him was revulsed and wanted to tear it apart with scissors.

Unfortunately, he'd never actually got to do either – the video had got muddled up and put in the case of a kids' video of *A Midsummer Night's Dream* Henry had been watching for inspiration. Which his gran had then borrowed to show to her great-grandchildren. Henry had nearly had a heart attack when he'd realised; he'd called up and tried to get it back but his gran, sounding very embarrassed, had mumbled, 'I've lost it . . . sorry, dear . . .'

All in all, Henry was very nervous about going to bed with Leila. She was obviously very experienced. And he was no Casanova. He'd had about three sexual encounters with women in the last decade. One with an actress after a rehearsal, on her dressing-room floor. One at a party, with a cute blonde girl with plaits. They'd gone upstairs to an empty bedroom and for once Henry had found himself enjoying successful sex. And then there had been Alice – his one and only long-term, full-blown Proper Relationship. Alice the Christian, who had pretended she was a virgin, making Henry swear to tell everyone else the same. In the bedroom, however, the Bible had gone out the window; she'd been voracious and obsessed with experimentation. Cucumbers, dildos, silk scarves, handkerchiefs, handcuffs, bedposts and furry rabbits – you name it, Alice had tried it. She'd always complained that Henry – because he liked straightforward, caring, missionary-position sex – was 'about as sexually inventive as a hot water bottle'.

And now Henry was driving all of them up for the wedding in Settle. And tonight he'd be in bed with Leila, and he was absolutely terrified.

'We are going to be *late*!' Leila snapped for the third time in a minute.

The car journey hadn't gone all that well so far.

Settle was a good six-hour drive from London. They had planned to set off at 6 a.m., but at 7 a.m. Jack had still been snoring in bed. Eventually, Susie had woken him up by jumping all over his bed, Katie had practically had to dress him, which had left Henry and Leila standing awkwardly in the kitchen, Leila sniping, 'God . . . I could *kill* Jack . . . if we don't leave soon, we'll miss the service . . .'

Having set off late, they got caught in the traffic on the M6. Jack went to sleep in the back, snoring loudly, and Katie, with Susie on her lap, had to keep holding her back and whispering, 'No, darling, don't wake him up.' Leila was in the front. She was reading a copy of *Marie Claire*; every so often she turned back and echoed a tip to Katie about putting egg yolk in your hair to make it more shiny or cucumbers on your eyes or yoghurt on your cheeks. All very girly, and despite a few lame attempts at joining in, Henry felt excluded and stupidly laddish.

Jack drove for the final half of the journey. By now they were very late and Jack, who was notorious for treating suburban streets as though they were Formula One race tracks, swerved round the country lanes at ninety miles an hour while Leila and Katie screamed at him to slow down and Susie giggled with excitement.

They zoomed up to the church in a spray of gravel and burst in just as the vicar was saying, 'And do you, Mandy Henrietta Mansfield, take . . .' Blushing frantically, they

120

all stood at the back like naughty children. Henry was touched by the service; he leaned down and said to Leila, 'Isn't it lovely?'

She nodded and looked up. To his amazement, there were tears in her eyes. He reached out but she shook him off irritably.

Henry hid a secret smile. *So*, he thought victoriously, *she is more of a romantic than I thought. Sweet.*

Then he turned and saw them, saw his father, and felt his happiness fade.

His father was standing at the end of a pew, near to the front. A Thai girl was by his side.

The one Henry had heard all about, but hadn't yet met.

Henry's eyes searched the crowds for his mother. Where was she? Why wasn't she standing next to dad? God, they could at least . . . behave . . . pretend to be married, for the sake of . . . well, everyone's embarrassment. He couldn't believe his father had brought the Thai girl. What were people going to think?

As the service came to an end, Henry saw his mother turn, looking for him. She was wearing a pastel green suit and her hat looked like a florist's shop. She'd told Henry she was 'so looking forward to meeting his new ladyfriend'.

Suddenly, Henry couldn't bear it. He hurried Leila outside for some fresh air.

There were a few wedding snaps, but rain was starting to spit from the moody sky. Then everyone got back into their cars and drove down the winding country lanes to the reception, which was being held at the local Hornby Laithe Bunk Barn.

'Wow, it's lovely!' Katie cried as they walked into the dark barn, the rafters strewn with balloons and streamers.

121

Then Henry saw the seating plan and nearly had another heart attack. Steve and his family were close friends of Henry's family and so everyone had been invited to the wedding. He and Leila were sitting with his grandparents. *Both sets.*

'God, sorry – they might be a bit mad,' Henry whispered in Leila's ear as they went over. Leila looked startled.

'Er, this is Leila,' said Henry, introducing them to his father's set, Jean and Gerard, who were both thin and pinched, sitting up straight like two old pieces of rope, and then mother's, Jenny and Terry, who were warm and jolly.

'I didn't know you were an actress.' His granny Jenny narrowed her eyes at Leila. Oh shit. She obviously recognised Leila from Jack's dodgy porn video.

'No, Leila is an agent,' Henry said firmly.

'An agent of . . . videos?'

'No, books.' Henry swallowed.

'Well, I do like women who dare to break out in their careers.'

Leila, obviously thinking Grandma Jenny had backward views on women's lib, smiled politely.

Somehow they made it through the dinner. Thankfully his father's parents, who always had to be in bed by ten or they spontaneously combusted or something, left early. Jenny and Terry, whose elderly bodies were still bursting with youthful energy, got up to go on the dance floor. There was only one other awful moment when Grandpa Terry whispered in Henry's ear, 'Thanks for that "How To" tape, by the way. Our nightlife is better than it has been in sixty years.'

Henry nearly spat his chocolate cake out. Great. His grandfather, who was ninety years old, had improved his sex life by getting tips from his girlfriend shagging his best friend.

Despite pressure to get up and dance, Henry stayed in his chair, preferring to watch, while Leila went off to find the loos. Henry hated dancing – he had no sense of co-ordination and he didn't want to risk embarrassing himself in front of Leila. His parents, Henry noted, were dancing. Thankfully, with each other. (There was no sign of 'The Thai Girl'.) Even if they did look like demented octopuses on roller skates, swinging their arms about in some manner they'd obviously learned from the sixties. For God's sake – his mother was menopausal, his dad had hardly any hair surely there ought to be a law against adults doing this sort of thing?

Finally Leila returned, weaving her way through the dancers. She had such an elegant stride – long-legged, hip-swinging, as if she was a model strolling down a cat-walk or a princess gliding down a red carpet. Everyone always turned to look at her.

Then, as a balding man on the dance floor caught her arm, Henry felt his insides curdle and he quickly hurried over.

'Hi, Henry,' his dad grinned. 'Just introducing myself.'

'Honestly, Henry!' His mother kissed him. 'You've been running away from us all afternoon.'

Henry winced as his father tried to engage Leila in a dance. Oh Christ. But Leila, to her credit, went along with it. She was a great dancer. She undulated in snakish coils, and as she raised her arms, her gold bracelet slid down her wrist and her black top rode up, showing off a strip of golden flesh, a jewel shining in her belly-button. As she twisted, the jewel reflected arrows of disco light, glimmering like a lion's eye.

'Well, she seems very nice,' said Henry's mum, edging Henry to the side of the dance floor. 'Though it's strange to wear black to a wedding.'

Henry rolled his eyes.

'Mum. Please. Don't. Leila always wears black. All the time. It makes her look thin.'

Henry hated the way his mother did this. She loved dissecting his girlfriends; she broke them into tiny pieces the way she ate her favourite custard-cream biscuits, analysing each crumb.

'I can feel a sadness about her.' Henry's mother lowered her voice.

'*Mum*,' said Henry.

Leila came striding up to him. There was a faint sweat glistening on her forehead from the dance, plastering tiny gold strands of hair to her face.

'Well, we'd better get going.' Henry took her arm hastily. 'We're staying with Aunt Moira and Uncle John and they're about to leave.'

Henry had deliberately stayed there, knowing his parents and grandparents were staying elsewhere.

'But they've only got one spare bedroom.' His mum looked confused. 'Oh, I see.'

'Come on, Hilda, they're not sixteen,' said Henry's dad, giving Henry a playful look. Then he gave Leila a lascivious wink. Henry boiled. Worse, Leila gave him a flirty wink back. His mother's lips pinched together as though she'd been stuffed and roasted in an oven.

'Come on,' said Henry hastily, 'let's go. They're waiting to give us a lift.'

Henry loved his aunt and uncle but he could hardly concentrate as he sat in their living room, sipping tea, nibbling chocolate biscuits and exchanging jolly synopses

124

of *what I've been doing for the past year*. All he was aware of was Leila's thigh, warm against his, as they perched on the sofa.

He could see now why Leila was such a successful agent. She charmed them as effortlessly and sweetly as she had his grandparents, discussing Aunt Moira's marigolds and Uncle John's model railway.

The best charmers, Henry realised, are the best listeners. They know how to make people feel special.

He felt a bubble of pride swelling up inside him and he put his arm around her, squeezing her shoulder and smiling down at her. She really was the best.

But up in the bedroom he suddenly felt awkward. He ended up getting changed in the bathroom while she changed in the bedroom. When he came out, she was sprawled on the bed in the most delicious, silky, thin-strapped, thigh-kissing night-slip-thing Henry had ever seen. It looked as though it was made from liquid silver; she writhed on the bed like a mermaid washed up on his shore. But even as he lay just a foot away from her, he felt funny again. Here he was, about to share the most intimate act with a girl he still hardly knew.

'Did you enjoy the ceremony?' he asked, playing for time.

'Yes.' Leila yawned, sliding her hands behind her head, drawing her hair into a long yellow peacock's tail which fanned up on the pillow. She drew a strand and twisted it around her little finger. 'What's up with your parents?' she asked bluntly.

'My parents?' Henry spluttered defensively. 'What? They're fine. They're great. They've been married for nearly thirty years, you know, but they're still madly in love. When my father proposed to my mother he got down on one knee and gave her a white rose, and he still has a single rose sent to her every morning.'

'How sweet,' said Leila, in a tone that suggested she wanted to puke.

'What about your parents?' Henry asked. He itched to stroke her hair. It looked like silk – no, more refined than silk. Like the finest spider-spun gossamer.

'Oh, we haven't seen each other for years.' Leila tried to keep her voice light but there was an acid ring to it. 'My Dad lives in Spain. He's in early retirement, so he spends all day chasing after young girls in bikinis who haven't the slightest interest in a pathetic, fat, balding man. As for my mother – she lives in Hollywood.'

'What does she do?'

'She's a therapist. It's such a joke. Have you ever heard of Affluenza?'

'A mental disease, isn't it? Rich people who can't cope with being rich?'

'Exactly. My mother charges them two thousand dollars a day to make them feel better about being wealthy. For crying out loud. She's on her sixth husband. Maybe her seventh. I lose count. She's a slut.'

Henry tried to hide his shock. Somehow he'd pictured Leila's mother as a frail, beautiful, Audrey Hepburn figure. A housewife who held elegant dinner parties in a large white house in Kensington. As for her father – Henry had imagined he would be a doctor, perhaps. Even a politician. Something classy and distinguished.

Leila yawned.

'Do you think families are important, though?' Henry asked.

'What is this, twenty questions?' Leila smiled. 'I'm pretty knackered.'

'Oh yes!' said Henry. 'Why not? I'll ask you twenty

questions, then you're allowed to sleep.' He tried to joke but he was hurt – didn't she want to get to know him?

'OK, ask away.' Leila yawned again.

'What did you think when you first met me?'

'What did you think when you first met me?' Leila echoed warily.

'Oh – I thought you were beautiful,' said Henry shyly. 'I thought you looked like Titania.'

'Who? Oh – I see. The fairy queen. Mmm.'

'What about you?'

'I thought you were gay,' Leila confessed.

'*What!*'

'Well, come on, Henry. You are a little effeminate and public-schooly. But look, it was only for the first twenty minutes.' Leila patted him as Henry, appalled, buried his face in his pillow. 'Sorry – I also thought you were very handsome and smart, OK?'

Henry lifted his face, still smudged with blushes.

'Next question?' Leila asked gently.

'What . . . do you think is the point of life?'

'God. I don't know. I don't believe in God, that's one thing.'

'You don't?' Henry had been brought up a Christian and now he was agnostic.

'No,' said Leila coldly. 'I do not. I think religion is the opium of the people. I think it's an emotional crutch. Life is hard and people are looking for ways to survive it – through God, or New Age therapies, or whatever – but when it comes down to it there's nothing out there at all. Just us and our seventy-odd years, our pathetic little stamp on this planet. So I think life is . . . is about making money. I'm a capitalist. A Thatcherite. I think humans are driven by greed, and the best thing is to just go for what you want and make as much money as you can.'

'Oh.'

'You look disappointed in me,' she said, almost teasingly. Was she just winding him up? 'I think you think too much, Henry. I bet you lie awake at night, wondering . . . wondering . . .' Leila paused, searching for something zany.

'. . . where all the radiators in this world go after we've finished with them?' Henry said, grinning as Leila laughed. 'True, I guess. But I think the point of life is to be happy.'

'OK. So exs. You're bound to ask me about exs soon. Yours?'

'The key one was Alice. We were going to get married, but I . . . changed my mind.'

'You did?' Leila looked surprised, almost impressed.

'She wasn't the right person for me. What about you?'

'Marriages – one. Still six to go before I get up there with my mother,' she said wryly.

'You've been married?'

'Divorced. God, Henry, you're looking at me as though I've just confessed I murder small children and lock them up in my freezer.'

Henry lay in silence, staring up at the ceiling. He remembered Jack mentioning that Leila had lived with a guy out in the US . . . but he hadn't clicked, or maybe he hadn't wanted to remember, that she'd been *married*. It seemed strange. Leila was such an independent spirit. She had her own job, her own place, her own money, her own social life, her own routine. He tried to see her in slippers and an old dressing gown, munching toast with her husband over the Sunday papers. Or driving to a garden centre and picking out conifers for their back yard. No – they were odd images.

He wanted to ask her more. He could have talked to

her all night. But Leila had slipped under the covers and had her hand poised on the light switch.

'I'm tired,' she repeated pointedly. 'Sorry. I've . . . had a hectic week at work, you know. I didn't get to bed until one o'clock this morning, after finalising a deal. Can we just sleep now?'

'Sure.' Henry climbed eagerly under the covers like a frisky labrador who'd just been tossed a ball.

Leila turned out the light.

They lay in the velvet darkness.

Henry could hear her breathing – light and ragged. He could smell her lavender scent, sense it quivering in his nostrils. He could feel the silk of her nightdress brushing the back of his palm. He was trembling. For a moment he wondered if he should wait – there was plenty of time, more dates ahead of them. Then he thought of Jack again, his wicked dark eyes shining with amazement. *Hey, Henry, what will Leila think of you if you don't make a move? She'll think you're gay.*

He reached for her. He groped blindly, felt flesh, her collar bone, her breast.

Then – *crack!*

She had grabbed his hand and nearly broken his knuckles. Suppressing a howl of pain, Henry nursed his injury in shock and disbelief.

Leila didn't apologise. She merely turned on her side, with her back to him, and went to sleep.

129

13
Jack

'Can I have a light?' A girl with a strong Australian accent asked him.

Jack looked up. A blonde in a bridesmaid's outfit was standing in front of him. She was very tanned, green-eyed, curvy, smiley. Another bridesmaid crept up behind her like a shadow; she was thin and floaty in her dress, like a ballerina in *Swan Lake*.

'Sorry, I don't smoke, I've given up,' Jack said with a wry smile.

The Australian blinked. Jack was sitting at an empty table, Susie on his lap, smoking a cigarette, a packet of Marlboros protruding from the pocket of his black tux.

'Well – you're not doing a very good job,' she said.

Jack grinned.

They both giggled.

'OK – I've *nearly* given up,' said Jack, finally getting out his lighter. 'Sit down,' he gestured, shifting Susie from his right thigh to his left; God, she was getting heavy now she was five.

The two girls pulled up chairs, pushing away debris from the wedding meal. Susie gazed at them with a faintly curious, faintly hostile gaze. She was enjoying the spotlight of Uncle Jack's attention. He'd looked after her throughout the whole wedding; made her laugh by singing hymns in a silly, high voice in the church, let her sit on his lap while he shared his buffet meal with her, played an ice fight under the table, taught her how to dance. Now, declaring she'd 'completely worn him out', he was having a fag break, watching the wedding winding down: people departing, putting on coats, saying goodbye, air-kissing. And Jack had just been thinking about opportunities to pull when, as though a genie had granted him a wish, the two bridesmaids who'd been sizing him up all evening had finally sidled over.

'Uncle Jack, can I have one?' Susie moaned as he shared out cigarettes.

'No, Susie.' Jack laughed; she'd been asking for the last hour and he'd kept telling her they would turn her lungs black and eat up her body.

Susie sulked. She wanted a go; Jack had proper, sophisticated cigarettes that blew smoke.

'Uncle Jack.' Susie kept demanding his attention. 'Why aren't you eating your cigarette? I eat the ones Mum gets me from the newsagent, they taste all sugary.'

To Susie's bewilderment, the girls exploded into laughter. Susie blushed, laughing too, though she wasn't sure why.

'Isn't she sweet?' The Australian patted her head. Susie rolled her eyes; she wasn't a dog.

'I'm Jessie, by the way,' said the Australian. 'This is Andrea.' She nodded at her friend, who smiled shyly.

'Jack.' Jack solemnly shook hands with both of them and they giggled again.

'I can see you've been enjoying the champagne.' Jack nodded at the empty buffet tables, where about thirty

131

green bottles were lined up like a fairground shooting stall.

'Oh yes—' Andrea sighed.

'We had two bottles,' Jessie interrupted, sharp as a tack, 'but we've given up drinking.'

'I see. I don't suppose you want any chocolate cake?' Jack, who didn't really have a sweet tooth, had left his portion. As he offered it to them, he saw their pupils dilating like cats eyeing cream and he smiled – the way to a woman's knickers was definitely through chocolate.

'Ooh, can't I have it, Uncle Jack?' Susie asked, kicking the table leg.

'You've already had three. You're not supposed to have any at all. Your mother will kill me.' Jack nodded at Katie, who was, oddly enough, jiving on the dance floor with a balding, middle-aged man in a stripey BHS sweater. She was obviously still feeling the effects of the champagne.

'I'm on a diet. I don't normally eat chocolate,' said Jessie, picking up a plastic spoon and taking a mouthful. She licked away a smudge of chocolate on her lips with a flick of her sharp pink tongue. God, thought Jack, flicking ash on to a paper plate, she is se-x-eee. He ran his eyes over her body appreciatively – long legs, big hips, a bit fleshy, but nice breasts. A good eight-and-a-half out of ten. He slithered his eyes up her neck, back to her face, and she held his gaze. For a moment they stared, sexual tension shimmering between them. Jack boldly stared her out until she lowered her eyes, a provocative little smile tugging at her lips. Mmm.

Then he realised Andrea was watching them. She was twisting the napkin in her lap into a painful origami shape, looking left out but resigned to it. Jack sensed that she was Jessie's sidekick, always cast in the supporting role. Still, she was pretty too, in an ethereal, waifish way,

132

with a cloud of strawberry-blonde hair and china-doll features. Jack smiled at her and she flushed, her thin lips quivering into a grin.

God, thought Jack, torn for a moment – which one do I fancy the most?

'Mmm.' Susie interrupted his reverie, slurping greedily from a glass.

'Susie, what is that?' Jack asked sternly, giving her a little tickle. She jumped, squirmed on his lap and looked up at him, all wide-eyed and innocent.

'It's 7UP,' she protested.

'OK,' said Jack. As much as he loved Susie, he couldn't help wishing she would go off and play somewhere. He glanced at the girls again.

'So, anyway – dear Jessie and darling Andrea – tell me how you came to be at the wedding.'

'I—' Andrea began.

'Oh, we both know the bride,' Jessie steamrollered over her. 'I'm her cousin and Andrea works with her on a magazine. I've been good friends with her for years, ever since we lived in Essex together . . .'

And then she was off. Five minutes later, she was still yapping. Jack almost wished he'd never asked. It was just a simple question that required a simple answer, not A History of Jessie's Life in Three Volumes, Part One. He lit another cigarette, carefully blowing smoke away from Susie's head, and glanced at Andrea. He couldn't help but feel sorry for her; another, more bastard part of him knew it was always a good pulling tactic to play the two girls off against each other.

'So, what do you do, Andrea?' Jack cut over Jessie.

'I interview celebrities.' Andrea went pink and sat up straighter.

'Wow – that's cool.'

133

'I interviewed Kelly Brook last month,' said Andrea, gaining confidence.

'I hope she didn't say too much about me,' said Jack. For a moment Andrea looked confused, then got the joke.

'Oh – don't worry – she told me all about your passionate affair but the tape recorder was switched off,' said Andrea with a wink, and Jack winked back, and they both smiled. Jessie narrowed her eyes as if she was about to explode.

'Andrea has made some right cock-ups, though,' said Jessie. 'She interviewed Alan Titchmarsh last month. Andrea totally lusts after him, don't ask me why, and she got all nervous and muddled her questions up and asked him why he didn't wear a bra. It was hysterical. I think he thought she was a right plonker.'

Jack, although he felt Jessie was taking a cheap shot, couldn't help laughing. Andrea tried to laugh too, but he could tell she was hurt.

'Well – if you're ever looking for a celebrity to interview, you can look me up,' Jack said. 'Obviously my life is just so colourful,' he added self-deprecatingly. 'I'm unemployed, broke, and I can't sing, act or dance. But still . . . I can play the guitar. Well, I can play a Nirvana song on the guitar. Well, the first few bars of "Come As You Are" . . .'

'What talent. Well, come on then – let's have your number,' said Jessie.

Jack paled. This was all a bit quick. Jack generally hated giving his number out to any girl, least of all before going to bed with her. He loathed the twist of guilt he felt in his stomach every time he heard the phone ring; he hated having to leave the answerphone on, or get Henry to lie and call them up and put them off. And Henry was so crap at making excuses. He never said anything sensible like, 'Jack's gone travelling.' Instead, he made up ridiculously elaborate excuses about Jack falling off a fishing boat in Norway and being eaten by a giant octopus, or being boiled alive by a tribe of Amazonian feminists in Papua New Guinea as an offering to the moon goddess.

He made an excuse that he didn't have a pen, but Jessie managed to coerce a Biro from a passing relative. Jack reluctantly scrawled his number on a piece of napkin, which Jessie rather ostentatiously folded up and put down her bra, patting it triumphantly. She gave him hers too, which he stuffed carelessly into his pocket.

'Well, I guess I should go to the loo,' said Andrea, as if she wasn't wanted any more.

Don't go, Jack wailed inside, willing her to stay, but she was already weaving her way out. Jack caught sight of Katie again – she was trying to edge off the dance floor, but the middle-aged bloke kept dragging her back, spinning her round as though they were dancing to country and western, not 'Come On Eileen'. Seeing Jack, she sent him a look that said, RESCUE ME. Jack paused, torn between friendship and a shag.

'Ah, in a sec,' he mouthed, giving her a thumbs up. Katie positively glared at him.

'Mum never had very good taste in men.' Susie sighed.

'Well, why don't you run along and dance with her?' Jessie asked, obviously keen to grab her chances.

'No,' said Susie curtly.

Good for you, thought Jack, smiling. Jessie frowned and put her hand on Jack's knee.

He suddenly felt a weary sense of *déjà vu*. How many times, in clubs or bars or hotels all over London, all over the world, had he been in this position? Chatting up two girls (for some reason, it was always two girls). Jessie and

Andrea, Debbie and Chloe, Marie-Claire and Jeanette, Heidi and Kristina, Zoe and Catrina, Katie and Leila. Flirting with both. Taking one back to bed. Telling her lies. Having sex. Leaving. *Au revoir*. He chain-smoked girls like cigarettes.

Mind you, he felt his libido stirring. He hadn't had sex since . . . since . . . Dominique. Then a brick of guilt squashed his desire. And look how she'd turned out. He couldn't face going through that all over again. It made him feel too mean.

Jack stubbed out his cigarette and took a glug of Susie's drink.

'Hey, you've got my glass . . .' Susie interrupted hastily, half-waking up from her sleepy daze.

'Susie – this is NOT 7UP!' Jack nearly fell off his chair. Oh God, Katie was going to kill him. 'This is champagne. I was wondering why you were so quiet,' he stormed, seeing Susie pull a sleepy, impish face. 'Right. To bed. I'll be back in a sec, Jessie,' he grinned.

It was the perfect excuse. As he picked Susie up in his arms, however, he saw Katie was leaving the barn, heading outside. He followed her. Henry and Leila were also exiting and Jack couldn't resist teasing Henry as they said goodnight, whispering, 'Don't forget to set the video.' Henry gave him a black look.

Katie was sitting outside on a large oblong stone by a field. Still carrying the sleepy Susie, Jack crunched over the gravel and grass towards her and sat down. He was about to apologise for deserting her when Katie put a finger to her lips. She pointed. Jack squinted in the gloom. Then he saw it. The red gleam of a coat. The flash of thin, fine paws as it picked its dainty, frisky way across the field. Then, seeing them, it froze suddenly, amber eyes glaring.

A fox.

They both paused, barely daring to breath. Even though Jack didn't go wild over animals like Katie, her excitement was intoxicating. She grabbed his hand, squeezing it tightly.

The fox ran away a few feet, then sniffed about, ears still pricked towards them.

'Isn't he lovely?' Katie whispered.

Even after the fox had disappeared, they carried on sitting there, enjoying the silence. Jack breathed in the country air – a mixture of elderflower freshness, animal dung, damp earth and greenery. God, he felt good. Miles away from London, from his problems, from Mick, from his debts.

'So, how's Susie?' Katie touched her face, but Susie carried on sleeping; Jack winced, hoping she wouldn't smell the alcohol.

Silence again. Up above, an airplane cut a twinkling path through the sky.

'Mmm, I think I might head out to France in a week or so,' Jack mused. 'I know a girl who works on the Channel Tunnel; she can get me a freebie.'

To Jack's amazement, Katie turned and gave him a look that nearly froze his bollocks off.

'But what about money, Jack? You haven't paid Leila any rent. And what about sorting out a new flat for yourself? God, Jack.'

'God Jack, *what*? What? All I said was that I wanted to travel, not rob a bank.'

Katie shook her head and muttered, 'Nothing.'

'Katie, I hate it when you do this in arguments.'

'What?'

'You say *nothing* when there clearly is *something*. And then you expect me to decode what you're pissed off about.'

'Well, I just think,' said Katie, a little more softly – which only made her words sting even more – 'that you should try and face things, you know. Whenever you go travelling, it's always because you're running away – from a girl you don't want to speak to, or a job you hate. Oh look, this is silly, let's not argue. Come on, we need to put Susie to bed.'

As they went to the car, Jack felt pissed off. As they passed the barn, he had a sudden urge to leave them and go back to Jessie. Jessie would never bloody harangue him. But no – he was too tired. He got into the car and Katie drove them to the hotel in silence.

★

In the hotel room Jack put Susie to bed, pulling the covers over her. He switched on a low lamp, bathing the room in a golden glow. Katie, letting out an exhausted sigh, sat down in a chair, took off her shoes and rubbed her sore feet. She drew a bottle of Evian out of her bag and took a few thirsty glugs.

Jack paused, then came to kneel beside her. He took her feet in his lap and gently massaged them. His way of saying sorry.

She smiled down at him, gently threading her fingers in his hair. Her way of saying sorry.

'Don't worry, Katie, I won't go off travelling,' he found himself promising, even though it made him feel tight inside, constricted somehow.

'No, it's fine,' Katie whispered, giving Susie a nervous glance. 'I know you're going through a difficult time at the moment.'

Jack hung his head and shrugged in a sulky, boyish way that suggested he needed a good hug. She spread out her arms and, leaning over awkwardly, her hair draping over her face, gave him a big, warm cuddle. It was only the feel of her softness that made Jack realise how upset he really was. Katie was right. He was running away from his problems. The trouble was, Katie just didn't know how big they were. He'd been drowning his worries about Mick and how to raise three thousand pounds without robbing a bank, but the champagne hadn't washed his problems away. They still floated to the surface like oil on water . . . Now, as he found his arms curling tight around Katie's waist and he pressed his head against her shoulder, shutting his eyes tight, he felt simultaneously choked up and soothed by her hands on his hair. She started stroking the crown of his head, the way he'd seen her do to Susie once when Susie had had a bad fall. Her fingers slipped down to the nape of his neck, light circles that seemed to drift down his spine like smoke rings . . .

And, all of a sudden, bang! He felt it. A change of mood.

A hot throbbing. A quickness in his breath, something catching in the back of his throat. His spine arching. He was suddenly acutely conscious of his fingers against her back, and he pressed them tentatively against the warm band of skin between her top and her skirt. It was as if a layer had been removed from his skin and he was super-sensitive to the voluptuousness of her breasts against his chest; her heavy, strong arms tapering into surprisingly slender wrists. He noticed a few freckles on the join of her hand and had an urge to bend down and dot them with his tongue. He lifted his head awkwardly, aware that she was sitting uncomfortably, but not wanting to let her go. She pulled away an inch and smiled down at him.

You're beautiful, he thought in amazement. In the golden lamplight her face had the serenity of a Madonna painted by Da Vinci. The tenderest of smiles curved at her mouth and her eyes were the melted blue of infinite compassion. He gazed at her lips – soft, like two slices of pear back to back. He closed his eyes and an odd rush of images collided and sizzled in the darkness – him slowly lifting up her top and pulling it over her head, her hair unfurling over her breasts, his teeth biting down the knotches of her spine, her pale skin against his, breathless gasps in a secret room, tumbles of love and lust as the dawn crept over them.

'There now.' Katie got up and moved away. He felt cold and lonely without her embrace. She picked up her bottle, peeling the blue label nervously.

'I—' he stammered, standing up. He still felt as though he was in a trance.

Katie, who was glancing at her daughter, looked up and whispered, 'I think you'd better go. I don't want to wake Susie up. You'll be OK?'

Jack didn't think. He just strode over to her. He took the mineral water bottle out of her hands and put it back down on the table. He drew her into his arms, hearing her faint gasp. And then he kissed her.

For a moment, everything was perfect. Later, when Jack replayed it all in his mind, he could have put them on a cloud and added Frank Sinatra crooning in the background, it was that perfect. A kiss of dreams. They locked together. She tasted beautiful. He could feel her lips respond, her tongue shyly curl against his, her hands smooth over his back, grab his shoulder blades, and he thought, *Why haven't I done this before?*

The next thing he knew, she'd hit him.

Something had changed; she had cooled, bit her lip, shrugged him away a little. He'd stood on tip-toe, yanking her back closer, refusing to let her go. She had drawn back with a sharp intake of breath, curled her fist into a tight ball and given him a clumsy punch on the shoulder. He felt as though he'd been hit by a tennis ball.

'Get out,' she whispered tersely.

'But – I—'

'*Get out!*' she hissed.

He couldn't believe it. His tender Madonna now looked like a creature from a horror movie. Her eyes were ice blue slits of hatred. Her shoulders were hunched.

'Katie—' He burst into nervous laughter, rubbing his shoulder.

Big mistake.

'You think this is *funny*?' she said in a shrill voice. 'You think this is funny? Oh, I'm a bit pissed, I didn't get a shag with the bridesmaids, so now I'll try it on with Katie. God, Jack.' She paused for a moment, pulling her feelings in. Then she wiped her hand across her forehead as though Jack was a horrible headache she wanted to flush away. 'Go to bed, Jack,' she said, turning away. 'You're pissed. Go to bed.'

If Jack had been pissed, he was sober now. Stone-cold, horrified sober.

He moved forward to touch her, but she recoiled violently, knocking the little table. Her bottle of mineral water wobbled precariously, wheeled on its side, then, just as Jack reached down to pick it up, fell to the floor, spraying water everywhere.

'I – oh God – God—' Jack searched around for tissues. He picked up a box of hotel tissues and, without thinking, held it out to Katie.

'Oh thanks, I'll clean up the mess, shall I?'

'I didn't mean—' Couldn't he do anything right? 'Look, Katie, it was just a kiss. I'm sorry—'

'Oh, leave it!' As he tore out a tissue, Katie put her

hands on her hips and gazed at him in weary exhaustion. 'Go to bed, Jack.'

Jack dropped to his knees, pretending not to hear. He dabbed a tissue and stared down with glazed eyes as the pink paper sopped up the liquid. And then he clicked. Shit. Keith. Fuck. How could he have been so insensitive?

'Katie—'

'Will you keep your voice down! You're going to wake up Susie. Leave the water, just go.'

'Look – I'm sorry – I know how crap you must be feeling, with the wedding and everything reminding you of Keith. But we're not all bastards, Katie—'

'How dare you bring Keith into this, Jack!'

Ouch. Sore point. Jack let the soppy tissue drop to the floor. His desire had gone now, died from flames to ash. He didn't want to kiss her; he just wanted to shake her. God, talk about overreacting. He'd only *kissed* her. She was behaving as though he was a rapist in a dark alleyway.

As he turned to go, he knocked over the mineral water again and heard her curse. Too angry to speak now, he purposefully left, striding to the door. Yet even as he walked into the corridor, he felt a boomerang urge to go back, to hold her. He turned, seeing her coming to the doorway; he spread open his arms . . .

'Don't you know, I bloody married Keith because of you!' she cried, then slammed the door after him.

14
Katie

Katie stood motionless for a moment.

She could still feel the aftershocks of slamming the door – tiny tremors echoing in the floor and walls, under her feet, squiggling over her body in little electric shocks.

She could hear her breathing, deep and harsh. Susie's breathing, light and soft in sleep. The wind breathing in the trees outside. The drone of a car. A creak on the landing . . . footsteps? In a reflex action, her hand flew back to the door, gripping it tightly, half expecting Jack to barge in again. Then she heard voices, a couple. Jack had clearly gone. Thank God.

She turned, went into the bathroom and closed the door. Right. Time to get ready for bed.

She picked up her toothbrush and scrubbed her teeth viciously, poking the bristles into every corner of her mouth until her cheeks ached and her gums bled. As if she was trying to rinse out every last drop of Jack's saliva, like poison in her mouth.

She threw her toothbrush back into the silver holder. It missed, clattering to the floor.

'Jolly well do as you're told!' She picked it up, threw it

back in, then caught herself. What was she doing – addressing an errant toothbrush as if it was alive, as if it was Susie? She was going bonkers.

She felt funny. And very hot. Like a volcano about to erupt. There were embers sizzling beneath her skin and heat spots on her cheeks and there was an itch crawling up the back of her neck like poison ivy – Katie always suffered from rashes under stress. Her heart felt tight and twisted and her fingers were tingly, as if, with a will of their own, they wanted to pick something up and smash it across the room.

She was still mad at Jack.

It was just the fucking cheek of it. Who did he think he was? Casanova? Who did he think she was? A prostitute? She'd always felt Jack had a slightly derogatory attitude towards women. A tabloid attitude – seeing women as sex objects. And she'd always felt she was the only woman Jack really respected, related to, saw as an equal. But now, now she felt he'd diminished her to the level of one of his bimbos. Bastard.

As she pulled off her dress, she caught sight of herself in the mirror. She paused, gazing at her figure; her voluminous breasts, billowing like saggy party balloons, the tyres of fat around her waist, her thunder thighs.

She pictured Jack standing in front of her, gazing into her eyes gently and cupping her breasts in his hands, fingering her nipples into points as he kissed her tenderly. For a moment the fantasy went all misty – then from nowhere came a nightmare image: Jack grimacing down at her, his erection shrinking to the size of a pea . . .

Yuk. Katie shuddered and hastily pulled on her pyjamas. She tied back her hair and started to smooth Oil of Olay over her face.

Still . . he was not a bad . . well, OK, admittedly a

quite good . . . a good . . . a bloody brilliant kisser. It was ironic, really – she'd spent much of the early years of their friendship wondering what it would be like to kiss him.

She'd never ever confessed to Jack that she loved him, of course. She kept it tight inside, only unlocking it at night when she sat up in bed writing long entries in her diary, analysing one tiny thing that Jack had said, pulling apart his sentences like petals from a daisy.

Only once, years ago, had she come close to telling him. They had been travelling home from a nightclub in London, sitting at the top of a night bus, both happy, drunk and exhausted, the edges of their hangovers starting to fog their brains. They'd been up all night; the sun was just starting to rise, slipping grids like long white fingers across the bus. Jack had been nodding off, his head slipping down on to her shoulder. As Katie had looked at him, at his scruffy head and stubble and long lashes that she always teased him for being girly, she hadn't been able to bear it any longer. She'd burst out:

'Can I kiss you?'

Jack had instantly jerked awake. He'd stared around for a moment, blinking, as if the words might have been spoken by some invisible woman behind him.

Then, staring down at his jeans, he'd addressed the scruffy patch on his knee.

'Er . . . I'm really glad we're friends, Katie . . . you're lovely, like my little kid sister . . . and that . . . oh wow, look, there's Big Ben.'

Katie had wanted to die.

They'd spent the rest of the journey gazing out of opposite windows, like strangers forced to sit beside each other on the Tube.

Funny, thought Katie, how just that one minute of conversation had been branded on her memory for ever.

And funny how that one-minute conversation had, looking back, been the beginning of the end.

That night, the moment she'd got into the flat, she'd burst into tears. She'd been really quite hysterical; Katie winced at the memory – she never cried any more, she was beyond that now. She'd stumbled around the flat in a blur. She'd sat down and tried to write her diary, clenching the pen in her hand, but the words had seemed to wilt and die inside her. Where could she begin? *The man I've been in love with for the last year has just announced he doesn't have the slightest feeling for me.* All she'd scrawled was: *I feel like I'm full of rotting flowers.*

She'd gone into the bathroom and been sick. Afterwards, she'd felt oddly cleansed, relieved, despite the pain at the back of her throat as if it had been sandpapered.

But life had somehow carried on. She had gone on a date with Keith and to her surprise it had been really quite respectable. He'd taken her out to dinner and they admitted that they'd been slightly economical with the truth about their jobs when they'd first met at the club. He had talked about his plans to set up a computer software business. He'd even worn a suit. When he kissed her in the taxi, she'd pretended it was Jack. When he'd taken her home and made love to her, she'd pretended it was Jack. The months had gone by and he'd kept taking her to dinner. She'd taken an odd satisfaction in seeing how dismayed Jack felt by their union, as she'd slowly, coldly, put 'Closing Down' signs up on their friendship. It was the best revenge – 'Sorry, Jack, I can't come out to the cinema, I'm going out with Keith . . . No, sorry, Jack, I can't talk on the phone right now, even if it is a girlfriend crisis, Keith is here.'

When Keith had proposed, it had been a shock. He'd

taken her to dinner, to Pizza Express, their usual haunt. And, just as she was dipping into a cheesecake, Keith had pulled out a little blue box. With a ring. She'd been so shocked, she'd merely turned white and blurted out, 'No.' In a whimper of despair.

Later, she'd wondered what the hell she was doing with her life. She loved Jack. She wanted to marry Jack. She wanted to go out to work and have him call her, for five minutes, to say he'd be a bit late home. She wanted every conversation to end with 'I love you'. She wanted to cook him gorgeous meals and spend every evening curled up on the sofa with him. She wanted to spend her Saturdays buying sexy underwear for a holiday abroad. She wanted to have his children and see Jack grow into a wonderful father. She wanted to affectionately argue with him over baby names. She wanted him to be by her side when she was having their baby, clutching her hand and telling her he loved her, so she could look up and smile at him through the pain and hold on tightly.

So she'd got up. Dashed to the phone. Called him. Once again, she'd been ready to say it. To say she loved him. And after twenty *b-rrings*, he'd picked up. He'd been laughing. There'd been sexy music playing in the background – some crooning jazz track, the saxophone reaching an orgasmic climax. And the laughter of a girl in his bed. And Katie had felt her heart sink and had admitted defeat. Her last flower of hope had curled up and died inside. He would never love her. There was no point in even trying.

Instead, she'd called Keith. It was 2 a.m. in the morning now and she'd apologised politely for getting him out of bed, and then, breathlessly, told him, *Yes Keith, I want to marry you.* His whoops down the phone had nearly burst her eardrums.

God, I was so naïve, Katie reflected now. She hadn't even worried about the fact she didn't love Keith. She'd been so relieved to have someone, anyone, who loved her, she'd airbrushed over that little flaw. She'd been twenty-three then. Stupidly, she'd felt she was being mature – she'd felt she was taking the grown-up, sensible view that passion was silly, that love, real love, didn't come overnight but would grow over the years.

Of course, it didn't. Love wasn't grey – it was black and white. It was there or it wasn't. She didn't love Keith and their marriage had been a disaster.

Still, thought Katie, going back into the bedroom and sitting on the bed, *the one good thing, the only good thing, that did come out of my marriage was Susie.*

She looked down at her daughter, sleeping soundly. Susie's eyebrows were knotted, her eyelids flickering as though she was suffering from a nightmare.

Katie frowned. She suddenly had an urge to reach out and wake her up, hold her, protect her from the world.

She slipped into the bed beside her and gave her a cuddle. She could feel Susie's heartbeat thudding against hers. Katie listened to the sound of their breathing slowly synchronising, their heartbeats pulsating in time, until they became one thump. She smiled, closed her eyes and kissed Susie's head.

She felt calmer. Her memories had reminded her that life was so much better now. She'd learned to like herself (well, on a good day). She was stronger, happier. She was single – but she was independent, no man to boss her about. She had a good job that she really believed in. She lived in a beautiful house, even if she was broke, and she had some fantastic friends . . . well, did have . . .

She'd say sorry to Jack tomorrow for overreacting, and for punching him. It wasn't his fault. He'd just been drunk, thoughtless, stupid . . . And yet, there was an odd flicker inside her, despite all the years of disappointment, despite all the stern lectures she'd given herself. A tiny flicker of hope that it was more than just alcohol that had caused Jack to kiss her.

The car journey on the way back was dreadful. The weather was cold and the car heater was broken, emitting only putrid, itchy air that reflected the atmosphere between the four adults. Henry drove fast, with a kind of reined-in road-rage.

Beside him, in the front, Leila was pretending to be asleep.

They'd barely spoken this morning. Henry had got changed in the bathroom while Leila snoozed. Then she'd gone for a walk and Henry had gone to have a quick breakfast with his parents and say goodbye to them.

He still felt sheepish about all the lies he'd told Leila. About his parents and their oh-so-ideal marriage. If only.

Their marriage had seemed perfect. For the first twenty-five years, anyway. They'd never argued. Never thrown crockery. Their conversation, admittedly, had circled around the mundane, but in a charming, easy way – 'Harold, shall we have baby sweetcorns tonight with the roast or carrots?' or 'There's a new car-boot sale down at the local church, we could throw out those old jigsaws, Hilda.' They had still laughed together; got drunk together; Henry had been aware from the noises in their bedroom that their sex life was still healthy. He'd always felt so proud of them, so lucky that their marriage was the one in three that had not ended in divorce.

He'd always thought: *I want my marriage to be like that when I grow up.*

But apparently not. A few years back, his mother had

called him and, after enquiring after his health and telling him his pet guinea pig had died, had added that she and his father were 'having some time apart'.

'What?' Henry had asked. 'What, Mum, what is it? Is Dad having an affair? You can tell me, you don't need to protect me.'

'No, Henry!' His mother had laughed, as if separating from her husband was a trivial thing she did every day. 'We've just . . . grown apart. We're stagnating. Like weeds at the bottom of a pond. We need a change of water (as if they were *fish*, Henry thought). We need space. We're still friends.'

Friends?! ★

Then she'd spent what seemed like the next hour debating whether to cremate or bury the guinea pig. Henry had sullenly suggested she roast it for Sunday dinner and she'd told him off for being 'sulky'.

Their divorce did indeed seem amicable. Henry's father mostly lived in his house in Notting Hill; he let Hilda stay in their country home in Hertfordshire. But worse was to come. A few months ago, his father had phoned up and, after asking what the cricket results were, and moaning about falling shares, had casually mentioned that he was ordering a Thai bride.

'What d'you mean, ordering?' Henry had spluttered. 'Dad! You can't *order* a girl. Not like McDonald's fries – "oh, and I'll have a bit of extra breast".'

'Actually, you can go into the specifications and everything. You can ask for any hair colour. It's like finding your own genetically-engineered woman.'

'DAD!'

Henry hadn't been able to believe that his father, always so sweet, so placid, was finding twenty-year-old girls who were no more than sexual slaves (on the internet, he'd informed Henry cheerfully). *His father,* who had always irritated him, perhaps because he reminded Henry of himself. He'd always been a servant to his wife, always eager to please. Just like Henry was with his girlfriends.

Despite his father's jollity, though, Henry sensed a deep sadness, expressed in an almost desperate desire to prove he was enjoying life as a single man. He'd had his hair cut in a trendy Robbie Williams style that looked absurd. His musical and TV tastes had descended to primary school level; he'd even started listening to Steps records. He took his Thai bride clubbing in the West End, where they danced away till the early hours of the morning; Henry winced to think of the other clubbers jeering and laughing behind his father's bald patch.

The divorce, however, had only made Henry more idealistic. *Now his desire had become: I want to have a marriage that isn't like my parent's. Something that lasts for ever. I want two point four kids, a job, a wife – the whole dream. I don't care if it's conventional.*

Henry knew from his brief forays into acting, from the actresses he'd seen hooked on coke who were desperate to flash their flesh for the tabloids, that fame and success didn't bring happiness. Love did. Love and a happy family life.

Which was why he was so upset about Leila. He wanted their relationship to be perfect. He had a sequence beautifully choreographed in his mind: a tender romance, maybe moving in together after a year, structuring a routine together, then a year later engagement, marriage. He even had romantic visions of them growing old together, perhaps living in a little cottage in the Lake District, where Leila would make jam, and real bread, and they'd take their dog for walks in the country, hand in knarled hand.

★

And yet he seemed to be stumbling and muddling his steps and treading on Leila's feet. Like last night. He shouldn't have tried to force himself on her. He'd never wanted to rush Leila into bed; he'd always wanted it to be love-making, not sex. He'd tried to behave like Jack the Lad, instead of just being true to himself . . .

His eyes flicked angrily to the front mirror. Jack was slumped in the back, resembling a corpse as he always did after a heavy night. Henry's eyes swerved to Katie. She was shooting Jack the most filthy looks, biting her nails to the core, irritably shrugging off Susie's demands for I-Spy. Henry was puzzled – perhaps they'd had a row. But when he looked again a while later, a funny little interchange occurred between them.

Neither of them spoke. Jack merely reached across and touched Katie's hand. She pulled it away, crossed her arms. He let out a long, cross sigh. Katie let out an even deeper sigh. Then she turned and glared at him. He glared at her. Then, mysteriously, they both started to laugh. Jack took her hand again and their fingers entwined like vines. They stayed that way for the rest of the journey.

15
Charlie

'What took you so long?' Puck demanded as he let me in through Jack's window. Then, before I had time to explain myself, he whispered, 'It's just as well you're late. It took him ages to get to sleep, what with reading and flicking through *Loaded* and sitting on the loo and feeding the cat and watching TV. I think he must be an insomniac; he stayed awake for hours looking at the ceiling. But he's dropped off now.'

We paused for a moment, watching Jack lying there, mouth slightly ajar, snoring peacefully. A copy of *On the Road* was still tweaked between his fingers. He turned on his side and his eyebrows knotted with the concentration of dream, then he sighed again, totally unsuspecting of what we were about to do to him. I suddenly had a terrible foreboding of doom.

It had been one week since Jack and his friends had gone to the wedding. Tonight was the night. The night we performed a spell to make Jack fall in love with the first girl he saw when he woke up.

'Here, I got all the equipment,' Puck went on, showing me the objects he had carefully laid out on the windowsill, like the tools of a surgeon: a pair of tiny manicure scissors, a rusty penknife, a roll of Sellotape, a roll of fine white cotton and, last but not least, a bottle of children's 'Bubbly-Fun' filled with rainbow liquid and a little plastic hoop to blow the bubbles through.

'What the hell is all this?' I asked. 'This isn't what the book recommended. Puck, this isn't *Blue Peter*, you can't just use objects lying around your home.'

'Well, where the hell was I supposed to get the saliva of a crocodile?' Puck demanded. 'Like, oh, I'll just take a quick trip to Australia. I'm sure Sellotape will be fine, I can't see how crocodile's spit makes a good glue anyhow.'

'But you know what Titania says,' I exclaimed. 'You only have to change one or two details and the whole thing can go in a totally new direction. We're dealing with a man's brain. Haven't you read *Frankenstein*? Victor aimed to create a harmless human and he ended up with a psychopath who pursued him to his death. Who knows what might happen?'

Puck suddenly gazed at me with a soft expression in his eyes. I felt my stomach turn like peaches in a liquidiser.

'D'you really think we should just give up before we've even started?' he asked, looking at me with the doleful eyes of a labrador pup. I couldn't tell if he was manipulating me or if his bewilderment was genuine.

'OK,' I sighed, 'I guess we may as well give it a go.'

Freud once said, 'The interpretation of dreams is the royal road to a knowledge of the unconscious activities of the mind' (ie: SEX!!). Our twenty-first-century scientists say dreams are merely a way of removing tension and clutter. Personally, I prefer the former idea. I'm sure dreams have meanings; think of the people who bought tickets for the *Titanic* and then decided not to sail because they had nightmares of its impending disaster.

But what is interesting about dreams is that even though you may think you're experiencing a dream that lasts for hours, in reality they only last a few minutes. Dreams tend to take place during the deepest phase of sleep, the REM period. If you wake up right in the middle of your dream, you'll remember it with complete clarity and vividness. If you wake up five minutes after your REM sleep has finished, you'll probably only remember a few hazy bits and pieces. If you wake up ten minutes after your REM sleep, you probably won't remember having dreamed at all.

One thing was for certain: no matter how Jack DeAntiquus woke up, there was no way he was going to forget the dream we were about to give him.

We made two mistakes with the spell to create a dream. The first was that we failed to plan properly. Sometimes I kind of worry that this might be the reason Jack is, you know, a little bit on the dotty side. Then again I don't want you guys to sue me, and we really did make sure at the end that we put his brain back together, honest. And I'm sure he had a tendency to be on the eccentric side anyway . . . Oh, look, just forget I said all this. I just want you to understand that we didn't mean to make any mistakes. Puck and I had read the page entitled 'Spell For Making A Human Dream About A Specific Subject' so many times that day we knew it by heart, but we still returned to read the first instruction.

Cut a small indent just behind the ear of the human [WARNING: Small fairies should not attempt this as it could result in death]. Then chant the following

155

incantation which will allow you to fold back the human head. With reference to the diagram on the following page, see Plate XVII, removal of the subconscious is a simple process that takes only a matter of seconds, without resulting in any harm to the human or causing them to wake. Using a pair of tweezers, extract the black roll marked 'X'. You may find that it is slightly wet so wait a few seconds for it to dry before unrolling. The length of the subconscious will depend upon the age of the human, though the eventfulness of their life is also a factor; I once removed the subconscious from a six-year-old which turned out to be an astonishing three miles in length. His parents had divorced at the age of two and since then he had been passed through six sets of parents, which perhaps accounted for this extraordinary phenomenon. I thus warn you to take care that you do not allow the subconscious to roll out freely or you may find yourself spending hours wrapping it up again at the end of the session.

Puck picked up the rusty penknife and took a deep breath. I crossed my fingers and practised the incantation over and over.

'Well,' said Puck, with a smile that was far too cheerful, 'wish me luck.'

The human brain is an astonishing sight, I can tell you. We couldn't believe it. There we stood on the pillow, looking into the brain of Jack DeAntiquus.

Amazingly the spell worked. It was easy-peasy (well, to begin with). Jack's subconscious slid out on to the pillow and for a moment we stood there, staring at the black reel. It really was just like a roll of film. Then Puck stood on top of the bedhead and held one end and I flew with the rest of it and landed on the golden doorhandle. There was still yards trailing behind me but we only needed the last few days or so.

Then we realised that we needed some Sellotape. Only the roll was still lying on the windowsill. Puck tried to tie the end of Jack's subconscious to the bed but as soon as he darted away it shot forward and wrapped me up. I was not amused at all. It took us several attempts before we managed to get it stretched out tight like an elastic band.

It was a fascinating sight. Every moment of Jack's life was captured, from the grey interior of a lift to the smile of a beautiful girl who passed him in the street, from a shot of the blue sky and floaty white clouds to a tiny ant crawling up the lace of his shoe. All that was needed were speech bubbles and it would have made a perfect cartoon strip. I was so overwhelmed I darted from one to another, the pictures flitting in a blur before my eyes. So often we had watched humans on the street and wondered, What are their lives like? Not the various parts they played on the stage of the world, but their inner selves, their spectrum of hopes and dreams and fears. I've so often thought, What would it be like to be inside someone's mind for just one day, to see everything from their point of view? Would the colour yellow still look the same? What would it be like to be a man? To be the Queen? Madonna: what goes through her mind when she poses semi-naked in leather? Or Tony Blair when he is making a decision that will affect the lives of the nation?

'This is awesome!' I exclaimed over and over. 'Being at the Tate is nothing compared to this. Hey, I'd love to see the earlier memories. Imagine seeing when he had his first date! Or when he was in the womb of his mother's tummy! Hey, Puck, d'you think if we wind it really far back we might be able to see what happened before he came here? What if he was Cleopatra in a past life? Did he go to heaven or hell?'

'Charlie!' said Puck, who was looking more nervous than wowed: somehow I think seeing the most intimate part of Jack suddenly made him realise what a serious thing we were doing. 'Look, we've got a job to do and it could take a long time so we need to start cutting and pasting, OK?'

As usual, Puck took the most interesting job of picking the pictures and then snipping them out while I only got to hold the edges out straight. We then had the task of splicing them together to form a dream.

The second mistake we made was to be too ambitious. Puck is such a fan of the cinema, and whenever we come out from a movie he always tears it to shreds and says he could have done much better. He wanted to go for an Oscar-winning three-hour epic that Stanley Kubrick would have been proud of, but we only had the location and time for a low-budget ten-minute 'Screen Two' sort of job.

Puck was soon swamped in the quicksand of his imagination. He walked round and round in a circle on the bed as though he was in some sort of trance, tossing out ideas like a magician with coloured scarves.

'What if Katie is lying naked on the bed? We zoom into a close-up of Jack squeezing a rainbow display of paints on to a palette. He paints her entire body, butterflies dancing down her spine, round juicy apples on her buttocks, italicised letters winding round her thighs saying *temptress* or *edible* or erotic chants in Greek and Latin. Shades of yellow from pale lemon to deep amber streaking from her eyebrows to the fringe of her hair as though her forehead is a horizon for the rising sun. Jack cannot resist leaning down and kissing her painted lips, turning his own crimson, his hands rubbing over her breasts, smearing his own masterpiece into a blur of colour—'

'Puck, Puck,' I protested. 'Look, the clock says it's nearly four. Puck, please, how on earth are you planning to find all this material? We'll need extras and everything – we'll need other people's brains. We just have to create a simple, sexy dream that makes Jack fall for Katie.'

'OK, OK,' he sighed, finally coming back down to earth.

This was the dream we finally came up with (bearing in mind Puck's predilection for food and sex). I set the scene as a half-full café in Primrose Hill. Jack comes in one sunny afternoon and orders a 'Chocoholic Sundae'. Then along comes Katie in a red bathing suit, superimposed from an episode of *Baywatch*, though I'm not convinced that Pamela Anderson's hourglass figure really suited her, and she did look somewhat curious with the facial complexion of an English rose and the rest of her body a rich golden brown.

In the next frame, Katie brings in the most delicious-looking sundae. The glass is simply bursting with scoops of vanilla ice cream and pralines and cream and mint-choc-chip, overflowing with rivers of hot chocolate fudge and butterscotch sauce, topped with almond nuts and hundreds and thousands and silver balls. She places the sundae on the table and Jack gazes up at her. Their eyes lock for several seconds. I did want to introduce some sexy dialogue at this point, or at least some background music like 'Bolero', but I hadn't the faintest idea how to do it so I had to make do with actions speaking louder than words. Katie now sits down opposite Jack, crosses her legs seductively and tosses back her hair; here I managed to include a great close-up of Jack's pupils dilating (we cut this sequence from a black pussy cat who was just about to pounce on a mouse). Katie leans across the table and takes a bite out of the ice cream. A few drops glisten on her lips. Then she starts to feed Jack.

At this point I searched long and hard for something appropriate, but all I could find was a baby ad and I didn't quite have time to perfect it since Jack ends up wearing a bib while Katie feeds him a mushed-up rusk from a plastic spoon. Still, the idea was there and I think Puck's barbed comments were just jealousy because he wouldn't have even managed to get this far if he'd been making it on his own. Finally, the film then jumped straight on to Jack and Katie making mad, passionate love on the red tiles of the café, which I admit did look a bit bizarre as all the other customers continued to chat and read the papers in the background.

'Oh, nice one, Charlie,' Puck said. 'Yeah, let's make love on a bed of bacon fat and dirty footprints.'

'Well, I found a shot of a four-poster bed, really romantic with wispy peach curtains and all that, but I thought it might look weird stuck in the middle of a café.'

'And so much foreplay,' said Puck. 'One minute they're smiling at each other across the table, the next they're tearing each other's clothes off. I worry for your future boyfriends, Charlie, I really do.'

'Hang about,' I said furiously, 'that's the bit I'm still working on, before you so rudely interrupted. And at least it's better than nothing, don't you agree?'

'I guess,' said Puck. 'I guess it will have to do. And now – the first person Jack sees when he wakes up he'll fall in love with. So when he looks at Katie at breakfast . . . well . . .' Puck made a bow and arrow motion. 'Cupid would be jealous of our great work tonight.'

16
Jack

Darkness. Jack blinked. Where am I, who am I?

His hand, like a spring, snaked down under the covers, curled round the waistband of his boxers and clenched his hard, throbbing penis. He had an erection the size of Big Ben.

At the touch of his fingers, skin against skin, his whole body juddered, as if he was wired up to an electric-shock machine.

Jack quickly withdrew his hand and rubbed away sleepydust from his eyes. God, he felt so . . . so . . . *rough.* Terrible. Unhinged. The upper half of his body was aching with a hangover, as though he'd just played a particularly vicious game of rugby. The lower half of his body, meanwhile, was flooded with sexual heat. Jack often woke up feeling horny in the mornings, but this was something else. It was as if every blood cell in his body was pulsating with lusty redness; his penis was still jerking about like a frisky dog starved of a walk. Feeling another shudder ripple through him, he suddenly felt a roaring, caveman desire to tear off the bedclothes, jump out of bed, rip off his boxers, throw down the nearest woman and make deep and violent

161

love to her; to bury his lips on her neck, feel her breasts filling up his hands . . . and oh God . . .

His brain, on the other hand, moaned if he moved his head by the slightest inch. His eyes felt white with heat, his mouth as though it was filled with sand, and there was a horrible, high-pitched ringing in his ears. He reached out in the pale darkness, his fingers fumbling thin air until they finally clasped the glass of water on his bedside cabinet. He downed the water greedily, spraying drops over his chin. God, what a hangover . . . How much had he had to drink? He couldn't even remember . . .

Five pints? Ten pints?

Hang on. Hang on a minute, he thought, blinking away. *I didn't even go to the pub last night. I stayed in. I was a good boy. I put Susie to bed and I went to bed too, at ten o'clock, with a cup of bloody cocoa.* It was now – his head swivelled to the clock radio on his cabinet – 4 a.m. So why the hell did he have a hangover after a few hours sleep and a cup of hot chocolate? It didn't make any sense.

Jack lay back in bed, groaning. Perhaps he was sickening for something. Perhaps that was why he felt so hot. Or maybe, a voice inside him said, he was getting old. His body was wearing out. Maybe he had drunk so much over the past decade that it was all catching up with him; his liver had been shrunk from a healthy purple-coloured vessel to the size of a small pebble. Maybe he was paying off past debts; maybe all the ten-pints-a-night of university drinking, those whisky-downing contests, had all been burning up inside him, slowly eating away at his cells and stomach lining, until his body could take no more . . . And now, now what? He would have hangovers without drinking. He'd have to become teetotal. He'd have to sit in pubs and primly sip orange juice with his friends. Instead of ordering pizza, he'd have to spend hours cooking brown rice and lentils and green organic mush. He'd have to stop smoking and start jogging and taking cold baths. Shit.

Stop it. He caught himself with a nervous laugh. He was getting carried away. But still . . .

Whether it was illness or paranoia, Jack felt sweat starting to dance on his forehead and trickle down his back. He rolled over; his bed felt crumpled and dirty. The pain in his brain had subsided a little to a soft, dull ache. He decided to risk the trauma of getting up and going to the kitchen.

In the kitchen, he didn't switch on the light. The moon was full and the whole kitchen was bathed in a silver light, giving it an oddly metallic feel, as though he was in the spaceship in *Blade Runner*. The tiles were wonderfully cold against his hot feet. He found a pint glass, filled it to the brim with cool water and downed it thirstily. He paused, clutching the glass, looking at his ghostly reflection in the kitchen window. He looked very odd – or was it just the light?

He was just turning away to rinse out the glass when a memory of the dream sliced through his mind. Him. Lying on a tiled floor. Making love to a girl. A hot, pumping, aching orgasm tingling through his body. Leaning down and kissing her smiling lips . . . kissing *Katie's* lips. Shit. Jack dropped the glass; it clattered, without breaking, into the sink, but the noise went right through him. How weird. Having wet dreams about *Katie*!

He needed a cigarette. He remembered he'd left his jacket strewn on the living room floor (no doubt Leila would tell him off later).

He went into the room and fumbled about in the pale blue darkness, locating a scrumpled packet of Silk Cut. There was one left – thank God. He opened the window and a gust of night air, cold and sharp as apples, blew in, scratching at his face. A wasp, sleepy and swollen with the end of summer, buzzed in too. Jack made a noise at it and tried to swot it out, but it disappeared into a dark corner. He gave up and slumped on the sofa.

Just what is this all about? he thought.

Why am I having sexy dreams about Katie?

Am I starting to . . . do I . . is this . . .?

Do I love her?

Jack laughed at the very thought. He needed an ash-tray; he picked up a little black pot on the coffee table. Leila's house was littered with this kind of trinket. As if avoiding his thoughts, he examined it, feeling the black chunkiness, looking at the 'Made in Africa' label. Probably cost Leila a million quid, he sighed.

The thing about Katie was – he loved her but didn't fancy her. Jack didn't believe in the whole *When Harry Met Sally* thing. Jack knew that people thought about sex all the time – whenever you met someone new, whether it was a friend, a friend of a friend, a bank manager, anyone, whether you liked it or not a part of you, subconsciously, computed within the first three seconds: *Am I attracted to them? Do I want to go to bed with them or not?* And the first words he'd thought when he'd met Katie, as cruel and blunt as it was, were: *Too fat.*

He'd realised Katie had a crush on him. She'd been different then, in her early twenties. She'd been more romantic – he remembered fondly how she'd cried when he'd taken her to see *Four Weddings and a Funeral*, and then forced him back five bloody times. He'd noted her blushes, her funny smiles. He was flattered but ignored it, pretended it wasn't there. She was the first girl he'd ever really been friends with and Jack didn't want to spoil it. She made him realise how much better he got on with women than men. She was his first real girl*friend*.

Of course, he did love her. He loved her as a sister.

164

He'd only realised just how strong his love was when she'd married that awful git, Keith. Why, Jack had never known, though he suspected she'd been in love with her dress, with the ceremony, with the whole idea of love a lot more than the actual man. Of course, before the wedding he'd told her he thought she was making a mistake and she'd practically spat in his face. Told him he was jealous. Told him he had no right to interfere. Told him to shut up. Jack had shut up. Katie was right; it was up to her who she married. But a few years later, when she'd divorced Keith, Jack told her it was the best decision she'd ever made.

And yet . . . images of his dream kept swirling and swimming in his imagination. What would it be like to go to bed with Katie? This was the trouble – his feelings for her were so cloudy, like muddied water. Like that other night, last week, when for some odd reason he'd felt so compelled to kiss her. Jack's hand instinctively crawled up his T-shirt, fingering the bruise where she'd hit him. Over the past week, he'd watched that bruise turn various colours of the rainbow, from deep purple to black-blue to green-yellow to bright orange. He winced.

No – he couldn't try anything on with Katie. Not when his feelings were so vague, so impossible to define. He wasn't sure if this was about love, or lust, or maybe even just sheer curiosity – after all, Katie was the only girl he'd known for eight years that he *hadn't* slept with. And it wasn't fair to mess her around. Since the divorce, she'd been tougher, harder, and uninterested in men. And what if, say, they did go to bed together and the sex was fantastic, then what? Jack had never been able to commit to any girl. The thought of settling down with Katie, being stuck in one house, shot fear through him. No. It was no good.

Yawning, Jack lay back on the sofa. The cool wind was starting to chill him, but he couldn't be bothered to get up. He yawned again, hearing the drone of the wasp, irritating and yet hypnotic. Slowly, he drifted into an uneasy sleep, pregnant with waiting . . . for the morning, for the click, for the spell to work, for the woman he would fall in love with at first sight to wake him, like a prince waiting for his princess.

17
Leila

. . . O . . .

   O . . . yes . . . O . . . yes . . . . O O O

   Yeeeeeeessssssss . . . yesssssssssss . . . she thought, OH, yes, yes, YES!

'Oh yes,' he barked into her ear and for a moment Leila blinked, losing the scale, her crescendo interrupted. For a moment she'd been enjoying the sex so much, floating in the sparkly darkness of gasping ecstasy, that she'd forgotten the man who was making love to her.

'Oh yes, baby, yes,' he repeated, thrusting harder. A little too hard. It hurt.

'Oooh,' she picked up, but it was no good – somehow her concentration had shattered. Her orgasm, like a will-o'-the-wisp, had vanished in a puff of smoke.

She frowned, watching him move above her, his wrinkled face scrunched up, his greying fringe falling over his eyes, beads of sweat dancing on his forehead, and she felt a shudder of revulsion and stared past him to the glittering chimera of the hotel lamps. She wondered idly for a moment if the couple in the room above were doing the same thing, and in the room above them, and had a

167

horrible vision of the whole hotel filled with identical thrusting robot couples all committing unenjoyable adultery. Finally – about bloody time too – he came, and then collapsed on top of her in a tired, panting heap.

Leila felt him go limp inside her like a dead seahorse. She felt squashed and suffocated.

'Excuse me,' she said quietly.

'Oh baby.' He was still showering her neck with tiny bud kisses, as if *that* was supposed to give her post-orgasmic tremors, for fuck's sake.

'Excuse me,' she said more loudly, hearing sarcasm bite her voice.

'Uh – sorry,' he mumbled, red-faced, withdrawing and rolling over on to his side.

Leila got up and, calmly picking up the clothes she'd left on the floor, stalked into the bathroom. She could feel his eyes following her. Men – slaves to passion, slaves to female looks, she thought coldly, but an odd sense of pride swelled inside her. She was in control; she had him wrapped around her little finger. Good. Then she slammed the bathroom door after her.

The bathroom was like a crystal palace, mirror upon mirror showing reflections of her pale, naked form. She had a sudden urge to crush her fist into the reflection and shatter it to bits. Swallowing back the sensation she sat down on the toilet, bending her head between her knees and combing her fingers through long tousled hair, feeling the blood rush to her head.

Sex, she thought dully. One of life's great mysteries. The Catch-22. A sugar-coated poison pill. Why was it that it could trick you into such a thoughtless frenzy? People risked marriages, their entire wealth, their children, their jobs, the presidency of the USA, all for one moment of wham-bam, a few gasps of bliss . . . and then this. The anti-climax. The emptiness. The devil must be laughing at us all, she thought. How could she have felt so wonderful five minutes ago and now so hollow, as though her heart was made of deadwood? She couldn't even cry; that would have been too emotional.

Back in the hotel room, Mr Winterton was getting dressed. Mr Winterton. That had always been part of their flirtation in the early days. Whenever Zoe had put his calls through with a cool, 'Mr Winterton on line one,' Leila had found herself coyly singing out, 'Hello Mr Winterton, how are you?' or whispering, 'Hi, Mr Winterton, sorry I'm late,' when she slipped on to the brown leather stool beside him in Pret A Manger where they met for illicit cups of coffee, or shrilling, 'Bend down, Mr Winterton!' in their games of S&M.

Leila watched him now. She was ready to go; he was still getting dressed, zipping up his trousers, smoothing down his hair. He looked better clothed. Naked, with his pot belly and double chin, he always seemed something of a buffoon. But as he dressed, each layer – the shiny family-crested cufflinks, the greyhound-smooth jacket – gave him an incredible sense of power and dignity.

I'm so perverse, she thought, crossing her arms. Why was it that she yearned for him most *afterwards*, as he was leaving? Seeing him put on his wedding ring, she knew he would go back to his wife and three children, take them to church, enjoy a roast dinner, go for a crisp autumn walk, play tag or catch leaves. While she, what did she have? A job everyone thought was so prestigious but she quite liked. A nice house that she shared with a fat loser and her daughter, which was now being invaded by an unemployable womaniser. Oh, and a pathetic boyfriend. Nothing. She had nothing to go back to.

'Well, goodbye,' he said.

As he leaned in for a kiss, she turned her head sulkily, refusing to let him. But in a moment of unexpected possessiveness, he caught hold of the necklace at her throat and yanked her face round to him. She let out a surprised hiss.

'I'll see you next week,' he said.

'Maybe,' she said, then spat in his face.

They kissed goodbye violently.

He got a taxi home. She hated that most of all, though she never showed it. The way he never bothered to check if she could get home safely. Just a little thing, a gesture to show she was more than a body to him, that he actually cared. And today, of all days, just as she watched his cab briskly turning a corner, she realised with a thud that – oh shit – she didn't have much cash on her. She couldn't get any more out because she'd forgotten to pay her last Barclaycard statement and there was a freeze on it. She'd have to get the Tube.

It was 7 a.m. on a rainy Sunday morning. Leicester Square Tube was icy cold and desolate. The wind tossed empty wrappers across the grey platform. Rats scampered in and out of the tracks. A black man was sweeping up. Leila tapped her ticket with her fingers.

Finally, the train groaned in. Leila carefully chose a seat by the doors. She picked up an abandoned copy of the *Guardian* and tried to ignore the old woman in the corner who was dressed entirely in dark colours, like a huge black widow spider, and was fidgeting and muttering biblical expressions. A nutter, clearly. Leila's hand tightened on her handbag in her lap and she flicked to some article by Suzanne Moore on the collapse of the modern marriage. Her fingers went to her throat and she

170

winced at the slight soreness from the way he'd tugged her necklace. Bastard. He'd given her the necklace the previous evening at dinner, to placate her. Recently she'd been playing one of her malicious 'I'm going to tell your wife' games (she had no intention of telling anyone, of course, she had just as much to lose). Leila had only fully understood since her affair why husbands bought mistresses gifts – it was the only thing the women could have to physically prove that the men might just care about them more than their wives.

By the time she'd changed at Holborn for the Northern Line to Chalk Farm, Leila was fed-up and exhausted. The article was vaguely interesting – it described how in ten years' time most women would be out-earning their partners, which made her think of Henry with guilt. Bugger Henry. She didn't want to think about any of that; she just wanted to snuggle up in bed and sleep for ever.

Outside the sky was threatening. It was only when she reached home that she realised, fumbling in her handbag, that she'd forgotten her keys – again. Oh fuck it, she thought, ready to smash the window.

Peering in through the ground floor window, she saw Jack lying on the living room sofa, his mouth open. Even through the double-glazing she could hear his snores. But, even more disturbingly, she could see his penis, fully erect, poking out of the hole in his boxers. God, didn't men ever stop thinking about sex?

Still, waking Jack – even if she did disturb a wet dream – was better than getting up Katie or Susie.

Rap! Leila banged sharply on the window. *Rap. Rap!*

It took quite a bit of banging before Jack finally rose, and for Leila to see through the glass of the front door a figure staggering sleepily towards her.

Leila crossed her arms and rolled her eyes.

There was a lot of clicking and rattling as Jack struggled with the locks.

Finally the door opened.

Jack stood there, gazing at her. His dark hair was puffed up in a cloud, as though he belonged in a 1970s movie. He looked like he'd been abducted by aliens. His eyes were saucers. And he was just staring. Staring and staring until she felt her eyes swim as though she was being hypnotised and she snapped out of it.

'Jack?'

'Yes?' he whispered.

'Can I please walk into my own house?'

'Yes,' he stumbled aside.

For a moment, Leila was suspicious that the reason for his weird behaviour was because some sixteen-year-old he'd had a one-night stand with was hiding behind the sofa. But she was too tired to confront him; her feet were like heavy weights as she dragged herself up the stairs.

'Leila?' A whisper from below.

'Yeah?' Leila paused at the top step, looking down. Two dark eyes peered up through the banisters.

'I think I'm in love with you.' His voice broke.

Drugs. He'd obviously just taken an E. Leila shook her head numbly and went into her bedroom, locked the door and collapsed into bed.

On Monday morning Leila came into work to find a huge slush pile on her desk. Big brown envelopes, big white envelopes, all fat with books from wannabe writers desperate for a lucky break.

'God,' said Leila, doing a double-take. 'Oh well, it makes good firewood, I suppose.'

'It must have been because of that article on you in *The Times*,' said Zoe.

So there had. An article on the best literary agents in London. Leila had been listed in the Top Ten.

Moaning about how on earth she was going to get through all this (Leila didn't trust handing anything to a reader, who might miss a gem), she sat down, secretly pleased.

But, upon opening the envelopes, she found it hard to concentrate. Leila didn't drink, generally. And when she did, she rarely drank in large quantities – she didn't like to lose control. But she definitely had a semi-hangover, a dryness in her throat, a fuzziness around her temples.

Well, what a weekend she'd had.

After spending Saturday night in a hotel with Mr Winterton, she'd ended up spending Sunday with Henry. He'd phoned in the afternoon, whingeing about wanting her to come and watch him in a rehearsal and meet his acting friends. Leila, after putting up a fight, had finally snapped, 'Oh, OK, I'll come then!'

Putting down the phone, she'd sat down in front of her dressing table mirror grimacing at her reflection. She looked like shit. She hated going without sleep. On a good eight or nine hours, she was bright and fresh; on any less, she was a hideous dragon behaving as though she had PMT. Last night she'd had one hour. But she could hardly say to Henry, 'Oh well, I'm sorry, but last night I was shagging another guy in a hotel room, so I'm too knackered to come.'

Maybe it was all a sign that it was time to dump him.

He was just too keen. It was ironic, because when she'd first met him in Odettes bar, he'd seemed so confident, so aloof, the way he hadn't asked her if she'd like a drink, made her do the chasing. When he hadn't come back to her place, she'd thought he was a manipulative bastard. When he'd called the next day, she'd refused his calls three times, but he'd kept ringing, ringing and ringing and she'd thought, *God, this guy is arrogant*. It was only recently that she'd started to realise she'd got him all wrong. That Henry had done all those things because he genuinely cared.

In fact, he cared too much. He called every day. He sent her flowers. He cooked for her. Not just baked beans on toast but proper four-course meals, like bloody Jamie Oliver. He was besotted. And she was worried. She'd met types like him before. This was the trouble with men – they were either bastards or nice guys. Neither were quite satisfying. Like Mr Winterton and Henry – two sides of a coin.

She'd been having an affair with Mr Winterton for six months now. It had started after a random encounter in a hotel at the London Book Fair and carried on ever since. Odd nights here and there, arranged by brief e-mails. No emotion. Just sex. Leila, who found it hard to balance the demands of work and a long-term relationship, enjoyed it because it was low-maintenance. After all, Mr Winterton was never going to call her and ask her to go out to dinner to meet his parents the same night she was booked for a book launch. He couldn't make any demands on her, or restrict where she went, or who she saw. He couldn't fence in her life, call the shots. She had her freedom . . . and yet . . . it was a soulless relationship.

Henry, on the other hand, was sweet. But he worried her. She sensed that his love for her was insecure, clingy; that he simply wanted to find a nice girl, any girl, to be with, and eventually marry, and spend the rest of his life smothering in a big blanket of possessive love.

Or maybe it was just her.

Lying on her bed, resting her cheek on her pillow, Leila

174

mused about how crap the laws of love were. *Why?* she thought cynically, *do I always do this? If I have to chase a man, I fall for him, then as soon as I've got him, or it gets too easy, then I want to push him away.*

To her surprise, meeting Henry's friends wasn't the nightmare she'd envisaged. Leila didn't tend to like actors very much – they normally had egos the size of America. But they all turned out to be fairly warm (perhaps because it was a small, amateur theatre company). She was also expecting Henry to drool over her and ignore his friends, but to her surprise he ignored *her*. They took over two tables in the pub and he ended up caught in a throng on one of them. Seeing her stuck at the next, he mouthed 'You OK?' and she nodded, but after that he spent most of the time talking to a girl called Emma. Leila didn't like her much. Nor did the crew, from the underhand comments that were dropped. Emma, just because she'd had a chorus part in *Cats*, was convinced she was going to be the next Sarah Brightman and she was flirting with Henry, giggling girlishly and buying him drinks. Leila pursed her lips. Perversely, it only made her start to want Henry again. She almost enjoyed the feeling of jealousy.

Then they all went back to Henry's place and played Abba and smoked twiglets and one of the particularly insane characters in the group, Muzzamel, set light to his feet by pouring Sambucca over them.

I haven't had this much fun in ages, Leila realised. *I'm obviously going to too many dinner parties where people discuss the merits of Rushdie versus Amis.* This was fun; it was like being young again.

It was around midnight when Henry suddenly flipped 'pause' on the CD player and said, 'OK, everyone out! Time for beddy-byes. I just feel too guilty keeping you all up at this hour. Time to go hooome,' he concluded in a sing-song.

Everyone either grumbled or giggled, reluctantly pulling on their coats and scarves, embracing Leila and saying how lovely it was to have met her. There were a few saucy comments – 'Don't stay up too late, you two,' and 'Sleep well!' – and a very snide remark from Emma, who threw herself at Henry in a lascivious hug goodbye and said in a loud, acid, five-cups-of-cider voice, 'Don't forget, you have to be at rehearsals *early* tomorrow.'

She gave Leila a murderous look and left. Leila ignored her, twisting her hands in her lap, suddenly feeling cold and funny and turned-off. *Here we go*, she thought wearily, *now it's time for obligatory sex.*

One of the refreshing things about Henry was that he'd been sweet about waiting for the right time for them to jump into bed. But Leila didn't feel ready. Soon . . . but not yet. *Maybe I'll just have to go through with it*, she thought dully, *like I do with Mr Winterton. Close my eyes and shut out the pain.*

Henry came over and fiddled with the CD player. Leila wondered if she should pretend she felt sick. Oh God. He was putting on an awful track too. Mariah Carey.

Leila stumbled to her feet, just as Henry turned and took her hand.

'I need to—' she muttered, ducking her head as he curled his arms around her waist and planted a soft kiss on her head.

'Let's dance,' he whispered.

They swayed. Leila's limbs felt as tense as springs. She really did think she was going to be sick. She stared hard at the button on his shirt, the white threads coming loose. She pictured the button falling onto the pavement, lying in a dirty puddle in a London street. She wondered

176

if she should tell him she wanted to break-up in order to stop the sex, but the moment seemed wrong, she didn't quite have the impetus.

Henry moved in a little closer. His body was warm and she found her hands creeping around his waist, feeling the taut roughness of his belt.

They were the same height, cheek to cheek. She could feel his stubble. Leila irritably curled her neck away, resting her chin on the curve of his shoulder, gazing at the flicker of candlelight dancing across the walls and a pair of crushed white paper cups, one leaking wine, like blood, on to the carpet. He pulled her in a little closer, so that their bodies were tight, hard together. She drew in her breath. Still, he didn't make any attempt to kiss her. She looked at the sky, starless, and felt a stab of fear; she suddenly felt glad to be inside, snug and warm, away from the dark world outside. The music swirled over them. She found her limbs loosening, sinking into him. She closed her eyes and began humming dreamily.

They swayed on the soft carpet for some time. The song finished and they stood still, lost. Leila felt deliciously warm. She raised her head hazily. If he'd picked her up and carried her into bed, she wouldn't have protested.

Henry looked down at her with sleepy eyes. She felt an unexpected flutter in her chest, as if a butterfly had wriggled its way out of her heart. It was a sensation she hadn't felt in a long time.

He's lovely, she thought. The butterfly caught in her throat, made her feel breathless.

'Well, we'd better get you home, dearest,' he said, smiling.

Oh no! As he turned to get her coat, she curled up her

fists. Her groin was wailing. She resisted the urge to leap on him and cry, 'Get me into bed, you idiot!'

He helped her on with her coat and even did up her buttons.

Normally this sort of paternal gesture would have annoyed Leila, but she found herself giggling and saying, 'Thanks Daddy,' which set Henry giggling too.

For a moment she considered taking the lead herself – it would be so easy to reach up and kiss him . . . but Henry was turning to find his keys. He looked back, shy and uncertain. The moment had passed. Leila repressed a smile and mouthed, 'Ready.' Dear old Henry, she thought affectionately, always on the wrong foot, putting his piece on the wrong square, doing the wrong thing at the wrong time.

It was a short walk from Chalcott Square to Princess Road. It was raining hard, but they were both on a high and hardly noticed. Henry kept doing a silly monkey walk, then pushing Leila into hedges and tickling her. He left her outside her house with a long moonlight kiss and a shy wave. As his lips touched hers, Leila suddenly had a memory of Mr Winterton leaning in for a kiss only the night before and the butterfly seemed to sink and die inside her. She went in feeling very sad and confused.

She'd only felt more confused this morning.

Twenty-four hours ago, she had wanted to dump Henry. Now she was sitting at work, staring into space, and wondering what it would be like to go to bed with him. It was a fantastic sign, a sign of real longing, but it also made her feel vulnerable, nervous.

Am I falling for him? And if so, what should I do about Mr Winterton?

The phone rang and she jumped, laughing at herself.

178

'Call for you.' Zoe said briskly,

Oh please, please, let it be Henry, she found herself begging.

'It's Jack De Antiquus.'

What the hell did he want?

'Can you tell him I'm in a meeting? Thanks.'

18
Jack

Something very strange was going on.

It was an ordinary evening – a Tuesday night.

Jack was faintly aware of a slight impulse floating in the riverbed of his consciousness as they sat in the kitchen, eating together. Katie had cooked herself a Quorn meal (she'd offered to cook some for Jack too but he'd politely declined). Jack had ordered a four cheese and pepperoni pizza from Pizza Hut, and he proceeded to devour it joyously while Leila watched in disgust, taking tiny, dainty spoonfuls from her pot of organic yoghurt. It was then that he noticed something – the way her tongue, small and lithe, like a kitten's, swirled around the metal of the spoon, the white yoghurt soft against the pink. Then, aware that he was staring, he glanced away, stuffing a pizza crust into his mouth.

Conversation was slightly stilted. Especially when Leila started ranting about an evil builder who had recently fixed her downstairs toilet and had apparently left a 'huge gaping crack'. Jack and Katie exchanged glances; Jack was sure it was just the tiniest of hairline cracks, knowing Leila.

After stacking the dishes ready for washing up, Katie sat down and started stuffing envelopes (as far as Jack could see, working for a charity consisted of nothing *but* stuffing envelopes). Leila picked up a copy of *The Bookseller* to analyse the bestseller charts. Jack half-heartedly played with his Gameboy, ignoring Leila's pained glances as he beeped and shrieked his way through Tomb Raider.

'Jack, could you stuff some envelopes for me?' Katie asked.

'I'm busy. And –' Jack knew what was coming next '– don't ask me for any donations, I'm broke.'

'Jack, come on. This is important. There are people out there who can't even afford to eat, you know. Who have barely enough money for one grain of rice – while you have a Nintendo Gameboy.'

'What would a starving African orphan want with a Nintendo Gameboy?'

'Jack!'

'Sorry!' Jack pulled a boyish, apologetic face. 'OK – I'll do the envelope-stuffing. Well, in a minute.'

He felt sure these leaflets were for a worthy cause, but ninety-nine per cent of the people who got them through their door would just chuck them in the bin. Then, seeing the disapproving look Leila sent him, he felt guilty. Finishing off, he got up and offered to help with the washing-up.

As Katie started to slosh water and spray in washing-up liquid, she sensed Jack's presence behind her and it made her uncomfortable. Since their kiss she felt funny around him – it was as if Jack was an electric fence and the slightest touch sent volts of awkwardness through her. As Jack took a soapy plate from her hands, their fingers brushed. Katie recoiled and the plate smashed to the floor. China lay in white fragments. Leila raised her eyes heavenwards.

'Katie!' Jack told her off.

'Don't Katie me. This is your fault!' Katie knelt down, yanking out the red dustpan and brush.

They knelt there together, Jack sweeping and Katie tearing off strips of kitchen roll to wrap up the shards of china.

'Hey – careful of that bit—' Jack reached over and she felt the length of his bare arm against her thigh. She jumped again; the china sliced her skin, drawing blood.

'Ow! Jack!'

'Don't Jack me. I was just trying to tell you to be careful of that bit of glass by your knee.' He took hold of her finger, and gently licked away the blood. It was oddly erotic and Katie pulled away.

'Jack, you're revolting, disgusting! Don't – just don't touch me, OK?'

'Sorry.' Jack drew back, sheepish and suddenly self-conscious. 'I – look – I wasn't about to leap on you. Is that why you're so weird with me?'

'I'm not weird with you.'

'You are. Yesterday in Safeway I brushed your arm by, like, *one millimetre*—'

'What!'

'Yeah! When I was trying to put in some Walkers' crisps and you gave me a lecture about hydrogenated vegetable oil, you acted as if I had *leprosy*. I don't want you to think that every time I touch you I'm going to maul you or something.'

'I don't,' Katie said, turning to the bin, face flaming. Did he have to discuss this with Leila in the room?

'You do. Look, I'll have you bloody know that a lot of women would like me to leap on them,' Jack blustered, grinning.

'Doubt it,' said Katie, putting on an airy voice, trying to make light of it. 'You're such a shit kisser. Urgh. God. It was like getting off with a dog's backside.'

'Oh, well, Katie,' Jack retorted. 'Since you can only manage to pull complete dogs, I guess you'd know.'

'OK – more like a washing machine,' Katie mused. 'Only not as clean. Still, bad breath is something that can be sorted out, Jack,' she added, knowing Jack was obsessed with personal hygiene. 'Haven't you seen the ads on TV for Lysterine—'

'Katie!' Jack burst into furious laughter. 'Right!' Picking up a terry cloth, he proceeded to flick soapy water at her until she was screaming in protest, and he had pushed her up against the sink.

'Admit it!' he cried, roughly pinning her arms behind her, 'I am a good kisser. I am a spectacular kisser. You loved it!'

'Bleurgh!' Katie made sick noises. Jack flicked a quick look at Leila, who was pretending to be engrossed in her magazine. He leaned in closer to Katie, his thighs pinning her against the hard, cold edge of the sink. Katie could feel the end of her ponytail dipping into the soapy water as she leaned backwards and she let out another slight scream, still struggling. All she could see were Jack's dark eyes, gleaming playfully, his mouth tugged up in his lop-sided smile.

'You want to kiss me,' Jack crooned in a sing-song voice. Their lips were inches apart. 'You love it, Katie.'

'I'm going to spit in your face if you don't back off.'

'You love it—'

'Children, children,' Leila sighed, looking up in disdain.

Instantly the mood was broken. Jack let Katie go, still laughing, and giving her a little play-kick. Katie kicked

183

him back, missed, pulled a face and hastily turned to the washing-up, trying to control the tumultuous beating of her heart. Leila stood up, sighing.

'Jaaack,' she said, twirling a strand of blonde hair around her little finger. 'I was just wondering if you could check something out for me. I'm convinced I've got sparrows nesting in my drain – could you take a look?'

'Sure.' Jack put down the plate he was drying.

Leila and Katie exchanged looks of surprise.

Since Jack had moved in, Leila had been constantly trying to wheedle him into doing DIY jobs, like changing lightbulbs or putting up shelves in the study. Whenever she asked him, she stopped her usual sniping and went all purry and smiley and *Oh Jack*-y, which Jack loathed. He didn't mind doing odd jobs – it was fair enough when Leila was letting him stay. But he did hate women like Leila who were convinced that all men were ruled by their dicks, that they only had to flash a bit of flesh, toss back their hair, and the opposite sex would melt in a pool of testosterone and do whatever they commanded. Jack wasn't stupid. Leila could strip naked if she wanted, he wasn't going to repaint her house for free.

So Jack felt as surprised as they did. Why, all of a sudden, did he feel so compelled to help her?

'Oh, I need some air,' Jack shrugged, then realised that didn't make a smidgen of sense.

He'd felt a bit funny around her for the last couple of days, as a matter of fact. Even since that morning on Sunday when she'd woken him up, appearing in the morning mist like an angel.

Fortunately, Leila didn't seem to notice. She led him eagerly up the stairs, chatting on and on about her drains, drains, drains . . .

As she brought him into her bedroom, Jack felt awkward, like a teenage boy sneaking into a prostitute's boudoir. It was a beautiful room – a white carpet (to match her cat, presumably, which was curled up in a ball on the bed), pale blue walls and huge white wardrobes filled with designer clothes.

The room was a dark blue-grey in the twilight. There was something smoky, dusky about her scent – a sweet swirl of lilac and bluebells. He breathed it in deeply for a moment, feeling it snake down his throat and coil in the pit of his stomach. God, she smelled gorgeous . . .

Down in the kitchen, he'd been aware of Leila surreptitiously watching his playfight with Katie. He hadn't meant to behave like such a flirt; yet the touch of Katie's body against his, the impression of Leila's eyes on him, had left him feeling oddly charged and erotic. He could still taste Katie's blood in his mouth, salty and acidic. He pushed his hands in his pockets, and watched Leila from behind, shoving up the sash window. A ray of light as she turned on a lamp caught the hairs on the back of her neck, a soft layer of down. Suddenly he pictured himself walking towards her, gently pressing his lips against it. It would feel like feathers, eiderdown. He imagined a hand curling round to clutch her breast, his kiss becoming vampirish. And then – wham! he felt blood in his teeth and an erection rearing in his trousers.

Jack started to panic, attempting to cover it with his hands. He tried to douse the flames with unerotic thoughts: tweed skirts . . . um . . . Mozart records . . . um . . . cold showers . . .

But – dear God – she was swivelling round now, leaning back out of the window, looking up. Her short grey skirt was moving up her smooth thighs, showing off her

185

pearly stockings, her breasts were riding up, her blonde hair cascading behind her . . .

'Jack?' she snapped. 'Will you please come and take a look?'

'Oh – yes.' Jack shook himself. Just what was going on?

He hurried over, turned round and leaned back out of the window. They were inches apart.

'See?'

As she leaned over to point, he felt her thigh brush his leg. She hadn't shaved her armpits. She'd hidden them away beneath her pink top but now that she was pointing, he could see the faint tuft of blonde hair. Normally it would have revulsed Jack, who liked women as smooth as marble. But for some reason, it really tickled him. He longed to stroke it . . . to lick it . . . oh yes . . .

'Can you see?'

Jack couldn't see anything. Just a drainpipe, the roof, and the cloudy sky beyond, huge and unbounded.

'Wow – doesn't the sky look amazing.' Jack leaned back further, unexpectedly moved. 'And the sunset – it's as if the sky's on fire . . .' he stammered.

God, that was an odd, un-Jack thing to say. He felt as though he was a doll, being controlled by a phantom ventriloquist who kept making him say corny lines that really belonged in bad poetry.

'What? See – see those twigs sticking out from the drainpipe? A nest! It's going to clog everything up. And try getting a builder at this time of year. I mean, I know I can't expect you to climb on to the roof, but maybe if we got a long, long ladder, you could . . .'

'Uh – sure – whatever. Anything for you, Leila,' he said, in a funny, high voice.

She swivelled round to look at his face. Jack felt the

breath knocked out of him. Then he saw her frown and he realised he was staring. Very obviously.

She knows, he panicked, *she knows . . . she knows . . .* What? he asked himself shakily. You fancy Leila? All of a sudden. Doesn't make sense.

'Miaow!'

Jack was thankfully saved by her cat, Candida, uncurling from the bed and padding across the room. Leila instantly scooped her up in her arms, stoking her, cuddling her face sideways into her snowy fur.

'Well, bye bye, Jack,' said Leila, giving him a mocking, teasing smile. 'Thanks for all your help.'

Jack got out of her room as fast as he could.

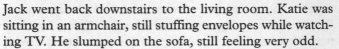

Jack went back downstairs to the living room. Katie was sitting in an armchair, still stuffing envelopes while watching TV. He slumped on the sofa, still feeling very odd.

'All right?' Katie asked, looking bemused. 'Well, Jack, I'm impressed with you helping Leila. You've obviously turned over a new leaf – you'll be on *Ground Force* next, replacing Alan Titchmarsh.' She nodded at the TV, where the great hero was wielding a spade with a cheeky grin.

'Mmm,' said Jack. He could feel a blush sweeping over his cheeks like a rash. Katie was so perceptive; she knew him too well. What if she guessed? 'Uh,' he yawned widely. 'I'd better . . . go . . . to bed.'

Upstairs in his room, he picked up Susie's Rubik cube, twiddled with it, put it down. Then he picked up his guitar, now coloured with Barbie stickers. He was supposed to be teaching Susie to play it but they'd only managed a few chords. He strummed lightly, careful not to wake her up in the next room, soothed as he played, his brain crunching over the mystery of Leila.

It wasn't as if he even liked her as a person.

He could remember their one-night stand. He remembered, with a fond smile, how nervous Katie had been then. She'd grown up to be so strong. Whereas Leila – well, Leila had been a bitch then and was a bitch now. She hadn't changed at all.

I didn't enjoy making love to her, he recalled. He'd been slightly drunk and everything had been dark and blurry, but he'd been high on anticipation, thinking, *God, this girl is gorgeous – making love to her will be incredible.*

Famous last words.

It had turned into a ridiculous power struggle. Both had fought to caress each other, as if competing to prove who was the best at foreplay. And Leila had kept kissing him, and opening his trousers before he'd undone her skirt, racing ahead; Jack always liked to set his own pace. She'd been so . . . aggressive! And for the climax, Jack had pushed himself on top of her, making love to her with burning passion, as if to show her who was boss. But she'd merely curled out from under him and gone on top. She'd made love to him, her eyes closed – which Jack had also hated. It had made him feel like a dummy, as if he was just a vehicle upon which she could enact her fantasies.

And, with his typical grass-is-greener syndrome, at the back of his mind he'd kept thinking, *Did I pick the wrong girl? Should I have gone with Katie? OK, so she wasn't as pretty, but she was sweet and kind. This'll teach me not to be so superficial.*

Afterwards he had wanted to cuddle her, but she'd walked out. Seconds later, he'd heard the shower. He'd lain there, feeling empty and bewildered and full of indignation, thinking: *Excuse me, but isn't this how women are supposed to feel?*

That was what he hated about Leila – she was too

much like a man. She was tough. She was ruled by her head and she was frighteningly intelligent. And look at the ruthless way she'd treated her ex-husband, Ray. Jack didn't know much about their marriage or divorce but it was obvious Leila had used him, sucked him dry of all his money, and then left.

No – Jack preferred his women soft and feminine, who laughed at his jokes and adored him. He didn't feel he was a chauvinist, it was just his taste.

If only, he mused with Pygmalion wistfulness, *I could combine Katie's personality with Leila's looks, then I'd have my dream woman.*

So why the hell was Leila reducing him to such a quivering wreck, with an erection like a skyscraper?

Maybe it was just his general state of randiness. After all, only the other week he'd been finding Katie attractive. Maybe he just needed a good lay.

He put his guitar down and stripped off down to his boxer shorts. Looking at the dusty mirror, he patted his stomach, flat but with just the faintest swell signalling future danger – *I must stop drinking beer and get down to the gym.* He got into bed and lay there.

His bladder was full. He was about to get up again when he heard the shower go on. And then a voice, like a thrush, singing *American Pie.* Leila.

After that, the rest of the night was agony. He couldn't stop picturing her in the shower, the water sluicing over her curves, beading on her back. Leila rubbing herself with a towel. Getting ready for bed, putting on that ivory slip thing he'd seen on her pillow. Sliding between the sheets, the cotton kissing her breasts . . .

Lust raged in him like a fever; he had to keep kicking off the covers and opening the window to let the autumn wind and rain stroke his body.

189

And then he heard it. A moan. Just faint, but there.

Jack gazed upwards, transfixed. Leila's room was above his. The ceiling was thin; he could often hear the murmur of her chatting on the phone. He strained to hear above the rumble of traffic. There it was again – another moan. Oh God, surely she wasn't satisfying herself . . . Oh God . . . He wasn't going to sleep a wink tonight.

In the morning, he heard the moans again. He frowned, delirious – surely she couldn't carry on *all night*? He'd left the window open and the room was now freezing. As he closed it, he noticed the bins below, blown here and there by the wind and rain.

And then it made sense. He'd just spent the night getting off on a load of squeaky dustbins. He really was losing it.

19
Katie

Katie would never have imagined that such a quiet evening would end in chaos. But then again, Jack always seemed to be bringing chaos with him these days.

She and Jack were planning to watch the lottery together that night, and so she spent the early evening helping Susie with a school project – an autobiographical scrapbook.

They'd bought a mauve scrap-book from Rymans and Susie had painted 'My Life So Far' in scrawly pink letters on the front. Now they were in the kitchen, the table cluttered with glitter, pens and Pritt Stick. Katie had got a big cardboard box of photos down from the loft. Looking at them made her feel strange – as she opened the wallets and albums, memories seeped out like smoke.

'Who's that?' Susie asked, peering at a picture of a young girl with very curly, canary-yellow hair. She was running out of the sea, licked by frothy waves, exuberantly waving a spade.

'Me!' Katie laughed. 'Me, when I was six.'

She suddenly remembered how happy, how alive she'd felt on that day. The sand squidging beneath her feet. The waves playing around her. The sky running on for ever, the wind chasing clouds across it. She'd danced around the beach, spurting with energy and love. *Where does it all go wrong, that Edenic fall from childhood to being an adult?* Katie thought despairingly. *I was so happy then, full of hope. I wish I could have stayed six years old, running on that beach.*

'Mummy, hurry up,' Susie moaned. 'We need some photos of *me*.'

'OK, OK, keep your hair on. Ah – here we are.' Katie smiled. 'Here's a photo of you – in my tummy.'

Keith had taken the photo. By the lilac tree in the back garden of their house in Hampstead. Keith had kept telling her how beautiful she looked and she'd never believed him. But she was glowing with impending motherhood.

As Susie messily glued the photo in, Katie found herself addictively flipping on through her wedding photos. A lop-sided photo of their house – Katie was never very good at taking pictures. A picture of Susie in her pram; under the shade of an oak tree. Her face was tinged green, like a wood nymph.

Oh, and a photo of Mum.

Katie always got a lump in her throat when she looked at that photo. Her mum, chin up, short curls wrapped in a purple scarf, baking in the kitchen, rolling-pin firm beneath her hands. You'd never have known she had cancer.

She had died just about the time that Katie's marriage to Keith had started to crumble.

It hadn't fallen apart due to anything specific. She'd begun her marriage willing to do anything to please him. Wash his dishes, mend his clothes, cook his meals. She felt people fell into two categories – those who took more love, those who gave more love. She was a giver; warm-

192

hearted and generous. She'd loved seeing the proud smile on Keith's face when she cooked a three-course meal for his business friends.

Where had it all gone wrong? Perhaps with the sex. It hadn't taken long for Katie to feel as though someone had tipped a sandglass upside down as her desire trickled away by the minute. Sex felt like rape. She became an expert at making excuses. Headaches, periods, ovarian cysts, candida. Or she would wake in the middle of the night and look at him, snoring, at his goatee beard and bushy eyebrows and shorn head, and simply *shudder*. Fear held tight in her heart – *what's the matter with me? Am I going mad? Why don't I love him any more?*

Deep down, she knew the truth. She'd never really loved him. Just married him on the rebound from Jack.

She'd nearly confided in her mother. Nearly. But her mother had been a Catholic. She'd believed in enduring, in suffering, in maintaining vows; Jack always joked that Katie had inherited a 'guilt' gene from her. So the words had remained pressed under her tongue, like a tablet. For a long time she'd been too afraid to voice her feelings, to make the abstract concrete – to make them real. While she hated Keith in her imagination only, she could still ignore it, pretend it was just a bad mood, a difficult day, PMT.

Katie had never felt so alone as when her mother had died. She was finally an adult. There was nobody to look after her. She had to look after other people, hold their lives together. Keith had barely comforted her; he wasn't insensitive, just didn't seem to understand.

'Oh – look at me, I've got chocolate round my mouth.' Susie picked up a photo of her sitting in the garden, surrounded by teddies.

'No, that's a mud pie!' Katie said fondly. 'You were always eating mud when you were little, it was terrible. I'd turn my back for a minute, look round and you'd have it in your mouth.'

'Urghhhhh!' Susie made puking noises, revelling in the idea all the same.

'Who's that? Uncle Jack?'

Susie held a photo of a man with long chestnut hair, standing in the kitchen, Susie on his shoulders.

'No, that's Darren. From GLENCO.'

GLENCO – the environmental group she had joined. God, it had felt so amazing to actually get involved, to be an individual, to do her own thing.

'But who's going to cook my meals?' Keith had demanded. 'And look after the house?'

Katie had realised then that that was all she was to Keith. Just a slave. A pretty little wife to iron his shirts and organise his dinner parties. He'd thought this was love; this was how his mother had behaved so Katie should do the same.

Seeing Susie gluing in a photo of a long-ago trip to the zoo, Katie felt a chill. She remembered staring at the animal cages, thinking, *I'm just the same. Trapped in a cage. Till death do us part.* She'd wished he would just do something, anything, to give her an excuse. Have an affair with his secretary. Hit her, even.

'No, Candida, get off the table,' Susie said sternly, as the cat bounced up, sniffing curiously. Susie laughed as Candida picked her way to the end of the table, glitter on her paws, leaving starry prints behind her.

And so she'd left. One Sunday afternoon. A day that had swerved towards unexpected violence. The final straw. As she'd packed her bags, there'd been blood on her clothes. But as she'd escaped, speeding away in her car, Susie crying in the back, a huge sense of relief had flooded over her. She'd yanked down the windows, feeling the wind billowing her hair back from her face; *I'm free*, she'd wanted to scream at the top of her voice, seeing the afternoon sky stretching out. *I'm me again!*

'Susie!' Katie suddenly realised Susie was rubbing Pritt Stick on to Candida's tail and showering glitter on it. 'SUSIE!'

'But she looks pretty, Mummy!'

Katie was about to start shouting. Then, seeing Candida's bemused face, she burst into exasperated laughter. 'Oh God, what is Auntie Leila going to say?'

'Oh shit.' Susie looked worried. 'Sorry, Mummy.' She clamped her hand over her mouth, seeing Katie's 'don't-you-dare-use-that-sort-of-language' face.

The scrapbook came to an abrupt halt. The evening ended with the awkward task of trying to get Candida into the bath to wash her tail. By the end, both Katie and Susie were laughing hysterically and covered in red scratch marks.

'Oh, you poor thing!' Katie tried to stroke Candida as she leapt out of the bath, shivering and dripping, but Candida stalked off in a huff and started to wash herself haughtily.

Katie put Susie to bed, gave her a fond kiss goodnight and turned out the light. God, she felt tired. She checked her watch. Jack should be here any minute.

Jack. Jack and that kiss. She still couldn't forget it. It had now been immortalised as a running joke between them. Katie kept teasingly calling him a letch and every time Jack hugged her or held her hand, he'd wink and say, 'You'll get a kiss later on, too, if you're lucky.' Though Katie felt relieved that she and Jack were friends again, the more the kiss was bantered about, the less erotic it began to seem – like a well-worn joke where the punchline falls flatter with every repetition. She could hardly remember how and why it had happened; she had just had a blurry image of being in that hotel room, and of that moment, just before he kissed her – a dark stillness, a sense of *rightness*, their lips inches apart, breath tight and shaky, everything as it should be . . .

But Jack quite clearly thought the whole thing was just a drunken, stupid mistake to laugh over. It was back to square one again. Back in the same old rut of friendship. Nothing had changed.

Biting her lip, Katie got out her lottery ticket. They always did the lottery together on Saturday nights – it was their ritual. But where was he? He was going to miss it . . .

Jack never showed. She watched the lottery on her own, and then the next programme, and the next, until she fell asleep on the sofa.

As the doorbell rang several hours later, Katie got grumpily to her feet. She was going to kill Jack for standing her up.

But, opening the door, her heart sank.

Jack was standing in the doorway. Blood all over his face. Blood splattered on his clothes. Eyes puffed up, tears streaming. Beaten up.

★

'Jack, what the hell happened?'

Into the bathroom. Where was the TCP? Katie flung open the cabinet. There were a thousand perfume bottles jostling for space – Leila's fern talc and Dead Sea salts and seaweed-and-jasmine-tea hair lotion and every bloody Body Shop combination you could find.

'Jack, oh my God, Jack.'

Katie sat him down on the toilet seat.

'Jack, what happened?'

Jack buried his face in his hands, tearful and wheezy, his fringe fluffing between his fingers. A slither of blood trickled over his T-shirt like burgundy wine.

196

'This guy . . .'

'Guy? What guy? Shall we call the police?' She couldn't find the cotton wool. She picked up her flannel, squeezed out the excess water, and knelt down before him. She gently washed away a streak of blood from the crevice of his cheek and dabbed at his nose.

'OW! That hurts!' Muzzily, he tried to swot her hand away.

'I know it does, darling, but you have to tell me what happened.' Had he been mugged? Attacked?

'I'm in love, Katie. God, I don't know what to do about it.'

'What? What?' Katie rinsed out the flannel again, wincing as she touched his tender nose. Was he delirious?

'I'm in love. You know you and Henry have been going on for ages about me falling? Well, I have. And I hope you're satisfied.'

Katie squeezed out the flannel again. Very slowly, very tightly. She felt a pressure around her jaw. She watched the pink drops slither down the sink. In love? Jack? In love? What? When? Why? How?

'Jack, what the fuck are you going on about? Why the fuck are you all beaten up?'

'Don't shout at me, I can't help it.' As his voice rose thickly, Katie fretted that he'd broken his nose.

'Well, what's the matter? What happened? Did you fall for some girl and she had a boyfriend? Were you pissed? For God's sake, Jack – can't you just – I mean – you can't go chasing after random girls. God. Men. The trouble you get into because your brains are chained to your—'

'It's a girl I've known for ages, and she doesn't bloody want me. You know, I've never been in this situation before. I don't know what's going on.'

'Will you just stop going on about this stupid girl!'

Silence. 'Here, I'll do it,' Jack sulkily pulled the flannel from her fingers, ineffectually swabbing his cheek.

'No, I'll do it.' Katie pulled it back, kneeling down before him again and washing away flakes of dried blood from his jaw.

'Oh, Katie, I'm sorry,' Jack burst out, pulling her into a deep hug. Katie found her anger melting away as she felt him clutch her hair, nuzzle against her. And then it hit her. *A girl I've known for ages . . . She doesn't bloody want me . . .* Surely . . . surely it couldn't be . . . but who else had Jack known for ages? Jack hadn't known any girl for more than five minutes. Except her.

'Ow,' Jack wheezed as Katie curled her arms even more tightly around him.

'Jack, who did this to you? I want to go and bloody smash their heads in right now.'

'Katie!' Jack squeezed her shoulder. 'You're so sweet. If I tell you, you won't kill me?'

'Who? Just tell me, Jack.'

'Well, well, I just went along to this party – bumped into Leila and Henry there. We were having a great time and then this guy just starts laying into me, about, well, about a hundred quid or so I borrowed, like, five years ago, when I was working with him on a building site and I wanted to get a flight to France. He'd said before that I could forget it but I guess he was pissed. He was waving around an empty cider bottle.'

'But that's terrible. You have to call the police, Jack.'

'Nah . . . I'm OK . . .' Jack got up shakily, grabbing on to the towel rail to steady himself, fingering his swollen nose in the mirror. 'Doesn't seem to be broken . . . I think the side of his fist caught me, luckily, otherwise it probably would be. I'm just – God, Katie – it was the shock. I've never actually been beaten up before. You kind of expect it to happen when you're walking home in the dark, not in the loo at some party.'

'So . . . so . . .' Katie swallowed. 'What does this . . . have to do with the girl?' Her eyes fell to his T-shirt, rucked up from the waistband, showing off a torn red Levi's label. Seeing the bare band of skin, she felt a sudden flare of desire. She couldn't look at him. She busied herself putting away the TCP, the bottle sliding between her sweaty hands.

'It's nobody you know, Katie,' Jack sighed miserably. 'Look, let's just forget it, OK? It's never going to happen.'

And a look of pain came over his face that was so jarring, Katie felt her heart sink into her stomach.

'So, did I win the lottery?' Jack asked, forcing a tired smile. 'Say something to cheer me up!'

'No,' Katie said coldly. *Nobody you know, Katie . . . Nobody you know.* 'We both lost.' *Nobody you know.*

20
Jack

Of course, he hadn't told Katie the whole story. Just fragments of the truth.

It had all begun early that Saturday afternoon. Jack often went to see his mum on Saturday afternoons.

He'd taken Henry along, at her request. Jack's mum adored Henry. It was funny – when they'd been friends at university, Jack had been terrified of bringing Henry over. Jack had once been invited to Henry's family home in the country – a huge sprawling manor in an acre of rose gardens, a cold building filled with golden candelabra, servants and loneliness. Jack had felt very self-conscious the whole time and had ended up making nervous jokes ('Your dog's looking a bit dead,' he'd remarked about the animal-skin rugs, at which Henry's mother had looked most offended) and muddling his knives at their four-course dinner.

He'd pictured Henry coming to his mother's flat: a peeling shoebox in a pee-and-graffiti-infested council block in Camden. And he'd avoided inviting Henry along for the next two years.

Finally, one birthday, he'd plucked up the courage.

And to Jack's amazement, Henry had loved it. He'd loved the way Jack's mum let them spend the afternoon chilling out and watching tennis or cricket; she'd even got into the spirit of it and shouted at the TV too, though she got the names wrong.

'I love your mum,' Henry had said wistfully, to Jack's bewilderment and pride. 'God, I wish I had your mum, Jack.'

Jack's mum was approaching sixty now. But while Henry's mother looked half her age, her smooth brown skin wrinkle-free from years of expensive face creams, her clothes elegantly fitted to her gym-toned figure, Jack's mum was very short. And very fat. Her grey hair was frizzy with a perm. She looked like an OAP.

'MUM!' Jack banged on the door.

He could hear the TV blaring. She always had it on full volume. She didn't even hear the neighbours banging on the walls for her to turn it down, her hearing was so bad these days.

'MUM!'

Finally, she appeared, her dark eyes sparkling like olives. Her wrinkled face was plastered with make-up, like a happy clown – turquoise, pink and red. She always shopped in Oxfam and she loved 'young' clothes. Today she was wearing a bright pink dress, a gold sequinned cardigan and gypsy earrings.

'Jack!' She gave him a hug, and then clutched Henry.

'Here we go.' Jack always brought her a pint of milk for her bones. Henry had brought along a box of Quality Street. She couldn't stop thanking him. Inside, on the table, a jigsaw lay in a half-finished zig-zag. She gave them tea and asked if Jack had a job yet (soon, he said) and interrogated Henry about his acting (she had it in her head that *A Midsummer Night's Dream* was a film and

Henry was about to become the next Mel Gibson). Jack, who'd been feeling bristly towards Henry since his lust for Leila had developed, couldn't help but hold up an invisible scoreboard in his head. Henry: one. Jack: nil.

Jack also failed the girlfriend test. He had to repress a smile when his mother started lecturing him about being left on the shelf.

'Mum – that happens to women. Not to men.'

'Look, I read the papers. Women are different now. They don't just want to run around after their husbands – they want their own lives. I've read about those girls who go drinking, those largerettes.'

'Ladettes!' Jack was in hysterics. His mum gave him a look.

'So, Jack tells me you've got a girlfriend,' she said to Henry, accidentally sitting on one of her embroidery sets. 'Leila? Are you to be married?'

Jack rolled his eyes apologetically. His mum, despite having had a terrible marriage herself, had an idealised view that every date led up the aisle.

But, to Jack's astonishment, Henry looked serious.

'Well . . . I don't know . . . maybe . . .'

Maybe! Jack couldn't believe it.

He'd assumed Henry and Leila were having some kind of fling. That they'd break up in a few weeks. That then Jack would be able to make a move without being too much of a bastard. Jack had accepted now that he fancied Leila, and the only solution was to shag her again and get her out of his system.

God. Jack wished they were back at university – when Henry and Jack had both fancied the same girl then, they'd fought for her over a game of tennis.

His mum was the only person Jack felt loved him unconditionally. Normally he left home feeling warm, as though her affection was a shield around him. Today he felt like a failure.

'Hey, Jack – Leila and I are going to a party tonight,' Henry said as they clattered down the grey steps, stepping over a scraggle of teenagers smoking illicit cigarettes. 'Fancy coming along? Might not be any good. In fact, it'll probably be one DJ playing an Aqua CD with a bottle of Virgin vodka, but you never know . . .'

Jack was torn. If Henry was serious about Leila, Jack should keep his distance. Out of sight, out of mind, and all that. But . . .

The thought of seeing her made him weak at the knees. He craved her like a cigarette.

'OK,' said Jack. 'Sure.'

Henry and Jack spent the rest of the day watching the cricket and turned up at the party at about 10 p.m. The party was in a tall house that throbbed with music, the windows full of silhouettes of people laughing, talking, smoking, kissing.

As they went from room to room, Jack found his heart hammering at the thought of seeing Leila. He searched through the sea of faces. In the daylight, the house might have been high-celinged with marble skirting boards. Tonight it looked as though it belonged in a '60s movie. Bright blue bulbs, like huge flies, hung naked from the ceiling, spreading an eerie glow over the swaying bodies. A dance track pumped from a stereo. Jack felt as though he was underwater, moving slowly, spacily, as if in a dream.

And then. He saw her. Standing by the windowsill. Sipping amber liquid.

God. Jack felt as though a firework had just exploded inside him and his heart was whizzing around like a

Catherine Wheel. The hair on the back of his neck felt as though a woman had brushed the end of a whip up the length of his spine. She was *gorgeous*.

'Henry!' The music was so loud, they could only shout. Or lip-read. She gave Henry a feline hug, then turned to Jack, playfully trailing her fingers along his jaw.

'Surprised to see you,' Leila interrupted, as if to say, *I know, Jack, I know this is no coincidence*. Jack flushed red, but then, to his surprise, she leaned over and gave him a hug and a kiss. 'You're looking great,' she whispered into his ear.

Jack was left reeling. He looked great!

He looked great!

He looked great!

He opened his mouth to tell her she looked more than great, but she had swirled away, dancing. And what dancing.

She curled her body around the notes like an undulating snake. Jack found himself falling into a kind of trance. He'd once tried opium, one crazy night in Thailand, and it had been a strange experience, blurring day and night, time and boundaries, leaving him smoky, his head full of stars. The same sensation came over him now. He couldn't stop staring at her. Under the blue light she was like a mermaid rippling through an ocean. Now and again, she tossed back a head of turquoise hair and looked at him, smiled, looked away. Jack smiled and whispered 'tease' to himself. He stepped forward hazily, about to join her dancing, when suddenly another guy was stepping out in front of him.

Henry. He gave a slightly sheepish laugh and winked at Jack, but Jack knew what he was saying. *Keep away. She's mine*.

Jack laughed too, shrugging good-humouredly, but

inside he was seething. He pretended to dance, pretended he wasn't watching. But it was impossible.

Henry was dancing like a kid at a school disco, shuffling from one foot to the other. But Leila was pure poetry. She swirled around him, brushing her body against his, curling her arms around his neck, sexy slow-dancing, grinding her groin against his . . .

Suddenly Jack could bear it no longer. He only just managed to stop himself from hurling his body at Henry, wanting to throw him out of the window, to feel the satisfaction of his body crashing through the shards of glass, so he could then gather Leila up in his arms, carry her into a bedroom . . .

He stood up straight and stalked past them, aware of Leila's head swivelling, startled that she'd lost her audience.

Jack jumped over two kids kissing on the floor. He needed a bathroom; somewhere private, somewhere to be alone. His face was boiling hot, his body was shaking as though he had a fever. He heard laughter in the distance and he felt as though he was slowly shrinking and shrinking, until he was only two-feet tall, a mini-man, surrounded by hysterical giants, their laughter growing louder and louder like thunder in his ears as he ran out into the hallway.

There! He spotted a retreat but a guy with red and yellow woven dreads was sitting in front of the door, staring down into a can of Budweiser as though it explained the answer to life, the universe and everything. Jack tried tapping him politely on the shoulder. The druggie rolled his eyes. Jack practically had to step on him in order to get into the loo.

'Hey, chill,' he said. 'Make love not apple pie . . .'

Jack snorted and slammed the door behind him. He

stared at his reflection in the mirror. He looked even more mental than the druggie. *What's happening to me?* he reeled.

Suddenly his lust flared again, igniting the anger of frustration, and without thinking, desperate to lash out, he smashed his fist into the sink, imagining it was Henry's head. Unfortunately, it was a good deal harder.

'Arghhhhhhhhhhhhhhhhhowwwwwwwwww.' Jack's yelp bounced around the bathroom.

Shit. Tears welled in his eyes. He wanted to cry. He kissed his knuckles, white from the bruising. It wasn't the physical pain that cut so deeply, it was the agony of this . . . this feeling inside, as though a knife had been messily thrust into his heart, slicing through aortas, splashing the blood of shame and misery throughout his cells. If this was love, he hated it. He didn't want it. And yet . . . and yet . . . he needed her so badly, he'd do *anything* just for one kiss. His hand was still trembling with the aftershocks of pain; he filled up the sink with water, wincing and biting his lip as it splashed over the wounded skin. Having filled it up, he dunked his head in. Ahh, the cool relief. He closed his eyes and listened to the dull thump-thump of the music. He opened his eyes again and saw the turquoise sink, triggering a vision of that turquoise room . . . Leila twisting her body around Henry like a snake . . .

Jack lifted his head out of the water, droplets splashing over the sink. He sat down on the toilet seat, feeling the water dribble down his back. He couldn't stand any more. He pulled out his erection with trembling fingers.

As he started to stroke, the relief was so painful he found tears slipping down his cheeks. He closed his eyes, stroking, his head drooping in defeat . . . and then his hand froze in mid-grip, appalled as he realised just what

206

he was doing. Wanking off! At a party! Over a girl! Just what was the matter with him? He fiercely brushed away tears with the back of his hand. Sad, pathetic, geeks did this – guys who had braces and glasses and whose idea of a chat-up line was, 'Is internet the new religion?' Guys who were always left talking to the pot-plant. Not him, not Jack, Jack-the-Lad who always got every girl he wanted. And if he didn't, he simply put her out of his mind, telling himself she was a lesbian, or frigid, or not worth his time, and moved on to another choice. A second choice. That's what he needed . . .

But all I want is her, a hollow voice whispered. *Who else looks like her? Who else has that smile, the way her lips curve to one side – mocking and flirting?*

Just the thought of her lips was enough to harden his erection and his grip.

The door burst open without warning. Jack's hand flew away, stumbling to tug up his zip.

A vaguely familiar-looking skinhead was standing in the doorway. He was wearing a black T-shirt and his body was covered with tattoos. Seeing Jack caught out, a slow smirk crept across his face.

'Excuse me!' Jack spat out. His voice was shaky with tears and he tried to sound gruff and hard. 'I'm using this—'

Before he could say another word, the skinhead came up and *wham!* punched him in the face.

'I — ' Jack saw the blood drip on to his erection. Stunned, he tried to kick out but his leg only caught in his unzipped trousers.

'You! You owe Mick! Four thousand quid! Now pay up!'

Then it dawned on Jack. Mick. The snooker match. The money he kept telling Mick was 'coming'.

'It's three thousand.' Jack heard his voice, all thick from the blood in his nose. He tried to sound strong. 'It's three thousand and it's coming next week.'

'Well, it fucking well better had.'

For a moment they glared at each other. Jack could feel his fists shaking. *Don't, don't punch.* He held back his pride. *Play it cool. Mick might have sent a gang to wait for you.*

Then, suddenly, the skinhead left, kicking the door shut with a painful slam.

As he emerged from the toilet, a guy noticed the green twist of tissue sticking out from his nose and made a joke about Kleenex being the new class-A drug. A beautiful Asian girl with long black plaits and yellow-framed glasses, who was hanging on to the guy's arm, burst into screams of laughter. 'Oh thanks,' said Jack. She looked guilty and called after him to ask if he was OK, but Jack didn't look back. He had to get out of this place, before the skinhead came back for more.

He stumbled down the stairs, dazed. The hallway was now a carpet of dross – a swirl of wrappers, crushed cups, beer cans, cigarette ends.

As he reached the front door, fear snaked up his spine. *What if it's a set-up?*
What if Mick's on his way to the party?
With reinforcements?

He paused, gulped.

Jack was normally an atheist but he found himself murmuring a prayer for his protection.

He stepped tentatively outside. He paused for a moment, feeling the wind like an acupuncture needle pricking his skin with a thousand sharp points. He started to stroll down the road. Hearing a noise, he jumped violently,

208

banging against a lamppost. His heart was hammering, his eyes darted nervously about, imagining blokes in balaclavas creeping like panthers from behind parked cars. But there was nobody. Just a couple strolling down the road, arms entwined, coming back from dinner.

Jack started to walk away very quickly.

It hurt. His body was aching to lie down. His nose felt as though it was screaming like a police siren and every few minutes he touched the skin tenderly, then yelped. He prayed it wasn't broken – he had no wish to spend the night in a no doubt underfunded hospital, sitting in a smelly waiting room surrounded by mad people with broken legs.

Even worse, it started to rain. And not just the usual British insipid spitting. The weather had obviously got muddled up and decided it was in Africa, because it came down in a monsoon deluge, buckets of water splashing out of the clouds. Jack was soaked within minutes, his fringe soppy on his forehead.

Getting the Tube home was horrible; people kept giving him funny looks, as if he was some kind of druggie or drunkard who'd just been caught in a fray. Jack hung his head miserably, shivering, feeling his socks squelch in his trainers. Suddenly he felt exhausted. He couldn't see any way out of his problems. He felt as though he'd fallen into a deep, dark pit and couldn't find a way to climb back out. Maybe he could apply for a bank loan. Or another credit card. He could always lie on the forms – exaggerate his income by a few ten-thousand. Put his job as 'Management Consultant'. Maybe. He started getting paranoid again – what if the skinhead had followed him home? As he walked back from the Tube, he kept looking back nervously, curling his fists tight in his pockets, ready to defend himself.

He kept hoping that Leila would be home; he pictured her stroking his wounds, soothing him. 'Oh Jack . . . are you all right?'

In the end it was Katie who was home, who ended up bandaging his wounds. In a funny way, Jack was relieved. Just being around Katie made him feel safe and sane again.

Jack was asleep.

Katie gazed down at him. Halfway through a late-night film, he'd started nodding off. She'd dragged him upstairs and he'd crashed out on her bed, groaning; the next second he was asleep. Seeing him wrinkle his nose in his dream, she felt a hot flood of emotion and turned away.

She went into the bathroom to chuck away the soggy cotton wool balls. They bobbed like rabbit tails in the loo. She couldn't believe it. Jack – in love! They'd always laughed about how crap their love lives were – Katie too emotionally bruised from Keith to give her heart away, Jack too laddish to last more than eight hours with a girl.

'We're such a pair, aren't we?' Jack would laugh, when they sat together complaining. 'You know, I bet in fifty years' time we're going to be in an old people's home together, still moaning. You'll be telling me about some guy who's pissed you off 'cos he keeps forgetting to put his teeth in when you kiss and I'll be trying to have my wicked way with the nurses and slipping gin into the Horlicks. Can you imagine?'

And now Jack had tipped the balance. They'd been jogging along at the same speed and suddenly he was shooting ahead, leaving her behind. What if it was serious? What if he got married? What if the girl was the jealous type and refused to let Jack invite her to the wedding?

What if every time she called, his wife made up excuses for him not to speak to her?

Going back into the bedroom, she gazed down at Jack again. *Just because I told you to grow up and fall in love, it doesn't mean to say I meant it*, she said silently. *And now where am I going to sleep?*

She and Jack had often slept together over the years. As in sleep, not sex. Crashing out in his grotty flat when Katie had missed the last bus home. Cuddling up together, gazing at the skylight, that magical square of starry black sky (curtains were beyond Jack), and inventing silly stories until they drifted off.

Tonight, Katie couldn't resist. She slipped under the patchwork quilt beside him. Instantly, instinctively, Jack reached out, cuddling her in his sleep, sighing his head against her breasts. She put her arms around him, gingerly resting her cheek on his head. They slept together, curled up like two kittens.

★

21
Charlie

After Puck and I had conducted the spell on Jack, I was expecting fairy life to return to normal. Well – in my dreams.

Puck and I were desperate to fly over to Primrose Hill and see the happy couple together, but it was impossible. For days it rained and rained, rained and rained, rained and rained. And fairies, unfortunately, can't fly in the rain – our wings get too water-logged and we sink like soggy tissues in a toilet.

The trouble was – would the rain ever stop?

I have to admit that us fairies were partly to blame. I'm sure you humans will remember the ghastly floods in the autumn of 2000. Now I don't want you to end up hating the fairy race but, ahem, I do admit we had something to do with it.

Obviously the British weather is traditionally erratic. But it would be a lot worse if it wasn't for the European Summit held every year in Brussels, where the Sun and the Moon, Wind and Rain, Summer, Winter, Spring and Autumn all meet to discuss the seasonal weather patterns.

Due to this conference, the Sun takes time off and as a result eclipses frequently occur – though you humans make up wonderfully new-fangled theories about them. Similarly, Puck and I have often found your weather broadcasts hysterical – if only your poor weathermen knew that Winter, hearing you predict sunshine, will often deliberately send out clouds just to make a mockery of your meteorological instruments.

The conference has a few poncy lectures, like 'Minimum Wages for Snowflakes: A Debate'. But the whole point really is just to have a big piss-up. There are elves and fairies, leprechauns and merrows, and everyone drinks too much red wine and ends up on the dance floor until 2 a.m. Winter is the worst, the most boisterous of the lot. Born and bred in Scotland, he has a thick grey beard and wears head-to-toe green tartan (no pants underneath, of course) and when he hits the dance floor it's like an elephant jiving as he swings pretty young sprites about until he passes out. Even as he's carried away by a band of snowmen, he can still be heard singing, '*I'm tired and I wanna go to bed . . .*' He always inevitably ends up on page three of *The Festive Gazette* with some young, fame-hungry sprite declaring how he tied her wings to a hotel bed and gave her one, like a Tory MP who has disgraced himself yet again.

The seasons are always given targets and benchmarks at the meeting. These, I suppose, are what you would call the laws of nature. The Earth, like the Gaia hypothesis confirms, is a self-regulating organism.

And then, in November, it started to rain.

Hard.

Up and down the country, on and on, flood after flood. We sensed something was wrong.

Well, Jack Frost was called in for a 'word' with Titania,

who in turn took a message to Winter. Only Winter, the cheeky old git, sent back a message saying that because scatty old Autumn had started so late the year before, he hadn't managed to start his shift until bloody December. It had been a real inconvenience. He was always getting slagged off for never giving humans a White Christmas and it was *never* his bloody fault. Especially since he'd spent so much time and money preparing snow and hiring a troop of clouds, who'd just ended up hanging around for weeks demanding overtime. So he'd decided Autumn could bloody finish early for a change, then she'd know what it felt like to have her schedule messed up.

Well, most of the fairy circle were outraged. Winter's name soon became mud and we were all discussing how we should get him back. Puck, having just watched *Ransom*, suggested we should gag and blindfold Jack Frost. Titania, however, had a more queenly way of dealing with the situation. We were all called to a meeting in the fairy circle where Oberon went to the toadstool podium and announced that, as it was a special occasion, Titania would perform a group spell. A spell to bring out the Sun.

Fortunately, the group spell worked and the rain stopped. In fact, it worked so well that we thought we'd give it another try now to stop the rain once more.

Normally, I loved group spells.

Normally, no matter how grumpy or irritable you felt before the spell, when you were standing there in the fairy ring, holding hands, knowing you were doing something truly noble to help the human race, there was a terrific sense of patriotism. All our tensions dissolved and we became one.

In the centre of the fairy ring was a cauldron, a half-

214

empty hazelnut shell, bubbling away with water. Next to it, there was a little table covered with herbs and various other foreign objects. Then Titania made her grand entrance.

Rumour had it that Titania's outfit had been specially designed for the occasion by Verslugace. The dress was made of the finest golden silk that swirled to her ankles, the train carried, as if she were a bride, by a couple of obsequious ladybirds. The bodice and hems and puff-cloud sleeves were encrusted with so many winking pearls and diamonds and yellow sapphires that I found it hard to look at her. I heard Rose whisper smugly that she had been the one to arrange Titania's hair, which now flowed in golden rivulets down her back, wreathed with tiny plaits woven with tiny buttercups. Gold bracelets jangled around her wrists as she clapped her hands and announced that the spell would begin. I grabbed the hand of the fairy closest to me, Pansy.

Usually the joy of a spell comes from the innocence, of observing but not really understanding what is happening. Of listening to Titania chant ancient fairy language, foreign, gutteral sounds.

'*Agni milee parame vyoman . . .*'

Normally I stand there with my eyes closed, hearing the words echo in my ears, snake down my spine, wriggle into my soul. I feel the chants dance rings around my heart until it swells with happiness and break the boundaries of my mind until all the usual buzz and chatter of useless thought and worry melts away and there is just infinity . . .

Today was different.

I knew what she was saying. Well, bits and pieces. Like a jackal, my mind kept picking up scrapings, chewing them for translation . . .

Fascinated, my eyes flitted open. All the fairies had their eyes closed, heads bowed. Titania's eyes were half-closed, her lips barely moving as she began to sprinkle sandalwood powder into the cauldron. Suddenly her eyes flitted up to me.

Our gaze locked. I gave her a guilty smile. She didn't smile back.

I shut my eyes.

'*Adhi visve nisedu*e . . .'

She knows, I thought in panic. *She knows I've broken the fairy Natural Law and misused the spells . . . She knows.*

Pansy's palm felt slippery and I took my hand out of hers to wipe sweat from my face; she started and I hastily took her hand again. We weren't supposed to break hands once during the ceremony. Titania had said, 'A chain is only as strong as its weakest link. The success of the spell depends upon us all. It is the strength of the group wish that will bring fruition: the whole is greater than the sum of the parts.'

Today I felt like an imposter. A rotten apple leaking bile into a fresh barrel.

A wild panic started to set in. I was convinced Titania could read my mind. *We did it for Jack*, I kept explaining, *we did it for Jack.*

'*Shantih shantih shantih.*' Titania's voice swelled as she reached the finale of the ceremony. We could open our eyes. She threw a garland into the cauldron and a flame licked up, dancing in the air like a blue snake. I blinked as smoke wreathed upwards. He was there! Jack! I could see him, vaporised in the smoke. Jack: his nose all bloody and broken.

Something's wrong, I thought, *it's all gone wrong.*

At the end, we all sat down cross-legged to listen to the musicians. I closed my eyes and tried to capture the

216

tingling feeling I usually got, as though the notes were dancing on my ribs. But I only felt flat inside.

Without a word, Titania turned and glided away. Mary cooed and hurried after her to pick up the train of her golden dress which was now trailing angrily in the mud.

The sun had now risen; it was time for bed. Each fairy went back to their flower in silence. We weren't allowed to talk and normally I loved this rule, carrying the silence away with me in my heart. Usually I drifted into a deep, soft sleep, like a child rocked by her mother, and I'd wake up feeling as though I'd slept for a hundred years. But the silence felt like a gag. I was bursting to tell Puck everything; my heart was scratchy and worried. He looked euphoric after the spell, his eyes glittering, his face slack and smiling. As I slipped beside him, he gently brushed his thumb against the back of my hand. I felt soothed, momentarily. Puck seemed fine; maybe it was all just me. But when I went back to my hollow in the trunk I discovered that Autumn had finally taken hold; the leaves had started to peel away and were strewn like tears on the grass. I went to sleep, gusts of cold wind blasting my body. I closed my eyes, searching for peace, but all I could hear was the noise of humans waking up; giants' voices, tooting horns and the chugging of monstrous motors.

Plop!

I was woken by a fat droplet of wetness exploding on to my head.

I blinked, seeing a patch of grey sky, a feeble ray of sunlight arrowing into my eyes.

Then I saw another droplet hurtling down from the clouds.

Plop!

217

It landed with almost gleeful rudeness on the end of a branch, rocking the leaves unsteadily.

And then another drop came. And another.

You humans have never heard the sound of rain. You hear only the splash of puddles, the tic-tac pitter-patter on rooftops and windows, the drumming on pavements. But if you had the delicate ears of a fairy or a bird, you would be able to hear that each raindrop, as it jumps from the clouds, sails through the sky and splats to the ground, lets out a squeal of delight, like a 'Whoopeee!' or 'Geronimooooooooo!' Raindrops, since they spend ninety per cent of their very short lives cooped up in a cloud like chickens in a factory farm, and the remaining ten per cent jumping out and committing watery suicide on a pavement or being disembowelled by an umbrella, are naturally slightly insane. They are a bit like lemmings and they figure that if you're gonna go, you'd better go with a bang.

I curled back up in my hollow, drawing leaves around me, but all I could hear was a mass of 'Whoopee!' and 'Way to go!'

'Shut up, shut up,' I whispered.

Finally, I fell into an exhausted, shivering sleep, filled with terrible dreams.

I had a nightmare that Jack was a huge giant, towering up in the sky. He had fallen in love but the girl didn't love him back – I couldn't understand why, it was so muzzy and murky. I was standing in the middle of Primrose Hill and all the other fairies had disappeared. I was alone, a tiny dot in an ocean of green loneliness. And I kept crying, 'Jack, Jack, I'm sorry!' But he couldn't hear me; he just howled, sending a thunder of pain across the sky, tearing lightning bolts out of his heart and hurling them down in his grief. I started to run, zig-zagging through the tall stalks of grass, blundering and stumbling and falling down in the mud, but all I could hear were his screams of pain. And then he started to weep, huge droplets of agony falling out of the sky, washing down over me . . . until I drowned in a pool of his tears . . . and woke up with a violent start.

Something is terribly wrong, I felt inside. *We have to find Jack. Now. We have to find him.*

22
Jack

Jack had decided. There was only one way to get Leila out of his system.

He had to find himself again. He *hated* being in love – well, lust – with her. Obsession was always portrayed in books and films as some kind of grand, sweeping, wonderful emotion that injected colour and meaning to life. Better to have loved and lost, than never loved and all those clichés. But in reality, Jack felt as though he was inhabited by a parasite. His obsession with Leila was making him useless. He longed to find himself again – the old Jack, who breezed through life without a care. He felt as if he'd been abducted by an alien who was intent on turning him into some kind of raging testosterone beast who couldn't sleep, eat or think.

And then he'd decided it was time to take control. Find a cure.

What was the antidote to Leila? To satisfy his desire, of course. To find a girl, take her out, have a night of wild wonderful sex with her. And all in front of Leila.

*

Finding a girl needed careful thought. He'd almost considered calling Dominique, but she'd probably turn up with a wedding ring and vicar.

No – he needed a girl who just wanted a bit of fun. A girl who was a bit of a tart, to be frank.

He flicked through his manky address book – Jenny (too frigid) . . . Kerry (too clingy) . . . Monica (always a bit too hard during oral sex – too dangerous) . . . Mandy. Ah – Mandy. She was a bubbly blonde who he occasionally bumped into in pubs and clubs.

But when he called her up, her flatmates informed him that she was away on holiday. Ibiza, of course.

Back to the beginning.

And then he had a brainwave – of course! Jessie! Jessie the Australian girl from the wedding. Jack picked up the phone and hammered in her number, laughing a little wildly.

Despite the fact that it had been a while since the wedding, she hadn't forgotten him, though she did make a slightly rude remark about Men Who Never Called. Jack, feeling a little sheepish, made an excuse that he'd been travelling.

'Look – there's a really lovely Greek restaurant I want to take you to. One of those ones where everyone goes wild at the end and smashes plates . . . You do? Great! Oh, and by the way, my friends are coming too – no, I mean, another couple – Henry and his girlfriend Leila. I thought a foursome would be fun . . Don't worry, Jessie, you'll love them. You might remember them from the wedding. Leila's really nice . . .'

And now he was standing in Leicester Square Tube station, by the shop that sold postcards and Union Jacks and other tourist paraphernalia, his eyes flitting over the hoards of commuters that were pouring up the escalators and through the barriers. Bored, he gazed at a map of the underground, tracing the rainbow veins, savouring unusual names.

'Hi!' A voice yelled in his ear.

Jack jumped, feeling as though someone had just stuck a pin in his eardrum.

'Uh – hi.' Jack kissed her. Instantly her perfume, a sickly rose, stung his nostrils. She stepped backwards, giving a little preen. Jack paused, thinking: *What?* Then, just like an actor who misses his cue and comes in late, he said, 'Oh – wow – you look great!'

She didn't look great as a matter of fact. Jack certainly didn't mind women showing a bit of flesh – but her dress was rather like the sort soap stars wore to award ceremonies to get them on the front page of the *Sun*. It was made of stretchy white lycra. It was very short, very low, and very see-through. And while Jessie wasn't fat, she wasn't thin either. The dress looked as if the stitches were about to explode over her hips and bust. Jack preferred girls a size ten. Still, her long blonde hair was gorgeous (shame about the roots). Shame too about the make-up. Jack preferred women without it – clean and natural. But Jessie's looked as though she'd plastered it on with a trowel, as if she'd used children's felt tip pens – blue eyeshadow, pink blusher, red lipstick.

It was a ten-minute walk to the restaurant and Jessie chattered all the way, about her granny (who was having a hip op) and her sister, Lucy, (whose husband was beating her up but she wouldn't leave him) and her cousin Benjy (who'd just been expelled from school) and how her shoes were killing her (she'd bought them for £5.99 from Shoe Express). Jack barely said more than one word, and that was 'Mmmm . . .'

'All right, love?' A car full of skinheads tooted at her.

Jack felt an odd stab of pride and shame that she was attracting such attention.

'Yeah, go FUCK OFF, you BASTARDS!' Jessie yelled, causing several heads to turn. She nearly poked Jack's eye out as she thrust up two fingers in a 'V'. 'Sorry, I hate it when blokes do that. Bloody sexist.'

Jack could see Henry and Leila in the restaurant, by the window, watching in amazement.

Inside, it was as cool and dark as a cave, and overflowing with leafy green plants. Ivy crawled over the ceiling, choking the framed photos on the walls.

'Hiya!' Jessie cried. 'Great to meet you all!' She swooped down and gave a startled Henry a kiss, right on the lips. She swung towards Leila, leaned in to kiss her too, but Leila recoiled, hastily extending a hand. She gave her a brisk handshake. Jessie bit her lip.

'Well – great to meet you,' she repeated, sitting down.

Leila ran her eyes over her and raised an eyebrow, a tiny smile pinching her lips.

'Your dress is very cold for November.'

'D'you like it?' Jessie chirped. 'I bought it in Camden market. Only three quid.'

'Wow, what a bargain,' Leila said coolly.

Bitch! thought Jack.

A second later, he crumpled inside. *But God, she's looking beautiful.*

He gazed at her from behind his menu. Her hair was woven into a golden coil, showing off her swan's neck, and she was wearing a slim black trouser suit, a few tantalising buttons undone. Beside her, Jessie looked like a Barbie doll.

'So, how are you finding England?' Leila asked, when they'd ordered their drinks. 'The weather's not as good as in Australia.'

223

'Oh great! The men are great, but actually I'm from New Zealand.'

'I apologise.'

'Big distinction. Girls have much bigger tits, guys have bigger dicks. Like, did you hear the one about the New Zealand guy and the Australian guy who were having a slash in the loo? "I'm going out with a girl called Wendy," said the Australian. "I have her name tattooed on my dick." Then he looks at the New Zealand guy's penis and sees a 'W' and a 'Y'. "Are you seeing my girl behind my back?" he cries in alarm. "No," says the New Zealander, pulling out his dick to its full glory. "It says: Welcome to New Zealand—" Jessie paused dramatically "—Enjoy Your Stay."'

Jessie screamed with laughter. Henry looked appalled, then quickly laughed too. Leila merely blinked and fiddled with a strand of hair, smoothing her fringe.

Jack had a feeling it was going to be a very long evening.

After dinner, they all caught a taxi back to Leila's house together. Nobody wanted coffee. Back in Jack's bedroom, he and Jessie sat on the bed, taking off their shoes.

'I don't think your friend Leila liked me very much,' said Jessie casually.

Jack paused, his hands on his laces, touched. He realised that perhaps Jessie's loud-mouth, rhino-skinned veneer was just a front, that she was just as vulnerable as anyone else underneath . . .

'Ah well,' he said, trying to smile.

'We were in the loo, and she said something which sounded nice but was really bitchy . . .'

Yes. Jack remembered that. She and Leila had gone off for a girly chat. He and Henry had been left behind. Jack, unable to bear it any longer, had gone straight for the jugular. He'd asked Henry. The question that had been burning in his soul for the last week. The sixty-four-million-dollar question.

'So – you and Leila. Have. You. Had. Sex?'

Henry's reaction had been quite odd. He'd turned pink. He'd picked up his knife, examined his reflection. He'd furrowed his fingers through his fringe. He'd picked up the menu, and said, 'So, how about baclava for pudding . . . so . . . well . . . we haven't quite yet . . . haven't had time – I mean, found the right time . . . no rush . . .'

'You haven't?' Jack had nearly shouted, he was so relieved. 'Fuck, Henry. Fuck. But you've been together for weeks now. Are you gay or something?' He'd bullied him mercilessly, knowing he'd hit a sensitive spot. Henry had flushed again and tried to laugh; he'd had a period of doubt about his sexuality in his teenage years. 'Come on, I did lend you that video. Didn't you pick up any good tips?'

'So, Jack, are you really good friends with those guys?' Jessie was asking.

'Uh?'

Jack came back down to earth. He gazed over at Jessie, her white stilettos on the floor, her shapely legs against the wooden slats of the bed. Then, suddenly, he heard a noise above from Leila's bedroom. Voices. The bang of the door closing.

'Ssh!' he hissed at Jessie.

He could hear the whoosh of curtains closing. A creak. Footsteps. A deeper creak, like springs in a bed. Oh shit . . . oh no . . oh God . . . they weren't . . . were they?

'Jack.' Jessie sprawled seductively across his bed, patting the pillow. 'Come and lie down, honey.'

225

And worse – what if it was his fault? Maybe by teasing Henry he'd only compelled him to . . . oh God.

Jack smiled quickly, then lay down stiffly beside Jessie. He suddenly felt gawky, like a teenage boy about to lose his virginity. As he was still staying in Susie's old room, the only light came from a frilly pink lamp by the bed. The day-glow stars still clung to the ceiling winking down at them.

He leaned over to kiss Jessie's thin pink lips, but after a brief smooch, she drew back.

'You know, you intrigue me,' she said.

Oh great. She wanted a pre-coital chat. A getting-to-know confessional session. Jack normally enjoyed getting to know a girl before a date. But this wasn't a date, it was a one-night – *no*, one-hour stand. He didn't want to talk to her any more; her accent, her flamboyant manner, her verbal diarrhoea were all getting on his nerves; he'd stop fancying her at this rate and his plan would fizzle, like a wasted firework.

'Tell me more about you, Jack. What about your mum and dad . . . ?'

'Well,' said Jack. Often he made stuff up, airbrushed over the awful reality, but tonight he was too tired. 'Well – my dad left when I was born. He was a bit of a lad, he loved women . . .' Jack, who'd never really known anything about his father, liked to think of him this way. 'He was Italian, my mum was English. Both Catholic. But she ran away from her family to be with him and they moved to London and unfortunately my mum thought it was love with a capital 'L'. Maybe it would have been, if I hadn't come along.' Jack gave a sad smile. 'I don't think he could cope with the thought of screaming babies. So he left. And my mum . . . she had a nervous breakdown, so for the first year I was mostly cared for by aunts and uncles, while she got herself together. She's fine now   she's lovely . . I mean, she lives on her own, in a flat in Camden and she's a cleaner, but she's happy, in her own way . . .'

'Oh God. Jack, that's terrible.'

Occasionally Jack had used this sob-story to milk female sympathy. Now he realised he was digging a deeper hole for himself in Jessie's well of affections.

'So how do you feel towards your dad?'

Jack gritted his teeth. Girls were always doing this – psychoanalysing him, assuming that he was some carbon-copy of his father. Maybe it was their way of explaining away their hurt and grief when he dumped them.

'How do you feel towards your dad?' she repeated.

'Nothing.'

'D'you want to see him again?'

'No.'

'Do you – oh!' She burst into giggles as Jack leaned over and silenced her with his lips.

After that, things hotted up. Passionate kissing. Short breaths. She wasn't a great kisser, unfortunately – she kept thrusting her tongue into his mouth like a leaping goldfish, and Jack murmured, 'Slow down,' but she merely laughed, didn't pick up on the hint. Instead, she murmured something back about being a wicked woman and rolled on top of him. Jack felt squashed, his bollocks caught at a funny angle beneath his jeans. He ran his hands over her back and as she leaned over to kiss his neck, he caught sight of his palms. To his surprise, they were covered with brown smears. He started in shock. *Do I need to wash? Am I covered with dirt?*

Then he twigged. She was wearing fake tan and it was coming off, leaving white and brown patches, like a cow.

Jack broke into a laugh. 'What?' Jessie asked. 'Nothing,' he said, and turned off the light. He rolled on top of her. There. That was better.

The darkness made everything more impersonal. It took away the edges of the room, blurred her face into a beautiful oval. He could almost convince himself that she was Claudia Schiffer, from the faint gleam of her golden hair.

Except Jack couldn't imagine that Claudia Schiffer (not that he was ever likely to go to bed with her, but still) would make such loud, animalistic noises. Jessie sounded like something off *Wildlife On One*. He almost expected Richard Attenborough to pop up at any moment and say, 'And the wild boars make an instinctive sound when mating . . .'

Glancing up at the ceiling, he almost wanted to shout: *See, Leila? Can you hear this? How much I'm making another woman happy? I bet Henry can't do this, can he?*

'Ooohhh yes,' Jessie carried on, pushing open her thighs.

At the same time, her noises were oddly erotic, highlighting her blatant, unashamed sexuality. Most women tended to be a little frigid and took a lot of work; no matter how much pleasure you gave them, there was always a Catholic guilt, a shame, a fear of showing their bodies. It sometimes seemed to Jack that women found having an orgasm as embarrassing as stripping off in a shopping mall in front of all their relatives.

Not Jessie. Her hands were flicking open his buttons, delving inside. Jack groaned, wincing as a plastic nail caught in his pubic hair.

'Mmm, you're a little limp,' she whispered throatily. 'I'm going to have to work you up . . .'

'Mmm,' he sighed, surprised. Jack normally had a permanent erection.

While she caressed him, he found his thoughts straying upstairs again. He strained to hear anything. But there was just silence.

'Oooh . . you are soft . . it's like a little pear . . . an overripe pear . . oh, now that's a bit better . . .'

The improvement coincided with Jack suddenly imagining Leila and Henry together. Locked in a tight embrace, Leila's slim, gorgeous thighs clenched tight around Henry's hairy ones. Henry's lips on her neck; her mouth curved in ecstasy . . .

He suddenly remembered the night he'd had sex with Dominique. She'd been virtually silent during the act itself and Jack had been amazed afterwards when she'd told him 'it was the best sex she'd ever had', explaining that often silent orgasms were the best.

What if – what if Henry was giving Leila the best sex she'd ever had, and they were drifting in silent spirals of aching pleasure?

Jack felt a bead of sweat slip and trickle from his forehead. He lifted a hand to wipe it off and he lost his balance, slipping on to Jessie, squashing her breasts. She yelped like a dog with its tail stuck in a door.

'Sorry, sorry,' Jack muttered, rolling off.

In the darkness, he could see the glint of her eyes, her teeth, her mouth twisted in a mocking sneer.

'Don't tell me, you have problems, right? I don't mind.'

'What?'

'You. You're flaccid. Limp. Can't get it up. I know guys like you – they come over all macho and strong and then you get into the bedroom and they're—'

'No! No!' Jack was outraged. 'No – I just – had a bit too much to drink. All those beers.'

'Yeah, I've heard that before. Don't worry about it, Jack. As we're not getting very far here, maybe I'd better go.' And she turned away, her shoulder blades gleaming as she pulled up the thin straps of her dress, fumbling about for her shoes.

'No!' Jack cried violently. 'No! NO!'

He sprung up and started to shower the back of her neck with little kisses. Instantly she melted, let out a little sigh and said, 'OK . . . that's better . . .' as he curled his hands round the front of her breasts. Then slowly sank back on to the bed.

He desperately wanted her to start moaning again. What if Leila kept hearing the noises and silences, stops and starts – what if she thought he was a terrible lover, keeping his girl on and off the boil?

But as Jessie's hands crept towards his boxers again, the whole thing became a terrible flop.

Jack tried to divert his attention to Jessie, focusing on stroking her, gently pulling up the hem of her dress and caressing her thighs, running his little finger along the hem of her knickers, teasing her in that way he knew women loved. Inside, his heart was racing as though he was in the middle of a marathon. He kept giving his penis frantic pep-talks, like a coach goading on a football team: *Now fucking wake up! Come on, what's the matter with you? You've never missed a winning goal in the past. Get a move on!*

And yet . .

'Oh no, don't stop,' Jessie cried as Jack took his hand away.

Jack, who had been acting on auto-pilot, quickly put his hand back again, stroking her forcefully.

'No – too hard!' she yelled.

For God's sake. She was like an aerobics instructor, shouting out instructions.

And then suddenly everything snapped. His arm ached. He felt exhausted. He didn't fancy Jessie. He'd rather go to bed with a hot-water bottle. This was all a farce.

He drew back, flopped on to the bed. Jessie looked down at him.

'Jack?' she asked. 'Jack?'

To his shock, he felt a sudden, terrible urge to cry.

'Jack?' she repeated more harshly.

He kept his eyes closed. He was terrified that if he tried to speak, the tears would spill, the whole story of his love for Leila would burst out . . .

Jessie's lips tightened. She smoothed her hair and stood up.

'OK, fine, I'm going,' she said, clearly waiting for him to beg her to stay.

Silence.

'OK. I really am going now. And don't c-call me again – you flat, tiny-cocked moron who can't even get it up! You're a bastard like your father.' And with that she left. The bedroom door slammed. The front door slammed. Her stilettos were like castanets on the pavement below.

Jack started to cry. He wiped back tears with the back of his hand, then punched his pillow. He felt sick with humiliation. He'd never, ever failed with a woman. Sex was his one talent. Orgasms were his forté. He'd always known how to please women, ever since, at the age of sixteen, he'd dated a woman twice his age who had lovingly taught him everything. And as for not getting it up! For God's sake, Katie was always teasing him about his virility. *Everything* gave Jack an erection, from *Sky* magazine to a vibrating bus.

He sat up, wondered if Katie would mind if he woke

her up. He desperately needed to talk to someone. But by now it was 4 a.m. Besides, Katie had been funny with him recently. He couldn't tell her about his love for Leila, and she seemed to sense he was keeping something from her; she kept asking, 'What's wrong?' and he kept saying, 'Nothing'. He'd never kept any secrets from Katie before and now there was an invisible rift between them.

He lay back down, longing for his dog. He hadn't visited her in ages. Suddenly guilty, he got up, buttoning his jeans. He'd go get Dido, take a walk, get some air, clear his head.

Outside, it was like walking in a ghost town. The streets were empty, as pale and grey as marble.

Steve was not especially pleased to be woken at 4:30 a.m. But Dido went completely wild to see her beloved master, barking and slobbering her wet tongue all over him.

'D'you want to wake the fucking street up?' Steve snarled, shivering in his boxers. 'And can you please choose a more sociable hour to collect your dog next time, OK?'

Sheepish and dazed, Jack took Dido for a walk on Primrose Hill.

After the crudity of his experiences with Jessie, the beauty of the landscape seemed china-delicate and fragile. It was that twilight hour between night and day when the world seemed magical, uncreated. Dew drops winked and whispered over the grass; a spider crawled on a sparkling web; birds began to coo in the trees.

Jack sat on a bench, watching Dido bound about and joyously sniff every tree as though on a treasure hunt. The view at the top of the hill was incredible – the long sweep of grass arching down to Prince Albert Road, the London skyline a zig-zag of cityscape, spires and flats puncturing the rosy puffball clouds. Jack felt a sudden lump in his throat, wishing Leila was here beside him.

God, this is ridiculous, Jack thought fiercely, wiping a tear away. *I've gone soft*, he realised in dismay. Physically and emotionally. Next he would be weeping at Lassie films. Writing sickly love poetry, making 'love' rhyme with 'dove'. He'd turn into one of those Romantic poets Henry was always raving on about; he'd end up dying at the age of thirty-one, too sensitive to bear the cruelty of life, of unrequited love . . .

How had it happened? Maybe I've just grown up, he reflected. Maybe it was inevitable. He'd been vaguely aware for some time now that one-night stands were no longer as much fun as they used to be. The string of Louises and Debbies and Claires and Chloes, Jennys and Lisas and Kathys. And Jessies.

Jessie's words still stung him. *You flat, tiny-cocked moron . . . you're a bastard like your father*.

Was he? Jack revulsed at the very thought of being compared to his irresponsible, cold-hearted, womanising, gambling bastard of a father.

And yet . . .

Anyway, he didn't want to sleep with random women any more. He couldn't do it – Jessie had proved that. Jessie had made him tired, disgusted.

No, he wanted to *make love* to a woman. To Leila. And more than that – he wanted to have a proper relationship. The type Henry was so good at. He wanted to . . . yes . . . he wanted to make a home with Leila. He could see it happening. Sharing a flat together, just the two of them. He'd get a job – women could never really respect a man who just bummed about all day. A good job. And in the evenings, he'd come home and he'd cook, beautiful meals rich with his love for her . . well, aside from the fact he couldn't cook.

233

No – he'd take her to restaurants, buy her the best food, watch her eat a three-course meal of pure ambrosia, with champagne and candlelight. And then he'd take her home and all through the night they'd make love – deep, tender, love – and with every touch, every kiss, he would show her how much he cared. And in the morning he'd bring breakfast in bed, on a tray with a rose, and he'd wake his darling princess with a kiss, and they'd make love all over again, until they were drunk on love.

Jack let out a faint moan. Let's face it, it was never going to happen. Because Leila, quite clearly, didn't love him. She was in bed with his best friend at this very moment, and they were probably making love, and it was killing him.

Back at the house, Henry was just as sad as Jack.

He was sitting by the window, grey clouds of smoke curling around his head. (Henry only ever smoked in periods of deepest depression.) He stared morosely at the grey streets, watched Jack returning, his dog frolicking around him. Jack the stud. Henry breathed deeply on his cigarette and felt jealousy surge within him. He'd had to put up with a whole evening of listening to Jack's sexual marathon. And yet, hey, Jack was the guy who was happy. He'd got his girl. Whereas Henry had been told yet again by Leila that she had 'her period'. She didn't feel like sex. She just wanted to sleep.

Henry gazed back at Leila, lying in her bed, the pink light of dawn caressing her body, making her look like an ethereal princess. *My fairy queen*, he thought sadly.

Didn't she understand that he just wanted to make love to her, not to use her, not because he saw her as a sex object, but to show her how much he cared? But no. She had her period. For the third bloody week in a row.

23
Katie

'How do I look?'

'OK . . . yeah . . . so Susie mustn't have any E-numbers, OK? No orange squash, just water. Yeah, I'll be back by eleven o'clock at the latest. OK, great, come round in a bit.' Katie, who was talking into her mobile to the babysitter, broke off and looked up at Leila, who was twirling before her in one of the most beautiful outfits Katie had ever seen. Katie gave her the thumbs up and mouthed 'Great'.

Yes, Leila did look great, and the smile on Leila's face as she twirled back to the mirror suggested she knew it. She was wearing a long shimmering dress, with slender straps, made of material that clung to her hips and slim waist and sloped gently over her breasts. It was a rainbow of blueness.

Katie, Leila and Henry were all going out for dinner that night.

'So, how's it going with Henry, anyway?' Katie clicked off her mobile. It suddenly struck her that for the first time in years Leila wasn't wearing black. Normally she looked pale and gaunt; the blue dress brought out the colour of her eyes and make her look younger.

'Oh, so so,' said Leila, slipping on her silver chain.

That was Leila. Queen of Cool. And yet Katie caught a flash of her expression in the mirror, a softness around her mouth, a shiny glow to her face. *I reckon Leila is much more of a closet romantic than she realises*, Katie mused.

'So, are you wearing that?' Leila enquired, in a tone that suggested Katie was wearing a black sack.

Katie was still wearing an outfit she'd put on earlier for an appointment with her bank manager. It had been hot and sweaty and despite her suffering, the bank manager had said an evil 'no' to Katie's request for an extension on her currently unauthorised overdraft.

'Er . . . well . . .' Katie came over and stood next to her by the mirror.

As soon as she did, she regretted it. She looked terrible in her blouse and red skirt, like a custard cream dipped in tomato ketchup.

She suddenly had a flashback, a memory of being a teenager again and getting ready to go out in Leila's bedroom. The way they used to steal Leila's mum's lipstick and red-slash their mouths, smear glitter over their cheeks so that they looked like Christmas fairies, and wear so much black eye make-up that bouncers sarcastically asked if they'd been beaten up. Leila always insisted they dress in identical outfits, like twins, which only served to highlight their differences – Leila slim in jeans, Katie fat in jeans; Leila with her 32A chest in a tight T-shirt, Katie with her 38DD chest in a straining T-shirt. Then they'd go out to clubs in Kingston with their fake IDs, fake date-of-births slipping off their tongues. The bouncers always let Leila through, but interrogated Katie.

'When were you born?' she remembered one goatee-bearded fourteen-stone monster shouting.

'18th November 1922,' she'd cried nervously, then

★

blushed when the bouncer informed her that made her sixty-six years old. They were sent home; Leila had teased her all the way back and promised not to tell anyone at school. The next day Katie had gone in to find every girl asking her, 'Hey, Katie – how old are you? Are you going to be drawing your pension soon? Where's your zimmer frame?' The entire school knew . . .

Back in the present, Katie found herself echoing something she'd often said in the past when standing in front of a mirror next to Leila: 'Maybe I ought to change.'

'No – no! You look great,' said Leila, but in a tone that suggested she knew she looked far better.

Which made Katie feel the size of a peanut (egowise) and the size of an elephant (bodywise). Huh.

As Leila padded off to the bathroom to rub an invisible speck of dust from her face, Katie frowned again.

You do look good, she told herself. She didn't normally feel so insecure about her appearance. Now that they were older, she and Leila had stopped competing.

Leila was softer now, and Katie was more careless. Katie had also realised that no matter how many millions of donuts she didn't eat, or how many millions of celery sticks she did eat, or how many press-ups she did, or how many early nights she took, she was never going to have the body of Elle MacPherson. And since she'd had a baby, her figure had flopped anyway, so she'd simply given up. She didn't need a man. Susie filled her heart and her days and absorbed every last drop of her love and energy. Katie ate whatever she liked now, and covered her size-fourteen-going-on-sixteen figure with baggy clothes.

'Oh shit,' said Leila, returning. 'Mr Winterton – this publisher I'm doing a deal with – rang. I have to go and close a deal; there's been a fight over contracts, Japanese rights, er, stuff, so I'm going to have to call off. But you go – you can still go!'

'Oh, well . . .'

'No, please, really,' said Leila, picking up her bag.

'Well, I guess.'

'Great! Great! I'll give Henry a call from the office. Must dash!'

It only occurred to Katie later that Leila had gone to the office, bizarrely enough, wearing her evening dress.

Having agreed to go to dinner alone with Henry, Katie instantly regretted it.

She really didn't feel in the mood for dinner tonight.

She was still knackered from being woken in the early hours of the morning by Jack having sex with some girl and her caterwauling echoing throughout the house like a banshee. Katie had tossed and turned, shoved in her earplugs oh-so-tight, put a pillow over her head, but nothing had cut out the 'Oh . . . Oh . . . Oh . . . Yes . . . Jack . . harder . . .' Then it had taken her ages to drop off again, she'd felt so angry. Just what did Jack think he was doing, treating the house like a hotel, a brothel? And she'd had to explain away the noise to Susie by saying Uncle Jack had had terrible toothache and had been in a lot of pain – and now Susie couldn't stop lecturing Jack and ordering him not to eat any more sweets.

Worse, Katie dreaded to think that this girl might be the one Jack was so deeply madly in love with.

She suddenly noticed a guy staring at her and she smiled, wondering if he knew him. He looked her up and down, then turned away.

Katie gnawed her lip. The Leila-mirror thing had got to her. A shaky paranoia was taking hold. She was convinced everyone was looking at her. The man at the bus

238

stop was now looking at the timetable, but she imagined he had his eye on her and was thinking, 'God, I'd never fancy her . . .' As she walked down Regent's Park Road, past the row of restaurants crammed together like pastel sweets, she was adamant people were looking out of the windows and pointing at her: 'God, what is that woman wearing? Why is she wearing that red suit? She looks like a tomato.' And, on entering the restaurant, Katie was certain the waiter gave her the cold once-over, as if to say, 'You're making my restaurant look *fat*.'

Worse, she was sure she could smell whiffs of BO wafting from her armpits. She'd been wearing the same blouse all day and it felt sticky against her skin. If only she'd changed . . .

In the Lemonia restaurant, Henry was waiting, dressed in a smart grey suit, his blonde hair gleaming, fingering a menu.

'Hi Henry, how are you?' As she sat down, her chair scraped.

Henry blinked. Katie wriggled. Why was he staring at her, raking his eyes over her? Did he think she looked dreadful too?

'Hi,' he smiled. He leaned over as if to kiss her on the cheek; then (perhaps it was her BO?) bent down and fiddled with his sock instead, smiling nervously.

'Is Leila . . . ?'

'She's, erm, not coming.'

'Oh.'

'She, er, she's working late. Big crisis at the office, some deal, Japan or something. Well – what shall we do?' Katie murmured.

'Would you like to stay?' Henry asked brightly. 'I mean – now we're here and everything.'

Katie paused, looking down. Her eyes swept across the

menu. The meal would cost at least forty pounds. Leila had offered to pick up the bill. But Katie could hardly expect Henry . . .

'I—' She was about to blurt out some excuse about not having a proper babysitter. Instead, all the stress inside her seemed to erupt. 'I'm sorry – I can't afford this.' She slammed down the menu miserably. 'I'm sorry but I saw my bank manager today and I can't even afford to eat, though from the way you're looking at me, you probably think I need to lose weight anyway. I can't afford to buy bread and jam, let alone pay ten pounds for a pizza, so I don't want you to think this is some kind of guilt trip, I don't expect you to pay, we can just—' Katie paused, seeing the look on his face. Oh shit, she was ranting.

'I – well – bye.' She was about to get up to go when Henry put out his hand, and gently nestled her back down. At the same moment, the waiter came up, twiddling his little pen over his pad.

'I'm just going,' Katie said, 'I'm—'

'No, you're not,' said Henry firmly. 'You're going to have a fantastic meal and I'm going to pay. OK?'

'OK.'

After the waiter had gone, Henry smiled at her softly, as if to say, *Don't be embarrassed*. But she was. Half of her felt wonderfully grateful, the other half deeply patronised. He was making her feel like a charity case, a damsel in distress, some poor urchin girl who needed looking after. She hated it when men did that.

They filled the silence by sipping their drinks. She was still worried that her clothes smelled all sweaty; she tried to keep her arms clamped down by her sides just in case the pong travelled across the table.

'So, did you have a run-in with your bank manager?

What did she do? Berate you? Tear up your cheque book? Eat your Visa card for her lunch. Ah, now you're smiling.'

Katie rolled her eyes. The smile was forced.

'Oh, it's not really her,' she sighed. 'She's in the right. It's me.'

'Really? According to most banks, the philosophy is "The customer is always wrong, and what's more, we'll slap on a twenty-five pound overdraft fee and send out stupid letters telling you how much we love stealing your money into the bargain."'

Katie managed another smile, but she wasn't quite ready to be cheered up just yet.

'It's money,' she sighed. 'Money, money, money. It annoys me how it does make the world go round. Money. It's all people think about, all governments think about. Doesn't matter if trains crash or we all eat GM foods and die, so long as they make a profit.' She realised she was in 'Greenpeace' mode and making a speech, and broke off quickly. 'Sorry. It's just – people say money doesn't buy happiness but it bloody does.'

'Oh, that's not true,' said Henry.

Katie took another sip of her wine and sat back in her chair. She couldn't help feeling irked and she tried to repress it, but failed.

'How can you say that?' she said in a light voice. 'You're sitting here in an Armani suit with a Rolex watch on your wrist, you own a huge house worth at least three million, and you've got a good income. How can you say you're not happy?'

'I'm not.' Henry gazed at her with his blue eyes.

'Well, why not?' Katie slapped the table, half-laughing, half-angry. 'C'mon. Haven't you always been rich?'

'Yes. My father is a self-made multi-millionaire. He

241

lets me stay in a house in Primrose Hill that he owns. I don't see that it's anything to be ashamed of; I don't see why I should feel guilty,' said Henry.

'No,' said Katie, though an unreasonable part of her did want him to feel so. 'But it's easy for you to say money doesn't matter because you've never been without it. You wouldn't know what it's like to cut out coupons from magazines, or to have a nervous breakdown every time your Visa statement arrives on the mat. Sorry.' Katie tried to control herself again. 'Sorry. That's rude.'

'No, I just think my life is a lot more crap than yours.'

Katie paused. *Yeah, right*, she thought bitterly, pushing around sugar crystals with her finger.

'I'm not that rich, anyway,' he said, casually picking up a knife and fingering the end. 'I had one hundred thousand pounds stolen from me several years ago. My entire savings account. I'm still borrowing from my father, and my father, being a brilliant businessman, is a terrible Scrooge. He charges me five per cent interest. Still, my stupid fault for getting it stolen, I suppose.'

Katie was ripe with curiosity, bursting to ask more, but the waiter arrived, bringing their starters: soft pockets of pitta bread accompanied by a gleaming plate of gooey hummus.

'So . . .' Katie said, biting into her bread. 'Wow, this is delicious—' She blushed as she accidentally spat a few beige specks on to the table, but luckily Henry didn't notice. 'So, how did it get stolen?'

'I was involved in a heist . . . No, only joking. It was my fiancée, actually. Alice. We'd been going out for four years and I wanted to propose. I mean, unlike most men, I actually wanted to settle down, get married, have children. I always knew Alice liked the fact that I had money, but I never . . .'

242

'What? You mean she   ?' Katie was aghast.

'Uh huh. She took the whole lot. One minute she was in my house and everything was hunky-dory and the wedding was only a week away. The next I'd gone away filming for a weekend – some crap film in Paris that just about made it to video, where I played a vampire suffering from anaemia – and I come back to find she's gone, left a note.'

'Oh my God. What a cow, Henry.' Jack had mentioned that Henry had had a rough love life, but Katie had never imagined it was this bad . . .

'To be honest, things weren't quite right between us,' said Henry. 'I mean, maybe it was a good thing – if we'd married it would never have worked, I can see that now. And I think Alice could too. I wanted to find The One, I wanted her to be Ms Right – in a way I wanted to change her, to turn her into my perfect woman. I think I stifled her, in the end. I think I was in love with an illusion.'

'That's still no excuse to wipe you out!' cried Katie. 'And you never got it back?'

'No. Never. I called her friends, but they probably covered for her. I called her mum, who was hysterical. She'd been looking forward to the wedding more than us. But anyway – that's all in the past now.'

'Now you have Leila.'

'Yes,' said Henry, but Katie was sure she caught a faintly sarcastic indent to his tone. 'So you see, I'm not rolling in it. I'm an impoverished actor. Well, nearly.'

'Yes, sorry.' Katie felt guilty, chastised.

'I know what it's like to give up money to do a job you really want,' said Henry earnestly. 'I love acting, but theatre work makes sod-all. Unless I do adverts – in which case I earn a great big wadge. But I don't get many, and

243

they're usually for some washing powder. I'm always cast as the nice smiley golden-haired husband with two kids who wakes up, shaves his sexy chin, comes into the kitchen and kisses his wife.'

'Oh Henry!' Katie laughed. 'That's just so you! It's true.'

'Oh, thanks very much!' said Henry.

'Oh – I didn't mean—' Katie caught his eye, and to her relief he was smiling. 'It's just – you're very handsome,' she said, blushing. Then, because she was embarrassed he'd take it the wrong way, 'In a very Mills and Boon sort of way.'

'Oh God!' Henry pretended to stab himself with the fork.

'Anyway,' said Katie, keen to get off the subject of Henry's looks. 'I know what you mean. I keep wondering if I should get a better job, a proper job, so I'd have more money for Susie and everything. But I *hate* the idea of meaningless work. I used to work as a temp, so I've been there. I love working for a charity – it just makes me feel as though I'm doing something worthwhile.' She paused, aware that she'd been doing most of the talking. Henry was probably very bored.

'No, I think that's so fantastic,' said Henry. 'I really do.'

Katie smiled as the main course came – stuffed vegetables. As she sliced open her green pepper, spilling a glorious tumble of beans and sweetcorn on to her plate, she felt a burst of happiness. It was so rare that she got to eat out. This was such a treat. Sod her weight, she wanted to enjoy every minute, every mouthful.

'So, what is up with you and Leila?' Katie asked, feeling a bit more comfortable now.

'Oh, well, there's her cat for a start.'

'What?' Katie laughed.

244

'I feel as though I'm in a love triangle.'

'*What*!'

'She's completely obsessed with it. It's bizarre – she's so hard and kind of career woman-ish, but get her near to the cat and she turns to goo and starts talking in this high-pitched squeak.'

'The relationship between women and their cats is very special,' said Katie. She felt she was treading a tightrope, trying to be loyal to Leila but desperate to gossip.

'And it's called *Candida*.'

'Well – the cat is very old, she named it when she was twelve. I don't think she feels she can change it now . . .'

'Oh, I'm sure the cat would need hours of counselling, Prozac, Rolf Harris . . . So you're not obsessed with anything? You don't have a pet gerbil called Syphilis lurking in your handbag?'

'No! No, I have a daughter. Much better than a cat.'

'You know, Leila and I had a fight the other day about what we'd call our children if we had them. Not that she wants them – she says she wants to wait till she's forty or something ridiculous.'

'Well, she is doing well in her job, Henry.' Katie kept defending her. 'Anyway – what names did you come up with?'

'Oh, hers were all boring. Mine were great. I love the names in Shakespeare's plays – I wouldn't mind calling my son Demetrius. Or Lysander! Oberon, even.'

'In that case I'm on Leila's side. Your children will commit suicide, Henry.'

'Oh, thanks very much. "What's in a name?"' Henry quoted. '"A rose could be called by any other name and still smell as sweet".'

'Uh?'

'Shakespeare. *Romeo and Juliet*.'

'I knew that . . .' Katie blustered, smiling; she didn't read much.

'Of course, Saussure said the relationship between name and form is random. But actually I believe there is a correlation – Sanskrit is an entirely onomatopoeic language, for example.'

'You've lost me.'

'Sorry – whenever I'm on a date and I get nervous, I start talking crap. Not that this is a date – I mean – oh shit. Anyway, Jack and I were discussing this the other day and Jack said if name equals form, I should call myself Charity, my old-banger car Faith and my willy Hope.'

'Honestly, typical Jack,' Katie laughed. A little too hard. What did Henry mean by *date*?

'Anyway,' Henry said quickly. 'I'm sure me and Leila will be OK. We're just . . .' He looked down. 'Going through a rough patch. How about you? How's your love life?'

Katie suddenly felt as though her happiness bubble had been punctured. *He made the slip about the date and now he thinks I fancy him,* she realised. *God, how embarrassing. Just because I said he was handsome. Men always take things the wrong way . . .*

'I don't want any relationships right now,' she said tersely. 'I've been married once and that was enough. No – I think Jack's love life is the most exciting at the moment. He tells me he's in love.'

'Is he?' Henry looked astonished, which surprised and disappointed her. She'd been hoping he might know more. 'God, who with?'

'Who knows.'

'I hope it's not Ms Orgasm.'

'Oh God, no – can you imagine that *every night*?'

'Don't!' Henry shuddered.

246

Somehow the ice was broken again.

They carried on chatting and laughing into the night, barely aware of the restaurant swelling, buzzing, and then emptying around them, till Henry suddenly checked his watch. It was 10:30 p.m.; time had flown by.

As the waiter came to take the bill, Katie leaned over to take a peek, then quickly clamped down her armpit again. Henry gave her a quizzical look, murmured that he'd get it, signed and then frowned at her.

'Katie – sorry if you think I'm being rude, but why the hell this 'arms glued to the side of your hips' thing?'

'Er – it's kind of like – I – well – look, I've been wearing this suit all day and I think I stink, OK? I probably do, and . . .' She was mumbling and bumbling; the wine had gone to her head.

'Oh God, terrible,' Henry said. 'The fumes have been wafting over throughout my dinner. It's been like sitting next to a living compost heap.'

Katie's mouth dropped in horror, then she realised he was joking. She sighed and got up. As she pulled on her coat, he jumped round to help, then put his head under her arm, doing a playful impression of an inquisitive dog pretending to sniff, and announced loudly that she didn't smell like a compost heap at all, she smelled of peaches and cream.

'*Henry!*' Katie swatted him away, squealing as he kept trying to force up her arm, and half of the restaurant turned round to look. 'Stop it, everytone thinks you're trying to grope me.'

'But I am trying to grope you,' Henry joked loudly as they left, causing the other half of the restaurant to turn round too.

247

24
Katie

Outside, Katie felt the cold air cool her burning cheeks. Then she caught Henry's eye and burst into laughter.

'Oh God, I think we've had too much wine.'

'Then have some more. If you're going down a slippery slope, you might as well slide all the way. I've got a bottle of Chardonnay at home.'

Katie paused. Suddenly she caught herself. This was all becoming a bit . . . a bit like a *date* really. She thought of Susie, who had gone to bed on the understanding that she wouldn't be home late. The thought of her daughter always made her feel more responsible and sober. And so she was about to turn around and politely say goodnight and ask for a cab when fate intervened.

A cab did indeed come schooming round the corner, and Katie raised her arm in a vague, guilty wave, even though she saw the 'For Hire' sign was out. The cab hurtled past at something like a hundred miles an hour, through a puddle, and splashed a huge volume of dirty water all over the tipsy couple.

'Shit!' Katie cried as they were left dripping and laughing

with fury. 'Oh well, I hated this stupid red suit anyway but you're all wet.'

'Bastard.' Henry flicked a 'V' sign, though the cab had long gone. 'C'mon then, back to my place – you can have a shower, borrow one of my jumpers. Hey, this is like one of those *Carry On* films, where the pervy bloke says, "And now let's get you out of your wet clothes."' He did such a good impression of Sid James that Katie burst into laughter.

'OK,' she said, 'but I'll have to be quick. I need to get back for the babysitter.

They shared more silly *Carry On* memories as they walked home, too engrossed in Matron and Barbara Windsor impressions to notice how miserable, cold and wet the night was.

'Of course, now I remember why your impressions are so good – you're an actor,' Katie said, shivering on the doorstep as Henry opened the door. 'Oh wow,' she sighed as he showed her in.

'My little council flat,' he said, looking slightly sheepish, as if remembering their earlier conversation.

Katie felt embarrassed for having given him such a hard time. It wasn't Henry's fault he was rich; it was hardly a crime. Wanting to somehow apologise, she kept making silly, wine-induced jokes as they went into the living room.

'Oh, this is your casting couch?' She collapsed on the chaise longue.

'Oh, definitely. Julia Roberts would never have got the part in *Pretty Woman* if she hadn't stretched out here for me,' Henry giggled, bringing her a towel. 'Now, I'm going to have a two-minute shower, then you can have one too.'

Henry was gone a lot longer than two minutes. Katie towelled her hair distractedly. In the past, wine had woken her up; these days it left her feeling sleepy, as if unravelling the tiredness already built up inside. She shifted; it was hard to get comfortable on the chaise longue, all blue satin and brocade, like something out of *Dangerous Liaisons*. There were large mirrors opposite and she started, catching a glimpse of herself. God, she looked a state. Her cheeks were red, her eyes were dark pools of mascara, her hair was a mass of damp straggles. This was a couch on which beautiful, elegant women belonged, sipping tea, or crossing their legs. Women like Leila. Katie had a sudden vision of Leila lounging across it, slowly sliding a foot in and out of a sandal, seducing Henry. She wondered if she and Henry had ever . . . on this couch . . . ever . . .

'Hi!'

She jumped violently. Henry was at the door in a dark green dressing gown. She noticed thick blonde hair tufting out of the top, then quickly looked away.

'Look, the shower's knackered – our bathroom belongs to a 1950s film. So there's only the bath aaaaaannnd – I know this is foul – but could you bath in my water? Sorry, it's so crap – I didn't switch on the bloody hot water in time—'

'Oh, no, no, it's fine,' Katie protested. 'I normally bathe with my daughter, which means a bath full of ducks and various lethal plastic objects. Really. I . . .' She wanted to add that it was fine, she could go home and bath, but Henry was already leading her upstairs.

'I'll root out a jumper and leave it outside the door,' he said.

'Sure – I'll be quick,' she said.

'Take as long as you like.'

Katie went in and locked the door.

It was a lovely bathroom. The bath was one of those deep, old-fashioned ones, propped up on bent white legs, with swan's neck taps. The water glimmered under the naked golden bulb. She peeled off her clothes, tied her hair into a scraggy knot at the top of her head and slid in. Ooh – it was hot – Henry obviously felt the cold. She trickled in more cold water, twisting the tap with her foot, then settled in, sighing.

Mmm, it was so good. A golden hair, one of Henry's, was drifting in the water and she twirled it around her finger. There was something dirtily erotic, she realised vaguely, about lying in the water with his skin cells and pubic hairs floating about, the water that had caressed him just ten minutes ago now lapping against her body. She pictured them in the bath together, Henry sitting in front of her, her legs curled around him, lightly scrubbing his back, sharing private jokes, giggling, private kisses, sighing . . .

God. She was having fantasies about *Leila's* boyfriend.

OK, so he was good-looking, but . . . Katie shifted uncomfortably. Well, if she was honest, she'd always had a tiny crush on Henry, but in a distant way, the way you admire a film star, never expecting anything to happen. He'd always been Jack's Friend.

It's just the wine, she told herself firmly, *and the shock of actually being taken out to dinner by a sexy bloke.*

For the first time in a while, she felt a bud of romance uncurling. She suddenly remembered what it was like to be wined and dined, to be made to feel special, to lock eyes across the table for that second too long and feel a lick of lust light inside. It made her feel vulnerable, troubled, and yet excited, alive. After all, since splitting up with Keith she'd gone out with a succession of no-hopers, with men she didn't really care for, almost as if from the start she didn't want it to work out, afraid of getting hurt again, trapped again. But Henry was different.

Things aren't going very well between me and Leila. His words echoed uneasily in her mind. Leila hadn't spoken much about him to Katie, but Katie had assumed everything was hunky-dory between them, that they were the perfect couple, blonde and beautiful together.

Then she felt horrible. She realised a part of her was pleased Leila's relationship was failing. And that was mean.

And maybe Henry was just a womanising bastard. Maybe he was just the same as all the rest. And she didn't really like men anyway. Suddenly petulant, Katie pulled out the plug. She wouldn't bother to wash her hair, it was getting late.

Wrapping her towel around herself, she felt her bladder aching. She unlocked the door and went into the little toilet next door, felt the warm urine piss into the bowl, went back into the bathroom, leaving the door an inch wide.

She was towelling herself off, humming something from a musical that she and Susie had watched on video earlier on, when suddenly she was aware of his presence. Henry. In the doorway. Watching her. How long had he been there? She tried to feign anger – it was rude, disgusting, indecent. Instead, she only felt . . .

'I – brought this jumper.' Henry held it up. He was still wearing his dressing gown. As he moved in closer, Katie smelled forest fern bubble bath and Johnson's baby shampoo.

He's going to kiss me, she panicked. She took a nervous step backwards, then saw the surprised look on his face. *He's not going to kiss me, I've got it all wrong*. She laughed nervously, apologetically. He took another step forwards. She mumbled something about the jumper not fitting, but the jumper was already on its way to the floor and

Henry's arms were around her waist. He pushed her up against the airing-cupboard; she felt the slats hard against her back, then his mouth was soft against hers, his hand delving between the folds of the towel . . .

Katie pushed him away, shocked. Thoughts were colliding in her mind. *This is terrible – but I fancy him. I can't believe this is happening. God, he's a good kisser – am I dreaming this?*

She stared at his dressing gown, seeing the damp patches from her breasts on the front, unable to meet his eyes.

'Henry – we can't do this. Shit . . . Leila . . . we can't do this, OK?'

'I know – it's terrible.' He looked genuinely upset. 'But . . . oh fuck . . . I just . . .'

And then he was kissing her again, pushing his mouth, insistently, against hers, warm and impossible to refuse . . .

Katie turned the key oh-so-slowly in the door. Even though she was coming back to her own home, she felt like a burglar breaking in. It was late now and she was terrified of waking Leila up, bumping into her in the hallway, having to look her in the eye and say, 'Oh, dinner with Henry was great . . . yeah, afterwards, I, er, went out clubbing with some friends.' Having to lie. Katie didn't think she could do it. She'd blush, stammer and stumble.

As she eased off her coat, she spotted the note on the little telephone table. Too scared to switch on the light, Katie held it up to the window, where the streetlamp fractured amber light on to Leila's handwriting. Katie jumped, paranoid it was going to say: *What the hell did you do with my boyfriend?* Instead it merely read:

Katie – I paid the babysitter, so you owe me £15 (she left at midnight). Susie is in bed. Hope you're OK. Sorry I missed dinner. Don't worry, we'll rearrange.
Leila.

Oh shit.

Katie hurried upstairs. On the landing, a small shape was sitting by her door. In the dark, Katie saw two frightened, reproachful eyes and the glitter of tears.

'You said you'd be back early,' Susie hissed. She made Katie feel for a moment that their roles were reversed. 'I was worried . . . I thought you'd *died*—'

'Ssh, darling, it's OK, Mummy's not dead. Come on, now, come to bed, you'll wake up Leila.'

'Don't want to,' she said petulantly. 'I want to watch TV. You missed the end of my video.'

'I'm sorry, I'll see it with you next time. Now come on!' Katie found herself yanking Susie roughly to make her get up, then feeling horrible when she started to cry even more. Eventually Katie promised her she could sleep with her, which she normally only did when Susie had nightmares, and succeeded in getting her into bed. Susie tucked her thumb in her mouth, a habit she retreated to whenever she was upset; Katie didn't have the heart to tell her off. She cuddled up against her daughter, listening to her breathing quieten as she slid into sleep.

Katie couldn't sleep.

All she could do was lie awake in horror, thinking *What have I done?*

25
Charlie

'Well, Charlie – do you want the good news or the bad news?' Puck cried as he came barging into my hollow.

'What?' I sat up in bed. I'd been ill for a few days with fairy flu and a nasty green rash on my wings. (Puck, the meanie, kept teasing me that it was gangrene but in fact I'd got it from accidentally flying past a human's armpit when they'd been spraying on some Impulse.) So Puck had been dispatched to check out our two lovebirds, Katie and Jack.

'Er, the good. I guess,' I said.

'The good is kind of bad too. Look, I saw Jack. He's not in love with Katie.'

'Oh.' I felt deadwood disappointment, like a hollow knock inside my heart. So the magic hadn't worked. We were idiots.

'The spell did work.'

'It did?' I jumped.

'It's just – he's fallen for Leila.'

'But – but what about Katie?' I stammered in horror.

'She's kind of fallen for Henry.'

'*Henry?* But I thought he was supposed to be in love with Leila.'

'He is. Was. Well, he's kind of fallen for Katie – actually, he's fallen for Katie even more than Katie has fallen for him.'

'God.' I shook my head in confusion. 'These humans are so *fickle*. "Fickle, thy name is man." They are willy-led wallies.'

'Welllll . . . it's just . . . I kind of did a spell on Henry,' Puck confessed, all in a rush.

'*WHAT?*'

'I did a spell on Henry. It was kind of an experiment, a whim . . . I was a bit pissed. D'you remember, the night after the floods, when the beetle dropped by and handed round some blackberry wine? Well, I had two bottles, and I just thought I'd fly over and see how the guys were doing. I asked you to come, Charlie,' he added in angry defence, 'but that was when you were starting to get sick. And then I saw how upset Katie was, now Jack's fallen for Leila, and she was so down on herself, as she's so – well – fat. So I thought if, you know, Henry fell for her, it would cheer her up. And I did the love spell on him, so it will . . . work slowly.'

'And wear off slowly!' I shrieked.

Silence.

I opened my mouth to have another go at him. Then closed it, chewing my lip. Maybe Puck was right. Maybe Jack had finally found his Jill. Maybe Jack was supposed to be with Leila, and Katie with Henry.

'Well, we wanted Jack to be happy. If he's happy with Leila, that's fine,' I said slowly. 'Although, they are a weird couple. They don't really go . . .'

'Like cheese and strawberries,' Puck giggled nervously. 'Or onions and cream.'

256

'Or HP sauce and Marmite,' I laughed.

'Yeah, well – the thing is, there is a problem. Leila hates Jack's guts.'

'Oh Puck, this is such a *mess*.'

I stood up and walked around my hollow in a daze. I ran my hand over the coathangers in my wardrobe, so they smash-tinkled together in an ugly cacophony. Puck winced.

'What are we going to tell Oberon and Titania?' I was only just starting to realise how terrible this was. 'We're not even supposed to be performing magic. And now Henry. That's *two* illegal spells. It's like Musical Chairs meets *Blind Date*.' Seeing the awful, nervous smile on his face, I snapped, 'Puck, this isn't a gameshow. It's real life.'

'Yeah, well, they're only humans, Charlie . . .' Puck trailed off, sliding out a copy of *The Brahma Book of Spells* from under his T-shirt. 'OK. Look. I have a Plan B, OK?'

'Oh God.'

I looked at the page he was pointing to, entitled

TROUBLESHOOTING

What to do if you accidentally give a friend warts . . .

What to do if the recipient of the spell mysteriously grows an extra leg . . .

What to do if you conduct a love/lust spell on the wrong person . . . (A-ha!)

These are extremely hard to undo, though the Brazilian Long-Toothed Sexy Hairy Love Spider can be used to undo a spell and ignite fresh love for the intended person, killing two birds with one stone.

'Oh Puck! You know how I HATE spiders!'

Secretly, I didn't think the Brazilian Long-Toothed Sexy Hairy Love Spider really existed – it was just a magical legend, our equivalent of the Loch Ness Monster or the Yeti. Or, that even if there were fragments of truth in the myth, it would take *months* to find. Or hopefully *years*.

Instead, it took two hours.

Puck, it seemed, had been doing his research.

'I took the liberty of making a few enquiries and eventually I discovered the whereabouts—'

'Oh, you took the liberty,' I said furiously, struggling to keep up with his pace as we flew away from the fairy camp. I kept coughing from illness and anger. 'You mean, you went behind my back.'

'—of,' said Puck, ignoring my tirade, 'a leprechaun who apparently is an expert in spiders. I checked him out and he's got a Brazilian Hairy whatsit spider in stock, the last one, so let's hope he hasn't sold it by the time we arrive.'

Chinatown was where we were now heading. We zig-zagged through the streets, scooting over glossy-haired girls, gaggles of tourists, men delivering boxes of iced fish, before Puck finally led us down a black cranky fire escape to the entrance of an underground Chinese restaurant. A chaos of smells were fighting their way out of the kitchen: whiffs of egg noodles, star anise and cardamom were mingling richly in the air. I caught a glimpse of a chef in a white hat, his crinkled face surrounded by billows of steam. Then Puck prodded me, drawing me round a pile of black dustbin bags to a tiny door, about a foot high, which was cleverly concealed by the rubbish. Puck rapped a sharp knock. I had a sudden flash of arachnophobia. I kept imagining that a spider was creeping up my leg, its

tiny, spindly, horrible, hairy, disgusting little legs squig
gling over my body, and I shuddered violently.

Suddenly the door burst open.

I let out a small scream.

The sprite who had opened the door jumped and Puck
started.

'Sorry,' I muttered. I felt as if my nerves were in shreds.

'Don't mind her.' Puck's pupils were already dilating at
the sight of the sprite, who was smiling sweetly. Only three
inches tall, she was entirely pink and sickeningly thin,
with a shapely, feline grace. 'We're just here about pur-
chasing a Brazilian Long-Toothed Sexy Hairy Love
Spider. As you do.'

'Sure,' she said, though a slight doubt seemed to flicker
across her face. 'I'll just call Peewing, he'll show you round.'

'We don't mind if you show us round, you're a fantastic host,' Puck flirted.

She laughed, blushed becomingly and buzzed off.

'Isn't she sweet?' said Puck.

I made a remark under my breath about her looking
like a bluebottle dipped in pink dye. Puck gave me a look
and said, 'Miaow.' I blushed, feeling horrible. Oh God, I
knew it had been a bad idea to come.

'Do come in, by the way,' the sprite called out, and I
tensed, paranoid that she'd heard my remark. 'Make
yourselves at home.'

Inside, the cavern was very dark, lit by only a few flickering candles hanging in lattice lanterns. I'd pictured
Peewing Wan Ho Leprechaun as a tall figure of tanned
genie-whirling splendour. In reality he was a shrunken
old man of four feet, dressed in ruby robes patterned with
gold Chinese dragons. He had a wide face, criss-crossed
with endless lines, a warm smile, showing broken yellow

teeth, pointy ears and friendly eyes. As he spoke, I caught a whiff of his breath, laced with chai and exotic spices.

He really was a lovely little creature. He showed us his collection of exotic creatures, from pink glow-in-the dark chocoholic giant millipedes (when he showed them a Mars Bar, they turned positively cerise, saliva dribbling over their coiled bodies) to lesbian stick insects, their gooey bodies tangled in bizarre positions as they performed sexy shows in their cages. With each one, I shuddered more and more violently.

'Amazing,' Puck laughed. 'But about the Brazilian Long-Toothed Sexy Hairy Love Spider?'

'Oh yes – my favourite little darling.' The Leprechaun turned, gingerly stepped over a row of cages, lifting his robes, and pulled, from a dark corner, a little cage, holding it up before us.

Inside was the most extraordinary creature. The spider was tiny – about the width of a two-pence piece. But she was the most incredible colour – the richest purple I'd ever seen; the deep mauve of bluebells mixed with the ripeness of plums and lilac. The light from the lanterns shimmered in gold shafts, highlighting her body here and there as she scampered, frightened, over the cage. Now and again, she let out little high-pitched squeaks. She sounded like a faulty fire alarm.

'Ah, she's a little excited,' he cooed at her. Whenever he talked to his spider, I noticed he crooned in a very soft, husky voice, which seemed to calm her down like a spell. 'Aren't you, my baby? My baby? She's called Mavis, by the way.'

'She looks incredible. How much does she cost?' Puck asked, straight to the point.

'A thousand petals,' he said casually.

I nearly freaked. A thousand petals! In human currency, this added up to about five hundred pounds. It was enough to buy a designer butterfly. I could even have surgery on my wings for that.

After a great deal of haggling, they finally settled on seven hundred and thirty-nine petals.

'How can we even be sure it will work?' Puck asked a little sulkily.

'Oh, but it will.' The Leprechaun looked slightly offended. 'Human consciousness is very malleable.' And, to his credit, he did give us a few gift-wrapped presents to send us on our way – a lovely little T-shirt made from pure spider's silk, with the slogan THE SPRITE GIRLS (the latest all-girl band in the supernatural world), and a strange little bottle, which he pressed into Puck's hands with a firm smile. 'This, my friend, contains the secret of all happiness. Save it for a celebration!'

The Leprechaun and the sprite came to the door to wave us off as we flew out into Soho, Mavis dangling from Puck's fingers, clinging to her cage and squeaking, 'Eek! Eek!'

26
Jack

Katie had once told Jack the reason why diets were doomed to fail: when your attention is on something it only magnifies it, makes the problem worse. The more you thought about *not* eating chocolate, she explained, the more you sat and visualised the thick brown creamy bar in the fridge that you *weren't* suppose to eat, and the worse it became, until eventually you had to fling yourself at the fridge, yank open the door, tear off the paper and gobble it all up.

Jack had always teased Katie over her lack of will-power.

Now he was in sympathy.

He'd tried his best. He'd decided to forget Leila. Sod her. She was an arrogant cow who didn't deserve him anyway.

He'd decided to make a fresh start. His life had been such a mess lately. That morning he'd set the alarm, got up early. He'd surfed the internet the night before and managed to key 'job' as opposed to 'Anna Kournikova' into the search engines, and had e-mailed his CV to a few IT firms. He'd breakfasted on bacon and eggs in a café and was now pottering about in Camden Market, looking for a present for Katie to cheer her up; she'd seemed down lately.

But as he browsed the stalls, he couldn't stop thinking about Her. He fingered beads and gold bangles, imagining them around her delicate Bambi-ankles. He flicked through a rail of tye-dye T-shirts, blazing spirals of amber, ochre and green, and pictured Leila in one . . . with nothing else. The rough pottery reminded him of a display in her bedroom. *Maybe I should just go and tell her I love her*, he thought. *I never actually found out for sure if she wants me or not. I mean – what if?* He picked up a packet of rose-smelling incense. *What if?* Suddenly he couldn't bear it any longer. He fled from the stall, his money falling from his hand, scattering the goods, ignoring the angry shouts of the trader.

It was early evening by the time he tracked her down. He'd borrowed Katie's car, yanking her keys off the kitchen peg; she'd told him he could use the car in an emergency, and fuck it, *this* was an emergency. He'd driven to Leila's office but she's already left for the day, so he thought she might have gone home or to Henry's. Katie's car was a red Fiat, and he drove in a kind of road rage, beeping his horn in the slow ant-trails of London traffic. There was a packet of Opal Fruits on the dashboard and he wolfed them down, chewing ferociously, the fruit flavours, lemon and lime and blackcurrant, fizzing angrily on his tongue.

He was just turning into Chalcott Square when his chewing slowed, his jaw went slack. She was there! In the taxi right in front of him. He quickly pulled in behind some cars, ducking his head as he watched her get out. She was carrying some flowers! Flowers! A spurt of strawberry jealousy burned in his throat.

She went up to Henry's door. *She had her own key.* God, they were practically married!

The door slammed, like a smug, grinning mouth.

Jack let out a deep, hyena moan of hysteria. He leaned forward on the steering wheel. *Very well*, he thought, *I'm going to sit here and wait. Even if it takes all night, I'll wait. I'll catch her when she comes out. Offer her a lift home.* But a deep wave of tiredness washed over him.

He could feel himself starting to nod off.

He shook himself, suddenly afraid, even though he felt heavy with a latent backlog of tiredness. The last few nights he'd had trouble sleeping. Every time he was about to drift off, desire would prickle him awake, and when he finally did drop off, nightmares gripped him. Every night they seemed to get worse. The dreams doused his mind in dark eroticism, leaving him foggy when he awoke, as though night still lingered throughout the day.

His head drooped. A flash of white light sliced through the darkness. He yawned. He was aware, just before slipping into unconsciousness, of a small voice by his ear whispering, *Don't panic.*

Jack slept. London buzzed. The city was only just waking up. People poured out of offices and into pubs. Tourists danced in a blue frenzy at the Hippodrome. Wine was sloshed, beer swallowed, music pounded. Jack slept on. Jack dreamed . . .

★

★

27
Leila

★

She was going to say it. She was going to say it. *'I'm sorry, but I think our affair is over, I just can't do this any more. I'm sorry but . . . it's not you . . .'* Leila climbed into the lift. It slid smoothly up to the fourth floor, to the room he'd booked. *'I'm sorry but I've met someone else. I actually love him, I think . . .'*

The hotel room was unlocked. She went in and shut the door behind her. He was sitting on the bed with his back to her. He suddenly looked such an old, sad figure. There was a bald patch at the top of his head she'd never noticed properly before. She had about as much desire to sleep with him as she did Robin Cook. She really would have to end it, she realised, in panic. There was no chickening out. She couldn't sleep with him, not ever again. Her desire for him, once a red flame of lust, was now pale ash, nothing.

'Derek . . .'

He turned, startled. Throughout their relationship she'd always addressed him as Mr Winterton. Her playful, pet name for him.

Leila sat down in a fancy hotel chair opposite him. She twisted her handbag in her fingers. He looked puzzled. She said, 'Look, I'm sorry . . . it's over. I can't do this any more. It's not fair on your wife,' she lied lamely.

Silence. The hum of traffic.

She didn't know what else to say. He just sat on the bed, staring down dully at his shoes, twisting his wedding ring. Her heart was beating madly, but at the same time she felt as flat as cola left out in the sun. The hotel walls seemed to be closing in on them.

Gingerly, she got up to go.

'Hey!' she cried as he suddenly yanked her down by the wrist. 'God – I—'

He forced her on to the bed, pushing his hard thighs against hers, pressing his fingers to her throat. And then he started to squeeze. *I'm going to die*, she panicked, feeling him suck the breath out of her like juice from a lemon. She tried to scream but just the faintest cry trickled out. She stared at the door, thick, locked, soundproof. Nobody would hear her dying. She'd just be a limp corpse on a bed. His face, manic about her, was red and swollen like a slab of butcher's meat. A huge anger roared inside her: *how dare he!* In a burst of inhuman energy, she kneed him in the groin. With a huge bellow, he rolled over, half-fell off the bed.

Leila jumped up, picking up her bag. One of her shoes had fallen off but she left it, fleeing to the door. Then she turned and saw him sitting on the bed, crying.

'Please don't go,' he pleaded. 'I love you . . . *I'll tell my wife . . .*'

For the first time ever in their affair, Leila felt sorry for him. She wanted to console him, but she was too frightened. She left the room, hurried into the lift. Guests in the lobby stared at this wild woman, her hair flying, hobbling out through the revolving doors with only one sling-back heel on her feet. The doorman politely hailed her a taxi, a smile twitching at his lips.

In the taxi, she tried to open the windows, then realised she couldn't. She felt like an astronaut in space, sealed in a vacuum. *In, out, in, out,* she kept telling herself, drawing in deep, shaky breaths. The echo of his touch, a sudden memory of his square nails digging into her throat, made her body recoil violently. Shit, she was supposed to be going to Henry's house, she couldn't turn up like this. She'd have to tell the driver to change direction; she'd have to call up Henry.

She picked up her mobile, trying to type in the numbers, then realised it wasn't switched on. She tried again; then, just as Henry answered, the sound of his voice touched her, and some instinct made her ring off. She hung on to the phone, clutching it in her sweaty hands like a rape alarm. She suddenly felt a craving, a need to feel his arms around her, to hear his soft voice, even if she couldn't tell him what had happened . . .

Her chin trembled; a few tears slid down it. It must be the shock. She wiped them away and leaned against the cab window, as the taxi crawled through the wet London streets . . .

'What are those marks on your neck?' was the first thing Henry said, after they'd kissed hello.

'Uh?' Leila froze, half-slipping her jacket from her shoulders.

He turned her round to face the large mirror in the hallway, propped up on an old Edwardian cabinet.

She watched as his fingers curled forwards, over her shoulder, to her throat, pointing to the marks. Two red claw marks, like swollen raspberries. Instinctively, she

267

pulled her scarf over them, but to her surprise, Henry fiercely pulled it away, frowning.

'They look like love bites.' His voice trembled.

'Oh no – they're wasp stings. Oh wow, what are you cooking?'

'Your shoes. You're wearing one shoe.' Pause. 'Did the wasps steal that too?'

Leila looked down at her feet. She suddenly had an hysterical image of Mr Winterton, back in the hotel room, cradling her shoe, the one remaining part of her, stroking it and kissing it, and a terrible smile quivered on her lips.

Then, to her relief, Henry suddenly burst into laughter too. She laughed; he laughed; he pulled her into his arms.

'You're having a crazy day, hey?' he said. 'Wasps and shoes, shoes and wasps. Are you OK?'

Leila smiled up at him, awkwardly.

She turned away, gazing at herself in the mirror again, her skin blotted with her sins. Henry slipped his arm around her waist and started kissing the back of her neck. Lots of little punchy kisses. In Leila's current mood, they felt like mosquito bites. After the shock of Mr Winterton, her skin felt as though it had been rubbed raw with a pumice stone.

'Er – why don't we watch some TV?' she suggested brightly, going into the living room. She picked up the control. 'Oh, look – *Family Fortunes*! Great!'

'*Family Fortunes*?' Henry frowned in disbelief.

'Maybe not. Oh –' she flicked to another side '– Anne Robinson!'

'Oh, even better,' said Henry, with playful sarcasm. 'We're spoilt for choice. Oh come on, let's just go to bed!'

Suddenly all boyish and excited, he picked her up and started to carry her upstairs. Despite herself, Leila kept laugh-shrieking as he told her to duck, mind that coat, mind that picture. 'Fuck it!' he cried merrily as a painting went crashing to the floor and he took her into the bedroom.

Sitting on his bed, however, she felt that familiar lurch of fear. After Mr Winterton, sex was the last thing she wanted. She craved the innocence of a cuddle. She tried not to wince as he sat down next to her and started to kiss her neck. He moaned; she feigned a moan too. He lay down on the bed, pulling her with him. She closed her eyes. She felt as though she had woken up in the middle of an operation, powerless to prevent the surgeon's hands, only able to watch in horror as he wields a scalpel.

I can't do this, she suddenly thought in weary despair. *I can't have a relationship. I'm not ready. I just want to cut myself off from all men and be alone again.*

His fingers dipped over her body and she couldn't help it, she winced. His fingers froze.

'Leila.'

She opened her eyes.

'Leila – do I . . . do you actually want to go to bed with me?'

'I do . . . I just . . .' She gazed at a picture on the wall. A Monet, a blur of green and pink.

'It's just –' he propped himself up on one elbow, '– you always seem so tense whenever I try to . . . and we've been together for quite a while and never . . .'

'I think . . .' She paused. Normally she'd just fob these sorts of questions off with a headache. Not that many men ever noticed anyway that she faked almost every orgasm, found loving sex a painful torture. But Henry's eyes were earnest; suddenly she was sick of lying. 'I just have this problem . . . I find myself separating love and sex . . . it's a bit hard to explain . . .'

'But I think love gives sex meaning. It's a way of

expressing love,' he said, and she could tell he didn't understand. He flopped back down on the bed. A silence stretched between them. She reached out, locking her fingers into his, wanting to explain, wanting him to unravel it all from her.

Suddenly Henry sat up on his elbow again.

'Tell me. Tell me the best sexual fantasy – no – the best sexual experience you've ever, ever had.'

Oh great. Now what was she supposed to say? Well, Henry, it took place last week, in a hotel room . . .

'Well,' Leila said carefully. 'I once – some time ago – had an affair with this older man.'

'What? An affair affair?' Henry looked shocked.

Shit, Leila thought, remembering Katie mentioning recently that Henry's parents had split up and he was very sensitive about traditional values . . .

'Oh no, no, I mean, you know, a love affair. It was ages ago –' Oh God, she'd go to hell for all this lying '– and I just – I don't know – he was very tough, you know? A bit of a bastard really. Mean and moody.'

'I can be mean,' said Henry, putting on a gruff gangster voice.

He sounded ridiculous. *Yeah, right*, thought Leila. Henry was about as mean as a Cliff Richard record. Released at Christmas. For his older fans.

'Henry, you're not mean,' she cried, suddenly, inexplicably irritated. 'You're . . . you're nice.' She spat the word out. 'You're really nice. You call when you say you're going to, you give me presents, you . . . you're nice.'

'Well, it's not a crime,' he pointed out and Leila felt a wave of guilt, realising that despite his put-on cool voice, her words had hit him like knives. 'I mean, loads of women complain about men standing them up, beating

270

them up, and so on. What's so terrible about being treated well, with love and respect?'

'No, no, you're right.' Leila realised she sounded perverse. 'I think it's just . . .' She searched for her thoughts, but they seemed blurry, confused. 'I mean – I think mystery is attractive in a man. Mr Winterton – this guy I had an affair with ages ago – I didn't really know him. So I couldn't find things to dislike. I had to make bits of him up. I didn't know his weaknesses – that he only bathed once a week, or that he secretly liked SClub7, or anything equally unsexy.'

'Oh,' said Henry. 'So. So then. You're saying that your sexual fantasy is basically shagging a faceless moody stranger who's really unpleasant to you. Christ. Sorry.'

'That's OK.'

'I wasn't apologising to you. I was apologising to Jesus.'

'What? Oh . . .'

'Oh, no, I wouldn't apologise to you, you bitch.'

Leila opened her mouth in horror, then smiled weakly, realising this was the new, mean Henry. 'Oh, ha ha.'

'I mean – look at you,' Henry went on. 'You have loads of faults. You wear black *all* the time, which makes you look as if you're permanently going to a funeral. You are the most anally tidy person I know. You like watching *Family Fortunes*, apparently. You are obsessed with getting ten hours sleep a night. You won't go to bed with me. You prefer the company of your cat to most men. And – admittedly only a little – you have dandruff!'

'I bloody well do not!' Leila cried.

Despite the fact that he was laughing and looking at her in a you-know-I'm-only-joking-manner, she felt bramble prickles of hurt and irritation all over her.

'Well – what about you!' she burst out. 'You sneeze all the time. You have hayfever even in winter, which is the

271

wrong season, you idiot. You bite your nails. You have this stupid habit of pulling your sleeves over your wrists and picking holes in them. You have enormous amounts of money and mostly you wear jeans and crappy old jumpers when you could wear suits. And you were nice, but now you're horrible.'

'Look at us!' Henry suddenly laughed. 'This is so romantic, isn't it? Insulting each other at great length . . .' He bit his lip and Leila looked down, picking at the quilt. 'Oh Leila, you know – despite the dandruff, every time I look at you, I do just melt. Sorry, that's too nice, isn't it? I mean, every time I look at you, I vomit.'

'You bastard!'

Exasperated, she grabbed the pillow and playfully hit him.

A pillow fight ensued, a breathless, laughing, shaking pillow-fight, a desperate way of defusing the tension, avoiding the issue.

Their breath was shaky, the bed covered with feathers. Henry blew a few silvery fluffs from Leila's hair. And then he leaned down over her, his face up against hers, his lips nearly but not quite touching.

It was a magical moment, a change of mood. For that minute or so, he hovered over her, their breath intermingling, until they found the same rhythm. He leaned down, his mouth just brushing hers. She arched up, he pulled away a few centimetres. Her breath caught in her throat. His eyes locked into hers. She felt his fingers trailing down, down, to the softness of her thighs, pushing aside the white cotton. He started to gently caress her. Something opened up. His mouth murmured against her, his fingers moved faster. He whispered, *You're shaking*. She bit her lip. His eyes were almost sad. He was staring at her so intently, so erotically, so romantically, she couldn't

272

find the words any more, just faint gasps, until finally, as she reached a climax, he pressed his mouth down hard and firm against hers, swallowing her orgasm.

Afterwards she collapsed back on to the sheets and he lay against her, his head on her breast, clinging tight. She held on to him too. The waves of pleasure were becoming waves of pain. She was panting, shocked. It was wonderful, it was horrible. He was just like Ray. Just like Ray.

They walked home in a pensive silence, hand in hand. They hadn't ended up making love, just held each other, talked quietly about nothing much. Leila felt choked up, strange. Henry had done it. He'd reached inside and prised open her heart. And what would he say if he knew, only a few hours before, she'd been in a hotel room with a married man, telling him she wanted to end their affair? What would Henry say if she told him?

He'd probably call her a slut. Maybe he'd even cry. He'd certainly never forgive her. It was better that he didn't know.

It's not my fault. She tried to talk the guilt away. *When I started going out with Henry, it was just a fling, nothing serious. I had no idea it would come to this. I can't bear to lose him. I haven't had something this precious since Ray.*

They were at her gate now. Henry had a funny look on his face. He shifted from one foot to the other.

'I . . .' He trailed off. 'I had something to confess – but . . . I – about me and K—'

Leila was suddenly frantic to change the subject. She had a feeling he was going to say something heavy and it terrified her.

'Did you – did you mean what you said about my dandruff?' she demanded, trying to laugh, to swivel the conversation back to jokes again.

'Of course not.' He kissed the top of her head. 'No – what I meant was . . . I mean . . . I love you.'

Before she could even digest the words, he'd hugged her, so she couldn't see his face. Leila blinked as he drew back.

Say it! she cried inside. *Say it, say it, say it.*

But she couldn't. She loved him, but something inside shrank away, like a snail retreating into a shell.

'Well, good night.' He bit his lip, tried to smile. ★

She watched him walk away.

Henry didn't call for the next few days. She thought nothing of it at first. In fact, it was a relief. Something was happening inside her. She felt a little like a caterpillar, cocooned in uncertainty and cynicism, but she could also feel something better, something more beautiful, emerging.

In any case, she wasn't sure what she was going to say to him, and she wanted some space, some time to get used to her changing feelings. Besides, Henry was always so intense. He called *every night*.

But he didn't call this time.

A few days went by and she felt a tiny pinch. OK, so she'd asked for this. But she missed having him there to sound off to, to rant to about the little trials and tribulations of her day. That was the nice thing about Henry; sometimes she'd find herself droning on, then catch herself and cry, 'Oh God, I must sound so boring.' But Henry always said, 'Leila, you could talk about the EMU and never be boring.' He was so sweet.

And then *another* day passed. On the Tube to work, *what if*s started to filter through her mind. What if he'd been run over? Fallen off a cliff?

She could call him, of course . . .

But Leila never called men. Ever.

She got off the Tube at Covent Garden, passing by the flower seller on her way to work. Every morning he called out Cockney banter to her, and she strolled past haughtily. But today she stopped unexpectedly, running her eyes over the rainbow display.

"I'll have the tulips,' she said impulsively. She'd buy them. For Henry. Take them to his place tonight. After work. She'd surprise him.

She knew it was weird, buying a man flowers, but she felt Henry would love them. He loved the countryside, nature, gardening programmes and sweet smells, and he'd said he loved tulips, so why not?

Back at work, she put them in the sink with some water. Running her fingers over the petals, soft and wet, she suddenly felt a light feeling in her heart, imagining the look on his face. She could hardly wait.

Unfortunately, at the end of the day she came back into the office kitchen to find some git had moved her flowers, dumped them on the work surface. They were now a messy, wilting, cerise heap. She swore, wet them and wrapped them up in kitchen paper.

She clutched them in her hands in the cab to Henry's. As they trundled through traffic, she started to worry again. Five days, he hadn't called. What if – what if Mr Winterton had contacted him? What if he'd turned into a male Glenn Close in *Fatal Attraction* and had called Henry? Would he ever forgive her? Shit, she thought, it's supposed to be husbands who are afraid of mistresses letting on, not the other way round.

Henry had given her a key to his house, right from the start of their relationship, as if he'd almost wanted her to move in immediately. She'd never used it before. She inserted the key, jiggled it in the stiff lock. She smelled the lovely old musty scent of his house. On the hall table was a huge display of flowers, a magnificent spray of lilies and tulips, making her own insipid bunch look paltry in comparison. Now she was nervous. What if Henry thought the flowers were too girly? She should have bought him socks. A tie. Oh well, they could laugh about it together . . .

'Henry, where art thou Henry?' she called out, laughing. Her laughter echoed eerily, then faded. A grandfather clock ticked heavily. The house seemed to shift and whisper. Maybe he was at rehearsals, maybe that was why he hadn't phoned. She felt a flicker of guilt; he'd asked her to go and watch him so many times but she'd always been too busy.

She was halfway upstairs when through the slits in the banisters she saw the living room door was slightly ajar.

'Henry?'

She wheeled down the stairs, pushed open the door, and saw Henry and a girl on the sofa together.

They were still halfway through pulling on their clothes – they'd obviously been frantically redressing since they'd heard her key in the lock. The girl had her back to Leila. She was blonde, plump, pulling on a flowery dress. Henry's shirt was still hanging open. He'd got his trousers up but the zip was undone. His face was sweaty, his hair mussed up. And then, as the girl said 'Oh my God!', Leila knew, knew that voice, but for a moment didn't really click, not even when the girl turned and looked at her. Leila felt she had to be a lookalike, a sister, a cousin, surely not . . .

'Katie?' she heard herself say. 'What the fuck are you doing here?'

'Look, I'm sorry.' Henry was blushing. 'We just . . .'

'We . . .' Katie started.

Silence. Words trailed off, hanging in the air like storm clouds about to burst. Leila just stood there. She couldn't believe it. This sort of thing just didn't happen to her. Men never did this to her. Men worshipped her. Men did not have affairs with fat girls like Katie. The world was turned upside down.

She looked from Henry to Katie to Henry, as if deciding who was to blame. She kept shaking her head as though trying to knock a coherent thought into place. And then, looking at Katie, at the sickening look of guilt and pity on her face, Leila felt an arrow of anger pierce the blankness.

'This is all because of Jack, isn't it?' she realised. 'Jack. He's been trying it on with me, he's in love with me, and you're jealous because you've wanted him all this time, and now you're getting back at me. Well, it's crap, Katie. Why didn't you fucking talk to me? I don't even like Jack. God, this is just the lowest, bitchiest thing to—'

'What?' Katie was obviously trying to feign bewilderment. 'No, Leila, it's not like that, we just . . .'

'You are such a bitch—'

'It just happened.' Katie spilled the words out in a rush. 'Ever since that night at the restaurant when you didn't turn up – and honestly, today I didn't mean to – I came over to tell Henry it was off—'

'Oh, and your clothes accidentally fell off,' Leila suddenly cut in, registering Katie's words. 'The restaurant. Since *the restaurant*? You're saying that . . . you've been . . . since then?' She turned to Henry, who was nervously edging behind the TV set. 'But we . . .' she trailed off, stunned with hurt. 'Our night . . .' That night had remained in her memory like a glass bubble, something pure and lovely to think about during the day when she was tired or stressed . . . and now Henry had taken the bubble and smashed it into pieces, shattering it every-where.

'I'm sorry – I wanted to tell you – I just couldn't quite – say it—'

'You are such a bastard!'

Suddenly Leila flipped. Rage swirled through her. She hurled herself at him, pushing the TV over, kicking him, tearing at his hair, pulling and tugging. He kept bellowing and ineffectually trying to push her away. Leila laughed, wildly. He was so polite, even though she was tearing out his hair. Nice polite Henry, who always seemed so reli-able. I trusted you, I believed in you, she found herself crying, I loved you.

She felt hands tugging at her waist and she realised Katie was trying to pull her away. She shoved her off and Katie skidded, stumbled backwards. Her flowery dress, still not done up properly, slipped halfway down her shoulders, revealing a dirty bra strap, a lump of breast. Leila squinted at her incredulously, her throat hot with tears. How could he? How could Henry prefer Katie to her?

She looked down. There were fair hairs in her hands, and the remains of the flowers. A few petals were still shimmering in the air. She tossed them at Katie, but missed, the stems flopping to the floor. Katie recoiled tearfully as Leila bunched up her fists. For a moment she felt like tearing Katie's hair out too. Then she thought, *Fuck them. Just walk away. Walk away.*

She turned and left.

Jack, still slumped asleep in the car, didn't even notice her go.

28
Charlie

★

★

Oh dear God, please can all this drama be over soon so we can just go back to normal again, I prayed as we flew over to find Jack, Puck leading the way. *I'm so tired . . . please can we get it right this time?*

The street looked expensive, a posh road of white birthday-cake houses. Puck eventually settled on the bonnet of a car, a red Fiat, where a dark-haired man was asleep at the wheel. Jack.

'Jack's asleep, he's on a vigil to wait for Leila to come out of Henry's house,' Puck explained in a theatrical whisper. 'That's Henry's house.' He pointed at a house across the street. 'So, we put the spider into Jack, it works its magic and spurts scarlet love juice to undo the spell, Jack wakes up, he sees Leila and, hey presto, he's cured. He won't love her any more. He'll think she's a dog. Then the spider spurts new purple love juice into his bloodstream so that the next person he sees *and* touches, he loves. Which is bound to be Katie. As soon as he wakes up, he'll wonder what on earth he's doing chasing after Leila, he'll drive home and Katie will be there . . .'

'There's still a lot of 'if's, Puck,' I said nervously. 'I bet it's all going to go wrong and he'll fall for a traffic warden or something.'

'No, because he has to *touch* this person too. Anyway, its frigging six-thirty in the morning. The odds are on our side today, Charlie. And with any spell there's always a slight risk. Now, come on. All we have to do is get our friend Mavis here –' he shook the cage and Mavis trembled '– to crawl into Jack's ear.'

'His what?' I shrieked.

But Puck had already flown on. The window of the car was partially open; I watched him flit through the gap, Mavis giving little mews of distress. Quickly, I flew in after him, wincing as I banged my wing.

'His ear?' I cried, watching Puck rest Mavis's cage on the dashboard.

Puck said something back which I didn't quite catch; with Jack's snores reverberating around the car, it was like trying to talk over thunderous pop music at a disco.

'His ear?' I repeated, flying up close to Puck.

'That's what it says in *The Brahma Book of Spells*,' said Puck, as if he was patiently explaining the alphabet to an illiterate child.

'Well, so far we've only turned Jack half-mad, so while we're at it, let's deafen him too, hey?'

'Charlie, don't you remember what Peewing Leprechaun said?' Puck said impatiently. 'The spider works by burrowing itself into the human heart. He wasn't spouting a load of poetic wank. He was speaking physically, not metaphorically. Now, there are a number of ways we can get this spider-thing into Jack's body. Through his mouth –' we both looked at his mouth, hanging open, dribbling slightly and winced, '– through his ear, or . . .' Puck's glance lowered down to his trousers. 'Well, there is a more kinky way . . .'

280

'Puck, that's disgusting!' I yelled.

'Right, so through his ear. Will you stop moaning and help me? I need you to hold the cage while I get Mavis to crawl out.'

'Oh God, I can't believe I'm doing this . . .'

Shuddering with disbelief, swearing never to speak to Puck again once this ritual was over, I positioned myself by Jack's ear by standing on tip-toe on the indicator stick. I felt like an amateur tightrope walker on a thin, black plastic rope. The cage wasn't all that heavy, but it was bloody uncomfortable having to hold it up against my chest, like doing weights without any relief. Puck seemed to take forever fumbling with the catch. But once the door was open, Mavis, who seemed petrified by the whole ordeal, curled up like an eight-legged hedgehog and refused to come out. Puck kept cajoling her but she wasn't fooled. She remained in a taut purple ball, her yellow eyes wide with disbelief. *Eek*, she kept squeaking at high pitch, *eek, eek, eek.*

My arms were starting to bulge with the strain of holding up the cage; I could feel sweat trickling down my back.

All the same, I could hardly say I blamed the poor creature. Through the dark bars of the cage, I could see Jack's ear-hole – a white mass of whorls, flecked with dandruff, greasy with wax, curls of coarse dark hair gently springing over it. It was a little like being pushed down a black-hole.

'C'mon Charlie, at least help,' Puck called over.

'I'm trying, my arms are about to fall off,' I hissed through gritted teeth, giving the cage a little shake. Suddenly, Mavis rolled . . .

. . . and rolled . . .

and in a heap of arms and eyes and antennae, fell into

281

Jack's ear. There was a final scream which echoed through his ear canal, fainter and fainter . . .

. . . until . . .

Silence.

I was so shocked and exhausted, I dropped the cage. It tumbled down on to Jack's denim jacket, before landing on the floor next to a trainer.

My eyes flitted up to Puck. He was looking slightly shocked too.

I looked back at Jack with horrid fascination. I had an odd, dirty, invasive feeling, as though I'd just robbed him or seen him undressing without him knowing he was being watched. I kept peering into his ear, worried Mavis would come creeping out again. I was so engrossed, I completely forgot that I was standing on the very edge of the indicator, leaning forwards like a diver about to take the plunge. Before I knew it, my feet had slipped and I was hurtling forwards into his ear, taking the same path Mavis had taken.

'*Ahhhhhhhhhh*' I cried. I felt Puck reaching out for me, his fingers brushing my foot, slipping away . . .

I closed my eyes, bumping down and round a dark tunnel, as though I was in a helter-skelter, until I found myself landing on something soft and wet. Jack's tongue.

'*Eek! Eek!*' Mavis was curled up in the corner of Jack's mouth.

I tried to stand up, but I felt as though I was in a sinking boat during an angry storm. Suddenly the sea was moving, as though a huge tidal wave had turned the boat over. I tried to cling on but lost my grip and went hurtling downwards through a thick green sea. With a loud *AAAAAATISHOoooooooooo*! I went flying through the air and landed on the dashboard. I lay there for a moment, drenched in slime and Jack's body fluids, aching all over, my mind dazed. I remember trying to stand, but my slippery legs buckled like a colt. In defeat, I sank back down on to the dashboard. Through a veil of slime, I saw Jack shudder, unconsciously wipe his nose in his sleep, and then carry on snoozing.

When I woke up again, it was dark and I was back home in my bed. I checked my glow-worm clock. It was only four in the afternoon. I didn't have to be up till seven. I had plenty more time to sleep.

But now I was awake, I couldn't drop off again. My body felt tired but my mind was still ringing with memories. After Jack had sneezed me out of his body, I had passed out for a while. I had blurred images of Puck carrying me away, of him rinsing me in the lake of Regent's Park, before tip-toeing me back through the fairy burrow, where he had deposited me into bed. He had tucked me in and given me a goodnight kiss, whispering that from now on everything would be all right. A warm glow had spread through my weak body and I'd smiled, touched by his tenderness.

I rolled on to my back, staring up at the ceiling. The wardrobe door was still slightly ajar. I pictured Mavis in Jack's mouth, her little feet scuttling on his molars and dentures, the way she had been idly picking black flint from one of his filings. Puck had assured me she hadn't been sneezed out when I had. I pictured her slipping by a silken thread, tied to the back of his tongue, down the ladder of his throat. Dancing on his kidneys, blown about by the huff and puff of his lungs, before finally finding his heart. I remembered Puck's quote from *The Brahma Book of Spells*: 'the spider burrows her way into the human heart and lives there for ninety days'. How would she get in? Perhaps she would roll up tight in a pulsating purple and scarlet ball, then slowly ooze into the red flabby organ, suck herself inside. Would she dilute his blood with purple poison? Would he feel it? And what if she reproduced? What if a sac of tiny little spiderlings bubbled and oozed on her back like something out of *Alien*?

After another hour of tossing and turning, I finally drifted off into a nightmare about Jack going to hospital, complaining that he felt under the weather. The nurses took an x-ray and a bemused doctor unfurled it to reveal a white skeleton blotched and blipped as though the marrow was being eaten up by cancerous cells. But on a closer look, the doctor realised it was hundreds and hundreds of tiny little spiders, all squiggling through Jack's body.

29
Jack

Jack woke up suddenly, hearing the soft female voice echo again in his head. *Don't panic*. He shook himself. There was a pain in his chest from sleeping on the steering wheel. His arms ached and there were creases on his face where the cuffs of his denim jacket had cut into his skin. Yet he felt wonderful. His head was lucid, as though rinsed with rainwater. His heart felt light. He blinked, rubbing his eyes, gazing out through the windscreen. Why am I here? Jack wondered in bewilderment. He shook his head. He felt like a character in a fairy tale who'd been asleep for a hundred years and woken up in a new era. Yesterday seemed a long time ago. He tried to extract some clear memory, some hook of normalcy and explanation. But there were only vague, blurry images – of Leila. Leila. He felt sure she had something to do with all this. But who cared about her? She was just Katie's friend, some cow who made his life a misery.

So what the hell was he doing here?

Had he taken an E by mistake?

Had someone spiked his drink?

What was the last thing that he remembered?

Nothing. He shook himself. There was a funny taste in his mouth, a bit like blackcurrants and syrup. He licked his dry lips and looked at himself in the rear-view mirror. His eyes looked bright, but there was a funny, purplish streak on his tongue and his teeth were aching as though they hadn't been brushed in years. His eyes dropped to the Opal Fruit wrappers scattered about his feet. They were probably bursting with sugar; no wonder his teeth hurt.

Katie would be furious with all the mess. Hastily, he picked up a handful of wrappers, scrunching them into his pockets. As he did so, he pricked his finger on a sharp black thing and picked it up, frowning. It looked like a cage for a tiny, tiny mouse. It resembled something from a Kinder Egg – probably one of Susie's.

He put the toy on the dashboard and shrugged again, looking around, trying to place himself. He didn't recognise the street, though it looked vaguely familiar.

In the wing mirror, he suddenly caught sight of a front door opening. Jack blinked. A tall man with ruffled blonde hair, wearing a green dressing gown, came out. Henry.

He was in Primrose Hill. Chalcott Square. Outside, for some bizarre reason, Henry's house.

Jack instantly hunched down in his seat. He didn't want Henry to see him; this was too weird and it was clearly drugs-related and Henry would only go and report it all to Katie, who was already in a strop with him. *Don't see me*, he willed Henry, *don't see me*.

Henry hugged the milk bottles against his chest. Then he glanced up and looked across the street. Straight at Jack. Recognised the car after a double-take.

Henry gave a puzzled little wave. Jack pretended not to notice.

'Hello?' Henry called out. 'Er . . . you OK?'

Jack groaned. Oh God, now what? He got out of the car and wandered uneasily up Henry's path, forcing a happy 'everything's normal' smile on to his face. He opened his mouth to speak, but there was a funny feeling in his chest. He paused, an 's' stuttering on the tip of his tongue, then dying away. He gazed helplessly at Henry, aware that he was staring but unable to control himself.

Henry's dressing gown revealed tufts of tawny chest hair, freckled skin. His face was soft, his eyes questioning. As the sun rose behind them, rays of light spilled on to his face, streaking his head with a golden aura. Henry screwed up his eyes. He bit his lips. Jack felt choked up. What beautiful, beautiful pink lips.

'Jack, *are* you OK?' Henry reached out and gently punched him on the shoulder.

At his touch, Jack felt lightning streak through his body. He gasped.

'Look, if you're pissed off about this Katie and Leila business, we can sort it out, but really, I don't think that now is the time . . .'

'Leila? What? I'm not here to have a go at you. I just . . . to be honest, I'm not sure why I'm here . . .' Jack gestured vaguely towards the car.

'Well.' Henry paused uncertainly. 'Er, well . . . maybe you should come in for breakfast?'

As Jack followed Henry into the hallway, it struck him that Henry was quite the most beautiful man he'd ever seen.

★

★

30
Leila

Ouch! Leila cursed, feeling sick as the red welt appeared on her hand. She paused for a moment, shutting her eyes. Her temples were throbbing with a headache, her forehead was rigid with stress. She saw them again: Katie and Henry. She opened her eyes and looked down, watched the blood slowly trickle across her love line.

'Shit!' she snarled. Since finding that bitch with her boyfriend, she'd stormed into the nearest bar, abandoned her usual mineral water in favour of shots of tequila, and proceeded to get off her face. At 3 p.m. the next day she'd woken up on top of her bedclothes with no idea how she'd got home. But slowly, the memories had filtered back. Katie and Henry. Spying a half-empty bottle of red wine next to her bed, she'd realised her head was pounding. In her bathroom she'd flung open her cabinet, which also doubled up as a paltry medicine chest, rummaging desperately for paracetamol, when she'd suddenly felt a white hot searing pain. A razor blade clattered into the sink; the Vaseline tumbled out after it with a clunk. She realised that – just to add to the general joy of the day – she'd cut herself somehow. *Wonderful*, she thought, with savage sarcasm.

Drawing out a bandage, she wrapped it around the wound. Blood instantly stained the white gauze. She sank down on to her heels and slumped back against the bath. There were a few hairs on the edge of it, from where she'd been shaving her legs yesterday. She remembered humming along to Carly Simon's 'You're So Vain' on the radio. She'd been so happy, and now look at her. She was a wreck. A jilted wreck, with a two-timing boyfriend and a bitch of a best friend. She wished they were here to see her. Then they'd be satisfied. Maybe they were laughing at her now. She pictured their conversation.

'Well, underneath her tough act, she's really insecure,' Henry would be saying.

Because that's what everyone wanted, wasn't it? For every tough career woman to fall apart, show her weakness. And Katie, with her snide sympathy, would add, 'Oh well, Leila's never been very good at sticking with relationships. Men always leave her, like Ray . . .'

And then they'd console each other. Kiss and hug and go upstairs and fuck and totally forget about her.

And Katie. God. The cow. Leila felt a rush of deep hatred. Their friendship had never been entirely easy, but for crying out loud, hadn't Leila always been a good friend to her? Supported her? Given her a place to stay when she'd left Keith? Her and her screaming daughter, even though Leila hated children, hated the mess, the going-to-bed tantrums, the sweet papers left on the sofa. Well, they could fucking well leave. Tomorrow.

Suddenly she had a horrible vision of Katie coming back to make amends. Leila got up, found her legs weak and shaky. She went into her bedroom, grabbed the bottle of red wine, found her Marlboros, tucked them in her pocket, retreated into the bathroom, locked the door and sat down. There was no lock on her bedroom door and she could just imagine Katie barging in, all soft and chubbily angelic: 'Leila I'm *sooooo* sorry . . .' That's what Leila hated so much about her. She was so *nice*. Leila had always suspected the niceness was just an act and now it was true. *People might call me a bitch*, Leila thought, *people might dislike me, but I am what I am. At least I say what I think; what you see is what you get.*

Feeling tears prick her eyes, she lit up a cigarette, breathing in a deep, shaky, lungful of smoke.

Ever since school, they'd always been Katie and Leila, good cop, bad cop. Leila knew deep down that she'd always been a bit jealous of Katie. Katie might not be pretty, but she was still just the girl Leila wanted to be. She was popular. Nice. The girl everyone liked. The type whom everyone went to with their problems.

Whereas Leila was always a girl everyone was wary of. Women saw her as a bitch or a slag, eyeing up her sexy clothes with jealous eyes, keeping their distance. And Katie had always had a kind of sweet innocence. She saw the good in everyone, and if Leila ever said a bad word about anyone, Katie would give a squeal of shocked laughter, but add in a small voice, 'But I think they're OK really . . .'

Leila was a cynic. She'd inherited this from her mother, who, as a psychiatrist, was always mentally dissecting people, putting them on a slab like a rat, slitting them open with a scalpel and probing their weaknesses. 'People are always the opposite of their outside sheen,' she'd told Leila. And it was true. Just like her father, the so-called family man, who'd turned out to have a mistress. And Henry, the so-called gentleman, who'd turned out to be a bastard. And Katie, the so-called nice girl, who was in fact a bitch.

Had their fling really been a one-off?

Or had it been a steamy, secret, behind-doors, dropped-telephone-calls affair which had actually been hotting up over weeks?

Leila kept running the memory files of her romance with Henry through her mind, trying to calculate when he might have started cheating. It wasn't as if she even liked him, of course . . . and yet. Leila remembered that soft feeling inside when she'd chosen the flowers for him. She could hardly believe she'd been so stupid. Because she did *like* him. He'd been the first man she'd opened up to since Ray.

She was aware that she'd spent the years after Ray developing a hard, scaly skin of cool unattainability. She'd only just been starting to shed it, to find a new Leila, a Leila who trusted, who cared.

But no, he'd turned out to be just like all the other bastards. Life had kicked her in the stomach once again. For a moment she really had believed in all that hearts 'n' flowers business; how could she had been so naïve?

She really was starting to cry now, she couldn't help it. It had to be the alcohol coursing in her bloodstream. She couldn't help longing for him to be here, to hold her and comfort her and kiss away her tears. And just why the fuck hadn't he called to apologise? Her handbag lay discarded on the floor; she half-crawled, half-leaned over to get it, pulling out her little black Nokia. Sure enough, the green light was flashing. You'd think if he really cared he would ring to apologise, with excuses like he was drunk, he didn't mean it, it was just a one-off, would never happen again. She checked her messages. One from Zoe asking if she was ill. She pressed 1471. Just the number of the office.

Oh God. She threw the phone into her lap. Nobody loved her. She was sitting here, crying, and nobody gave a *fuck*.

Leila got up and the phone clattered to the floor. She felt drunk again; everything was fluid and hazy. She put down the bottle on the toilet seat. She moved forwards; a second later she heard the crash and turned to see shards of green glass everywhere, the wine spreading like a ghastly pool of blood. Shit.

Locating a dustpan and brush downstairs cleared her head. The act was almost soothing. She found relief in the concentration of checking for every last fragment, even if her hand still ached.

Once she started, she couldn't stop. She had to keep tidying, she had to keep busy. She sorted out her dressing table, throwing away caked mascara and lipsticks she didn't like any more. She discovered the list for a dinner party she was planning and fiercely crossed Katie and Henry's names off. There.

She picked up her handbag and went downstairs. It was just getting dark outside and the air was frosty. She shut the door and walked down the street, wishing she'd put on her coat but too drained to bother going back for it. She continued round the corner, a sad lonely figure, her arms folded and her shoulders hunched, heading towards the graveyard.

31
Charlie

Puck and I were celebrating Jack's love life with a trip to St. Mary's graveyard. We'd brought along the Bottle of Happiness the Chinese leprechaun had given us. It was completely clear, like vodka, and the thin blue label on the side was a mass of odd letters, pictures, hieroglyphics.

Giggling and teasing each other that a genie would pop out, we found some acorn-cups to use as goblets and Puck unscrewed the bottle.

For a moment I saw bright white light and a yellow ribbon of air, like a translucent snake, which spun into my mouth, rippled down my throat. And then I felt a thud as I hit the ground and I was just floating, high above silver clouds, in streams of infinite light and happiness.

When I came to, Puck and I were lying in the grass.

It was literally like being filled with sunshine. My limbs felt as light as balloons. There was a beautiful taste in my mouth, like butter and thick cream and sweet sand grains and sun-kissed sea water. I thought I'd swallowed sugar-lumps of bliss. Even though it was twilight, my eyes were convinced it was day. There was a whiteness behind and inside everything. It was as though someone had taken a silver pen and sketched an aura around the trees and buildings. My sight was so refined, I could even see the air molecules, a mass of silver dots zinging and zagging and dancing in the sky.

I swivelled my head to look at Puck. His face was gleaming like a character in a film who's just seen an angel or a UFO. He didn't look at me, he just said, 'Wow.'

Is this what paradise would be like? I wondered dreamily. I realised then that the saying about heaven or hell being a state of mind was right. For a few brief hours, I had forgotten my worries, my stresses, myself. My doors of perception had been cleansed and I just lay in the grass, listening to my breath light in my ears and marvelling at how beautiful everything looked. The huge bruise-coloured clouds, rolling across the sky like majestic chariots. I looked at the pole-star and felt I could taste it, like milk and diamonds covered with dew. I watched a sycamore clinging to a branch before a final gust of wind brought it sailing down through the sky, like a dancing sprite.

I closed my eyes. A profound sense of beauty filled me up to the brim. I felt a ladybird's feet whisper across my face.

But the sunshine started to fade. Then came a feeling like a pin-prick in my heart. A tiny bubble leaked out, and it started to swell, and swell and swell, until I felt a tight pressure behind my eyes. Tears. I reached up and put my hands on my heart as though trying to trap the sun inside, but I could almost feel it trickling out through my fingers.

A shadow passed over the moon. I looked up at the tree-tops; they looked like claws tearing at the sky. I shuddered, blinking back tears again, a panic inside me.

What's happening? Am I coming down after a high? What is this?

But the melancholy only deepened, as though I was being drawn into a well of loneliness. I kept wanting to turn to Puck, but I felt strangely locked into the sensation, as though I couldn't make the effort to even twist my head or make a noise.

I could feel the winter coming. I could taste dead leaves in the air, rotting fields, twisted DNA, lost humans filled with regrets, a mutilated planet, the earth a dead, barren husk . . .

And I heard it. In the distance. Tears.

I shivered, wondering if it might be a ghost. Or even a sprite. Perhaps it was the scream of a dying tree. A month or so ago, Puck and I had found a hollow oak tree with a spirit trapped inside. She had died an unexpected death. A sudden road crash had caused her spirit to leap out into the nearest thing it could find. We'd attempted a few insipid spells but couldn't free her. It had all been rather hideously comic, actually. I could remember me attempting the magic and Puck getting in the way, over-excited and hopping about shouting, 'Come out, out, out; push, *push, push!*' All a bit like a pregnancy.

Remembering, I giggled nervously. Then my laughter died away as I saw her. The girl sitting on the bench.

She was in an odd position, head bowed, hair trailing over her face, nails clawing into her clothes. Her sorrow was so intense, I could see a dense grey cloud shimmering around her head.

It was so heavy that I flew backwards, compelled to run away. But she lifted her head, tossed back her hair, revealing her tear-stained face. Leila.

I was completely shocked. I was immediately convinced her grief had to be our fault. Mine and Puck's.

Taking Henry away from her, driving him towards Katie. Shit. I slumped to the ground by her side. What a mess.

For a moment I even wondered if Puck had put a spell on her too. But as I paused, listening hard to her thoughts, trying to sense her feelings, I caught the words, *He's dead, he's dead, Ray's dead.*

An odd chill swept over me. I felt myself sucked into a trance. I saw into Leila's mind, saw the sorrow spreading everywhere, and the roots, the cause: her previous husband.

Ray.

And then something happened to me that had never happened before. I think it can only have been the sunshine potion.

Normally, I could sit on a human's shoulder and listen to their thoughts. But when I perched on Leila's, I literally felt myself slip inside her. I became her. I felt transparent, as if I was being transported back in time, reliving a memory with her . . .

I found myself seeing it all through her eyes. Standing outside the grocery store. Hearing a shout. Turning and seeing my husband standing across the other side of the road. He waved and I smiled. He was clutching a carrier bag – later I saw he had bought me a hat.

He came running across the road. A taxi hit him at seventy miles-an-hour. They found out later the driver was drunk. He went to jail; my husband died.

For months after your death, I felt as though I too had died inside. Lying awake at night, staring into an empty space, never sleeping except for when I downed pills, waking up groggy, no idea of the time or the day, the sun spilling into the room, horribly aware that something was wrong.

In fact, I hated the sun. It was a constant reminder of that dreadful day, of burning tarmac, of the sun squinting in my eyes, as if trying to shield me from watching you. Your body ricocheting against the bonnet.

I hated the sun so much, I didn't want to leave my flat. So I stayed in. I had groceries delivered. I took time off. People rang the doorbell; I ignored them. People phoned and I told them I was fine. But the moment I put the phone back down on the hook, I'd flip from the strain of putting on such an act – I smashed glass, tore at the walls, broke nails clean off my fingers. I emptied a bottle of lavender perfume, your last present to me, all over my hair, so that I could treasure the smell. I didn't wash it, let it matt into a sweet-smelling mess. I ripped up your pillows and cried into the feathers until they stuck to my face. I tore apart your suits. I hated you for dying, for deserting me, leaving me. I drew your name on the walls in lipstick, as if I might summon your ghost, like the silly romance of *Truly, Madly, Deeply*. You never came.

After a few weeks, I realised that I was losing it. I was stuck in our flat: three rooms, twelve walls. I remember waking up one day and just crying and crying, for eight hours, on and on, until my body felt beaten up. I walked into the bathroom and gazed at the mirror. I looked dead. I pressed my nose against the cold glass and the terrible thought came: *It's going to be like this for the rest of my life*. Day after day. Without you. Nothingness. Forever.

Up until this point, I'd been rejecting life. But the will to live, to survive, to evolve, is such a powerful thing, impossible to deny. I went into my bedroom and, feeling like a puppet, I took off my nightie. It smelled terrible, of grief and tears and sweat. I pulled on some clothes. I

297

combed my hair and put on some dark glasses. I took my keys and bag. I went outside.

I felt as if I was walking on another planet. The noises were deafening. The screams of traffic, people chatting, children yelling, a motorbike. I went to the market. I asked for three oranges. As I paid for them, I felt tears in my eyes. The street trader was black and smiling; as his moccha hand touched mine, I knew I was back in the living world, I was forming a bridge, I was saying I would survive. Part of me felt angry, rebelling against it, wanting to go back into my flat and hide away. I did. But the next day I was up again. I decided to go back into work.

I hated their pity. Everyone saying they were so sorry. Every time I heard the words I felt as if needles were being slowly inserted inside me. I wanted to blank you out, to forget it all, but everyone kept reminding me. I wanted to scream at the lot of them, 'SHUT UP! I DON'T CARE IF YOU'RE SORRY!' Instead, I was polite. A week later, I decided to change my job. I moved back to England. To avoid any more pity, I told everyone, even Katie, I'd got a divorce. I'm sure they all thought I'd screwed you for money. I'd inherited a lot of money from you, enough to buy my own house in Primrose Hill.

I left your things in boxes, Ray. I kept my wedding ring and your letters. How come you never wrote me any love letters? All I have is bills. Stupid stuff. If only you'd left me something – a poem, a declaration of love, something. Did you ever love me at all? Sometimes I even wonder. Are you punishing me now? Henry is my first real boyfriend since you left me, and you know I'm never going to love him as much as you, you know Mr Winterton never counted – we laughed at him behind his back. But Henry . . . are you punishing me, Ray?

Blankness.
Ray?
Silence.

At this point, I couldn't take any more. I slipped out of her cloud of grief; I crumpled on the earth. I became myself again – Charlie the Fairy.

I couldn't believe it. So this was the real Leila. She wasn't divorced. She'd covered herself in a hard shell of grief, shut her friends out. And they had all been fooled – Henry and Katie and Jack. Thinking she was just some moody career bitch, when really she was carrying a lifetime of sadness inside. Learning to live with it. I felt indignant for her, proud. Nobody understood; they ought to have looked a little deeper.

I was tired, sucked dry, but I noticed her tears had dried and there was a faint peachy colour in her cheeks. By listening to her thoughts, I had shared the burden. For a moment I remembered what being a fairy was all about – to help, to heal. Despite feeling so drained, I felt almost peaceful.

'Ray, Ray, are you there?' she whispered.

'I'm here,' a deep voice chortled.

I blinked. A wild, hungry sound flew from Leila's lips. 'RAY!' she screamed.

'PUCK!' I yelled.

'Yeah, this is Elvis, calling from Radio Heaven,' Puck said. 'I'm just beaming down to let you know I'm alive and well and controlling Tony Blair—'

'PUCK, SHUT UP!' I yelled, hurling myself at him, sending him flying into the grass. We tumbled in the earth, as Leila began whispering Ray's name over and over, her shell of grief cracking open again . . .

★

299

I sulked at Puck all the way home.

'Well, I didn't know her husband was dead,' he protested. 'I'm sorry. It was just a joke. And anyway, why are you so upset? We're not humans, Charlie, we're fairies. We're not stupid. We know what happens to humans when they die, we know where they go. People only grieve because they don't understand all that and none of their religions explain it properly.'

'I know,' I snapped back. 'But, Puck, couldn't you see how upset she was? Sometimes you are so insensitive.'

'We were supposed to be having fun. Celebrating.'

'Well, you weren't there, Puck,' I snarled, blushing as I saw spit fly from my lips. 'She was hurting so much. I'm worried about her. We need to help her.'

'She's not our responsibility, Charlie. We were supposed to be looking after Jack. We've sorted him out. That's enough.'

'But . . .'

'You know what, Charlie, you're getting too emotionally attached. They're only humans, you know.'

'No, I'm not,' I protested.

We carried on arguing all the way home, but I knew inside Puck was right. I might have been a hundred times smaller than Leila, but I felt a deep, almost maternal concern for her. I wanted to take away her grief and make her see the joy in things again; it was such a waste that she was going to spend the rest of her life being so unhappy.

In the past, humans had always been a little alien to me; now I was beginning to have a better taste of them. I was realising just how much and how easily they suffered. It made me glad not to be human.

32
Katie

Oh God, what have I done?

Katie could feel another headache coming on. Normally she only liked to use herbal remedies – sipping hot water and taking an oil massage or a warm bath. But today she couldn't be bothered, she was too tired. She took two Nurofen from the cupboard. In fact, she'd had an almost permanent headache ever since Leila had found her and Henry kissing.

She recalled the scene with deep guilt, wondering how a few innocent kisses could have come to this. Of course, she'd expected their encounter after the restaurant to be the end of it – a one-off drunken mistake. But then, the next morning, he'd called her. At 8 a.m.

'You can't call me here!' she'd hissed. 'Have you forgotten I share a house with *Leila*? Are you mad?'

'We have to talk,' said Henry.

'We have to forget it happened,' Katie said firmly.

'Yeah, but we still need to talk.'

'What about?'

'Are you being weird with me.'

'I'm not – shit—' Katie could hear the creak of Leila's slippers on the stairs.

'OK, come to my house. Tomorrow?'

'Can't. It's Susie's school play.'

'The night after. Please. Come in the evening, Jack can babysit.'

'For God's sake, OK.'

'Great!' Henry's voice rose to the octave of the 'Hallelujah' chorus.

Right, thought Katie. *I'm going to tell him this is it. We had an accidental one-night stand. And that's it. I can't two-time him with Leila. No way.*

To make her point, she walked over wearing her oldest, most horrible clothes – the flowery summer dress she'd once bought in Oxfam, *reduced* to fifty pence because even old women wouldn't pay a pound for it. And a cardigan, woven with a picture of Dougal from the Magic Roundabout, which a friend had once given her for Susie (the friend in question had never had children and seemed to think that a size sixteen cardigan would suit five-year-old Susie somehow). She tied back her hair and left a smudge of mud on her face from gardening. There. She even considered not bothering to clean her teeth or spray on any deodorant, then figured she was taking it just a little too far.

And yet, and yet.

Little flickers of hope kept poking through from her subconscious like maggots. Visions of times with Henry. Silly, romantic visions, that belonged to adverts for fizzy drinks and chocolate bars – them both laughing over dinner, or driving through country fields, or signing for their first mortgage with shiny happy faces. And then the ads took on more erotic, post-9 p.m. watershed feel. Long, sexy kisses. Henry peeling off her T-shirt and . . .

oh . . . and . . . As she walked up the path to his house, she found herself flipping open her handbag and smearing on some cherry lipstick.

Katie, you're disgusting, she told herself, smearing it off again with a tissue.

As she knocked on his door, a big fat shark of nerves swam around in her stomach.

'Hi,' said Henry, opening the door. As he did, he spat milk at her. 'Oh, sorry.'

He was wearing pale blue jeans and a big, thick, green shirt. He was holding a bowl of shredded wheat in one hand.

'D'you want any?' he offered her.

'Er, no thanks.'

'I mean – I can get you a separate bowl.'

'Henry, it's six o'clock in the evening. I can't stay long, I haven't been able to find Jack and so Susie's gone to play with a school friend for a couple of hours. I think Jack's buggered off in my car.'

'OK. Right. Well. Let's go in. And . . . talk.'

In the daylight, Henry's room looked oddly disappointing. A few nights ago it had been filled with erotic shadows moving across the walls like Egyptian spirits. Now it just looked a mess. Books, dog-eared and crumpled, were everywhere. Coffee cups were lined up on the mantlepiece like ornaments – like a weird display in the Tate Modern. Katie removed *Kiss and Tell* by Alain de Botton from the chaise longue before sitting down.

Henry tactfully sat on the chair furthest away from her. The light fell on his face, highlighting the tired creases, the laughter lines fanning his eyes.

'Look – I'm really sorry about The Other Night (like a famous battle, it now had a proper name). It was a mistake. I'm sorry, I regret it all.'

303

'Oh,' said Katie.

She hadn't exactly pictured Henry getting down on one knee and proposing, but . . . well, she'd expected . . . at least a little bit of flattery, a bit of 'Oh Katie, you're so sexy, you were impossible to resist . . .'

But no. Of course Henry would never think like that. Because he was on a par with a male model, and Katie was much too . . . fat. A big fat mistake.

'It's just . . .' He paused. The sleeve-ends of his shirt had holes in them from where he kept dragging them over his wrists and he waggled a finger in the hole. 'Leila and I – God – my relationship is such a mess.'

'Do you want to talk about it?' Katie asked generously, swallowing back her hurt. Maybe it was the best thing, helping Henry and Leila to get back together. At last she could sleep with a clear conscience.

'Yes – well. I don't know where to begin. It's like going out with a brick wall. The beginning was great – you know, how you start off a relationship and it's all hunky-dory and dreamy sighs. I loved her. I really did. I wanted to be with her every second, I wanted to marry her. But the more I loved her, the more it seemed to annoy her. Y'know, if I phoned her up, she'd always answer with "Hi, Leila Clare here."' Henry enunciated her harsh, syllable-splitting manner of speech perfectly. 'She made me feel like a bank customer she wanted to get out of the way before moving on to the next. And if I bought her presents, she never liked them. I bought her this really expensive purple scarf once and she just looked at it and said, 'Oh, I've got one of those.' And she's so critical. About everything. Films and books and the government and people and all her exs. The world, according to Leila, is Crap. Except for her. And her cat, of course. I mean, if the cat had bought her that purple scarf, she would have

304

worn the bloody thing every day and bought Candida a whopper box of Munchies. I don't know. I didn't mind any of this in the beginning, I thought she was strong. And then I woke up one morning and realised I was just going out with a bitch. I remember it so clearly – it was the night before The Other Night, and I had all these strange dreams . . . kind of strange, sexy dreams about fairies and stuff, and I . . . I just . . . saw you and then I realised that I didn't even care that Leila hadn't turned up that night. My love had gone. It was as though I had a hole in my heart and every last drop had leaked away. I just thought – why bother?

'Mind you, I did see Leila after the restaurant and I thought to myself, *I'll break up with her tonight*. But she was all in a flurry – she had these wasp stings on her neck. Bizarre, I know. Anyway, she was upset and I comforted her, and we talked things through . . . and for that night I really felt perhaps it could work out between us. I genuinely felt some tenderness towards her. It was all quite touching.'

'Oh,' said Katie, thinking how very confused Henry was sounding. One minute he didn't like Leila, the next he did. 'So there is hope—'

'*Yes, but*,' Henry couldn't stop. 'When she'd gone, I lay on my bed feeling fed-up again. OK, so we'd had one lovely night together. But overall – you have to look at the long-term picture – she makes me feel crap. I can't be me. You know how different people bring out different parts of your personality? Some make you feel loud, some quiet, some serious, some jokey. Well, I never felt right with her. I felt as though I was trying out all these different Henrys – I'd be nice one day, nasty the next. Sorry, I sound like a schizo. But anyway. I don't know.'

'Well—'

★ ★

305

'She's just so much *work*. If Leila was a job, she'd be a job in the civil service, cleaning loos, for one pound twenty-five an hour. No job satisfaction, no pensions, no benefits.'

Katie burst into laughter.

'I'm serious. And yet I don't know what to do. She's like an oyster. You prise her open a bit and she just snaps shut again.' He clapped his palm shut in a theatrical motion.

'Phew,' said Katie. 'Have you told any of this to her?'

'Well . . .' Henry looked sheepish, as though the thought had only just occurred to him.

'Henry, this is silly. It sounds to me as if you've been storing this up inside. I mean, the first rule of any rela-tionship is communication.'

'Communication.' Henry rolled the word around his mouth uneasily, like a boiled sweet.

'Yes. At every step of the way, you need to say what you think, what you feel – and mean it. It's all about honesty. It's a cliché but it's true. Because ninety-nine per cent of our everyday relationships are based on lies. I mean, people generally do annoy each other, or misbehave, or have faults, or moan, or whatever. But if, every day, you actually told people what you really thought of them, the truth – well, at work you'd get the sack, you wouldn't have any friends, and if you told your relatives, you'd spend every Christmas Day alone. Most relationships do depend on lies and having to ignore the bad bits and just get on with it. But the best thing about a loving, roman-tic relationship should be that you can be yourself, and be honest, and say when life is getting you down, and show your weaknesses, and not pretend to be Superman. And if the other person upsets you, you can say so. I mean – say it nicely, of course. But with Leila, you've let it all build up, and in a way you've weakened the relationship by airbrushing over everything from the start, when in fact you should have said to Leila how you were feeling . . .' She suddenly trailed off. Who was she to lecture anyone about relationships when she had a failed marriage? 'Well – I speak from experience. We're often afraid of hurting the people we love with the truth, but in the end they respect us more, I think.'

'You're so lovely,' Henry suddenly said.

Katie blinked. Feeling uneasy, she picked up a book from the floor, *The Unbearable Lightness of Being*, and fingered the cover, avoiding his gaze.

'That bit you said about showing your weaknesses – that was lovely. I think Leila seems to hate all human weakness. But I mean, y'know, if I shouldn't lie, I shouldn't be lying to her about us, should I? I mean – about The Other Night?'

Good point. One which Katie had been trying to ignore.

She knew, just knew that Leila would never forgive her. She wanted to scrub The Other Night from their history books.

'Well, I also think . . . I think the main problem is . . .' Henry stopped.

'What?'

'. . . well, isn't you. You're you. And I think . . . I think I love you, not Leila.'

And that was when her resolve came to pieces.

Henry came over and started kissing her.

At first it felt surreal, as though it was happening to someone else. She was so used to avoiding relationships that her erotic hormones had shrivelled to a dry powder. She heard herself breathing shakily and it sounded odd; she felt herself parting her legs and then nervously clamping them shut again. She closed her eyes and suddenly thought of Susie on her knee, playing Tomb Raider, jiggling and screaming as they made it right through to the end. But then she looked up and saw Henry smiling, quite goofily, his eyes sweet with affection, and she let out a breathless laugh. He pushed her back down onto the chaise longue and she wriggled, found a book digging into her spine. Henry pulled it out; Proust's *In Search of Lost Time: Volume One*. 'Proust ought to have spent less time tying his brain in knots and more time doing this . . .' Henry joked clumsily, kissing her neck, and Katie giggled, her voice cracking as she felt his teeth on her skin.

More books were damaged as Katie slid underneath him; but neither cared. As they fumbled and moaned, tugging buttons and zips, the front cover of Rousseau's *Reveries of the Solitary Walker* was bent backwards and Dylan Evans' *Emotions* torn. Katie felt him slip down the straps of her dress, felt him lick the tip of her ear and whisper, 'You're so fucking gorgeous,' and his words squiggled through her, shot to her groin like excited sperm, and she moaned, running her hands over his back, arching her neck, feeling a dark bud of desire start to open, when Leila walked in.

Henry drove Katie home a couple of hours later. She spent the whole journey biting her nails in tense silence. Henry, feeling strained, put Vivaldi on. The violin flourishes danced around the car like annoying flies buzzing in her ear. She kept wanting to fling open the door and get out. For God's sake, how was it going to look if they pulled up at home and Leila saw them? As if they were a couple, that's what, as if their affair was more than just a mistaken moment of mad passion.

As he pulled up, she could hardly believe his nerve when he reached over and tried to kiss her again. He said something like, 'Katie, we need to talk about us,' in a terrible, pleading voice. Katie muttered something, scrambled out of the car, slammed the door, hurried up the steps, turned her key in the lock, slammed the front door and raced up the stairs to Leila's room. She knocked. No reply. She knocked again. Nothing. She'd ventured in. It was empty.

She noticed Candida sitting on the windowledge, pawing to get in. As Katie opened the window and Candida slunk in, damp-furred and purring, a breath of wind stirred a piece of paper on the dressing table. Katie picked it up. It was a guest list for Leila's dinner party. Her and Henry's names were sure to come off.

Katie barely slept. She tossed and turned, constant acupuncture pricks of guilt reminding her of what she'd done.

She had put the whole affair with Henry in perspective. Katie was a mother. She was twenty-nine. She didn't love Henry. He'd even offered to let them come and move in with him if Leila threw her out. But that was crazy. Henry was a lovely guy – sweet and kind and handsome. But she didn't love him.

Finally, at dawn, as milky light was flowing into the room, she heard the sound of a key, Leila's heavy foot-steps on the stairs. She lay there, arguing with herself. *Get up!* said her conscience, *comfort her!* But a more cowardly, small voice argued, *Leave her for a while, she needs time to calm down.* The cowardly voice won. Katie eventually got up and made breakfast, feeling all jumpy, waiting for Leila to come downstairs. But she didn't emerge. Feeling like a guitar string about to snap, Katie made her a mug of tea and left it outside her door with a soft knock. After returning from taking Susie to school, the tea was still there, covered with a huey film and with a dead fly floating on the top, its wings laced with stale milk.

Katie quickly realised that Leila was avoiding her. A temporary relief gave way to more nerves; she'd almost prefer to have the whole thing out in the open. She dreamed one night of being back in the council flat they'd lived in just after her divorce.

That tiny little flat in Birch Green. The walls all yellow from the last tenant's smoking, the stale smell of tobacco embedded in the grimy mattresses, the chipped windowsills. The kid who ran around at midnight screaming and smashing up cars.

If Leila chucked them out, they might well end up back there. After all, Leila had always generously offered Katie a ridiculously low rent of forty pounds a week. Elsewhere, it would be more like two hundred and forty.

And what about Susie? She was in a private school. Katie spent nearly all of Keith's mingey allowance on the fees – she felt it was worth it. Susie was finally putting down roots. But if Leila forced them to move, Susie would have to start all over again somewhere else.

Oh God, surely Leila wouldn't do that, would she?

33
Charlie

'So let me get this straight,' said Puck.

'Well – I—'

'Let me get this straight,' Puck repeated viciously. 'Let's recap on everything so far. First of all, Jack, who was supposed to fall in love with Katie as a result of our dream, fell for Leila. Henry, who could have enjoyed a perfectly happy relationship with Leila, who is tragically grieving over the death of her husband, then fell for Katie. Leila sees them together and decides she loves Henry. Henry still loves Katie, who still loves Jack. And NOW, Jack, who was supposed to bloody fall for Katie, is in love with *Henry*?'

'For God's sake, Puck,' I retorted furiously, my voice trembling with anger. 'Is this my fault? Whose idea was it to perform a spell in the first place, even though our magical abilities amount to little more than Paul Daniels with a pack of playing cards? And who went and put a spell on Henry without even asking me? You did. And whose idea was it to put a spider, of all things, in Jack's ear? I said it could go wrong, but did you listen? No. Anyway – we don't know for *sure* that he loves Henry. I just – well, we'll have to see when we find out what his thoughts are . . .'

Silence.

We were in Jack's bedroom, sitting on his bedpost, swinging our feet just above his head. He was having a late afternoon nap and I could feel his warm snores tickling the soles of my feet.

Puck and I had brought along some 'Perception Powder' – a concoction of dandelion and daisy pollen. According to *The Brahma Book of Spells* it made 'thoughts visible'. Whatever the hell that meant.

As I've mentioned before, fairies can sometimes hear human thoughts. But when humans are very upset, their stress can block their thoughts, coating them in a heavy tar of misery. I'd tried sitting by Jack's ear to listen to his, but it was just a mangled mess of broken sentences – a bit like listening to a radio station on a fuzzy frequency.

We drew the powder out from my little beetle-skinned handbag and sprinkled it around Jack's head. It sparkled in the air like Christmas tree glitter.

'Wow,' said Puck.

It was an extraordinary sight. Jack's thoughts were all visible. We could see *I'm hungry* in bright rainbow letters. And *HOW AM I GOING TO PAY MICK BACK?* in bright pink screaming-to-be-heard letters.

Puck reached out and caught the last sentence. It tried to wriggle away like a fish, but he sniffed it. Then he took a cautious nibble and gagged.

'Urgh – it tastes all bitter, like bile. Urgh.'

Curious, I caught the *I'm hungry* and took a little bite myself. It tasted all watery and hollow. As I swallowed it, I suddenly felt my stomach groan, rumbling for food.

312

'Hey, this is really weird!' I said. 'We are what we eat!'

'Oh God, look!' Puck nudged me, as *Henry* came wafting out from Jack's head. The letters were a soft pink, suspiciously romantic. 'Mmm, it tastes like rose petals and jam.'

And then I saw a dreadful sight.

The words *OH HENRY* floated out.

Surrounded by tiny hearts.

I nibbled one, stunned. It tasted beautiful – like candy sugar and liqueur chocolate, like melted honey and golden syrup, like sweet peachy wine and hot treacle.

It tasted of love.

Puck and I just stood there, thoughtful crumbs on our lips, swallowing hard.

Oh God. Of course. Who was the first person Jack had seen? Henry. And Puck and I were so, so stupid. Sex didn't matter; whether Jack touched a man or woman, a spell was a spell. Love was love. We'd assumed, foolishly, that there would be some kind of logic to the love potion the spider was injecting into his veins. But love had no reason. You only had to look at half the couples in London to know that. So why had we assumed that Jack would discriminate, that he wouldn't fall for Henry the moment their fingers met.

We started arguing again. Puck blamed me; I blamed him.

'Well, what are we going to do?' I cried. 'What do you suggest now, Puck – buying a lesser-spotted sexy hairy elephant or something?'

Puck glared at me; I glared at him. Then, suddenly, we both burst into wild, tear-streaming laughter.

Despite my panic, I'm ashamed to admit that there was an odd feeling of pleasure in my stomach. I suppose

I was enjoying the crisis; I suppose I was relishing the thought of Puck and I having to brainstorm all over again; I suppose a tiny, wicked part of me thought the whole thing was hilarious.

'Maybe we should make Katie and Leila lesbians too,' I spluttered. 'Perhaps everyone would be happier that way.'

'OK,' said Puck, still giggling. 'Sober up, Charlie! Let's see if *The Brahma Book of Spells* carries any solutions.'

Luckily, there was indeed a footnote in small print on 'What To Do If The Brazilian Long-toothed Sexy Hairy Love Spider Is Inserted Into The Wrong Heart'.

In such a case, it is vital that the spider is removed *as soon as possible*. The spider's poison increases in toxicity hour by hour, so the longer the spider resides in the heart, the more powerful the passion will be. The only solution is to flush the spider from the body. In order to achieve this, a simple but potent laxative needs to be digested by the human, to pull the spider out from the heart through to the anus, where it will be expelled from the body.

'You see,' said Puck, with a wicked smile on his face, 'for everything in nature there is always an opposite. For every poison, there is always an antidote. It just means poor old Jack is going to have to spend much of the evening on the toilet.'

The book concluded:

You will know that the spider has been expelled from the body when you see and hear a large purple explosion from the anus, like a small bomb going off.

By the time Jack had woken up from his afternoon nap, it was six o'clock and Puck and I were fully armed.

With wonderful irony, Jack decided to cook himself baked beans on toast. We tipped in the laxatives as he stirred them in the pan.

Unfortunately, he didn't seem to be very hungry. He flicked through a copy of *Loaded*, ate a few mouthfuls, went to the bin and *threw his meal away*. A few globby beans rolled down the black plastic sack on to the lino. Jack threw his plate into the sink and went into his bedroom.

'Shit!' said Puck.

'Well, he ate some, didn't he?' I pointed out.

The question was: had he eaten enough?

In Jack's room, Puck started to get agitated. Jack had been to the loo once but there was no spider. Now Jack was lying on his bed in the dark, giving long, depressed sighs, fingering a small white cellophane packet in his hand. I kept getting strange vibes from it, the type I normally felt if I was near to a goblin: a feeling of ugliness, rottenness, evil.

Jack put the white packet down on the table and went back to the loo again. Puck let out a laugh of relief and fluttered after him.

'C'mon, Charlie!' he called, but I lingered, fingering the packet. There was a tiny tear in the left corner, a single crystal loose. I pressed my finger to it, pushed it against my gum. A bitter feeling sizzled in my mouth, so strong I gagged and spat the crystal out, retching and shaking. Cocaine.

Was it a reaction or a vision? I suddenly saw a night-mare stream of actions and reactions. A dealer. A dark pub. A young girl, thirteen years old, blonde plaits. Experimenting. Impressing her boyfriend. A bad reaction, hospital corridors, funerals, tears. All in a three-second rush of image and feeling.

What's he doing? I fretted. *Why the hell is Jack, a perfectly nice guy, selling drugs?*

Of course, I knew. He still owed Mick three thousand pounds from that disastrous snooker game. Shit.

In a panic, I picked up the cellophane packet and flew out to the kitchen. Jack had left the cupboards open and I searched wildly. There were jams, marmalade, syrup, Typhoo tea, coffee and – ah! There! Sugar. A great big bag. I flew up and tried to tug it, but it was like a ten-ton truck, far too heavy for me to lift. I pushed it in despair and it suddenly flew on to its side with a bang.

Whoosh! A stream of sugar came pouring out.

I watched the sugar waterfalling over the floor, then picked up the cellophane packet and carefully tore it open, picking at the tape with my teeth. I carried it to the sink and poured out the cocaine, sprinkling some over the taps by accident. I smoothed out the cellophane over the kitchen surface and brushed the spilt sugar into it, until it looked roughly the same size and shape. Then I sealed it up again. It looked a little messy, but nothing too suspicious.

Back in the bedroom, I put the package down on the bedside table just as Jack came back in, looking rough. Puck looked even worse.

'Did it come out?' I asked.

'No,' said Puck. 'No, it bloody didn't. Fuck, Charlie, he doesn't even do it . . . he just sits on the loo and groans and nothing comes out.'

'Well, it's got to eventually,' I said brightly.

'I don't think so.' Puck looked down at Jack, who was lying on the bed, groaning and rubbing his stomach. 'He's fucked, Charlie; we're fucked, everything's fucked.'

34
Jack

Dear Mr Heinz. Jack was composing an extremely angry letter of complaint in his head that night as he sat up in bed, groaning. *I am writing to enquire just what the fuck you put in your baked beans . . .* He knew that he'd feel better tomorrow, that he'd never get round to writing it or sending it, but it made him better. Marginally.

God, what was wrong with him? His stomach felt as though it was trying to regurgitate itself; his head felt as though it had been battered with a sledgehammer.

He tried to ease the pain by pushing up the pillows behind his back, but a terrible pain slashed his groin again. He leaned back; horror stories from newspapers, of live toads found in salad packets, rats' tails in burgers and earthworms in chicken nuggets, flitted through his brain.

'Katie . . .' he croaked ineffectually towards the closed door.

He remembered then that she was staying over at her friend Kerry's tonight, where Susie would have a sleepover with her school-friend Amelia. Which only left Leila, and Jack couldn't see her bringing in water and paracetamols with a Mother Teresa smile on her face. He'd have to make the long trip to the kitchen himself.

He pushed back the covers and swung his feet out, but the slightest movement sent an odd wobbly pain through him, as though his body was a precariously balanced pack of playing cards about to spin apart at any moment. He tried to stand up but collapsed on to the floor instead. He could feel his sweaty forehead pressed against the brittle carpet. Someone help, he mumbled, but the only result was fluff in his mouth.

He closed his eyes, suffering another wrench of pain. *I'm just going to lie here and fucking well die.*

And then, opening his eyes a slit, he saw his mobile, lying with his usual random messiness on the floor. His fingers crawled across to it; he dialled.

'Hello?' A brisk, polite voice.

'Henry?' he wheezed. 'It's me . . . Jack . . . I'm dying . . . I think I'm fucking dying . . .'

★

Hours seemed to pass before Henry came over. Jack lay in a kind of daze, but the shriek of the doorbell stirred him back into consciousness. He heard Leila's footsteps down the stairs, her surprised 'Oh Henry!' and then the pinched disappointment in her voice when he said he was here to see Jack. And then the door opened and two faces were looking down at him, Henry looking troubled and Leila gaping over his shoulder.

'Oh God!' she mumbled. 'What's happened to him?'

Jack saw two pairs of feet moving towards him: a pair of glossy red heels and a pair of sexy, slightly worn-in brogues, plus the black hems of smartly pressed trousers. Then there were hands moulding into his body and the floor was rolling away from him, his ribs were hitting the mattress, and he was groaning into his pillow. The covers

319

were being pulled up over him. A face appeared, red-lipped and narrowed-eyed, a taloned hand smoothed back the hair from his forehead.

'Jack, what's the matter, have you been taking drugs?'

'Baked beans,' he moaned. 'I'm sick. Bloody baked beans . . . must have been . . . off . . .'

A pause. Then Henry's voice, kind and compassionate, saying, 'I'll look after him.'

'Well . . . well . . .' Leila spluttered.

'Don't worry, really,' said Henry. 'I'll get him some water and he'll be fine, then I'll go off home. Just a little food poisoning, I had the same last week. Prawns, past their sell-by date.'

Jack watched them out of the corner of his woozy eye. They stood, awkwardly, looking at the walls, ceiling, shoes, anywhere but each other.

Strange, thought Jack. They've obviously had a tiff.

'Well, I'm going to bed,' said Leila, looking exhausted. 'I've got the dinner party tomorrow.' She gave Jack a look, as if it was outrageously rude that he had chosen to be sick the night before her party. 'I have to get up at six, to go into work, rush home at lunchtime, clean the place, set up the table, organise the cooking, everything. I have twelve guests coming. I need to sleep—'

'It's OK,' said Henry. 'Go to bed. I'll make sure he's OK.'

Leila turned, letting out a huffy breath. But as she reached the door, she looked back and said in a small voice, 'Well, get well soon', though the words and her gaze seemed directed towards Henry.

Henry went out to get a glass of water, which he put on the bedside table. He drew up a chair. Silence. Jack felt waves of heat from sickness and embarrassment coursing over his body. He wished Katie was here; she'd

320

be laughing and bringing him grapes and old Monty Python tapes. Henry was just making him feel worse, sitting there in awkward silence, tapping his fingernails against the chair. *Tap, tap, tap*. In Jack's sick state, the noise was magnified to the sound of a hammer. *Tap, tap, tap*.

'Could you stop doing that?' Jack hissed.

'Sorry,' said Henry. He sounded hurt. Then: 'I was just thinking up songs.'

'What?' Jack whispered.

'Songs. For your funeral. You're dying, right?'

Jack curled his hand into a weak fist, but there was a smile edging at his lips.

'Fuck off.' Pause. 'What songs?'

'Oh, "Angel" by Robbie Williams.' Henry hummed a few bars in his exquisite voice, then trailed off.

'You play Robbie Williams at my funeral, I'll kill you.'

They looked at each other and burst into laughter.

Jack's laugh caught in his throat, turned into a coughing fit. Jack sat up, choking, as Henry patted him on the back and handed him the glass of water. He took a few sips, his eyes watering. Henry kept his hand on his back. Jack felt an odd tingle shiver down his spine; Henry rubbed lightly. It reminded Jack of being a little kid in the bath, with yellow ducks and wrinkled skin, the way his mum would rub his back when he had wind. He held the glass tight. He felt Henry's caress move a little higher, to the top of his spine, and then to the back of his neck, where his hair licked the skin. Henry lightly brushed his fingers over the fine hairs. Jack savoured the sensation for a moment, the compassion in his touch; then something wild and angry rose up in his chest and he flinched, quickly flicking Henry's hand away. Henry started; Jack's hand wobbled and a splash of water spilt on to the bed,

321

leaving a spreading dark stain. *Like semen*, Jack found himself seething, as if he'd just ejaculated.

'God, are you OK?'

'Fine.' Jack thumped the glass down on the bedside table, sploshing a few more drops. He pulled the covers up tight around his head.

'The sheet's all wet.' Henry rubbed the damp patch.

Jack could feel an unexpected erection rearing and he gripped the covers even more tightly.

'I'm fine!' Jack rolled on to his side, his head throbbing. 'Can you please leave me in peace?'

He heard Henry mutter something like, 'Sure . . . you just sleep . . . I'll be here if you need anything . . .'

Like what? Jack thought with ferocious sarcasm. *A blow job? What are you implying, you faggot?*

Jack closed his eyes, trying to force sleep. But a fog of pain whirled behind his eyelids. His body kept alternating between icy cold, teeth chattering, and boiling hot, as if his chest was an overheated car engine. As a fresh wave of sweat swept over him, he was dying to push down the covers and feel the cool air. But he still had a bloody erection – it had to be his nerves. And then what? It might be dark but what if Henry noticed? God, he'd think Jack was some kind of nancy. When Jack was sure that if there was a nancy around here, it wasn't him.

Something funny was going on.

Jack knew sod all about gays. The only image he had of a gay man was a stereotype: a thin man with a squeaky voice who liked tight tank-tops. When he'd first met Henry at university, he'd been convinced he was gay – his effeminate build, fine blonde hair, slightly shy, girlish smile, floppy wrists, elegant manner, and the worrying way he preferred watching a Walt Disney to, for example, a Bruce Lee.

But Henry was straight. Or so he said. Well, ninety per cent straight, he'd affirmed later. Jack remembered once reading a copy of Stephen Fry's *The Liar* and asking Henry if it was true to life. Henry, who'd been to a private boys' school, had blushed and muttered something about 'experimentation' and 'prefects' and 'peer pressure'. Jack hadn't pushed for any more details; he really did not want to know. And Henry seemed normal; he'd been out with pretty, if slightly odd, girls. He'd had a solid, long-term relationship.

But what if, what if, for all these years, Henry had been hiding, repressing, or even nurturing a secret lust for Jack, which was finally starting to show itself?

Jack tried to sleep, to push the idea away, but he couldn't help flicking through the files of his memory. The more he thought about it, the more his imagination ballooned – showers they'd taken together, football matches, punches on the shoulder, Henry buying Jack pints. OK, so Jack was always broke *but* . . . And what about that time, that student play, where Henry had worn a dress and played an insane Lady Macbeth, carrying around a Spot the Dog? Ah, they'd all laughed at the time, *but* . . .

Jack wasn't homophobic, gays were fine, everyone had a right to their own choice without ridicule or prejudice, but when it came to Henry and him . . . well, that was sick. Sick, sick, sick. Jack could taste the bile in his throat.

He nestled in bed, trying to shut it all out, but as sleep drew him down a panicky thought flicked it suddenly away. What if, when he fell asleep, Henry reached out . . . and . . . drew back the covers . . . Shit. Just why had he called Henry up and asked him over here? What signals did that send? Jack was a grown man; he could look after himself. Why was he calling Henry and asking him to be a nursemaid? Jack felt his body tense. Well, if Henry tried anything, *anything* on, Jack would bloody turn round and sock him one right in the face. God, it was disgusting, it was vile, imagining the two of them together . . .

'You – you – if you think you can – you scum!' Jack suddenly burst out.

'What?' Henry, who'd been nodding off in his chair, started awake.

'Go – just get out – I know what you're sitting there thinking.' Jack clutched his feverish head. 'Get out.'

'What?'

'I'm not sick, I'm fine, just go, go. Now, you gay fairy; get out.'

'A fairy?' Henry blinked, his elegant eyebrows knotting. For a moment he stared at Jack, and Jack shrank back against the covers, a blush heating his face. 'No – I – no. What's all this about?'

'You know. Just – you hanging about – you – get out. JUST GET OUT!' Jack felt his sore throat rasp with hoarse anger. 'GO!'

'OK, I'm going, I'm going.' Henry stood up, shaking his head in disbelief. 'You're just sick.'

'Really?' Jack coughed. 'I think you're the one who's sick. Bye, you faggot-who's-trying-to-take-advantage-of-his-sick-friend.'

Henry's lips tightened. Then he left, slamming the door.

Jack sank back into his pillows, drenched in sweat. God, that had been a narrow escape. He heard the crash of the front door – good, he'd gone. He turned off the lamp.

And yet, as he lay in the darkness, in a cold sweat now, he wished he hadn't asked Henry to go. A funny part of him wanted him back, sitting in the chair, watching over him while he slept; in a funny sort of way, he missed him.

35
Henry

B-rring, b-rring, b-rring, b-rring . . .

Henry fingered the row of twenty-pence pieces on top of the yellow plastic phone.

B-rring b-rring . . .

He knew it was stupid. Katie had asked him not to call her. Leila might answer; in which case, he was poised to slam down the phone.

B-rring b-rring . . .

She wasn't in anyway. Yet he didn't want to hang up. Just in case.

B-rring b-rring . . .

Henry sighed and put down the phone.

He checked his antique watch, thinking for the thousandeth time that he must get a new strap; the black leather was now held together by a safety pin. It was 3:34 p.m. He was sitting in the hallway of the Caledonian theatre. Rehearsals would start in five minutes.

Henry really didn't feel up to it. He'd taken his lines for *A Midsummer* into the bath with him last night after he'd got back from seeing Jack. Henry normally loved a good hot bath while he learned his lines, letting the words seep into his head like steam. He had an excellent memory and normally remembered them straight-off. But they'd just slipped in and out of his head like butter. The bath reminded him of Katie; he kept picturing her in the water with him, sitting behind him, her soft breasts pressed against his spine, her beautiful, slightly pudgy hands soaping his shoulders.

She wouldn't even speak to him at the moment. Henry couldn't believe it. Life was following the same tracks all over again – Katie had become Leila and somehow he'd turned himself into a victim once more, a Petrarchan lover tortured by an icy mistress.

'Henry!' Emma came strolling down the corridor in her fur-lined black jacket, her hair wrapped up in a pink tye-dye scarf, her blonde extensions trailing down her back. 'Come on! Rehearsals are NOW, you moron!'

Emma was playing Titania.

The rehearsals were unexpectedly eventful.

Eventful because they were even worse than Henry could possibly have imagined. He stumbled through his part like a drunkard on a tight-rope, trying to gain a foothold, to cling to the script, then realising he was in the wrong place and having to start all over again. The director, Jan, was hoarse from shouting at him by the end. Several actors kept giggling, which started Henry off, and a kind of schoolroom hysteria swept through them like a contagious cough.

Unexpectedly, Jack had turned up.

He was sitting a few rows back, between a tower of scripts and a seat festooned with wigs, which resembled a pile of multi-coloured octopuses. He was looking well – he seemed oblivious to his insane moment of fever last night when he'd inexplicably accused Henry of being a fairy. He even helped Henry out by mouthing some words in the right places.

But when Jack started to get restless, and put on one of the blonde wigs, pursing his lips girlishly, the whole stage dissolved into open hysterics.

'For God's sake, Henry, sort it out!' Emma screamed.

'Sorry,' said Henry sheepishly.

'All right – I give up for the day,' said Jan, giving Henry a filthy look.

Jack came back to Henry's house. He was in an odd, hyperactive, giggly mood. He kept trying to force Henry to come out to a nightclub with him to pick up some girls. But Henry hated clubs and he was far too knackered and, despite his smiley veneer, upset from Jan's tirade. Then Jack refused Henry's offer of a cup of tea, saying he wanted to get pissed and watch a movie. So Jack went off to the video shop and Henry asked him to get something gentle and romantic. Jack returned twenty minutes later with a six-pack and a video, which he furtively removed from under his jumper. It looked like a blank tape.

'The guy at the video counter's a friend of mine,' said Jack, grinning. 'He's been promising to let me borrow this for ages. It's called *Food for Thought*.'

'What – is it some kind of cookery programme?' Henry asked hopefully, thinking of Nigella Lawson.

'No – it's porn, Henry, you mug!' Jack laughed, gently whacking him on the head with the cassette. 'I'm feeling randy.'

Henry winced; he'd been looking forward to being consoled by pleasant scenes of Italy, beautiful young English girls, and elegant dialogue. Oh well . . .

'Come on.' Jack bounded upstairs, the six-pack rattling.

'Er – there's a TV and video in the living room,' Henry called up.

'Yeah, but can we use the ones in your bedroom. The TV screen's better.'

Henry blinked – er, what? The screen in his living room had been bought along with his new DVD player, a large glossy black affair that made you feel as though you had a cinema right in your own home. The TV upstairs was a small portable with an aerial that had to be twisted into the shape of a weird scarecrow in order to pick up a crackly reception. But Jack was already upstairs, so, anyway . . .

He went into the kitchen and picked up two glasses for the beer – a pint glass for Jack and a small beaker for him. Henry hated pint glasses – he found them too fat and clumsy.

Upstairs, Henry heard the tinkle of Jack going to the toilet. God, his bedroom was a tip. The bed was rumpled and the blue, crinkly curtains were still dragged shut, as if he was ashamed of letting the sun look in.

Jack came back, tugging his zip, to find Henry bending over, stacking up a pile of old books. *God, he has a cute butt*, Jack thought, then shook himself.

'It's so weird.' Jack slotted in the video, 'I just had a pee and I swear my piss was kind of . . . *purple*.'

'Purple?' Henry flopped on the bed, facing the TV. 'Have you been eating beetroot? Hey, you were pretty ill last night, Jack.'

'Yeah, that was weird.' Jack shrugged, joining him on the bed, shoulder to shoulder. The tape was clearly a bootleg; Jack fast-forwarded through the silly advert with two bad actors at the beginning, warning you not to buy dodgy videos for fifty pence from market traders, and through the previews for interestingly titled films such as *Nurses at Night: Part III* and *My Wet Pussy Meets New York*. Porn really wasn't Henry's cup of tea and he was mildly embarrassed. But even so, lying there on the bed and sipping beer, Henry felt a warm relaxation ooze through his body. Suddenly he had a rush of affection for Jack. He'd succeeded in taking his mind off Katie. Women were so complicated, as friends or lovers, twisting you in cat's cradles of emotion; friendship between two blokes was simple, easy, no frills, no pretences, just lounging on a bed enjoying a relaxed evening.

Frequently when they watched videos together, Henry was slightly irritated and amused by Jack's inability to keep quiet. Jack was so lively, he tended to start chatting halfway through a film, so Henry had to keep telling him to shut up, or else Jack would shout at the hero during unbearably tense moments in the plot. Today, however, Henry was thankful for Jack's restlessness and chatter; he really had no desire to focus on the current sex scene, which consisted of two girls wearing aprons (and nothing else) having an erotic food fight in a kitchen. *Tacky*, thought Henry, wincing.

'Are you turned on?' Jack asked playfully, as he swigged back his beer.

'Are you kidding?' Henry rolled his eyes.

'I wonder if women really like having beef stuffing licked off their breasts,' said Jack, shooting Henry a sideways glance.

'Not something I've ever tried, being a vegetarian.'

'Still, ice cream might be good,' Jack mused.

'I've tried ice cream.'

'You're kidding?'

'Well – it was with my ex, Alice. She went through

this phase of being very bored, sexually. So she wanted to experiment. We were making love on her parents' bed one evening when . . .'

'Go on.'

Henry blushed. 'She asked me to go down and get some ice cream, and spoon it up her – you know, and lick it. So I ran down, but there was none there. So I grabbed a piece of rhubarb instead, thinking it might make a nice vibrator. Unfortunately, it got stuck. I couldn't pull it out, it sort of got wedged.'

'Shit!' Jack nearly spat out his beer.

'I know. Alice was livid. She had to call her mother and say she'd accidentally put the rhubarb in thinking it was a tampon. Her mother had to get it out with oil and every-thing. It was so embarrassing.'

'Rhubarb and tampons – easy mistake to make.' Jack was still shaking with laughter.

A brief silence. Squeals from the TV set.

'Women,' Jack sighed, scrumpling up his can. 'Who needs them? Sometimes I think they're so much hassle I may as well just give up and become gay.'

Henry choked on his beer, swallowing it back violently, feeling bubbles fizz up into his nose. Jack – gay! What a thought. He pictured Jack in a London club, dressed in a tight pink T-shirt and cool shades, bobbing to Kylie. He shook his head, smiling.

'Can I ask you something, Henry?' Jack suddenly looked serious, a rosy blush warming his cheeks. Henry nodded, watching Jack make circles with his forefinger on the bedspread. In the background, Henry was vaguely aware of two men, one tall and blonde, one dark and short, tearing each other's clothes off, shirt buttons tic-tacing to the floor. Come to think of it, Henry noted, there hadn't been any heterosexual sex in

330

the film so far at all – just girls and girls and boys and boys. Jack was always saying he wished he could have a threesome with two women; he was obviously hoping for some lesbian orgy, the pervert, Henry thought with a smile.

'So,' Jack continued in a rush, 'is there anyone, you, er, fancy at the moment, Henry?'

'Me?' Henry jumped, thinking of Katie. He paused for a moment. The beer had softened his inhibitions and he wondered if he should tell Jack everything. But then he remembered Katie's sharp words: '*Henry, I don't want you to tell anyone about us, OK? Not just for my sake, but for Susie's.*' And there was no guarantee Jack wouldn't go back and say something.

'Er . . . well . . .'

'There is, isn't there?' There was a sharp, rough edge to his voice as if he'd swallowed sandpaper. 'Who? Who?' Jack demanded passionately.

Jack was looking at him with such fiery eyes that for a moment Henry fretted: *Has Jack guessed anyway about Katie?* Jack was very protective of Katie; Henry hoped he wasn't about to be thumped.

'Er, yes – Jan, Jan,' Henry improvised wildly.

'Jan?' Jack spat out.

'Er – she's the director for the play I'm in, you met her today,' Henry said uneasily. He hoped he wasn't about to start a rumour.

Behind them on the video, the dark man was now kneeling down and slowly licking cream from the blonde man's penis.

'Oh – her. Her,' Jack realised. 'What, that small Japanese dwarf? That bitch? She's foul. What the fuck do you see in her?'

Henry was taken aback by Jack's aggression.

331

'Well – she's pretty, and, er, short,' Henry said randomly.

'Short? You'll squash her to death in bed. She'll be Flat Stanley – afterwards you'll have to plump her back up again.'

'Well, maybe I could go for someone a bit taller . . .'

'Oh no, Henry, you don't want a tall woman – it's like shagging a giraffe, I'm telling you. So . . . so . . . does Jan like you back?' Jack's voice dropped into an intense whisper, as he savagely twisted a ringpull between his fingers.

Maybe Jack fancies her, Henry thought in bewilderment, *maybe this is why he's going so weird on me*.

'Er – no,' said Henry hastily. 'She doesn't. Look, I'm not all that hot on her, really – it was just a passing crush, not worth mentioning to Katie, or anyone. Actually, please do promise not to tell anyone because she's engaged to Rupert – you know, the guy on stage? The one playing Demetrius? Tall, red-haired?'

'Oh him. Yeah, he was very handsome,' Jack mused.

'That's very sweet of you, Jack,' Henry said playfully, smiling.

'Don't worry, he's not nearly as handsome as you,' Jack said quickly, then, seeing Henry's startled expression, added hurriedly, 'I mean, from Jan's point of view. I'm sure she lies awake at night fantasising about you. Er, also from a general point of view, you are, er, so – so – so – aesthetically pleasing, Henry. Your hair is wonderful, it's like . . .' Jack struggled momentarily, fingering the air as if trying to pluck out a metaphor. 'It's like pure gold, pure honey.'

'Oh, thanks,' Henry was faintly cheered. Normally Jack, who was so competitive, could be a bit derogatory about Henry's looks or talents. Only jokingly, of course, but the sting was still there.

Jack got up and started burrowing in Henry's wardrobe. He gaped at the hundreds of shoes, and the ties hanging like a row of tropical bird plumes and the designer suits in grim grey and charcoal and black, from the days Henry worked in the City before becoming an actor.

'Can I try this on?' Jack asked impulsively, pulling out a suit from the wardrobe.

'If you must.' *And I expect I'll be the one who has to tidy up*, Henry thought with a weary sigh, watching Jack eagerly tear off his shirt.

Jack looked good in the suit – suddenly he appeared taller, leaner, like a model in a Calvin Klein ad. Then he tried on a white suit and a panama. He tugged at something from a hanger which swirled out like a silky canary. Henry explained it was a cravat ('You what!' exclaimed Jack).

As Jack carried on messing about, Henry yawned sleepily, his eyes travelling back to the video. Now the two men were making love on a table. A close-up: the dark man's hair was slick with sweat; the blonde leaned over him, lovingly licking his ear. Henry watched curiously. Next the screen flicked on to two nurses and, despite the crudity, Henry felt a slight erection hardening in his trousers. Self-conscious, he sat up, looking over to see Jack standing in front of his mirror, struggling to tie the cravat.

'Could you help me tie this, darling?' Jack feigned a camp voice and a floppy wrist. 'Wow, I love playing fancy dress.'

'Jack, what has got into you today, are you insane?' Henry laughed, sliding off the bed and coming over. As he struggled with the cravat his nail accidentally cut into Jack's skin. Jack shivered, and moved closer to Henry.

333

And suddenly the air felt ripe, the molecules sparked with fire. Henry swallowed uneasily. Jack's face loomed even closer, and all Henry could see was the crooked shape of Jack's nose, a nose knocked out of shape from a drunken fight one night at university with a jealous boyfriend enraged to find Jack had had a one-night stand with his girlfriend. *Bump!* – their noses knocked and they broke off laughing. And then Jack planted a kiss at the corner of Henry's mouth, pressed his lips against him. *I'm kissing Jack!* Henry thought in amazement. *No – he's kissing me.*

'Jack!' Henry exploded, pushing him away. He wiped his mouth with the back of his hand. Yuk.

'Sorry – did I taste of beer?' Jack clamped his hand over his mouth.

And then a smile started to quiver on Henry's lips. Jack was obviously having a laugh, pulling his leg. Jack loved nothing more than a good wind-up.

'Ha,' Henry chuckled. 'Taste of beer? God, for a moment there you had me. Yes, you did! You tasted disgusting.'

'Did I?' Jack paled. 'Oh no, and I wanted our first kiss to be so perfect. Shall I go and clean my teeth?'

'No, don't worry.' Henry's laughter died away. Jack was looking worryingly convincing. He was starting to freak Henry out a bit, actually.

'I – I need the toilet,' Henry said, feeling that a little space might be a good thing.

He tried to make for the door. Unfortunately, Jack was standing in the way, his eyes sparkling wickedly. Henry darted to the right; Jack darted to the right. Henry sprang to the left; so did Jack. Henry clenched his fists, trying to be jolly and hide his irritation.

'Jack, this is, er, very funny, but I do need the loo. So . . can we, er, stop joking about?'

'You're right, Henry, this isn't a joke,' said Jack with frightening vehemence. Then he reached up and gently stroked the back of his hand against Henry's cheek. 'I wanted to sit down and talk it all through with you first, but my passion overwhelmed me. Honestly, this isn't about a one-night stand, I swear. It's just – your lips! They're so, so, kissable; they look like apple slices baking in the sun . . .'

'Jack, what the hell are you talking about?' Henry spluttered, backing away nervously, but the next thing he knew, Jack had tripped him up and he was on the bed with Jack's heavy weight on top of him.

'Jack – get off!' Henry tried to stand but Jack had pinned him down and was starting to tickle him. 'Ow! Oh, ow, Jack, that's enough. Let me up. Ow, stop it! Look, I'll do anything. I'll buy you another beer! You can have my suit, just STOOOOOPPPP!'

'OK – but only if you—'

'Just get off me!' Henry squealed as Jack's fingers dug deeper into his ribs.

'Only if you kiss me again. One kiss is worth a million suits.'

'No way. What the hell has got into you, Jack?'

Jack's face dropped and he brushed the tips of his fingers against Henry's forehead, then, catching Henry unawares, he leaned quickly down . . . and . . . *kissed* . . . him. Again!

'Jack!' Henry screeched, rolling his head aside, but Jack only trailed a stream of bud kisses across his cheek and jaw. 'God, you're disgusting! Get off! What the fuck's got into you? Just get off!'

'Men always say no when they mean yes.' Jack smiled lovingly.

'Jack! Get off! Jeez, is your testosterone in such over-drive that you have to leap on me?' Henry tried to joke

335

again, but Jack showed no signs of loosening his grip and he was twice as strong as Henry. 'Jack – now – I mean it. I am going to get *cross*! Let. Me. Go.'

'God, you're so sexy when you're angry!' Jack laughed, as if it was all a fun game and Henry was playing along.

And then the penny finally dropped. Henry looked up into Jack's eyes. And he saw a look of complete tenderness. And the realisation hit him like a punch in the stomach: *Jack really is serious* . . .

Henry was so shocked by the revelation that his best friend was seriously trying to get off with him that a surge of brute force rippled through his body.

'Jack – just fuck off! Stop it! Get your hands off me and get out!' Henry yelled. He didn't care about using force any more and he shoved Jack away violently, rolled aside, off the bed, and stood up, smoothing his ruffled hair.

Jack stood up too. His fingers trembled like a butterfly's wings.

Silence. They stood and stared at each other. Jack's eyes were naked with hurt; Henry's blinking with bewilderment.

Behind them, the video finished. The last credits rolled. The screen went blank and the video whirred to a stop.

'Look,' Henry said, more quietly, 'I've had enough, all right? I'd just like you to leave.'

'Well – fine,' said Jack furiously. 'Fine. I mean – I'm entirely to blame – making a move when you've been leading me on all day! Don't deny it. The way you kept staring at me flirtily in rehearsals, and buying me beer. OK – I bought the beer – but *you* brought the glasses and you got me up here in your bedroom, wearing those sexy clothes—'

336

Sexy! Henry looked down at his blue jeans and crisp mint-green shirt incredulously.

'But – no – this is fine. I've got other friends to meet anyway,' Jack snarled, his voice catching with tears. He hurriedly stooped down, bundling up his clothes against his chest. Henry blinked in disbelief as a small white packet fell from the pocket of Jack's jeans; Jack's fingers curled around it, his eyes flitted back to Henry, then he quickly scooped it into his palm.

'Jack, where are you going?'

Jack was already walking towards the door.

'Jack?' Henry hurried out on to the landing. 'For God's sake, man, you're wearing a white suit and a panama.'

Jack was already storming down the stairs.

'*Jack!*'

Jack paused, halfway down, and gazed up at Henry. 'I'm just going to meet some guys. I'm sorting out that stupid bet I made a while back, just some money. Is that OK with you? OK that I'm meeting some *guys*? Or, no, maybe you're thinking I'm getting involved in some kind of gay gang-bang? Can't you just give me a break?'

'You're going to meet some guys? In that outfit?'

'So what? I'm so sorry, you sad, cruel-hearted, narrow-minded, man-hating git, but yes, I am. I like it and I feel like wearing it.' Jack clattered down to the door.

'JACK!' Henry came bounding down the stairs two at a time, only just catching him in time. Jack paused on the doorstep, chewing his lip sulkily, his dark eyes cloudy with confusion and desire.

Henry clung to the door-frame nervously. 'I, er, I think maybe we should talk about this? I don't know what's going on – but – look, just come back after your meeting, OK? Let's sit down and talk it all through.'

'You want me to come back?' Jack's face lit up with

fresh hope. 'We can talk about us. Maybe things will make more sense if we discuss it.'

Oh God, thought Henry.

'Well, great!' said Jack, all boyish eagerness now. 'I'll be really quick – just ten minutes. Don't go anywhere or do anything. Promise?'

'Promise.'

Jack started to walk away, but, sparked by a flare of passion, he turned back and tried to kiss Henry goodbye. Henry hastily turned it into an Italianate kiss-on-both-the-cheeks, cringing as a neighbour strolled past with their dog, shooting him a shocked look. Jack, oblivious, broke into a tender smile.

As he watched Jack walk off, a jaunt in his step, the sunset shiny against that ludicrous suit, the jeans swinging from one hand, Henry felt deeply uneasy. Something was very wrong with Jack.

Back in the house, Henry showered vigorously and slapped on aftershave, but he couldn't stop worrying about Jack and what he was up to. Jack – gay! It was absurd. What was the world coming to? Next it would be snowing in June, or Clinton would declare he was becoming a monk.

36
Jack

Jack couldn't quite believe what he was doing, either.

Here he was, sitting in a pub, looking suspiciously like Quentin Crisp, about to pay Mick back his three thousand in grams rather than notes.

Jack felt queasy with hypocrisy. He *hated* drugs. His younger sister, Kelly, had gone to Manchester University and got into the druggie scene for a while, progressing at an alarming rate up the ladder from pot to coke to heroine. It had been a horrible experience, visiting his sister and seeing her pasty, spotty face, the tell-tale powder in her nostrils, her weird mood swings, as if she had permanent PMT. Eventually Jack had persuaded her to stop, with lengthy lectures that she was going to end up in rehab, with damaged braincells, no nose and no life, that there was nothing remotely cool or glamorous or interesting about her drug-taking. Kelly had finally come off the stuff. But she'd still ended up flunking her degree and was now working as a waitress, doing an Open University degree in the evenings.

Jack loved his sister with such fierce protectiveness that he couldn't blame her. Instead he'd demonised the dealer who had got her started, caricatured them in his mind as an evil bastard from a Boche painting. And now Jack was sitting in a pub about to do the same. He didn't feel good. And yet he didn't know what else to do. He'd got the stuff from Maribelle, a stinking rich Sloane girl with a drug habit who'd never forgotten Jack after a one-night stand. Jack felt rotten for using her. But he'd pay her back. And it bought him time, precious time.

People know that I'm a dealer, he kept fretting, the envelope greasy with sweat in his lap, tucked beneath his wallet. Then he'd remembered wryly, *Actually, they're all looking at me because I'm wearing a white suit and panama.*

The suit, Jack was rapidly deciding, was a bad idea. It had seemed, well, funny at the time. He wasn't quite sure why he'd put it on. But now he was getting weird looks; the barman had served him as though he had leprosy, dropping the ten-pence change into his palm from a great height as if in terror of their pores colliding.

'Jack!' Mick appeared in the doorway, nodding. Seeing the suit, a wild smile tugged at his lips.

Jack gulped.

Mick hadn't come alone.

Behind him were six rather butch blokes, who gathered around Jack, pulling up chairs, their eyes bulging at his outfit.

'You look gorgeous,' said one sarcastically. He had a bulging beer belly and 'Paul' tattooed on each bicep. 'Where did you get the hat?'

'Love your tattoo,' Jack replied sharply. 'I guess if one arm falls off, you've still got one left to remind you what your name is.'

The guy looked as though he was about to sock Jack one, but Mick, like an owner restraining a Rottweiler, put a warning hand on his shoulder. He pulled up a chair, turned it backwards and sat with his long, khaki-trousered legs stretched out, cupping his hand around his dodgy little roll-up as he lit up.

'I'm going to a fancy-dress party,' Jack added with a splutter. God, he felt like such a dick. Just what had he been thinking of?

'So, have you got the stuff?' Mick went straight to the point. 'No – DON'T put it on the table – d'you want the whole pub to see it?' he hissed in a whisper.

Jack, flushing, slipped it underneath.

He could hardly believe how easy it was. For a second, Mick's grubby fingernails brushed his, then it was gone. The deal was done. He was free to go. He waited for the relief to wash over him, but it didn't come. He just felt rather ill.

'OK,' said Mick, slipping his hand with practised casualness into his trouser pocket. 'I'll just take a trip to the boys' room to check it out.'

'Check?' said Jack. 'Why d'you need to check?'

'To make sure it's decent stuff.'

'Of course it's decent. I got it off a top-quality dealer,' Jack lied.

'Yeah, like your car. The engine blew last week. You also neglected to mention that three of the doors are held on by Sellotape.'

Poor Michelle, thought Jack, with an unhappy pang.

Mick disappeared into the Gents, his desert boots leaving a slightly muddy trail of prints behind him. Jack sat at the table. He was locked in on all sides. How long was this going to take? He felt as though he was sitting in a dentist's waiting room. Or worse, that Mick was subjecting him to one of those long, drawn-out Japanese tortures. The pub was boiling; the suit stuck to him like a wet-suit. It all reminded him too much of that night in the pub

341

when he'd lost the snooker match. He could feel the same tingling in his thighs, the same acid fear in his stomach, as though an ulcer was about to erupt. *When I get out of here,* he promised himself, *I'm going to learn my lesson. I'm never, ever, going to have any dealings with Mick again. Or anyone dodgy, in fact. I'm going to bloody do as Katie says and get myself a nice, honest, decent job where I don't have to sit in a pub in fear of being clubbed to death by a group of thugs.*

He couldn't sit still any longer.

'Where are you going?' Paul snarled as Jack stepped over his legs.

'Just to the fruit machine,' said Jack sullenly.

He had a few coins to slot in. A cherry, a dollar, a watermelon. Jack put in his last pound, knowing he wasn't going to win. Today wasn't a lucky day. He wanted to get out of here. He just wanted to be back with Henry, talking about their relationship . . . confessing their feelings for each other . . . kissing . . . lying in bed, their arms around each other, shutting the world out, encased in a bubble of love.

Then he heard the creak-swing of the toilet door opening.

The moment he saw Mick's face, he knew. Mick was smiling, but Jack could see the poison in his eyes. He just knew. It was a no-win situation. He'd been set up.

He opened his mouth to speak, but his legs had a mind of their own. They started to run. They carried him through the pub doors, out on to the pavement, and up the road.

Footsteps were pounding behind him. Jack felt the wind tearing into his lungs as though it wanted to rip them out. He swung round a corner, fleeing past a bus-stop, an odd lady with a pug dog. Past a restaurant. Should he go in?

Say he was being attacked? Call the police? His legs kept going. The tendons in his shins felt as though they were being stretched like elastic bands. If only he'd stayed at Henry's, followed his gut feeling. Oh shit, they were coming closer. Six of them. One of him. Should he try to fight them? No, no chance. He pictured their fists smashing into him, his face a pulpy mess, his teeth lying in blood, and forced himself on harder, gasping in pain. *Oh God*, he whimpered, *please don't let them catch me. Please don't let them get me. Save me, God, please.*

He looked back – he was gaining ground. Then he heard a cry, someone calling his name, and he swung round, saw his love, felt his heart leap. He ran into the road and the world turned upside down.

The blue sky was bitten into by metal teeth. Everything cracked, then collapsed. He could taste tar in his mouth. His body was screaming with pain.

Afterwards he could remember just one moment in exquisite detail – the car tyre that he'd stared at before passing out. The black tyre, putrid with petrol smells. The grey mirrored plate; the nut in the centre. Elongated faces reflected in it: Henry smiling at him like an angel. The zig-zag in the rubber that grew wider and wider into furrows of darkness, before blackness swam over him like ink and he was just a body lying in the road, surrounded by passers-by asking if he was OK.

★
★

37
Charlie

Jack's body lay in the middle of the road. Screaming, I swooped down over his head – just as it hit the road. I'll never forget that moment – the impact of flesh against tarmac. His face squashing up, his cheekbones crunching, his eyeballs laced with purple rolling upwards, his rib-cage snapping. And then stillness. His body limp, like a ruined ragdoll; I half expected to see his flesh tear open and yellow stuff come crumbling out.

Instead, there was blood. It started to drip from his nose, and then gush, and then pour . . .

'Oh my God, oh my God, blood, blood everywhere, oh my God.' I could hear my voice muttering a stream of incoherent curses.

Slam!

The truck door swung open. A man in jeans and a stripey yellow and red checkered shirt, a baseball cap plunged over his greasy curls, got out. He walked over to the body, slow heavy steps, like a cowboy checking out an Indian he's just shot down.

He knelt down in front of Jack. As he bent over, I caught a whiff of his breakfast breath – fried bread and

344

eggs. I felt bile in my throat, green bitterness mixed with the salt of tears.

'You OK?' he whispered.

Silence. Drip, drip. Jack kept on bleeding.

'Is he OK?' A skinhead, one of Mick's cronies, his face now as pale as the skull on his T-shirt, took a few steps forward.

'Of course he's not OK!' I screamed. 'He's dead. You humans! You monsters, you've killed him!'

The skinhead started to gabble about not meaning any harm. Jack had owned them money, Jack had got scared and taken flight, they hadn't meant him any harm . . . He reached down to touch Jack and I spat at him.

'Idiot, you can't move him! He'll die!'

'Hey!' The truck driver caught the skinhead by the arm. His calm was amazing; his voice cool and measured. 'You had better not move him. It's dangerous; he may have broken his back.'

'Right.' The skinhead stumbled back. He kept shoving his hands in his pockets and then taking them out again, looking helpless. 'We can't move him,' he parrot-echoed to the bundle of onlookers who were slowly gathering round. 'It's dangerous, you see.'

'Aren't you going to call an ambulance?' one Japanese girl shrieked.

'Yeah, right!' The skinhead was gibbering now, spit forming on his lips like a baby. 'Call an ambulance.'

The truck driver pulled out his mobile phone. Despite his calm manner, I could see his hands trembling. He stared down at his black Nokia.

'Well, go on then, call!'

But he just carried on staring, hypnotised. He looked up, a red flush seeping over his face. I realised then that his calm exterior was shock.

'I can't – I—'

'It's, er, nine, nine, nine,' said the skinhead helpfully, shoving his hands back in his pockets.

'Thanks.'

It was almost too surreal – as if they were politely sharing the number of a local pizza house. I'd always thought shock made people act with frantic speed; but the humans seemed to be behaving as though they were in slow motion or underwater; clumsy, blinking, heavy. And Jack was lying there on the road, and every second was so precious. His heartbeat was slowing, his breath thinning, his body compressing like a burst balloon with the air gushing out, as if letting out a big sigh. He was slipping peacefully away . . . but no, no, NO, it wasn't good enough. *Jack, you've got to live*. I found myself jumping up and down on his neck, my hands grabbing tufts of his hair, yelling, *JACK, wake up JACK*, into his ear. *WAKE UP, JACK, WAKE UP!*

'His head keeps shaking, he's having a seizure, look!' the Japanese woman cried, pointing.

I danced even harder on his head, determined to shock him, drum life back into him.

'JACK, JACK, WAKE UP JACK! JACK, JACK, WAKE UP JACK!'

'Charlie!'

Suddenly a hand was curling around my waist and I was being lifted up into the air. I screamed and tore at the hands, but they had an iron-grip. I half-twisted round, saw Puck, heard him mutter, 'You're hysterical'. Then I bit him. Puck let out a howl and dropped me. I went flying back down on to Jack's head, slithered down his nose and fell into a pool of blood. For a moment I lay there, sloshing in redness, millimetres from his face. The look carved on his features terrified me: his pale pink lips

346

were frozen in a snarl, his pupils two black pin-points of accusation. As if he knew it was our fault, as if his look was his silent final word of revenge and retribution. I tried to scramble to my feet but I slipped and reached out, grabbing Jack's nose, the blood pouring over my hands, splashing my skirt and face, and I started screaming again. I could see blue lights and white doors slamming and a figure walking towards me. It was the Grim Reaper, his attaché case swinging, coming to take Jack far, far away . . .

It was Puck who came for me again. *It's the ambulance, Charlie*, he told me, *Jack's going to be all right.*

He dragged me by my wings up, up, up. When I bit him again, he slapped me round the face, so hard I felt the whiplash like an adder's sting in my neck. I started to sob, feeling the pain raw in my cheek, and I tried to struggle again but Puck was too strong for me. He held me upside down, my wings grasped tightly between his fingers, my head squashed uncomfortably against his waist, so I had a half-angle view, through the crook of his elbow, of the scene below. The ambulance men scything through the crowds . . . people parting . . . I felt tears blur in my eyes and I blinked, watching a tiny teardrop fall and splash on to Jack's forehead before the ambulance men wrapped him up like a mummy and Puck flew us away from everyone and everything.

Finally we came to a halt, just above the clouds.

For a moment we hovered, hands held tight, eyes frightened. Puck's face was smeared with blood. I looked down and saw blood on my palms and I tried to wipe it on to my dress. It was everywhere, wet and shiny, red and ashamed. I felt defiled and dirty with guilt.

'Oh Puck,' I sobbed. 'What are we going to do?'

347

'Charlie, don't worry,' he said, taking me in his arms and holding me in a tight hug.

I'm a murderer, I said to myself silently, as though trying out my new identity like a suit of clothes. *I'm. A. Murderer.*

And then I saw them. In the distance. The flock of birds. Coming towards us.

I felt my heart skip several beats.

'Puck!' I squeaked. 'Puck!'

You humans may not realise it, but the natural world does have police. If you ever spot a starling hanging about your garden, sitting on your fence, casting about a beady black eye, it's really a cop keeping an eye out for magpies stealing human jewels, or cuckoos laying illicit eggs, or earthworms smuggling fertilisers.

But if you ever look up and see starlings flocking in a V across the sky, you know there really is trouble.

They're not migrating – they're coming to arrest a criminal, to throw them into jail – tiny, horrible, smelly cells in the River Thames, guarded by water rats, where the prisoners are fed nothing but dirty polluted water and boiled river fungi and fish poo.

And now they were coming for me and Puck.

38
Katie

'The point is, Leila,' said Jeremy, his eyes gleaming like pebbles behind his wire-rimmed spectacles, 'that we simply live in a different era—'

'A more advanced era,' Penny interrupted, fingering a pearl earring in her tiny lobe.

'Not necessarily. I'm saying that, over time, people have stopped believing in magic, and we have sacrificed magic for materialism. I was reading the other day that there is good reason to suppose the Inca tribes had *sidhis* – the ability to fly over tree-tops. Or take the Aborigines – their lives in the Australian outback may be simplistic, but they certainly don't spend their lives addicted to Prozac or paracetamol in order to survive each day. And take Shakespeare. Look at *Macbeth*. The play is littered with omens. It's about natural law and the way nature reacts to, or reflects, human sin—'

'Yes, Jeremy darling.' Leila put her hand on his sleeve. 'But are you suggesting that the horoscopes in the *Daily Star* are true? If so, you're insane. I love you, but you are insane. Pass the butter, please.'

'No, Leila,' said Jeremy, blushing slightly. 'I'm just

saying that it's all about *belief*. Adam woke from his dream and found it true. We create our own worlds. If, collectively, the human race did believe in omens, then perhaps omens would work. Maybe our fate does hang in the stars. After all, our visions of life are so narrow. We're all sitting here at this dinner party, unaware and barely caring about what is happening next door. Or in the next street, or over in America—'

'Britney Spears is probably having a boob job,' Penny said quietly, with a smile.

'Or in the universe at large,' Jeremy continued. 'We're just one tiny planet in a vast cosmos and I think it's egotism that makes us think our tiny, insignificant lives are so special, so individual, and we can't accept that perhaps our existence is just one tiny blip in the whole order reflected in the planets.'

'Jeremy, I think you've been watching too many documentaries on Channel 5,' said Leila.

A ripple of laughter. Leila smiled and took a sip of soup.

In the kitchen, Katie grimaced as she accidentally cut her finger instead of the courgette. Wincing, she tore off a strip of kitchen roll and wrapped her finger in it, the blood soaking through the flowery pattern. She could hear the pretentious conversation from Leila's dinner party slipping through the serving hatch between the dining room and kitchen. She wasn't sure how much more of oh-look-I'm-so-intelligent-I-can-read-*The-Sunday-Times*-and-regurgitate-journalist's-opinions-at-dinner-parties chit-chat she could bear to listen to. Only five minutes ago they had been arguing with fierce passion as to whether Anne Robinson was an A list, B list or, hey, B++ list celebrity.

A, B, C. Katie couldn't stand any of that. Hierarchies,

divisions, labels. As far as Katie was concerned, friends were people she chose because they were good people. Not because they had a posh car or a big house or a nice Oxbridge accent.

Anyway, it was clear that in Leila's little world, Katie was C double-minus. Leila had asked Katie to cook for her dinner party. 'Just three courses,' she added airily. Katie had made up an excuse about being busy, but then, Leila had added lightly, 'Look, Katie, I do let you stay here for forty pounds a week, which is terribly cheap, and I just think it might be nice if you could help out now and again.' Katie had felt her heart turn to ice. Despite the fact that she knew she half-deserved it because of the Henry thing, she still felt furious. Jack had cheered her up by offering to help. But it was now 8 p.m. and, as usual, there was no sign of him.

Thanks very much, Jack, Katie thought sourly, her bad mood thickening by the minute. *Nice to know I can depend on you.*

'Can I lick the bowl?' Susie begged for the seventh time that hour, swinging her legs against the stool.

'No! It's olive oil and yoghurt dressing.'

'So, I can add some chocolate sauce. Ooh, it's the phone!'

Was it? Katie really couldn't be bothered to answer it. It was probably one of Leila's friends, apologising for being late because their fucking chauffeur had a cold or something. She threw the scraps from the fruit salad into the bin, a rainbow mush of pips and cores and skins and rinds.

The phone kept ringing.

'A very persistent caller,' Jeremy remarked in the dining room.

'Oh, Katie will get it,' said Leila loudly.

351

No, I fucking won't, Katie thought savagely. But she found herself trudging into the hallway, beckoning Susie with her (she didn't trust her with the chocolate truffles). God – it must have rung about twenty times now.

When she picked it up, a voice said, 'Katie?' Henry. She nearly flipped. All her pent-up rage was redirected at him. Didn't he understand that, no, she did not want to go out with him? Ever.

'Henry, I'm busy.' The line was crackly, Henry's voice sounded like a warped creature from *The X-Files*.

'No . . . Katie . . . listen . . .'

And then his words started to seep in. Jack. Accident. Hospital. Henry's voice, not passionate but desperate. *Beep, beep,* the call ran out. Katie put down the phone. She turned and grabbed her coat from the hook, not noticing that it was her light, summer jacket. She tugged Susie into her duffel coat, fumbling with the smooth pebble-shaped buttons, ignoring Susie's cry that they were done up the wrong way. Then she ran out into the street, waving for a taxi, ignoring Leila, who had stalked into the hallway, demanding to know why the second course was so outrageously late.

Hospital. Reception. A black girl, hair coiled into hundreds of tiny, pink-beaded plaits. He'll be in intensive care.

Shiny plastic floors. Shoes click-clacking. A man in a wheelchair, his voice creaking. An endless maze of signposts. Susie begging to buy sweets from the machine. 'Later, later,' Katie said. She turned left, stumbling. She wanted to curl up her fists and scream, 'CAN'T ANYONE IN THIS STUPID PLACE TELL ME WHERE THE FUCK TO GO?' An Indian doctor. Clipboard. A moustache, like a bristly black caterpillar, balanced on his top lip. Where can I find intensive care? she asked. Third floor, he said. He didn't even look up from his notes.

I'm just another visitor. Jack is just another body using up a bed.

'Take the lift, it's quicker,' he added, looking up briefly. Olive eyes, soft with sympathy.

'Thanks.' Katie suddenly felt her chin tremble, bit back an urge to hug him.

The lift was so slow. It pinged on floor one, floor two. A throng of nurses came in. Susie held Katie's hand and asked if Uncle Jack was dead. Katie shook her head firmly. Susie kept quiet. The nurses chattered like birds in a cage. *Did you go out last night? Have you seen* American Beauty? Katie leaned her head against the cool of the mirror. *Oh yes*, Katie replied inside, *I've seen it. I saw it with Jack, sitting in the Odeon, sharing a big box of salty popcorn, and afterwards we went out to the Coffee Republic and sipped mango teasers and had such a good chat. How, how, can we have leapt from that to this? How could he have been laughing then and dying now? Can't you make this lift go any fucking faster?*

Ping.

'Come on, Susie.'

Intensive care.

One of the luminous lights in the corridor was broken, flickering weakly on-off, on-off, yellow-black, yellow-black, like a disco light. There was an air of frantic tension. Doctors rushing. Masked green figures moving about like grim reapers. Nurses unsmiling. Everyone aware that they were walking on a knife-edge, trembling between life and death.

A nurse asked who she was. Katie stuttered and stammered *Katie DeAntiquus*.

One of the doors opened and a body covered in a sheet was wheeled out. Susie asked if it was Uncle Jack.

'No,' Katie managed. 'Don't stare.'

'Sorry.'

Katie watched the trolley rattling away down the corridor, the sheet shifting slightly, revealing a dead foot. Her stomach turned and she tasted acid bile in her throat and she was terrified she was going to be sick. *It's an omen*, she panicked as they approached the ward, and even as they opened the door and saw Jack caught in a web of machines and wires, like some broken android in a sci-fi movie, she just knew in the pit of her stomach that he was going to die.

39
Charlie

Click! The starling snapped the handcuffs on to Puck's wrist.

Click! The starling snapped the handcuffs on to my wrist.

I stared at them sullenly. Puck and I had had no time to escape. The starling police had circled us in a black fog. I'd tried to push through, but they had beaten me black and blue with their wings until my mouth was full of ebony feathers. Then two starlings held us down and cuffed us as the Chief Inspector, Stan the Starling, approached.

He looked like a bloody criminal himself. He had a black eye-patch over one eye and a twig cigar protruding from his mouth, dropping acorn-cigar ash. I'd heard the most terrifying stories about him. How he *enjoyed* torturing his victims; how, imitating the infamous scene in *Reservoir Dogs*, he'd once caught a thieving magpie, locked her in a police cell, and slowly pulled out feather by feather, one black, one white, one black, one white, until, half-bald, she'd squawked her confession.

'You can't do anything until we've called our lawyers,' Puck said cheekily.

355

'*Lawyer!* It's a bit late for that now. I've been keeping a *close* eye on you two over the last few months,' he said, looking me up and down like a sleazy frog. 'I know what you've been doing. Stealing spells. Breaking fairy Natural Law. Tormenting innocent humans. And now you have – potentially – killed someone. Titania has given me a permit for your arrest. I'm afraid you're being taken to The Tower.'

The Tower!

Puck and I were stunned. The Tower was for . . . real criminals . . . suffering the worst punishment. Death. Not hanging – our equivalent of capital punishment was being lined up at dawn while a flurry of birds plopped on us, until we fell in a suffocating heap on the floor. We would, literally, be pooed to death.

Before we could protest, the Chief Inspector flapped his wings and muttered, 'Right, Bob, you're leading, but don't take the flock through another bloody pylon, OK? My wings are still frizzled at the end from the last time.'

So we set off in a procession across the sky. I felt as if it was our funeral march; I could hear the heavy organ notes pounding in my head. As we swooped down towards the Primrose Hill canal, I noticed a human couple pointing at us, making a remark about birds migrating. *God, if only*, I thought.

The strange thing was, I didn't feel any fear. It was such a shock that all I could feel was white blankness, as if I was just witnessing the whole thing from a distance.

And then I caught Puck's eye. He flicked his wings in the direction of the canal. Glancing sideways, I noticed a gap in our entourage; one of the starlings had slipped away to chat-up a red-breasted robin. I felt my heart start to thump, thump. We passed over another tree and I saw a family of squirrels; seeing us, the mother pulled her

356

young close to her and I felt a sick wave of shame. I looked at Puck again.

'LEFT TURN!' Bob shrilled.

'NOW!' Puck yelled.

We cut out in front of them. A terrible pain sliced through my wrist as Puck tugged the handcuffs too hard. Then we were flying, wild and free, in the sky.

The wind roared in our ears. The starlings were squawking like mad. *Flap, flap!* I heard their wings beating madly behind us. I felt a wing-tip brush mine and I flew even faster, feeling my own wings grow hot with pain.

'The clouds!' Puck yelled.

We flew straight into the dense white mass. It slipped past us like water, but the starlings (who have much thicker wings) were immediately clogged up. As Puck and I schoomed away, I saw them all banging into each other, piling up in a black heap like a collision on the M25. Victory soared inside me. We had escaped!

'DOWN!' Puck yelled.

We hurtled downwards like a rollercoaster without brakes.

To my confusion, the canal banks were crammed with birds. A collage of blue and grey dotted the green. Pigeons and blue tits were spread out on the grass with picnic baskets; sparrows clustered on hedgerows, thrushes and robins partied on riverboats.

And then there was the piercing noise of a microphone.

'And I'd like to introduce the 34th Royal Bird Beauty Contest,' cooed a nightingale in a voice of pure silk, so soft she must have swallowed a bottle of Fairy Liquid. 'Now, the second round of contestants will each say a few words.'

Behind her were a row of birds in mossy bikinis, their breasts and beaks shining.

'Quick!' Puck cried. He pulled me behind a thick flock of pigeons, who didn't notice us – they were all too busy cooing for their representative, Camilla Pigeon.

'Hello birds.' Camilla stood before the mike, her wing-tips clasped shyly in front of her. 'I'd like to stress that I believe in World Peace [cheers], the RSPCB [cheers] and the abolition of Ken Livingstone. He might want the pigeons removed from Trafalgar Square – I say remove the HUMANS! [Riotous clapping].'

Then, as I saw Chief Inspector Starling fly down and take the mike, I grabbed Puck's hand and we ducked down.

'I have reason to believe there are two dangerous fairies hiding amongst you,' he said harshly.

A kerfuffle ensued between the birds. As a pigeon turned and fixed her beady eyes on us, I cringed and gave her a pleading smile.

'Are you a fairy?' she asked cautiously.

'Ah, no,' said Puck, putting on an Aussie accent. 'We're, er, two mutated dragonflies from Australia. We've just come over and we're lost. We were looking for the Houses of Parliament.'

Pigeons have the IQ of a potato (they always come last in the Bird-Brain of Britain awards). But they also have hearts of gold. To our relief, the pigeon offered to give us a lift. She tucked us under her wing and we flew out, unnoticed, high above the tree-tops, until she finally gently deposited us at the Houses of Parliament.

Puck and I hugged each other in relief. We were safe. For the time being.

Now we just had to find out whether Jack was still alive.

40
Henry

Tragedies bring people together. Shock heals rifts, transcends grudges.

Henry and Leila, who had vowed never to speak to each other again, found themselves sitting together in the hospital canteen, exchanging terse words of grief. Katie wouldn't come down; she wouldn't leave Jack's side, was comforting Jack's mother and sister, so Henry and Leila took it in turns to bring them sour-tasting cups of coffee from the machine.

It was late and they were both haggard with exhaustion. Henry invited Leila to come back to his place for a bite to eat. He felt glad to have someone to talk to. Katie, in shock, would barely say more than a few words, sitting frozen by Jack's side like a mannequin, as if terrified that she was supporting his heartbeat by her constant attention, that if she looked away he might slip from her. Henry couldn't help feeling jealous every time he saw her. The look in her eyes. The love. And then he felt awful, because Jack was his best friend, and he wanted nothing more than for Jack to wake up, to be alive again, laughing with him down the pub or playing tennis.

Back at Chalcott Square, Henry pushed open the door, embarrassed by the unopened post splattered over the mat, the Mount Everest of washing-up in the sink, the half-drunk bottles of red wine.

'Have you been having a dinner party or something?' Leila let out a high laugh, rinsing two mugs under the sink.

Henry tried to smile. He'd been drinking a lot the last few nights, trying to burn up his grief with alcohol, slumped in front of the TV in a numb daze. Since the accident, his life had been shaken up like a snow-scene, everything whirling.

Outside the kitchen window, a sudden explosion showered green sparkles across the sky.

'Shit – it's my neighbour's fortieth birthday party,' said Henry. 'I completely forgot.'

'Shall we go?' Leila asked. 'He only lives next door, after all.'

Henry frowned in disbelief. He couldn't understand why Leila was being so light-hearted, so breezy about the whole thing. Didn't she understand that Jack might die?

In the living room, they sat on the chaise longue with a tray of crackers and cheese and a bottle of wine. Henry felt funny, sitting with Leila on the same place where he and Katie had been discovered by her. They sat in awkward silence for a few minutes, their munching and crunching magnified. Then Henry moved to an armchair and flicked on the TV, channel-hopping. Leila self-consciously picked up a crumpled old copy of the *Daily Telegraph* that was lying on the coffee table.

'I just feel so guilty about Jack,' Henry sighed, barely noticing that they were stuck on *Blind Date* – one of his least favourite programmes. 'I feel . . . somehow as if it's my fault. Because I was with him before he . . . I mean – I think if I had just looked out for him, maybe he'd still be OK.'

360

'Well, you did pay off his enormous debt to Mick,' said Leila archily. 'I think Katie was very impressed.'

Henry narrowed his eyes. This was not a time to behave like a bitch. He opened his mouth to say something more, but Leila instead remarked, 'Oh God, it says here Gwyneth Paltrow and Ben Affleck are back together. Can you believe it?'

'Really?' said Henry, in the coldest, most sarcastic voice he could muster. 'At a time like this, all I can think of too is the wonder of Paltrow's love life. Indeed. And do you know what they were wearing when they got back together? Gucci? Do tell.'

Leila slowly looked up from the newspaper, shooting Henry a look of pure venom. Henry looked sheepish and muttered sorry. But for God's sake, he thought, what was up with Leila? She hadn't cried once over the past few days. She'd come to the hospital, yes, but she'd kept a brief vigil, standing by the window, barely looking at Jack, watching ambulances come and go, people come and go, people live and die.

She has no depth to her, Henry realised. *She is totally, utterly soulless.* He wished he could ask her to leave, but he wasn't that cruel. So they sat and watched fifteen minutes of *Blind Date* in a black silence.

The ads began. Henry reached for the wine.

'Did I ever tell you about Ray?' Leila asked suddenly.

'I hope she picks number three . . . what?' Henry replied.

'Ray. My ex-husband. I've never really told you about him.'

'Right.'

Here we go, thought Henry, outraged. With Leila it was all me, me, me. If it had been Katie, they'd be talking about Jack now, sharing their grief, cheering each other

361

up – talking in that completely honest and sincere way Katie did. But all Leila could do was rant on in some self-pitying fashion about her ex.

Leila paused and swallowed theatrically, as though she was about to begin a grand soliloquy. Henry repressed an inward sigh and took another swig of wine.

'I first met him when I went to America. I moved over there when I was twenty-one years old – it was just after Katie and I had met Jack and become friends. I felt sad to be going, to be leaving Katie, even though on the outside I had started cutting her off. I behaved like a real snob, felt she wasn't good enough to be my friend any more.'

Nothing's changed, thought Henry snidely. But his good manners forced him to nod with polite interest.

'I guess it was all my stepfather's fault. I'd always wanted to have a career, but he was a real chauvinist. He stopped me going to university, told me I couldn't stay at home, that I had to go out to work. Katie and I ended up being secretaries, temping. Katie never had any ambition really – she just wanted to get married and have kids.'

'Nothing wrong with that,' said Henry sharply.

'Sure,' said Leila quickly. 'But I'm not . . . like her. I felt so repressed, so angry all the time. I hated being a secretary – doing basic, menial work when I knew I was more intelligent than my boss, typing his stupid fucking letters and making his stupid fucking tea. I was so bored, I thought I'd die. So I got myself a proper job. My ex-boyfriend, Manuel, swung me a job in America, working in publishing – I'd always loved reading so it seemed like a dream come true, even if I was starting at the bottom.'

Another one of her exs, Henry thought contemptuously. They seemed to be scattered around the globe like satellites, all mirroring how fabulous and gorgeous Leila was, all desperate to have her back.

362

'So I was snobby to Katie – I felt I was cool, in a different league to her now I had this flash new job. It was crap really, because when I got over to New York, I was even worse off. I was staying in this crappy apartment, sleeping on Manuel's sofa, and when he realised I didn't want to get back together with him, he was furious. And I started working for my new boss – Ray.'

Pause. The theme music to *Blind Date* jazzed out from the TV; the credits were starting to roll.

'. . . hmm,' said Henry distractedly, wondering what was on next. Then he realised Leila was passing something over for him to look at. A photo.

'That's him. Ray.'

It was a small photo of a tall, dark man standing outside a house. Henry was quite surprised. He'd expected Leila to have gone for some supermodel, but Ray was slightly overweight with a strong face, a black moustache and smiley eyes. Still, he definitely had a certain charisma . . .

'Yeah – I didn't expect to like him at first.' Leila took the photo again, fingering the dog-eared edges before slipping it back into her handbag. 'It wasn't his looks that were his allure – it was just something indefinable, some self-assurance about him. Actually, I hated him to begin with. He was my boss and I was working as his secretary. Filing and making tea – no different to my job in Britain, I thought. Only it was worse – because he actually was more intelligent than me . . .'

Henry raised his eyebrows, surprised. Leila (who'd once boasted her IQ was high enough to be in MENSA) admitting that someone was *more intelligent than her*. Wonders would never cease.

'Anyway – there was a sexual tension there from the start. I didn't even think about wanting to go out with him

363

though because I was set on my career and I didn't want to get distracted. I decided I didn't even want to get married, so I would never have to suffer the fate my mother did in her first marriage – being ordered around and bossed about by a man, cooking his meals and playing his slave. No – I wanted my own independence. But, as I said, there was something there between us . . .

'He liked me. Ray was pretty intimidating but I stood up to him. Actually, I was really bolshy. I was always cheeking him and telling him I could do his job better. He was too busy to read his slush pile and I told him that he was missing tons of great talent. He would take me out to dinner, saying he needed to discuss work, and I'd be very sarcastic. I'd try and wind him up by saying, "What – why the hell d'you need to wine and dine me just to discuss a paltry press release. D'you fancy me or something?" But I always went, and I loved it. I loved teasing him and being teased by him. But whenever he did take me out, he never laid a finger on me, and it drove me crazy. I kept thinking that he didn't like me – I couldn't work out where I stood with him. At the same time, I liked the suspense . . .'

Henry felt a flicker of recognition there – a hint of Leila's game-playing, her emotional snakes and ladders.

'. . . but at dinner we'd talk for hours. Hours and hours. He told me that he'd been married before and was now in the process of being divorced. He had a son, who was six then, whom he hardly ever saw. His wife had hated him being such a workaholic, she'd wanted to move to Long Island, which I saw at once was a complete joke. Ray was like me – seething with ambition. He was thirty-six years old – older than me by about twelve years – but I liked that because he was mature. Now and again I did try and date younger guys, but they had nothing interesting to say – I just liked their looks. I'd bring them into the office, just to wind Ray up, make him jealous. But he *still* didn't make a move on me.' Leila smiled fondly. 'And then I found it.'

'Uh?'

Henry was feeling so fed-up, so pent-up with anger, that he was trying to shut her out by watching the commercials. His lips twitched at a particularly amusing one advertising beer, which involved a talking kangaroo and a lascivious tortoise. He took another gulp of wine.

'On his slush pile.' Leila sounded irritated. 'I found a brilliant book. A masterpiece. I did it all by myself. I proved I was right.'

'Oh, great,' Henry sighed.

Pause.

'So then what happened?' Henry forced himself to ask, raising his glass once more.

'Well, Ray did the dirty on me. He took credit for the author I'd discovered. Well, he was the editor. But at the time I fumed. So I left.'

'You walked out?'

'Yes. I joined a rival firm. He went mad. For two entire weeks, he ignored me. Wouldn't take my calls. Nothing.'

'Well, you can't expect men to chase you for ever,' Henry said. Who did she think she was – some sort of goddess?

'And then,' she went on, her eyes opaque with fond memories, 'I got so mad I went storming up to his apartment, interrupted this dinner with humungously important people, and just threw myself at him. It was embarrassing.' She let out an unnaturally girlish giggle. 'He was so relieved, so hungry for me, he sent them all home! After we'd made love, we had seven orange tiramisus left over to eat. We fed each other. We stayed up all night, talking. And a year later, when we were married, we celebrated our anniversary with orange tiramisu. Not that it even tasted that good – it was one of Ray's wild concoctions. He fancied himself as a cook, but he was crap. I used to have to eat the most frightful shit to please him. But I loved him. I loved him so much.'

'So when did things go wrong?' Henry asked resignedly.

'When he died, I guess.' Leila let out a small laugh.

'Mmm . . .' How long was this going to go on for? He wished she would hurry up and get to the divorce papers. His eyes flicked to the clock. Nine p.m. He was . . . hang on. Hang on! 'What did you say?' Henry was so startled by her words, as they finally rattled into his conscious mind like stones, that he turned and half-sat on the remote control, flicking to BBC2 and nudging up the volume in the process, a cookery programme blasting out like a heavy metal concert. There was a clumsy moment when Henry took several gos to turn it down. Then he turned and sat on the edge of his seat, gazing at Leila.

Her shoulders were slightly slumped and she suddenly seemed to Henry like a modern-day Miss Haversham. In the gloom, her blonde hair looked grey. There was an expression on her face he'd never seen before, as if she had finally lifted off her social mask. Sadness was etched in her mouth, dull in her eyes.

The silence stretched out like a sheet of glass waiting to be shattered. Henry hardly dared to speak. He felt as if he'd swallowed a bubble of shame.

He came and sat on the arm of the chaise longue, facing her. He rubbed her shoulder very gently and muttered something soothing, nonsensical, 'OK . . . it's OK . . . cool . . .'

'He was hit by a taxi. It's so . . . so unfair. Ray and I – we had it all. A perfect marriage. If you look around, there are so few people who really have decent marriages. They're either stagnating, or just surviving, or having affairs, or secretly loathing each other. And why do they live but Ray had to be killed? You once asked me if I believed in God, but I can't see how any God with any compassion would . . . let it happen . . . like that.'

'Ssh . . . it's OK.'

'It's not OK, Henry. I've cheated on you. I've cheated on everyone. Ever since then, I've only had flings. I guess I channelled all my energies into my career – I felt it was something I could control. People are so difficult . . . I know this is going to sound fucked-up, but I've had so many affairs. It all started with this guy a while back – well, to begin with, he didn't tell me he was married. I suppose it sounds perverse, and I didn't want to break up marriages but I wanted to make a mockery of them. There was some kind of justice, some revenge, in ruining other people's marriages the way mine had been. Horrible, really. I was starting to feel tired of it – this thing that men won't leave their wives is a fallacy. Men do leave. A while back, one tried and it was such a mess – I didn't want him, his wife didn't want him. I ruined him. I think that shell-shocked me, so I went for a year of enforced celibacy. Then I met this guy, Mr Winterton, and it all started again. And then I met you.'

Silence.

Henry could feel his chin trembling and he coughed quickly, trying to steady himself.

But he couldn't help it. He felt all his grief about Jack and Katie building up inside him like a pressure cooker. The wine had liquefied the sugar cube block of emotions inside his heart. All his pain was dissolving, loosening.

367

And for the first time since he was ten years old, he felt tears trembling. He tried to flick them away but Leila noticed.

'Henry,' she smiled, 'I'm the one who's supposed to be crying.'

'I'm sorry.'

They both laughed wildly – echoed a moment later by a burst of canned hyena laughter on the TV.

'Er . . . I . . . would you like some tea? Anything? Some chocolate – no, no, you don't like chocolate. Well, some tea, then?' Despite Leila shaking her head gently and saying she was fine, Henry went ahead and made her a cup anyway, spooning in three sugars. The teaspoon shook, some sugar sprinkled on the surface. He was really very drunk.

He came back into the living room and pressed it into her hands, slopping a few drops on the sofa. Before she'd even had time to take a sip, however, he took it out of her hands again and leaned over, pulling her into a hug. He could feel the tension in her hands, her neck. He'd always felt in the past that when he held Leila it was like holding a wire doll. Now he understood – she was clinging to all that pain, holding it tight inside. He kept stroking her hair and saying, 'You can cry, I don't mind. Don't be embarrassed, you can cry it out all out.' But she just remained stiff. Dry-eyed.

Henry knew that what he was doing was a big, big mistake but somehow he couldn't stop himself. It was partly due to his guilt, partly a desperate desire to unlock Leila. He leaned over and kissed her.

A second later he pulled back, horrified with himself.

Henry, what are you doing? How does it look? You're trying to get off with an ex-girlfriend, who you recently cheated on with her best friend, who has just told you the saddest story

368

you've ever heard about her dead husband. You're behaving like a total bastard.

He gazed at Leila. Her eyes were wide. He half-cringed, expecting her to slap him. He almost wanted her to slap him; he deserved it.

Instead, to his shock, Leila started to kiss him. Not her usual soft, tight kisses, but deep, wild, frenzied kisses, as though she wanted to drink him in.

Everything happened so quickly, but later Henry saw the whole sequence as a series of snapshots. Leila running into the hallway, pulling him after her. Tugging him up the stairs. The crumpled sheets. Leila lying back on the bed. Making love in the dark. The open curtains, the sky brilliant outside. Fireworks exploding into beautiful shimmering flowers of green and pink and blue that echoed over Leila's body like jewels. Henry was too panicky to attempt foreplay; she was too impatient to bother. But seeing her start to cry, he tried to withdraw, to crush his desire, suddenly hating himself again. *Just what are we doing?* But it was too late; his body ejaculated obstinately, shamelessly. Henry rolled aside, took her face in his hands and kissed away her tears.

She turned away. Henry remembered that she'd once said she hated anyone to see her crying.

Afterwards they lay there, listening to the bangs and whizzes outside.

He could see her silhouette in the dim gloom. Her shoulders were shaking, he could hear little sobs. He wanted to reach across and comfort her. But somehow the sex, instead of uniting them, had wedged them further apart. He felt sick with shame. He'd taken advantage of her; all right, so she'd initiated it, but still . . .

He felt stone-cold sober now. Everything was frighteningly clear. The rumpled bed. A damp patch beneath his

369

left buttock. The cracks in the ceiling, a spider running across the white islands. *What have I done?*

He got up, yanking on his clothes.

'I'll be right back.'

He nearly tripped on one of her shoes, regained his balance, went to her side. He smoothed her fringe away from her red eyes and gently kissed her forehead. 'Wait here.'

Henry knew his behaviour was becoming increasingly insane, but panic was taking hold of him like a puppeteer and he was giving in to it.

It was only when he got into his car that he realised he'd forgotten his shoes and the pedals felt gritty and grimy beneath his socks. As he drove, rain started to spit and he switched on the windscreen wipers, comforted by their whirr. He kept his eyes fixed on the yellow street-lamps, trying to concentrate on looking for what he wanted. But visions of Leila, of her body beneath him, her mouth in a gasp of grief and orgasm, kept flashing before him.

It all fitted into place now. The way she behaved. Her cageyness. Her fear of intimacy. Her odd moods.

She was terrified of falling in love – to her it must have felt like diving into a deep ocean when she hadn't learned how to swim. So she'd been taking tentative steps forward, testing the water, waiting, but no, Henry had been an insensitive git, he'd tried to rush things, to force her to jump, pushing her all the time. And then, just when she'd finally started to feel ready for a relationship, what had he done? He'd given up on her, lost his patience and slept with Katie.

And worst of all, Henry knew, deep, deep down in the pit of his heart, that he still loved Katie. And now he'd

370

only made everything a million times worse. What if Leila wanted to get back together? He couldn't reject her, not after this. So what was he supposed to do – live a lie or tell her the harsh truth: *I'm sorry, Leila, but I only slept with you because I was trying to say sorry?*

He returned to his house about fifteen minutes later, racing up the stairs two at a time. He was worried that she might have gone, but she was lying on the bed, picking a thread, her eyes red and dull. She started at the bulge beneath Henry's jumper and then, for the first time that day, a look of pure delight spread over her face as a paw and a cross, whiskered face emerged.

'I've brought you Candida,' he said. 'She was outside the front door, waiting for you to come back.'

'Oh, Henry. Thank you. You're so sweet.'

Leila cradled Candida gratefully in her arms, showering her with kisses. But Candida wriggled free, sniffing about the unfamiliar and un-Leila-smelling surroundings.

Henry lay down too, cuddling up against Leila. Candida finally settled in a soft, round ball between them. Leila needed to be surrounded by warmth and love, Henry had decided on the way back. He would stick with her. He might not love her, not the way he burned for Katie, but Leila needed him. He owed it to her.

'D'you feel a bit better now?' Henry whispered, stroking the delta of flesh between her neck and jaw.

'Not really.' Suddenly her mood had chilled.

'I do know what it's like to grieve for something you love, Leila.' Henry tried to bond again. 'I once loved this girl, Alice . . . it was some time ago, before I fell for Katie – I mean, for you,' he spluttered, realising the *faux pas*.' She didn't die . . . but she left . . . and I woke up every morning missing her so much. I know what it's like.'

'Oh, do you?' Leila rose, folding her arms. Her hair, which had been neatly tied in a plait was frayed, mussed up.

'Leila, are you OK? Where are you going?'

'D'you think that, just because you've *fucked* me, you *know* me? D'you think I really enjoyed that then? Oh yes, Henry, yes. What a comfort. You don't know fucking anything about me. Ray was just one part of me . . . you don't know me . . . you don't know anything.' And, with Henry blinking and protesting in disbelief, she scooped up her precious cat and strode out.

41
Charlie

I'd expected that it would take ages to find him; he moves swiftly, from place to place, person to person, working tirelessly throughout the night. I'd been terrified that we'd be too late, that we'd miss him.

But Puck, by good chance, heard that he was in town. We found him in a pub in Notting Hill. Not the grimy pub I'd been expecting – somewhere seething with stress and evil and ways to end goodness. Instead, we discovered him in a posh wine bar on Soho Street. He was sitting at a corner table, in a dark suit, with his back to us, chatting to a girl.

The girl looked as though she worked in a PR firm. In her mid-thirties, she had a smooth brown bob and was wearing a navy suit. Her legs were crossed, her fingers playing with her wine glass, smoothing up and down the crystal flute. As Puck and I sat on the bar, watching, I felt an odd thrill. She *fancied* him. I watched him lean forward and gently caress her jaw-bone; she shivered, her pupils dilating, trying to swallow back her quickening breath. She really had no idea. It was sexy, in a horrible way – like watching a TV movie from the safety of your living room, knowing the vampire is about to strike.

'You really are . . .' He leaned in, whispering something we couldn't hear.

'Excuse me,' she bit back a smile. 'I just need the Ladies. I'll – I'll be right back. Oh God. Just wait, I'll be right back.'

A few minutes later, we heard the screams. Two other Essex girls went into the loos, talking about blokes; they came out white-faced and stammering. The pub fluttered with kerfuffle; some people, as if fearing a bomb, hastily downed the last of their drinks, picked up their purses and made a swift exit. The landlord, a small tubby Italian man, picked up the payphone and started to punch in the number for emergency services as his wife flapped around him, waving a beermat and gabbling in frightened Italian.

But it was all futile, of course.

Her time had come.

Her moment was up.

And while everyone else was panicking, he still sat there at his table, calmly nursing a glass of whisky in his hands, occasionally lifting it to his lips. I noticed he curled his lip over the rim of the glass and pretended to sip, feigned a swallow.

'All in a good night's work,' Puck called over.

He turned away from the table and swung his gaze on to us. I couldn't help shrinking back against the wood of the bar. It was quite a long time since I'd seen The Grim Reaper. I'd forgotten just how terrifying he was.

Of course, he doesn't look like the silly figure you see in films. No dark robes or a shadowed, pale face.

The Grim Reaper looks like your average City worker. He wears a dark, pin-striped suit, cufflinks, black shiny shoes. He has a head of thick, sculptured grey hair, a patrician face. He has a cruel mouth and the most terrifying eyes you've ever seen. They are so distinctive, so mesmerising, that to blend in he wears a pair of wire-rimmed spectacles, though to my mind they only magnify his eyes, black and hollow like two bullet holes in his face.

And he always carries an attaché case. He never carries a scythe – there's no need, for his ways are far more subtle and sinister. When a person's time is up, The Grim Reaper knows. He's there. And it's a quiet case of *veni, vedi, vici*. He'll breath cancerous poison into your cells with a single kiss of death, release a deadly virus into your bloodstream by drugging your drink, or in his mind silently twist an invisible fist around his victim's heart until the last drop of life is squeezed out of them.

'My dear Puck . . . Charlie,' said The Grim Reaper. Despite the pleasant words, his tone was a monotone of pure ice. He always sounded like a vicar saying the 'ashes to ashes' speech for the thousandth time.

'Hiya, Grim, howsitgoing?' Puck, in his nervousness, was trying to be ultra-relaxed. He sounded like an American rapper. I nudged him.

We gently flew on to The Grim Reaper's table, settling down by his glass of whisky and gazing up at him.

'It's a shame about the girl,' he said. But, being The Grim Reaper, he couldn't seem to resist adding, 'Well, everyone's time to end comes one day.'

Charming, I thought.

Puck, however, remained cheerful.

'Oh no, Charlie and I are going to live for ever, we've sold our souls to the devil . . .'

'I hope you got a good price,' said The Grim Reaper, a

375

faint, ironic smile creeping across his face. Like Oberon, I sensed he had rather a soft spot for Puck's boyish wit.

'Speaking of negotiations . . .' Puck began, then swallowed. 'I, er, hear that shares in Hell Inc. are on the increase. Have you managed to bump off any politicians yet?'

'I'm working on it. Their time will come when it comes.'

The Grim Reaper, a little like an elephant hunter searching for the most prized skins and hides, always has a few people on his hit list. But, as he noted with a faint sigh of resignation, he was not in control of choosing the moment of death.

'Their time will come when it comes,' he repeated, glancing away. I stared in fascination at his long, thin, pianist's fingers, curled tight around his glass.

'Like the girl over there,' I said, seeing the landlady burst back into the Ladies, wailing and making a huge fuss. 'The one you were having a quiet drink with, who's now lying dead in the loos.'

'Heart attack,' said The Grim Reaper. 'She's smoked thirty cigarettes a day for the last twelve years. It was supposed to be lung cancer but I couldn't bear—' He paused, corseting his words. 'It was a nicer, cleaner way to go than years in a grimy NHS bed eating shit.' Somehow, hearing him swear was shocking. 'Even if she was only thirty-four.'

I saw the sadness in his eyes and my gaze flickered back to his hand, to the wedding ring glinting pale gold in the dim light. I'd always wondered about that. Who was his wife? Did he marry her when he was human, if he ever was human? Did he miss her?

'Poor woman. Oh well, there will be articles in the papers about how people are being affected by stress at a younger and younger age,' Puck laughed bitterly.

'Quite.' The Grim Reaper smiled thinly. 'Good to keep them on their toes.' He paused, lowered his eyes and pinched his lips in contemplation; then he launched into an unexpected speech. 'People over here don't value their lives at all. They don't realise how lucky they are. They sit in this pub, moaning about their boss or having to work till 6 p.m. – they should see Sarajevo. Just having to sort out all those poor souls leaves me exhausted. People always talk about things they dream of doing, places they want to go to, people they wish they could confess they loved. But they only value things when they're lost and then it's too late.'

Oh God, now he was starting to get heavy on us. I was too depressed about Jack to muster up a decent response.

The Grim Reaper picked up his glass as if to drown his sorrows; then, remembering he was only acting, put it down again.

'Ah well.' He drew back, checking the thin silver watch on his wrist. 'It was lovely to—'

'Wait,' said Puck desperately, 'we were wondering . . .'

'We just—' I squirmed uncomfortably.

'I – there's this guy . . .' Puck started again.

'Oh yes?' said The Grim Reaper dryly.

'His name is Jack DeAntiquus. He's twenty-nine years old and just too young to die.' Oh God, now Puck sounded like a guest making a charity appeal on *Oprah*. 'Look, he's a great guy – young, handsome, full of so much potential, with so much to give – and basically, well, we were kind of wondering if maybe he could, to put it simply, live.'

The Grim Reaper chuckled.

'If he's in a coma, you'll soon know one way or the other.'

There was the sound of sirens in the distance. The

landlady was having hysterics; she kept ranting at her husband that they had to close the pub early. But he'd reacted to the shock by slipping into a state of ultra-calm and was petulantly arguing that it wasn't *their* fault a girl had had a heart attack and dropped dead in their loos, why should *they* lose an evening's business and spoil all the young people's fun? In any case, the young people were already exchanging furtive glances and the pub was emptying; soon we'd be the only ones left.

I pictured Jack in the hospital. I had a sudden flash: nurses' faces above me, a white pad being strapped around my arm, a needle being gently inserted. Could I feel him? Was I Jack?

'Look!' I suddenly exploded. 'Don't you care at all? You just gave us all this shit about appreciating every minute, and yet Jack is dying and we're going to get the blame. We're probably going to be hung, drawn and quartered. Can't you just *try* to do something?'

The Grim Reaper kept a polite smile plastered on his lips as he suddenly noticed the handcuffs on our wrists, but a muscle flickered in his temple. Looking slightly surly, he paused, then picked up his briefcase and flicked it open, yanking out his laptop. It looked like any other laptop but – believe it or not – this was in fact his Doomsday Book, the small encyclopedic calculator of all deaths present, past and future for every single human in the entire world.

I peered over the top, watching him type in:

JACK DEANTIQUUS

A few seconds passed; the machine whirred and then:

Jack Michaelangelo DeAntiquus –

'Michaelangelo!' Puck spluttered sarcastically.

Born in 1972, Camden, London
Death 23 April 2050, drowning, River Thames.

'Fantastic!' I burst out. 'He's not meant to die for what – another fucking forty-nine years. That's great! C'mon, he will be saved right now, won't he?'

'Correct,' said The Grim Reaper, sounding rather disappointed.

Puck and I let out a huge sigh of relief.

'However, I can't guarantee that he won't be brain-damaged, or lose a limb,' The Grim Reaper added, with relish.

Puck and I drew in our breaths again. And then The Grim Reaper punched in a few more buttons and started to make funny noises. Like 'oooohh' and 'gosh'.

'What?' Puck cried.

'I'm afraid it really doesn't look too good for you fairies, though,' he said, pursing his lips. 'As far as I can tell, your entire camp is due to be wiped out during the next three months.'

'Whhhhhhhhhhaaaaaaaat?' I cried.

'Yes. Let me see.' His eyes glinted behind his glasses. 'Oh. An incinerator, about to be built in Camden, close enough to pollute Primrose Hill fairy camp. Yes. Plenty of those about at the moment, I'm afraid – it's human policy. Do all kinds of nasty things to humans – birth defects, neurological difficulties, respiratory diseases.' You could almost see The Grim Reaper rubbing his hands in delight.

Of course. The pollution would creep into the humans in invisible whispers, the disease slowly eating up their cells, wiping out their organs. But us fairies were far too small and sensitive to cope. I pictured the wind, like a foul, diseased breath, carrying the pollution and vomiting it on to the fairy camp. We'd all be wiped out within days.

'Well, at least we'll die heroes,' Puck's voice trembled. 'We'll die knowing we helped some humans to enjoy a little more happiness.'

I knew Puck was trying to be brave, but I couldn't cope. I could feel a sob swelling like a bubble in my chest. I pictured Puck and I breathing in the deadly gases, our wings caked with tar, struggling to some gutter, dying together in a pile of old mushy leaves.

'Oh Puck,' I whimpered, tears starting to stream down my face.

'Oh Charlie.' Puck put his arms around me and enveloped me in a warm hug.

'Now, now,' said The Grim Reaper, looking slightly amused, as though we were behaving like something out of *Gone with the Wind*. 'The humans are on your side. Jack's friend, Katie, is campaigning against the incinerator. She may win. Don't forget that nothing is written in stone,' he added bitterly. 'Taxes are even more certain than death – despite fate you always have free will. And if that will is strong enough, you can, just through your actions, rearrange the future that hangs in the stars for you.'

42
Jack

'Can you hear me, Jack?'

The first thing he was aware of was the beeping.

He struggled to reach out, to bang the faulty black button on his alarm clock. He was lost in the past, when he'd worked as a courier and had had to rise at six every morning to deliver brown paper parcels to the East End.

But his hands refused to obey the frantic messages from his brain. One fumbled as though his fingers were stuck in glue. The other was holding something soft. A hand. He wiggled his fingers and felt the hand tighten, squeeze. He found himself squeezing in return. In the darkness, he was aware of warm, pudgy flesh, knobbly joints. Nails indenting into his palm. He heard a voice saying, *Jack, are you awake?* and he felt his eyelids flitter. The room was foggy and an angel was smiling down at him. He felt a pressure in his body somewhere, but he was still floating, trying to find the outlines of his form, his boundaries. He jerked his leg, felt a heavy weight of cloth.

'He's moving. Oh. My. God. He's moving.'

The room dipped and dived like a rollercoaster into a

black tunnel. He closed his eyes again and held on to the hand. Katie's hand. Refusing to let go.

When he woke up again the next morning, he found that he was in hospital. Katie was by his side.

'What the fuck am I doing here?' There was a disgusting taste in his mouth. As he spoke, he could almost see clouds of stinky breath. His tongue felt as though it was coated in the fur of a dead rat that had been trapped in a sewer for the last week. 'Shit – I need to clean my teeth. Urgh. God.'

To his amazement, Katie burst into giggles. She kept laughing, holding his hand so hard it hurt.

'What? Was I in a fight?' Jack asked. His ribs ached as he spoke. He gazed at his legs, his arms, for plaster. None.

Then, just as Katie started to explain, he remembered. Smashing into the car, his body spiralling in the air, the crunch of his head on the road.

'Mick! Shit! I owe him some money!' Jack tried to sit up.

'Ssh, Jack, it's all right,' Katie swallowed her giggles, pushing his hair back from his sweaty forehead. He was sweating all over, in fact. The sheets were too hot; he felt as if he was being mummified. 'Henry paid them off. It's fine.'

'Shit . . . Thank God . . . so I'm OK?'

Katie went on to explain that he wasn't quite OK. Fortunately, the car hadn't hit him full-on, otherwise he might have suffered a broken back. But, as it had been a near-miss and he had been hit from the side, he had suffered concussion, injuries to the left side of his body, a few broken ribs and a sprained wrist.

As she spoke, Jack gazed up at her face. Her hair fell in dirty clusters. There was a dark ring of coffee around her mouth, as though she had pencilled the edges with eye-liner. Her skin was dry and flaky, her eyes dead with insomnia and worry. And when he saw tears of relief start to slide down her cheeks, he wanted to comfort her, and felt oddly ashamed. But he was too tired. So tired. Overwhelmed with shock, a thick sludge of exhaustion was travelling over him. He didn't have the energy to talk any more. Just sleep.

As Katie went to get a nurse, Jack tugged her back.

'No,' he muttered.

'What?' she said, her voice all thick and snotty. 'What?' she sniffed.

'Please, just stay here.' He kept his eyes shut. 'Just stay here and hold my hand.'

Jack spent the next four days in hospital, during which time he grew thoroughly bored.

'Do you know?' he once said to Katie. 'There are seven marks on my ceiling. Seven blemishes in various shapes and sizes, all of which I could describe in depth. One of them looks exactly like the mole my French GCSE teacher had on her neck. That's how bored I am.'

Thank God for Katie.

Her visits were the highlight of his day. If he had the energy, they talked incessantly. Katie was forced to reiterate exactly what was happening in *Neighbours* and *EastEnders* (Jack had started moaning that he ought to have his own TV, that the NHS was a waste of taxpayers' money – until Katie had pointed out he'd never paid tax), or just supply general gossip on Leila and Henry (who apparently had had some kind of row and weren't speaking to each other again). Katie brought him cigarettes – though she cruelly only allowed him one a day, telling him he had to give up now. And if he was too tired to chat, she read to him from the *Sun* and they giggled over the problem pages. Or from *On the Road*, her voice like pure honey, washing over him like a healing balm.

She also cheered him up by bringing along his camera with a new film. It was ages since he'd taken any photos. Jack enjoyed the challenge of having to make boring scenes interesting. The knarled face of his surly nurse, a spray of magazines across a chair, a mint-green splash of disinfectant across the bathroom tiles. He even photographed the blemishes on his ceiling on one particularly radiant sunset, when inky red light ran across the ceiling like marbled paint, making the marks seem like mysterious blood stains. Jack decided to caption the picture 'THE SCENE OF THE CRIME'.

Occasionally, Leila and Henry visited too. Separately, though.

They only made him feel very awkward. It was just too weird having Leila being so *nice* to him, saying he could stay as long as he needed to. And then, because she couldn't think of much else to say, she'd absent-mindedly eat all his precious grapes. The only way to make her go, Jack realised tiredly, was to mention Henry was coming. Then she got flustered and left quickly.

As for Henry, it was just as bad. The first time he came in, Henry spent about ten minutes asking him how he was before Jack had the courage to bring up his brief flirtation with homosexuality.

'Forget it,' Henry said instantly. 'I'm trying to,' he joked feebly.

It wasn't mentioned again.

In quieter moments of reflection, Jack relived his time before the accident. It seemed as if it had all happened so, so long ago. As if he'd been a different person. His life before the crash now seemed to him like a mad rollercoaster, as if he'd been inevitably hurtling towards a destructive end. Selling drugs, falling for Henry, trying to seduce Leila. Madness gone mad. In a funny way, Jack was almost glad he'd had the crash. It had slowed him down, brought him back to normality. Now he was ready to get his life back on track. He just couldn't wait to get out, to go home with Katie, to have a proper hair-cut and a shave . . . and a long, luxurious bath . . . and a decent copy of *Loaded* . . . and a long session watching the cricket . . . and getting his film developed, and, best of all, a good old deep-pan crusty four-cheese and pepperoni pizza.

43
Charlie

'Oh God, Puck – does it have to be the Houses of Parliament?' I cried miserably, gazing up at the dreaded building, its spires like huge vampire teeth in the blood-coloured sunset.

'Come on, Charlie, there's nowhere else to go.'

I yelped as Puck tugged me on. We still hadn't managed to get our handcuffs off and my wrist now had a nasty red sore, a bracelet-shaped scar, circled around it.

Since being ostracised from the fairy camp, Puck and I had been roaming around like New Age travellers. We'd tried kipping in a cage at London Zoo, but the giraffes kept mistaking us for leaves and nibbling us. Even now we knew that Jack was alive and free from his spell (thank God!) we realised that we would still not be welcome back at the fairy camp. Not until we had fulfilled our task of making him happy by New Year's Eve . . .

As soon as we flew in through the doors of the Houses of Parliament, I felt as though the gates to the Garden of Eden had clanged shut.

In the supernatural world, the Houses of Parliament

are more than just a place for MPs to hang out and bicker. It's our equivalent of Amsterdam. An atmosphere of stress, grit and restlessness, exacerbated by years of political disillusionment, hangs about the building like smog. And yet its central location in the heart of London makes it very handy for sprites, goblins, fairies and other creatures to spend some time. It's a stopping-over place, an in-between-places hideout, full of oddballs and crooks, New Age travelling sprites selling crystals and cheap vanishing spells, sailors, and goblin drug lords quietly hustling in bars, uttering in people's ears, 'Half an ounce of puffclock seed . . . ?' Only last month a fairy from Kew Gardens had been found dead in one of the rooms, suffocated by a twig in her mouth during a seedy sexual act.

The next time you watch *Prime Minister's Question Time*, take a closer look behind the rows of green seats at a long skirting board nicknamed 'The Ark'. Here there are endless mouse-holes, some dating from the 1950s, some more modern, which have been turned into hostels and hotels.

Puck and I began our weary trek down the row. The first was a grimy hole with an earthworm hanging outside that glowed an unusual, rich red colour. We paused uncertainly, then jumped as a beetle in drag emerged, waggling her scarlet-tipped antennae at us seductively.

'Hello darlings,' she said in a thick Australian accent, snapping her claws and raking her beady eyes over us in a manner that made me shudder. 'And what exactly are you looking for? I can see from those cuffs that you like a bit of S&M?'

'I'll give you S&M – Sod off and Mind your own business,' said Puck sourly and she flounced back into her hole.

A few feet on we came to the next hole. It looked a lot better, with a white painted sign saying 'Luigi's Guest Home, established 1950, bed, breakfast and dinner, including ten varieties of toadstool'. But Luigi, who turned out to be a large Italian spider with a moustache, took one look at us and our handcuffs and shook his head, saying they were 'full up'.

'Bastard,' I muttered. I felt as though my heart was sinking into my stomach. I felt so rejected. I felt like scum.

We dragged on to the next place. This one was a rather small, grubby hole. A mouse with large ears and wearing an apron appeared.

'Evening,' he said, slightly suspiciously.

'Good evening,' said Puck, deliberately putting on a posh voice. 'My name is Pease High-Spriteington-Floo and this is my wife, Cobwebsbottom. We are travelling actors.'

'Actors!' The mouse's face instantly lit up. 'Have you been in anything famous?'

'Er, no,' Puck muttered.

The mouse looked disappointed but let us in all the same.

Inside was a dark, oval bar and a café where a very old mouse, so thin and gaunt he looked like a shrivelled mouse-dropping, was hunched on a stool, moodily sipping beer. Gazing over us, he gave a nod; we smiled back, self-conscious and uneasy, as the mouse led us down into a draughty, low corridor where we had to stoop to avoid hitting our heads.

'My name's Mickie, by the way,' he added, pulling a big circle of keys from his waistband.

Puck and I instantly exchanged glances – *Mickie Mouse* – and involuntarily let out sniggers. Immediately,

Mickie turned to us with a glare. His warm manner had frozen into hostility. 'Yeah, my parents had a sense of humour too.'

'Sorry, sorry,' I said.

Mickie gazed at us, his eyes falling to our wrists. Puck and I leaned in together but it was too late – he'd already seen the cuffs.

'Er, Char – I mean Cobwebsbottom gets stage-fright,' Puck joked weakly. 'I had to chain her to me to stop her from running away.'

He paused, as if debating whether or not to throw us out. Then he said abruptly, 'It'll be seventy-five petals a night.'

Oh well. It seemed better than nowhere.

'Great,' said Puck, forcing a smile.

Unfortunately, we paid up before we'd seen the room. It looked like something a water rat would sleep in. A single bed made from pieces of old crate nailed together. A saggy mattress that looked as if it was full of mouse droppings. Shivering under a thin blanket made from itchy badger-fur, Puck and I curled up together in a nervous, cold sleep, cuddling together for warmth and comfort.

We went to visit Jack in hospital the next day. Henry was just leaving and we both wriggled uneasily – Henry was the only human left who was still under the influence of a love spell. And, judging from the tender looks he gave Katie as she left with him, it hadn't worn off.

Well, today we weren't using any magic on Jack. Spells were now a swearword for me and Puck. We were just going to try subliminal thought-manipulation. It wasn't half as strong as magic, and sometimes it took weeks to work. But it was our last hope.

It's very simple and a bit like Louise Hay (perhaps she's been in contact with fairies) and her theories on positive thinking. It's just dropping repetitive ideas into the subconscious. The human mind, you see, can be trained like a dog.

So, as Jack drifted into sleep, Puck and I positioned ourselves on either side of his head, whispering, *Please Jack, please prevent the incinerator from being built, please Jack*, praying that he could hear us.

Returning to our bed and breakfast, trying to ignore the din of Prime Minister's Question Time, we noticed that there were ominous yellow posters pinned up all over the Ark. The black letters blazed:

WANTED
TWO ROGUE FAIRIES ON THE RUN
POTENTIAL KILLERS
REWARD: 2000 PETALS EACH

'Wow!' said Puck in a shaky voice. 'It looks like we're famous.'

'Puck, this is dreadful.' I went pale. OK, I know this sounds vain, but I couldn't help grimacing at the photos. Puck's was great – he looked all dark and debonair, a quarter-inch of thistle-stubble peppering his jaw like a pop star. But my photo was one of those dodgy passport snaps taken inside a 'PHOTOS IN JUST FIVE MIN-UTES' toadstool cubicle. I looked like a ghost. With bad acne. God, if I was going to be a criminal, I could at least appear *glamorous*.

That was the trouble. None of this was glamorous. Puck and I had often talked about running away in the past. In my fantasies it had always seemed so exciting; I'd pictured us as the fairy equivalent of Bonnie and Clyde or a couple in a Tarantino movie – sexy, wielding guns, exuding danger, dashing from place to place in a whirl-wind of violence and romance. Instead, we were stuck in a squat – homeless, friendless and penniless – and about to be recognised at any moment. Could things get any worse?

I just prayed that Jack would save us. He was our last hope . . .

44
Jack

To say Katie was surprised when Jack volunteered to help with her campaign against the incinerator was a bit of an understatement.

The night he'd come home, she'd cooked him a special, super-healthy meal of rice and vegetables, to make up for all the hospital sludge he'd been forced to eat. His sprained left wrist was still in a sling and Susie found it very amusing that Katie had to help him chop up his food and then fork it into his mouth as though he was a baby.

Jack, then, predictably, spent the next few days camped out on the living room sofa with the TV on non-stop. Katie had expected him to stay there for the next three months; *Jack is a lazy sod – he'll milk his 'recovery period' as much as he can*, she'd thought affectionately.

So she was amazed when Jack, who in the past had referred to her more eccentric colleagues as 'mad long-haired Greenpeace lentil-shaggers', threw himself into her environmental campaign with great gusto.

There was only a week left before the council made its final decision as to whether to grant permission for the incinerator to be built, so Katie was bowled over by his help. It was so much more fun having someone else to stuff envelopes and draw up petitions with rather than doing it all on her own. She'd always been nervous about phoning up councillors, but Jack, who was both very persuasive and a bit of a bully, was brilliant at bringing them round. Whenever Katie had tried to get local papers to cover the issue, they'd devoted about three lines to it; when Jack sold them the story, they splashed it across their front pages, with a huge picture of Jack standing grimly in front of the waste site.

A week later, they gathered at the council offices for the final vote. Many of the hardcore protestors had turned up waving placards and wearing wacky costumes, including one guy who was dressed as Darth Vader. Susie was thoroughly enjoying herself; she had put on her fairy costume from the school play and was waving around a glittery wand and crying, 'I'm going to cast a spell so we get an incinerator.' Jack had to keep correcting her and telling her, 'No, Susie, we're *against* it, OK?'

Inside, the public had to stand in the gallery in silence, gazing down on the councillors below.

'That article in the local newspaper really worked,' Katie whispered to Jack, thrilled. She'd worried that about three people would turn up. But the gallery was packed, frothing with people of all ages from Camden, Primrose Hill and beyond.

The rule was that the public had to remain completely silent while the councillors discussed each issue and then voted. Jack found the rule hard to bear. They had lobbied the councillors with phone calls and even managed to meet a few for a presentation. But many were still ill-informed or brainwashed.

'An incinerator will actually purify the air,' a councillor

below, who looked about a hundred and sounded as if he was about to drop dead at any moment, called out in a quavering voice.

'Oh bullshit!' Jack yelled down. 'The evidence shows they cause respiratory diseases. They're not ionisers, for God's sake—'

'ORDER, ORDER!' The clerk banged his gavel.

Jack sullenly bit his mouth shut. Beside him, Katie gave him a reproving but proud smile and took hold of his hand. He squeezed it tightly, but anger still burned inside him. *Calm down*, he kept telling himself – it wasn't normally in his nature to get so het up about anything. When the councillors started to vote, it all became too much. He felt blood throbbing in his temples. The air was thick; there were too many people about. He told Katie he needed to go; she glanced up in alarm as he pushed his way out, the door slamming behind him.

Outside, he lit up a cigarette. God, this was stressful. He could see now why Katie was so passionate about her job. Oh dear – where would it all end? Next he'd be fighting for dolphins and rainforests when, let's face it, it was all pointless, everything came down to money. He'd just end up one of those sad, bearded protestors who didn't wash and smelled of animal poo.

A few minutes later, Susie appeared, her wand limp in her hand.

'Well?' Jack cried.

'I think we lost . . .'

'No, we didn't!' Katie emerged, laughing. 'Susie, we're against the incinerator. Oh Jack – we won the vote! We did it!'

Afterwards, they had a wild evening of celebrations. A horde of them swept down to the pub for several rounds of rowdy pints. Every so often, Jack kept giving Katie mad hugs, punching the air and crying, 'I don't fucking believe it – WE DID IT!' At around nine o'clock, Katie felt that Susie had had quite enough excitement and illicit beer and dropped her off home and put her to bed.

'Come on!' said Jack, grabbing Katie's hand. 'Leila's home, so we can leave Susie. Let's go and have some dinner. I'll pay. Or Barclaycard will.'

Katie wilted for a moment. She was absolutely leaden with exhaustion. It was as if she'd been surviving on adrenaline for the last three weeks; she'd felt she needed a wheelchair to get herself home, a stairlift to cruise her upstairs and tip her into bed.

Yet something, a restlessness, a sense of anticipation sparkling in the air, made her want to stay up. After all these weeks and weeks of hard work; they deserved to have some fun.

They ended up at the Pizza Express on St. Martin's Lane. The waiter showed them to a secluded table at the front, shielded by a large bookcase of old, tatty volumes. Katie gazed up at the sky, icy-clear, speckled with faint stars, and her heart skipped with happiness.

'Oh wow, I can't believe we WON!' she burst out.

'I know.' Jack shook his head, grinning. 'It's been such a wonderful, fantastic, cool, bloody brilliant evening!'

'Phew, I feel so tired, though. As if I could sleep for a week. I wish I could go on holiday.'

'Well, I'm thinking of going off travelling. Why don't you come too? Come on – we can go together. Let's just pack our bags tomorrow and take off somewhere!'

'What? No – I mean – I'm broke, and what about Susie?'

'Ah well . . .' Jack lowered his eyes. 'I think I might take off for a bit on my own then.'

At first Katie thought he meant a weekend away in Paris or Amsterdam. Then Jack quietly informed her that, no, he was kind of, probably, planning to go to Europe. *For a month . . . maybe more . . .*

He was leaving in two days' time, he added casually. Or so.

'I see,' said Katie.

'What? What do you mean, "I see"?'

'Nothing.'

'*Nothing*? Katie, you always say *nothing* when you mean *something*. Look – I'm sorry – I will really miss you. I will. I just – since the accident, I've been feeling a bit restless. I've really enjoyed helping you with all this campaigning – I wanted to get my teeth into something. But now I want to start earning money again – I have to pay Henry back. I want to take some photos, really good, quality shots, to build up a portfolio, so maybe I can get into photography again. And I can't just ignore Leila. I've been kipping at her place for months now.'

'Well, there are plenty of decent places to photograph here,' Katie said desperately.

'Like what, Burger King?' Jack said with a defensive edge to his voice.

Katie knew Jack well enough to know that he hated being nagged. He had a stubborn streak that often prompted him to do the reverse of whatever he was being pressurised to do.

'Anyway,' said Jack, putting his hand on her wrist. 'Come on, let's order.'

Katie couldn't focus on her menu; she gnawed her lip, picked at stray skin, gazed out into the dark street where a crowd of students were emerging from a performance of *Art*. She knew it was irrational but she couldn't help taking Jack's decision to leave personally. *I stayed by his side every bloody day and night during the accident – and now he's better, he's just going off and deserting me.* She frowned. A deeper, more frightened voice argued, *I nearly lost you, Jack. I really thought I'd lost you for ever. I feel the way I did when Susie was two years old and she disappeared in a super-market. For weeks afterwards, I wouldn't let her out of my sight, I was so terrified of it happening again.*

Anything could happen while Jack was travelling. A plane crash. A fight in a bar. Some mad Australian game-keeper accidentally shooting him. OK, so it was silly. But it could happen.

She felt as if all her euphoria over the incinerator had trickled away. She didn't even care any more. She realised then that the reason she had enjoyed the campaign so much was because she'd got to spend more time with Jack.

'What did you mean, Katie, when you said that you married Keith because of me?' Jack asked, out of the blue.

'What?'

'Ages ago. That night I behaved like a real letch and tried to kiss you in the hotel room. You said to me, "I married Keith because of you," and ever since then I've always wondered what you meant. After all – if you think back . . . well, I was always the one who told you *not* to marry that jerk.'

'I . . . I . . .' Katie was lost for words. 'Well,' she said lightly, trying to make a joke of it. 'I guess – when in doubt, blame Jack.' She laughed. 'I blame everything that's gone wrong in my life on you. All your fault.'

'Oh, thanks,' Jack said, smiling, but then he looked serious again. 'So, do you ever think you'll remarry?'

'God, I don't know. Probably not. Once was bad enough.'

The waiter came to take their orders – Soho Pizza for Jack, Fiorentina for Katie. They shared a garlic bread for the starter, which arrived swiftly. They tucked in eagerly, their knives and forks chinking, both starving after a long evening's drinking.

'Maybe you will find a new man, you never know,' Jack said idly, wiping away butter from his chin.

'What is this, the Jack DeAntiquus dating agency?' Katie laughed.

'Maybe we should fix you up with the waiter, he so obviously fancies you.'

'What? He does not.'

'He does, Katie. You ought to be more confident – you never seem to think anyone fancies you. Look – I ordered a pizza and the waiter rolls his eyes as if he might just bring it, if I'm lucky. You order and he looks as if you've just proposed to him. He went totally dewy-eyed.'

'Jack, keep your voice down, he's at the next table,' Katie hissed, laughing.

Katie was even more embarrassed when Jack went off to the loo and on the way back appeared to have a few words with the waiter, shooting her raised-eyebrows glances as if he was setting up a blind date.

'OK – I just asked him if he was free later tonight and he said he hopes you practise yoga because you're going to need to be very flexible to cope with his sexual prowess—'

'Jack, you DIDN'T!'

'Nah, I just told him we wanted some wine. OK – where were we? So, come on. Tell me. Who would be your ideal man? If you could marry anyone?'

'Brad Pitt . . . OK, seriously. I guess my standards have actually gone up since last time round. I mean – when I was twenty, I was in love with the idea of love and marriage, but now I'm more practical, which actually spoils romance in a way. I'm not looking for a man who brings me flowers, though that would be nice. Or a bastard – I don't want a man who's going to control me or expect me to bend my life around his. Just someone who is *nice*. Without being a wimp – he has to have an edge, and a sense of humour. I don't even care if he's good-looking. I want him to be brilliant with Susie, and caring, and relaxed, and if I'm tired be willing to take Susie to school, and not expect me to give up my charity work so I can stay at home and cook for him.'

'Well, hey, Katie, this is the twenty-first century. I don't think blokes do expect that any more.' Jack took a sip of wine.

'But they do,' Katie said hotly. 'They do. I mean, I've only dated a few times since . . . and they say, oh yes, Katie, I want you to do your own thing, but they don't mean it. Deep down, they're thinking, *I'm sure this charity thing is just a hobby, I'm sure she'll give it up eventually*. I'm not a feminist but it would be nice to find a man who would share the cooking.'

'Fair enough,' said Jack. As the waiter arrived with their main courses, Jack watched him closely as he put down Jack's pizza with a scowl and Katie's with a beaming flourish. Jack widened his eyes at her meaningfully and started humming the wedding march under his breath; Katie kicked him under the table, trying not to laugh.

'Mmm, this is gorgeous,' Jack tucked in. 'God, d'you remember – the very, very first night we went out for a meal was a trip to Pizza Express?'

Katie wasn't sure what prompted her to say what she said next. Maybe it was the wine, or the curious intimacy of the evening.

'I had such a crush on you, you know, back then.'

Jack's head sprung up like a jack-in-a-box. 'You did?'

Why the hell did I say that? I've spent eight years holding that in. And now I just blurt it out.

'Oh, it was just a silly thing. You know. I don't want you to get big-headed now, Jack,' Katie wielded her fork at him. 'You were a lot more handsome then, you didn't have the grey hairs you do now,' she added viciously, knowing Jack was very sensitive about the occasional ones he found dotted in his hair.

'Thanks. But did you really?' Jack persisted. 'You really fancied me?'

'You know I did, Jack,' Katie said, trying not to sound irritable. This was too surreal – after eight years of sweeping the subject under the mat, now all of a sudden they were shaking it out, wiping away cobwebs and calmly discussing it over pizza. 'It was perfectly obvious.'

'I do remember you being all weird and shaky.' Jack admitted. 'And do you remember when I offered you a cigarette and you pretended you could smoke and then almost coughed your lungs up?'

'Oh, don't! Anyway—' Katie wanted to change the subject, but Jack wouldn't let it go.

'So how long did it last, your crush?'

'What about you?' Katie picked on a subject that had been chewing away in her mind for some time now too. 'What about this girl you were so in love with a few weeks back? You never talk about her any more. You know, when you were in hospital, it struck me that I ought to call her. I went through your address book but, God, there were forty thousand girls' names in there. I asked your mum, too, but she was all fraught and worried and forgetful. So I just left it, and you never brought it up or asked for her . . . so I assumed it was over.'

'Oh, her. Her,' Jack laughed awkwardly. Ahem. His obsession with Leila now seemed as embarrassing and distant as a passing teenage crush. 'That . . . didn't quite work out.'

But he said he loved her. Katie frowned, cutting up the last square of her pizza. *Is this Jack's idea of love? God, he's fickle.*

'She dumped me,' Jack improvised hastily. Nearly true. After all, Leila had idly flirted with him, then tossed him aside. 'But back to my earlier question, which you so craftily side-stepped there, Katie. You and your crush on me. How long did it last?'

'Oh Jack, you're not going to let me forget this, are you? Promise me you won't tease me all night? OK – two weeks, at the most. Until I got to know you and realised what a stupid bastard you are,' Katie added with a smile, thinking through gritted teeth, *Only the last eight years, Jack, but, hey, some of us are more observant than others.* 'Sorry. Look – I really am going to miss you if you go. I was kind of planning all sorts of things for Christmas . . . but . . . it doesn't matter.'

'I'm going to miss you too,' said Jack earnestly. ★

'Let's have a toast.' She raised her glass. 'To your swift return.'

They chinked glasses and, even though they couldn't afford it, ordered pudding, not wanting the meal to end, wanting to savour every minute. They stayed in the restaurant right up until the lights were dimmed, the restaurant was empty, and the waiters politely asked them to leave.

Back home, they didn't feel like going to sleep. Somehow there was a strange sense of anti-climax, as if there was still so much to discuss, so much to do and share, but too few hours left.

Going into the kitchen to make bedtime drinks, Katie caught sight of Jack's old, dirty trainers lined up wonkily by the back door, and a wail of affectionate misery coursed through her. *I don't want him to go. Who's going to tease me at meal times? Buy lottery tickets with me and watch the draw? Come out for a walk with me and Susie on Sunday evenings? Calm me down when I'm fighting with Keith over the monthly payments he never coughs up?* She wanted to run to Jack, get down on her knees and beg him to stay. Instead, she got two cups out and switched on the kettle.

She had just gone back into the living room with two steaming cups of hot chocolate when there was a white flash and she very nearly slopped them both down her front.

'Jack!' she half-cried, half-laughed, putting down the mugs and staining milky rings on the coasters.

Jack was standing by the window, fiddling with his camera.

'I want some photos of you so that I can remember you when I'm away travelling,' he said, trying not to look sad. 'Come on – just one more. No, not there – the light's crap as it is. Over there by the picture.'

Katie let out a theatrical sigh and fluffed her hair, wishing she'd washed it. She sucked in her cheeks and swanked her hips, doing a piss-take supermodel pose.

'No – Jack – that was a joke. You weren't meant to take a photo!' Katie screeched as he snapped away. She pointed her finger at him and he took another of her looking all cross and indignant. 'JACK!'

'Sorry!' Jack had to put his camera down, he was laughing so much.

Finally, after Katie had been allowed to brush her hair properly, Jack positioned her again, sitting on a chair and staring straight into the camera. Jack knelt down before her, gazing into her eyes and tweaking back a few strands of hair from her face. His touch was so tender that she flapped him away like a fly and told him to 'bloody well get on with it'. Jack, peering through the camera and adjusting the distance, thought how beautiful she looked, clear-skinned and without make-up, glowing under the golden lamplight. Katie, trying not to move her lips, hissed for him to hurry up. Jack smiled and took a shot.

He ended up taking the whole film.

They slept together again that night. Not sex. Just sleeping. Just as they had done so many times before. Only this time it was a little different.

It was Jack's request and Katie relented easily. Jack loved cuddling under her quilt – the patchwork one her mother had handed down to her, a sprawl of navy and ochre, stars and stripes, flowers and faces. Feeling slightly odd, Katie self-consciously covered herself up, putting on a pair of leggings, thick green Milletts walking socks and a baggy grey jumper with a hood, which caused Jack to sarcastically remark, 'Are you dressed for the Arctic?' as he peeled back the quilt.

Katie, who was pretending to be engrossed in her Jilly Cooper, did a double-take. He was wearing boxers. Hang on – *black* boxers. With a *fine gold trim*. She recognised them because they'd once had a confiding session about the underwear they wore on first dates to impress. The black ones were Jack's pulling pair.

'What are you wearing those for? Trying to look like James Bond?' she muttered, slotting her bookmark into her book and putting it on the cabinet.

'Do I get a bedtime story?' Jack snuggled up to her, warm and almost naked.

'No,' said Katie firmly.

'Do I get a goodnight kiss?' Jack picked up their joke again. Only this time neither of them laughed. Katie coolly flicked the light off and for the first five minutes

403

they had their usual fight ('Katie, you're stealing the covers!' 'Jack, this is *my* bed!' 'Katie, can we *please* open a window, it's too hot!' 'Well, I'm cold! You keep pulling the covers off and my feet are freezing!') Then Jack warmed her by curling his bare feet against her wool-clad ones.

'Better?' said Jack.

'Mmm,' Katie replied. Just what was going on here? She had the tiniest, most delicious feeling that Jack was . . . *but no – No!* she told herself. Remember the last time in the hotel. Jack gets horny and he . . . but this was different. He wasn't even drunk. And yet . . .

Oh God, I'm never going to get to sleep tonight, she sighed inwardly, rolling on to her side away from him and nestling against the pillow.

Then, as Jack rolled over too, sighing, and cuddled up against her so they were like two spoons, she felt her heart almost stop. His chest stretched along her back, his arm was slung casually over her waist. The silence was unbearable. She was terrified he could hear her ragged breathing. She listened to the night sounds – traffic, voices shouting, the distant ripples from the canal, faint music from a party on a houseboat. Every cell in her body was tingling with desire, swimming with lust. She kept half-praying, half-hoping that he would . . .

45
Katie

She woke up some time later to find the bed empty. She blinked at the clock. It was 2:45 a.m. She must have dropped off for a while. Even though she'd been sleeping, part of her subconscious had stayed awake, acutely, deliciously aware of his warmth beside her. But now he was gone. She splayed her fingers across the sheets, feeling reassured by the warm patch from his body heat. In the darkness it felt shiveringly erotic and she smoothed her fingers over the sheets again, tracing the creases, the indents of his body. She heard a creak and pulled back jumpily, waiting for the flush of the toilet, the splash of water in the sink. But there was just the wind, and the creaking of the house as it stirred in its foundations. She frowned, got up, pulled on her dressing gown – deliberately opting for the silky purple one Jack had brought back from Japan for her years back, patterned with black-ink sprays of flowers. Her old pink one she kicked under the bed.

Padding down the stairs, she felt silly. What was she doing, putting on a sexy dressing gown and chasing after him? He was probably just getting a drink of water. But then she heard the ripple of guitar notes from the living room; his playing sounded edgy, strange and he kept swearing under his breath as he went out of tune. She poked her head around the door.

'Hi,' she whispered.

Jack was sitting on the sofa in the milky darkness, plucking at his guitar.

'I couldn't sleep,' he whispered back, his eyes glinting like a cat's in the gloom.

'You know,' she giggled. 'You had me then. I actually thought you might have taken off and gone travelling.'

'Oh well . . .' Jack looked down at his fingers, adjusting a chord. 'I, er, I don't really know about this travelling thing. It was just a vague idea. I think I might stay put for a bit longer.'

'Oh, right. Well, that's great.' Pause. 'Er, would you like a hot drink?'

A few minutes later she came back, bearing two large mugs swishing with hot milk. As she bent down to put them on the coasters, she added, 'You're so good at the guitar. I'm jealous, I admit it.'

'Come and have a lesson,' Jack laughed.

'What – at this time of night?'

'Why not? I feel on such a high, I can't sleep. Come on, it'll be a laugh!'

Katie opened her mouth to say that she'd never had any inclination to learn the guitar; she'd always refused his past offers to teach her Nirvana's 'Come As You Are'. Sadly, Katie's musical tastes were governed by her daughter's, which didn't aim much beyond Britney and Kylie.

But Jack's eyes were glinting playfully and, impetuously, she said, 'Go on then, but we have to play quietly, Leila and Susie are asleep.' Shutting the door behind her, she sat down beside him on the sofa.

'No, like this,' said Jack.

He sat back, spreading open his legs so she could sit in front of him, his thighs curled around her, her back to his chest. She felt as though her stomach had just jumped off a diving-board and plunged into her groin. She tried to keep her hands steady as he hoisted the guitar on to her lap and positioned her fingers on the strings. The battered brown wood was splattered with stickers from foreign countries, along with Susie's Barbie stickers, plus numerous scratches, dents and grooves.

'What are these?' she joked nervously. 'Knotches on your guitar for all the girls you've been with?'

'Of course not.' Jack sounded upset.

'Sorry,' she blushed.

'Look, stop talking and behave.'

'Yes sir.'

'Or you get lines.'

'Ooh.'

'Come on. This is E-flat.'

And then: 'Come on, Katie.'

And, once again a few minutes later: 'This is easy. Concentrate, girl!'

How can I concentrate, Katie wanted to wail, *when you're so close to me?*

His warm breath was tickling her ear. Then, finally, just as she had succeeded in getting the note, she felt him lightly kiss her neck. She pictured the steamy imprint of his lips on her skin. She could feel desire licking in her stomach like a fire, her breath cloudy with love and lust. Then, as he trailed more breathless kisses over her cheek, she let out a groan. He caught his fingers in her hair, twisting her head back and putting his lips to hers, his hands cupping her breasts, his erection in her spine. The guitar slipped from her hands to the floor with a loud *twang!*

407

Even though she'd known it was going to happen, had somehow felt the knowingness tingling in her spine ever since she'd woken up, stood on the stairs and heard the nervous twanging in his guitar playing, even though she'd been waiting for this moment for so many years, her desire turned to blankness at first. As though it was happening to someone else. His tongue slipped into her mouth, his hands smoothing over her hair and arching down her back. Then, as his hand slipped between the silky folds of her dressing gown and burrowed under the thick jumper, his fingers cold against her skin, she let out a slight yelp of pleasure and shock and pulled back, overwhelmed. She gazed at Jack. He was staring at her with such earnest intensity that it was all too much; she burst into laughter.

'Well, I'm glad you find me so amusing.' Jack looked genuinely hurt.

'Oh – God – no, I'm sorry.' Katie flushed like a schoolgirl. She *felt* like a schoolgirl. As if this was her first kiss – knock-kneed and not sure where to put herself, how to touch. 'I'm just – this is all so weird and unexpected and – well – a surprise. A nice surprise, but . . .'

'I've been wanting to kiss you again for quite a while,' said Jack.

'What, since Dominique? Since Jessie?' Katie couldn't resist.

'Katie – I'm serious. I have been wanting to kiss you for ages, only last time you hit me. Seriously, I'm not drunk now, I really— Look – we've been friends . . . and . . . things change . . . and things grow . . . and I've kissed you . . . and there you go.'

'Oh right, that makes everything clear,' Katie giggled.

Jack gave a sweet, shy smile, rolling his eyes at his own inarticulateness. He leaned in again and they shared another light kiss, but Katie pulled back before it became too passionate. Jack, sensing that she needed to talk, got up. For one neurotic moment, she thought he was going to walk out; instead, he turned the light on. Her eyes stung, adjusting to the glare. She laced her fingers together awkwardly as he closed the curtains, then came and sat beside her.

For a moment, they sat like a couple before a marriage guidance counsellor, all stiff and awkward, staring at the ticking clock on the mantlepiece, their breaths catching with desire.

'This is so surreal, isn't it?' said Jack, and Katie felt relieved. 'Come here.' He spread open his arms and she cuddled up against him.

'So when are we getting married?' Katie asked.

'What!'

'I'm joking, Jack.' She pulled back. 'I'm just nervous . . . I mean – are we? You know? Are we – is this a one-night stand or are we getting it together?'

'We're getting it together, I think,' Jack said nervously. 'That is, if you want to?'

'Of course I want to.'

Jack broke into a huge smile.

'Then we are.' Jack rubbed his nose against hers and, just as he was about to kiss her on the lips again, Katie let out a weak yawn, then stifled it in embarrassment.

'Sorry.'

'Am I that boring?'

'No! I'm just exhausted, darling,' Katie kissed his cheek and Jack felt a warm glow at the imprint of her lips. *Darling*. He liked that. *Darling*. He could get used to that.

'Why don't we lie down here?' Jack pulled some green cushions up for pillows. 'Just crash out and sleep and . . . maybe talk more in the morning?'

'So are we getting together because . . . you . . . like me?'

'Of course I like you.' Jack kissed her cheek. 'I've liked you for a long time. I've just been nervous . . . you know, I'm not exactly wonderful at relationships. All the time we were sitting in the restaurant tonight, I could hardly focus on my food. I kept looking at you and I just wanted to grab you right there and take you on the floor – sorry.'

'No – this is – wow,' said Katie. How could she have been so oblivious to it?

'But I admit – I was nervous too. I guess that's why I suddenly blurted out this idea of going off travelling. I wanted to run away, because, well, I knew we had something special and I was scared – I'm scared now – of messing it all up. I mean, I know this sounds a cynical thing to say only five minutes after we've got together . . .'

'No, go on,' Katie said uncertainly.

'Well, who knows what will happen? Half an hour ago I was lying in bed and thinking, What if it doesn't work out? What if, in a few months, it goes wrong and we end up hating each other? That's why I wanted to hold back, that's why I escaped and came down to play my guitar. Plus the fact that I had a huge whooping erection and I was convinced you were lying there thinking what a filthy pervert I was. Which I am, of course.'

'Oh, Jack, you're so funny.' Katie kissed his nose. 'But look – all this stuff about not working out – don't worry about it. Let's just . . . just take it as it comes, OK?'

'Yeah, take it as it comes.' Jack repeated. They lay in pensive silence for a few minutes, Jack gently stroking her shoulder in soft circles.

'Are you warm enough?' he asked fondly.

'I'm fine—' Katie broke off, yawning again, and Jack

410

smiled, lovingly stroking a few strands of hair behind her ears.

'You need to go to sleep.' He had his watch hand curled around her and he rubbed the watchface against the sofa to swivel it to face him. 'God, it's fucking three-thirty – where did the night go? Definitely time for you to go to sleep. Come on.'

'OK.' Katie pursed her lips and they kissed goodnight. She cuddled into the crook of his arm, feeling warm and protected, as if she was a little girl and for once someone was looking after her. Jack smoothed a few more blonde pencil-strands from her temples and gazed at her sleeping face. When they'd slept together way back in their early twenties, she'd always slept with innocent peace. When they'd shared a bed a few nights ago, he'd woken up ten minutes before she had and seen her face knotted with stress, as if her subconscious worries were scuttling across her mind. But tonight her expression was soft and serene. *I've made her happy,* Jack realised. But his flush of pleasure was edged with discomfort. He suddenly felt as though he was holding her life in his hands, like a fragile ornament that he mustn't drop.

As dawn tip-toed its pink feet under the curtains, Katie slept on, snoring faintly. But Jack stayed awake, frowning up at the ceiling, absorbed in thought.

46
Leila

B-rring, b-rring . . . b-rring b-rring . . .

Arghblerughwhatthefuckisthephoneringingforatthis-
timeofnight? Henry attempted to roll out of bed and
succeeded in falling to the floor. He groaned, curled his
fingers around the phone chord. It clattered to the floor
with him, the receiver banging against his head.

'God . . .' Henry finally untangled himself and picked
it up. All he could hear was silence, and then a shaky
breath. Great – it was a nutter. Ringing him at . . .
Henry's eyes travelled to his clock. Five o'clock in the
morning.

'Henry?'

'Leila?' he asked in shock. He opened his creased eyes
which were sticky with sleepydust. Leila? Leila, who had
refused to speak to him for the last four weeks; who, when
he'd tried to call her for a friendly chat, had said coldly,
'Go screw yourself.'

'I need you to come over,' she whispered shakily. 'I'm
with this guy and he's scaring me, I don't know what to
do. He's asleep but I'm scared. He's got a gun.'

'Shit? Who? Where?'

'I don't know. I'm in . . . I'm in . . . Euston Road.'

'But what, who?'

Click.

At last, he found her. Leila was waiting outside a big house, her hands coiled around two black railings. Shivering in a thin black dress. Seeing Henry pull up, she started walking away rapidly. What the fuck . . . ?

'Leila!' Henry called out of his car window. She turned, looking at him sulkily, then got in, slamming the door.

'You OK?'

'Fine,' she practically spat at him. 'You took your time. I managed to get out.'

'Well,' Henry snapped defensively, 'I didn't notice a guy chasing you out about to put bullets in your head.'

Leila peeled back her sleeve and showed him the red scar of a Chinese burn. Henry felt his stomach turn in horror. 'Luckily, he passed out drunk. OK? Look . . . can we talk about it . . back at your place?' She swallowed, narrowing her eyes.

Back at his house, Henry let Leila in. He left her there while he went to get coffees; he needed air. He strode down to Starbucks and bought an Earl Grey for him, a black sugarless coffee for her (Leila's favourite – he still remembered). He nearly slipped several times on the way back; the pavements were sheened with ice and his breath made white dragons in the chill, the heat from the cups stinging his icy fingers. Balancing the cups on top of each other, he dug for his key and went back inside.

Leila was in his living room, fiddling about like a restless cat. She was fingering the chess board spread out on the coffee table. *The Times* lay rolled next to it – Henry had been practising a Grand Master game last night.

'Want a game?' Henry asked casually.

413

She shrugged.

So they sat down and laid out the pieces. For a few minutes, as they let their drinks cool, they played in intense silence. Henry was white, Leila black.

'So are you going to tell me what's going on?' Henry enquired, sliding forward his pawn in *en passant* and capturing a piece.

Leila knawed her lip. What could she say?

Well, Henry – I don't know.

It had all started after Henry had slept with her. That horrible night. She'd just snapped. It was as if a giant hand had reached down and scrambled the jigsaw of her life into a jumble of pieces.

Or maybe it had been the excess of time on her hands. The days, normally a treadmill of reading and meetings, had become slack now that Christmas was approaching. Publishers had started winding down. Leila hated it; she needed things to *do*.

She'd gone to the Christmas publishing parties in the evenings. She'd played her role as the agent; professional, efficient, charming. She'd exchanged a hundred air-kisses and *darlings* with editors. Afterwards, she hadn't gone home. She'd felt herself bubbling with a restless, pent-up energy, like a shaken-up coke can. So she'd gone to clubs instead. Bars. She'd broken her tee-total ban. She'd knocked back cocktails. She'd smiled at businessmen. Exchanged seductive conversations, played games, told lies, accepted their expensive drinks, brushed fingers, brushed legs under the table. Gone back to apartments. Thrashed about in beds. Passed out. Woken up before dawn, in the bleak blue light. Felt hollow. Sifted through wallets to find out the names of men she'd slept with. Showered in foreign bathrooms, discovered hidden wedding rings left by the sink.

Afterwards, she'd go straight to work, skipping sleep, feeling dead with exhaustion. Yet every evening, like an alcoholic helplessly reaching for the dreaded bottle, she'd found herself going through it all again. Ten o'clock came, the parties wound down, and she would think of her bed at home, the empty peach sheets, a night of loneliness. And couldn't face it. She'd preferred nameless sex, just for the comfort of a warm body next to hers, an arm slung across her naked waist, a heartbeat echoing hers.

She had been aware that she couldn't carry on like this. She'd had a nightmare that she was walking through a dark forest, her eyes pinned through the floor of leaves and twigs, knowing that there was a trap, that one misplaced step would send her sliding into darkness. She'd known she was on the edge.

And then, that morning, she'd discovered that she'd picked the wrong man to go home with. She'd had a funny feeling about him from the start when she'd picked him up in the Hippodrome. He was tall, dark, Armenian-looking, but his eyes had been like lasers and his speech slightly slurred. Back at his flat, he'd roughly persuaded her to have anal sex, which she'd hated. Going to the loo in the night, she'd found two bags of coke stashed behind his toilet. A gun in his bathroom cabinet, along with dildos and handcuffs, a mask and a gag, and she'd been so frightened she'd been sick, spewing up in his beautiful, shiny white toilet. Then she'd tip-toed into his study and punched in Henry's number with trembling fingers.

As Leila relayed her story, Henry didn't say much. They carried on playing chess as though she was simply talking about the weather, his brow wrinkled in concentration.

'I don't know what to do.' Leila fingered the smooth wood of her knight. 'I just don't know what's happening to me. You know me, Henry – I'm a complete control freak and now . . . now . . . Am I going mad, d'you think?'

'No, no, I think it could be a good thing.'

'How?'

'Maybe there's been some grief tied up in a knot inside you and it's coming out. You're getting it out of your system. And I think you'll come through, and maybe feel relieved at the end. It's a kind of therapy. I think.'

Leila looked momentarily relieved – sharing her problems had made them seem smaller. But then a sadness came over her again and she said, 'I need a drink,' and got up, went to his drinks' cabinet, sloshed vodka into her coffee, knocked it back defiantly. Then she came and stood behind him. Reaching out, she gently ran the tip of her fingernail along the back of his neck. He shivered.

'Leila, please sit down,' said Henry, feeling oddly like her father.

She sat down, pouting, shaking back her hair. She fingered her bishop, sliding her finger up and down over the smooth wood, tweaking her nail into the sculptured head. Henry put his hands around hers. She looked up sharply. Under the table, Henry felt her leg curling against his. He pressed his hands tighter and stared straight into her eyes, his gaze firmly unsexual, but full of warmth and compassion. Leila's leg wilted; her mouth thinned. She tried to pull away but Henry held on, ignoring the chess pieces that swirled and spun and went tumbling to the floor.

'Leila—' He tried to hold her gaze, but she looked down. 'Leila. Look – I – I've never had a girl as a friend before. I've always been a bit, well, frightened of women. And I know I made a hash of our relationship and I don't think we can go back now, because – to be frank – I did still have feelings for Katie until recently—' He felt her tense. 'Although they are wearing off, actually. I realise

416

now I'm not meant to be with her, it's obvious she's meant for Jack. I guess there isn't much spark between us – Katie and I, I mean. But it is a little soon, after all the things that have happened, and I think I need time, we both need time. But I still really, really care about you. I want to be your friend – look, I love you. I want to help you through this.'

'I know,' she crumpled, her hands suddenly slack in his like wilting flowers. 'But I don't . . . I just . . .' She kept trying to swallow back tears, to find her voice. 'You know, I remember you once saying that you wanted to be happy, and that once you'd found that, you'd feel you'd found the point of life. But – I just can't see anything to live for any more. I hate life. I hate everything.'

Henry reached over and gave her a tight hug. She cuddled against him and he kissed her cheek gently, tasting a salty tear. Then Leila pulled away, saying she needed to get home, get ready for work. He watched her go to the big oak mirror on his mantelpiece and do herself up in the dusty glass, put on layer upon layer of make-up.

They walked home in near silence. The world was waking up, cars slamming, children off to school, milk carts droning.

Leila was limp with rejection. A friend. A *friend*. What was that supposed to mean? She had male friends. They were all her exs. But they were friendships she engineered, because all Leila's exs, no matter how badly she'd treated them, wanted to get back together with her. She would often flirt with them, chat to them on the phone (normally moaning about her present boyfriend), dangle a carrot of maybe-we'll-get-back-together, then whisk it away if they ever got serious.

Leila's male friends all doted on her. They bought her flowers and flattered her and took her to dinner.

417

I don't believe it, she thought, gazing up at Henry's profile, his smooth Greek nose. *I still love him. We've completely reversed. Now I love him more than he loves me, and it's too late. I've blown it.*

They said goodbye; he gave her the sweetest, tenderest kiss on the cheek, like a duck feather brushing her skin. As he walked away, she felt anger fermenting inside her again like sour vinegar. Maybe she'd stuff the office, go straight to a pub, drink, find a man, fuck, and drink till she ended up dead in some stranger's apartment or passed out with alcohol poisoning.

But then Henry turned, gave her a tiny smile, and she remembered his words – 'Leila, I'll always be there for you, call me at any time, day or night, and I'll be there for you,' – and she felt soothed. Somebody loved her. Even if he was a friend, he loved her.

Inside, the house was warm and welcoming after the winter chill. Laughter and bright voices bounced from the kitchen like party balloons. Suddenly feeling slightly cheered, Leila strode inside to find Katie and Jack sitting at the breakfast table, both fighting playfully over the last piece of toast.

They really ought to just get it out of their systems and shag, Leila thought crudely, getting the Nescafé out of the cupboard.

As she pulled open the cutlery drawer, she knocked a spoon to the floor. Bending down, she saw something under the table that made her start. She rose up quickly, digging the spoon into the coffee granules, distractedly twisting dark furrows. She gazed at the oval curve of the spoon, which reflected back the scene behind her: Jack's hand, under the table, playing with the hem of Katie's skirt, caressing her thighs in light circles.

Turning back slowly, she gazed at Jack. He looked tired, but his face was bright with euphoria. And Katie. She was blushing slightly and her face was pulsating with blood, her lips ruby red, eyes sparkling.

'Well, you're both looking very happy,' she said slowly, smiling teasingly.

Katie and Jack exchanged anxious glances: had she guessed?

'Oh, well,' Katie blushed. 'We, er, we went along last night to the council meeting. We won our fight against the incinerator so . . . we're both happy, yes.'

'Good,' said Leila, pausing, waiting for further information. But Katie just ducked her head shyly.

They were interrupted by Susie, dashing in at top speed, thumping herself down on the bench and crying exuberantly, 'Time for Coco Pops! I can't wait till tonight when Uncle Henry babysits me.' She shot Leila a sly glance. 'Are you going too, Aunt Leila?'

'No thanks – Henry and I are no longer – we're – just – we're friends now.' Leila was shocked at how much the words hurt her.

As she left she suddenly caught sight of Katie gazing over at Jack, her eyes soft with love, and Leila tasted jealousy like bile in her throat. She'd always found Katie's unrequited love for Jack rather pathetic, if not masochistic, as though Katie was the heroine in some eighteenth-century Brontë novel, moping about for the lost dark handsome stranger in her life. Leila had always thought, rather smugly, *If I was in that situation, I'd just screw my feelings for Jack into a tight ball, throw them away, move on and show I didn't need him, show I can be self-sufficient and independent.*

But now the waiting had paid off: Katie had got her man. It really looked as though she was getting together

419

with Jack, at long last. Meanwhile, the tables had turned and Leila was the one frozen in a friendship based on unrequited love. She cringed at the parallel, and as she strode out of the kitchen for a brisk shower, a fresh resolve spurted up inside her. *If Katie can do it, so can I. I'm going to get him. Friends for now, but not for long. I've never been rejected by anyone. I'll get Henry back, sooner or later . . .*

47
Katie

There were thirty-five minutes left to go.

And then Jack would be there.

Katie gazed over at the kitchen table, covered with a white sheet (there'd been no tablecloths – argh! – and Leila's dinner party ones were at the dry cleaner's). Candles winked, reflected against the two gleaming white plates. She smiled dreamily.

Ever since the kiss they'd shared last night, she'd been feeling euphoric. It had finally, finally, *finally* happened between them.

She'd woken up this morning with fear tight in her chest, frightened that he would have thrown a commitment-phobic fit and jumped on the first plane to Australia. Instead, he had hoisted his bags into her room (Jack was far too lazy to bother unpacking) and they'd shared breakfast together. Leila had walked in and she'd been bursting to tell her, but held back for fear of Susie finding out. Katie had asked Jack not to mention their relationship to Susie yet; Katie wanted to discuss it with her gently and carefully. But Jack, unable to keep his hands to himself, had kept curling his feet against Katie's under the table, and every now and again, as Susie slurped her Coco Pops and Katie distractedly nibbled her toast and Jack gazed down at *The Times* without taking a word in, they'd catch eyes. And giggle-smile. Remembering last night.

Finally, as Susie had gone ahead and got into the car to go to school, Jack had caught Katie in the hallway, pushed her up against the coats and stolen a kiss, saying 'I can't wait until tonight, it's too long!' The kiss had trickled into her stomach like liquid bliss. Katie had punched him off, laughing.

Jack was spending the day with Steve doing Christmas shopping (Katie suspected they would end up watching sport on TV instead). Katie, however, hadn't spent the day mooching about the house in a lovesick glow. She was no longer the sort of romantic who put butter in her tea or called all her girlfriends and repeated every word of Jack's conversation. As though she was afraid to indulge in her feelings, she only became more practical, more in control. She'd spent the day briskly making lists and finishing off chores – getting decorations down from the loft, wrapping up presents, sending out a hundred Christmas cards and ticking off names on a list, sorting out lost friends' new addresses and updating her address book.

But as she was hoovering, or unrolling wrapping paper, or making a cup of tea, she'd suddenly remember: *Jack kissed me last night!* And a firework of happiness would explode inside her. *He kissed me, he really kissed me!*

She'd felt exhausted from lack of sleep – they'd only managed about five hours – and yet when she'd climbed into bed to steal a quick afternoon nap, she hadn't been able to drift off. She had lain there, with her eyes closed, a high-pitched buzz in her ears, and fantasies had stolen across the blackness: Jack and her waltzing into the bedroom laughing, Jack stroking her hair back and kissing her ear, his hands clasping her shoulder blades as they sank down on to the covers . . .

They had planned a romantic dinner. Leila was out (she seemed to be out all the time these days – Katie suspected she might have a new man). Henry had agreed to babysit Susie, to take her along to his rehearsals to that she could play dressing-up.

Now a risotto was simmering on the stove, and she had put on her best long black velvet dress and was fidgeting, smoothing her fingers over her shiny cheeks. She'd wanted to wear make-up but Jack kept insisting she looked better fresh-faced.

She was just waiting for the minutes to pass and for Jack to come back.

She flipped through a tatty copy of Leila's *Vogue*. She yawned again, tiredness from last night still catching up on her. Her eyes wandered to the washing machine, a colourful whir of small jackets and jumpers and Susie's Disney-patterned socks. She suffered a flicker of memory and felt suddenly troubled, a cloud passing over her happiness. *Do I really want to get into another serious relationship?* she wondered. *What if it all goes wrong like it did with Keith?*

The spin and gurgle of the washing machine brought back memories of the day she had left him. A Sunday morning in August three years back. Their marriage had been a tatty mess by then, held together by a few threads. And it was as though all the things she hated about him, the sniping about her charity work, the snide comments that she was putting on more weight, had been gathering momentum over the last few weeks, rolling into one big ball of fury, rolling faster and faster.

Katie had always imagined that marriages ended with a huge screaming match or a dramatic event as they did on TV – a wife walking in and seeing her husband with his secretary, that sort of thing.

She hadn't expected her drama to unfold at 11 a.m. on a perfectly ordinary Sunday morning when she'd just put the washing on.

Keith was sitting at the breakfast table. The tension was thick between them; they'd just had a row about his refusal to raise her minute household allowance for groceries and clothes. *He treats me as though I'm a selfish teenager asking for an increase in her pocket money,* Katie mused.

She dished up his breakfast, fat sausages and eggs and fried toast, on to a plate. Resisting the urge to chuck the lot over his lap, she politely handed it to him. Keith looked up from his crossword, his fingers curled so tight around his pen it had indented pink marks into them.

'I don't eat fried food any more. You know the doctor told me to lay off.'

'Sorry, I forgot,' she lied. 'I'm sure you can eat it just this once.'

Katie put down the plate with a little thump, splatting a few drops of oil over his crossword. Keith looked up at her and that – that was the moment. He saw the hate in her eyes. She'd grown used to concealing her feelings over the past months and years, smoothing her anger into a smile. She couldn't do it any longer. She stood there, staring at him, venom in her eyes, silently declaring war. He stared back, shocked. The next thing she knew, he stood up and hurled the plate at her. The plate missed. Shattered on to the floor, fatty sausages skidding everywhere. Katie found her survival instincts kicking in and

424

crouched down by the washing machine, shielding her face. Keith came at her, cracking over the china with his fist curled. Later, she wondered with a shiver whether he might have killed her. He certainly looked as though he wanted to.

And yet a strange calm came over her. A relief that emotions were finally being expressed. She took her hands away from her face. She really didn't care that he was hitting her. For the first time in her life, she wasn't afraid of him. Keith, realising this, looked shocked. He trembled and recoiled slightly, as if he expected her to retaliate. Then he took a sad, shuffling step backwards and walked out. There was a clink as he picked up his golf clubs from the hallway. The front door slammed. The gravel crunched as he drove out.

Katie knew the pattern.

Later, he'd return. With flowers. Apologies. Patronising comments on how everything would be better if only she would put more effort into being a good wife.

Well, not this time.

She took Susie to a friend's house. Spent the afternoon packing, jumpy with nerves. Every time she heard the vroom of a car passing by her window, she peered through the net curtains, convinced it was him. She was so scared that she wouldn't make it, that she'd just push her cases under the bed and make his tea and lose her nerve and life would never change.

She struggled with the heavy cases, bumping them down the stairs and putting them into the boot of the car. Later, when Susie was dropped off, Katie ushered her upstairs to pick out some toys, saying, 'We're going on holiday. Come on, hurry up.'

Susie had forty-eight teddy bears on her bed. All

arranged in a painstaking collection. She stood before them, pondering, slowly picking up a panda bear, then putting him down again and frowning.

'Come on, Susie.' In a panic, Katie ran downstairs, grabbed some Tesco's bags from the cupboard under the stairs, ran back up and started to shove the bears in. Susie started screaming. Katie tried to soothe her by bribing her with a bag of crisps she'd been saving for the journey. *Hurry up, hurry up.* Finally, she grabbed the four bags, picked Susie up in her other arm, ignoring her cries, and carried her down the stairs. Susie dropped her crisps; they crunched like eggshells underfoot. Glancing back, seeing the shards, Katie giggled hysterically, imagining Keith's face when he saw the mess.

She gently placed Susie in the back of the car, clicked on her seat belt and drove away into the darkening afternoon.

She could hardly believe she had escaped.

'You OK, Susie?' Katie asked.

Susie turned away, shutting her out, sniffing, staring out of the window. Big houses sailed by with grim mouths; lampposts stooped over them with long arms; trucks rumbled by like monsters. Susie gazed at the bags of toys half-squashed under the seats, and reached down, the seat belt cutting into her, ignoring mum telling her to sit still. She lifted out Humpty, the kooky blue octopus with long arms, and hugged him tight, burying her face into his blue mustyness.

That night Katie stayed with Janine, a friend from her temping days.

They stayed there a week and moved on. And moved on. And moved on.

Until eventually she came to live with Leila.

It was awful at first. Once the initial euphoria had

passed, panic attacks set in. How would she live? Was she being a terrible mother, ripping Susie away from her home and her father? She had no money. Would Keith give her a settlement? It wasn't as if she had caught him *in flagrante* with his secretary or anything. She had no idea how divorce worked; it wasn't something she had ever imagined happening to her. Her mother's words echoed through her mind as she tossed and turned at night, Susie in bed with her: 'A Catholic marriage is for life.'

She didn't know how she would have survived without Jack.

He was always at the end of the phone, even at 3 a.m. in the morning when Keith turned up drunk on her doorstep demanding to see Susie. He persuaded her not to go back to Keith one fraught day when she woke up penniless, unable to even buy food for her evening meal, frantic that she'd made a terrible mistake. He took out a loan for her, helped her to find a lawyer, to find a charity job that brought in some money. He helped her to become strong again, to put the past behind her and move on, to learn to enjoy life once more.

Back then, she'd sworn never, ever to marry again. Never to fall in love. She had Susie and that was enough. She would focus on giving her a brilliant upbringing, that was the most important thing.

But, of course, time had softened her. She'd dated here and there. But never fallen in love with anyone other than Jack. And here she was, sitting at the kitchen table, feeling a wobbly sensation of excitement and passion, knowing that tonight, tonight she and Jack would be making love for the first time. *Jack's different from Keith*, she reassured herself.

You're getting a little ahead of yourself here, Katie thought with a wry smile.

She got up to check the risotto again and then she heard the key in the lock.

He. Was. Here.

In the hallway, she glanced at herself in the mirror, adjusting her dress. She looked not so much the Lady In Red but the Michelin Man in Black.

Jack was wearing a suit, carrying a small spray of white roses. He looked so gorgeous! She put her arms around him, breathing in the scent of his aftershave, smoothing a hand over his shaven jaw, kissing his brown neck. She pulled back.

'Wow – you look older – mature, I mean – you look great,' she gasped. 'Oh, thanks for the flowers. Take your jacket off, or keep it on if you like, it's cold isn't it, brr, I've only just got the central heating on. Oh wow these flowers are lovely – they really smell – a lot of flowers these days don't seem to smell of anything much, do they? Sorry!' She realised she was gabbling.

'Don't apologise.' Jack smiled again and she noticed then that it was a slightly forced grin, but she was so excited she carried on, regardless, sitting him down, slapping his hand as he stole a hunk of bread, letting him uncork the wine, laughing as the cork went diving into the risotto, fishing it out and serving up the meal.

She sat down next to him, waiting for him to say how great it tasted. He didn't. He did, however, slurp with eager hunger. She smiled. Jack and his huge appetite. He'd probably only had something rubbishy like McDonalds for lunch; he was probably starving.

'So, how was your day?' She buttered her bread.

'Oh good. Steve and I got some Christmas shopping. Stuff.'

'Stuff?'

'Yeah, stuff.'

428

'Good stuff?'

'Pretty good stuff.' Jack smiled feebly.

'Great, I've done mine. I just didn't know what to get for Susie – she wanted a Barbie house but I just couldn't afford it, so I got her some new Barbie outfits in a sale, and a skipping rope, and some chocolate, but I don't know, it's not quite the same.'

'Yeah.'

Silence.

'Cold out, isn't it?'

'Yeah, brr,' Jack said through a mouthful of risotto, emitting brown flecks on to the tablecloth. 'Oops, sorry.' Forgetting he was wearing a suit and not one of his usual crappy T-shirts, he automatically went to wipe it with his sleeve, but Katie hastily passed him a napkin. 'Sorry.'

'Don't – I'm ashamed to admit this, but I'm afraid the tablecloth is actually a sheet.'

'Is it?'

She'd expected Jack to laugh but his mind seemed to be elsewhere. He looked out of the window at the dark night and the candlelight danced sad ambers in his eyes.

Maybe this is all too formal – maybe I should have just ordered a takeaway pizza, she fretted, bolting down her food in her fear. *Maybe all this suits and flowers business isn't really Jack.*

'Katie.'

'Yes?'

'I'm sorry, it's no good.' He pushed his plate away and for a moment she thought he was referring to the food. Too salty? Overcooked?

'I mean – look – I love you, Katie.' He stumbled over the words, blushing. Even though Katie ought to have felt joy, she didn't. Somehow they only made her feel

429

worse. They were a warning flare, a flash of fire and a scream that Jack was about to say something terrible.

'Look,' she cut in, trying to divert the words she was terrified of hearing, 'I don't expect you to make a big commitment, Jack. I'm hardly asking you to get married, for goodness sake. D'you think, after my crap marriage to Keith, that I'm dying to put a ring on your finger? Well – I'm not. I've never even thought about it,' she lied, and then added more truthfully, 'Look, I'm scared too, OK?'

Jack looked straight into her eyes, crushing his napkin between his hands.

'Yeah, I know Keith treated you badly. And you deserve a whole lot better, which is why I don't want to hurt you.'

'You won't hurt me.' Katie laughed brittly. 'Look – I don't know myself how it's going to go between us. I might well change my mind in a few months.' (*As if,* she thought inside.) 'You can never tell at the start of any relationship whether it will work. It's a toss of a coin, it always is. You just have to take the plunge and give it all you've got, because if you stand back half-heartedly, and only put half of yourself in, well, it won't work.'

'It's no good, this just isn't going to happen, Katie.'

Silence.

Katie bit her lip. She stared down at her risotto. At the sprinkling sparkle of salt crystals. The green slithers of courgette. She remembered chopping those just an hour ago, humming happily along to an old Bangles' song on Capital Radio, feeling her love flow from her heart into her fingers, into the food, determined to make him the most scrumptious meal he'd ever tasted. And now this. *I knew,* a small voice crowed inside, *I knew this was all too good to be true.*

'Last night—' Katie heard the pleading in her voice

and tried to straighten it out, taking a nonchalant sip of red wine. 'Last night, *you* made a move on me. *You* said you wanted to settle down. Now you're saying you don't. Just what is going on, Jack?'

'That's the point.' Jack reached across and tried to take her hands but she pulled away, folding her arms. 'I really care about you. (*Oh I see*, thought Katie, he's gone from 'I love you' to 'I care'.) That's why I'm saying this now – before we get really close and it all goes wrong.'

'If you're expecting it to go wrong, it will, won't it?' she snapped. 'Look, Jack – all relationships take work. They're not like a job, but they take time, and energy, and communication.'

'This is all me, Katie.'

'I knew you'd use that line.'

'But I'm not – I'm not using a line, OK? I've never been in this situation with a girl before. I'm not using any lines, I'm being honest with you, and it's hard, because I feel like I'm being a bastard—'

'Yes, you are, Jack.'

'I'm just not ready yet. Maybe in a few years, I don't know.'

'Oh, and you expect me to hang around waiting, putting my life on hold for you?'

'No. That's why I'm saying this. I want you to have – a good life, and a good love life. You deserve love, I don't. I'm crap and I'm useless at relationships and right now I hate myself.'

'Oh, stop being so self-deprecating, tying to make me feel sorry for you.' Katie knew she was becoming more and more caustic as Jack became more quiet and humble, but she couldn't help it, her anger was percolating inside her.

'I'm sorry, but I feel constricted in relationships. I feel

431

as though I lose myself. I just like being independent and free and being able to wake up in the morning, pick up my rucksack and take off.'

'Look, Jack.' She tried to smile, to cajole him, but it felt like one last attempt at lassoing a wild horse. 'You *can* travel. I said myself that I don't want to constrict you or control you. That's what Keith did to me and it's the last thing I'd ever do to you. Don't you see – I love you. I love you,' she said more confidently. 'I want to be with you. I'm not like the other obsessive girls you've been with who call you every minute on your mobile and expect you to drop your friends and your life for them – did I mind today when you went off with Steve, even though we'd only just got together? God – no.'

'Oh, Katie, you're so lovely.' Jack suddenly rose from the table, came around the side and awkwardly pulled up her limp arms, drawing her into a hug. Despite everything, she found herself melting into him, falling for him all over again.

'Please, Jack.' She lost her guard, curling her fingers into his belt-loops. 'Please, can we just give it a go? Try and see what happens? I love you so much, I think we'd make each other really happy—'

'I'm sorry, but—'

'OK. Fine. Whatever.' She pulled back, deciding to feign calmness. But it didn't work. Not when Jack was stood there, forlornly chewing his lip, his dark eyes sad and bewildered, looking like a lost little boy, so unbearably sweet. Not when he then blurted out, 'Can't we just be friends again, like we were before?'

Katie meant to say yes, shake hands, get rid of him, go upstairs and cry her heart out. She nodded mutely. But then, as Jack gave a sigh of relief and happily reached to hug her again, she found herself crying, 'Friends? You

432

want to wrap a neat little "let's be friends" ribbon around our break-up? Well, I'm sorry but it's too late. How can we be friends after this? Eight years I've been waiting for something to happen and—' Oh shit. She saw his face. She'd let the cat out of the bag. 'Look, I'm sorry, but I can't. At this moment in time, I – I don't even like you, Jack. I hate you. You've just – just – used me.'

'No—'

'*Yes*! You were probably too knackered to find anyone else, so it was like, "Oh, let's try Katie." Well, you can treat other women like that – but not me. I thought you had more self-respect for me.' She ran out of breath, feeling tears sharp in her throat, swallowing them back. Jack just stood there, not even looking apologetic but glaring at her. She had a wild urge to punch him. Instead, she started to stack up the plates, scraping food into the bin, tossing the knives and forks into the watery jug by the sink with an angry clatter.

'If you really think,' he said quietly at first, his voice then rising furiously over the noise of cutlery, 'that this was about a one-night stand, and if you really think so little of me, after all the things we discussed last night, well, then I don't think that shows you have much *respect* towards me.'

'Oh, look—' She broke off, crashing plates into the sink, swirling up dirty water. 'Just –' she felt so churned up, she wasn't even sure what she wanted to say next '– just go, Jack. Just fuck off and go back to Steve – just go.'

'Katie.' His voice softened. 'Come on, let's talk about this like adults.'

'Adults?' she laughed. 'When you have the emotional maturity of a sixteen-year-old boy who can only have one-night stands with women who look as though they belong on page three of the *Sun*? This is why we don't go together, Jack. You're right. I do want commitment, I do want marriage even. I want something steady and long-term and solid and that's nothing I should be ashamed of. It's not a crime. I shouldn't have to hide my feelings and pussyfoot around you. Whereas you're still at the stage where you consider a second date a huge leap forward. It's ridiculous. There's an age gap between us, Jack, and it might not be in years but it's there in maturity.'

'Well, thanks a lot, Katie.'

Jack turned, fiddling with the oven gloves slung over the edge of the chair. Then, to her surprise, he said, 'You're right, Katie. I'm immature. I'm just not ready now. And I'm sorry. And I love you. And that's all I have to say. So . . . I . . .'

'Goodbye, Jack.' Katie turned to the window, washing up briskly, willing herself so hard not to cry, to keep her chin from wobbling.

'Well, bye.' Jack shuffled out. 'But I do hope we can be friends and everything . . . well, bye.'

When he'd gone, Katie waited for the tears to flow but they obstinately dried up; the hurt had burrowed deep down inside her, solidified, too raw for tears.

She finished clearing the table, washing up, drying up. Putting away the tablecloth and the candlesticks, as if eliminating every last memory that the meal had ever happened. There was a sharp throbbing at the top of her nose and a headache starting to dig at her temples. Finally, she called up Henry and asked him to bring Susie over. When he asked how the meal was, she just said, 'Fine.'

A few streets away, Jack woke up in blind white pain. He saw a curl of blonde hair and felt relief, snuggling against

434

her breasts. Katie truly was the best cure for any hangover.

Then he realised. This wasn't Katie's comforting,
plump warmth . . . but the thin, skeletal ribs of a girl he
didn't know, some nameless, faceless girl he'd met last
night. He felt despair fill him like smoke as he remembered. After the fight with Katie, he'd gone back to the
pub and drunk until his head had been a swimming pool
of beer and somewhere along the way a girl had
appeared, comforted him, organised a taxi. He struggled
for a moment to recall if they had . . . but no . . . no, they
hadn't. She had tried to cajole him; she had sat him
down on the bed and tried to undress him, but he had
kept drunkenly pawing her away. She'd poured him
whisky, which he'd spilt on her gorgeous counterpane;
she'd tried to push cigarettes into his mouth but he'd
kept moaning that he'd given up, Katie had made him give
up, until the girl had finally flounced out in exasperation.
He smiled painfully at the memory. Later, he'd been
vaguely aware of her returning, her breath smelling of
whisky, her snapping at him to roll over and give her
room to sleep. She had slept beside him, passing out at
once, snoring loudly.

He stared around the bedroom. It was white, beautiful,
empty. No posters. Nothing. He longed for Katie's
cramped bedroom, her piles of books, old clothes in plastic bags to be taken to charity shops. Never had he felt so
bereft, as though the beer had drained everything away,
flushed out his heart and internal organs and left nothing
inside.

He got up, dressed quietly, 'borrowed' with great
shame a ten-pound note from the folded roll by her bed.
Went out into the white gloom, back to Leila's house.
Ten minutes later, his stuff bundled into no more than

three carrier bags, he hailed a ghostly taxi to Heathrow Airport.

Three days later, in the last post before Christmas Eve, the present came. It was addressed to *Susie, c/o Katie*. Susie, seeing the huge brown box that Henry had to help Katie carry upstairs, hid behind the door later that evening when Mum thought she was asleep. As Mum tore away the brown tape, swearing and struggling to cut open the corrugated card, Susie felt a flare of excitement. It was the Barbie house she'd wanted. Oh wow, oh wow, oh wow. She couldn't understand why, when she'd just got the best present she could ever dream of, Mum was sitting on the bed crying, holding a card that said, *Love from Uncle Jack xxx*.

48
Charlie

Just when I thought things couldn't get any worse, Puck suggested, 'Look, Charlie, surely it wouldn't do too much harm if we just did one more teeny-weeny, ant-sized spell on Jack? There's only a week left until New Year. You know what Titania threatened from the start – if we don't make him happy by New Year we'll never be able to return to the fairy camp.'

And I flipped.

'PUCK! If it wasn't for those stupid spells, you and I wouldn't have to be in this dire little squat.' I glanced around our tiny bedroom. 'It's no good, Puck. We have to give up.'

Puck's face fell. He looked so sad, I wanted to reach over and hug him.

We'd been hoping that we might be released from our task; we had sent messages to Titania, Queen of the Fairies. We had flown around the House of Commons during Prime Minister's Question Time, stolen a hand-kerchief and Tony Blair's fountain pen (he had looked somewhat surprised to find it missing), and scrawled a message on the cotton, relating how Jack might not be happy but he was at least, er, alive. We added in a casual PS how we had saved the fairy camp from the incinerator, in the hope that that might be enough for us to receive a royal pardon. We had sent the message via Pigeon Post, paying our way by stealing Murray Mints from the back-benchers' pockets (pigeons love mints). But we had never received any replies.

The WANTED posters for our arrest were still splat-tered all over the place. We had tried to disguise ourselves – Puck had grown a thistle beard and he had streaked my hair blue using the last ink in Blair's fountain pen. But time was running out . . .

'Look,' I went on, more softly. 'I think Jack and Katie will finally get together eventually. Just through evolution. It has to happen somehow.'

'No.' Puck shook his head vehemently. 'It's not that easy. Look, I know this sounds crazy, Charlie, but you know when we went to see The Grim Reaper? Well, I lis-tened to his thoughts. I tell you – his brain is a lot more fascinating than his laptop. And I saw – I felt – Jack's future. All laid out.'

'You did?' I asked suspiciously. I had always been the psychic one, not Puck.

'Jack and Katie might never make it together. They might do – but might not.'

'What? Why?'

'Because they are humans, Charlie. Look – d'you remember that night when we first decided to make Jack happy? We flew around Waterstone's in order to learn about human culture, and decided love would be the answer? Well – if you take a look at any romance in their books, from Shakespeare's *Romeo and Juliet* to *Anna Karenina*, do they ever finish with a nice, shiny, Walt Disney happy ending? NO! People die. They slit their

438

throats or drink poison or whatever. But the point is, love causes more pain than pleasure.'

'OK, OK,' I blustered, hating to hear such cynical words. 'What about – hey – Jane Austen. *Pride and Prejudice*?'

'So? I hardly think Darcy and Elizabeth will last. They don't even kiss in the book.'

'Puck! You're hysterical. What, d'you think that, had the story continued three hundred pages on, Elizabeth divorces Darcy because he has a small penis. Come on!'

'Charlie, you're missing the point! They're books! People learn lessons in books. That's the whole point – characters develop. Everything ends neatly. In real life, people hardly ever learn from their mistakes, they just go round in circles repeating them over and over. OK, so Jack loves Katie and Katie loves Jack. But is love and life ever that simple? All marriages begin to suffer wear and tear, threads come loose, and holes appear. Love finds it hard to bear the strain of life's tragedies and challenges – mortgages or lost jobs or deaths or a foolish affair. Love can harden over time into a deep companionship, or it can be corroded by boredom. Maybe Jack and Katie will be married happily ever after. Or maybe Jack will slip up, suffer the restless bug, and desert her to go travelling. Or maybe Katie will be too cynical to trust her feelings again. Who can tell? They have the potential to go either way.'

'So? You could say that about any couple, Puck. Give the poor guys a chance.'

'That's my point, Charlie. How many humans ever do get it right? One in three marriages ends in divorce. How many happy couples have we seen on our travels round London? One in fifty?

'So, what's your answer?'

'I found it in *The Brahma Book of Spells*.' He thrust the

439

book into my hand. 'Small print! A permanent love spell that can never be undone. Yes – Jack loves Katie, but this will be the final icing on the cake. It means Jack will love Katie for ever more. So much he won't want to leave the country because every minute of every day, he'll want to be with her. His heart will be knotted to hers by an invisible rope of complete devotion. Love conquers all! When people really surrender their hearts, they're ready to give up everything, lay down their lives for another person. They'll never control that other person, or try to change them, or love an ideal – they'll just love each other for what they are. And because Jack will want only the best for Katie, he'll grow up and become strong; and Katie will realise men are OK and the bitter splinters in her heart will get eased out. This isn't a fairy-tale – this is real life.'

'ENOUGH!' I cried. I could feel anger exploding in my heart. Because I was so moved, I so much wanted Puck's speech to be true, but I knew it was just lies. Puck's usual bullshit. 'I'm sorry, Puck, but I've heard all this before. I'm leaving. I'm leaving this stupid planet Earth.'

'What? OK – if you don't want to save the humans, be selfish—'

'Selfish! OK, I really am going now, Puck.'

'Good. Go then.'

'Fine, I'm going.'

'OK. See you around.'

I flew out, clutching *The Brahma Book of Spells* tight to my chest.

Up above the clouds is the ISA (International Supernatural Airport). This is the airport that ships anything and anyone from fairies to three-headed aliens to any

440

location in the universe. The huge glass building had been erected nearly a decade ago, but its over-hyped construction, followed by a reputation for complete ineptitude, matched that of the Millennium Dome. A typical journey involved getting on a spaceship that was supposed to arrive on Mercury within six hours . . . and getting out nineteen hours later on the frosty green rings of Saturn, wondering what the fuck had happened. Apparently, since the fairy government had sold the airport to public companies, they had scrimped on safety spending and the hyperspace bypasses were riddled with poor tracks and black holes.

On this occasion, I really didn't care.

'Can you give me a ticket for the next take-off?' I said as I went up to Departures, where a sprite was tapping away at a computer. 'I'll go anywhere.'

'I can do you a two-week trip to Venus with a special Venus Fly-Trap spectacular,' she said, which basically meant a strip show. Venus – planet of love, luxury and hedonism, stardust cocktails and nights of never-ending ecstasy.

'OK, fine.'

'Or, if you have a Young Person's Sprite card you can get twenty-five per cent off a trip to Mars, planet of sports, fire and aggression, where the Green Martians will be playing the Red Martians at hedgehog tennis. Lovely for a suntan.'

When I snapped that Venus was just fine, she shot me a look that said the-customer-is-always-right-but-boy-I-wish-they'd-be-polite. The machine spat out my ticket.

I waited for my flight, flicking through magazines, reading a long article about the aliens on earth who were currently masquerading as humans. As my flight was announced, I felt suddenly uncertain. *Am I behaving just*

441

like Jack DeAntiquus? I wondered. *Down on earth, he too is running away from Katie, from his problems.* My eyes kept flitting to the glass doors. As if expecting someone to come and stop me.

Nobody came.

I boarded the plane.

I took a seat next to a mermaid. The sulky air hostess gave us a demo. The spaceship chortled and spluttered into life. I watched the earth spin away from me. From a distance, on a warm day, the earth can look glorious, like a throbbing golden ball of energy and light. Tonight it looked tired; a weary planet, exhausted by human greed and misery, cities and towns resembling grey spots, like polluted cells gobbling up the last of Nature's greenery. *I don't belong there*, I thought, *I'm glad to be going*.

The flight was to last eight hours. The only view was endless, depressing blackness. There was a hoard of alien giraffes on the plane; the kids weren't potty-trained and they trailed green goo up and down the aisles. Their mother kept mopping it into pooper-scooper bags, looking flushed and sweaty. I sighed, flipping through *The Brahma Book of Spells*. A page whirled out – torn from my fight with Puck. My eyes skimmed over it.

And suddenly my heart almost stopped. ★

The easiest spell to make humans fall in love is to find a daisy and peel off the petals while incanting '(s)he loves me, (s)he loves me not' (a game which has trickled into popular human culture). If the spell ends on an auspicious 'loves me', boil the petals in hot water and streak over the lovers' eyes . . .

Oh my God. It had been here all along. A permanent love spell. Oh. My. God.

. . . while whispering your wish from the deepest silence within, where thoughts begin as seeds . . .

And then all the lights went out, and the spaceship was plunged into darkness. Nobody reacted too badly. We were used to the ridiculous delays, the announcements crackling over the tannoy: 'We do apologise but there has been a signal failure with a star going out but you are all welcome to a complimentary beetle biscuit from our buffet . . .'

I closed my eyes, trying to find silence inside. Unfortunately, I was interrupted a second later by the spaceship tipping over with a violent jolt. Screams clawed the air. Giraffes wailed. The spaceships shuddered and shook like a metal bull on heat. I tried to hang on but I felt my seat-belt rip away and found myself crushed under the weight of a half-elephant, half-pixie whose pierced tusks jangled silver bells in my ear. *I'm going to die*, I thought with a strange calm.

The spaceship suddenly plummeted with a loud *whoosh*, like a lift with snapped cables. Silence. A creak. A shaft of yellow light. A voice over the tannoy:

'This space flight has now landed safely back at the airport. We do apologise for the slight disturbances on our journey and are offering five petals off any Skunk Perfume in the foyer . . .'

Shaking violently, I crawled out of the spaceship amidst a chaos of furious customers and shrieking giraffes . . . to find myself engulfed in a pair of arms as someone flew out of nowhere, yanked me into a violent hug and whispered, 'Oh Charlie, oh, by my wings, I really thought you'd died.'

Puck pulled back, holding my face in his hands and staring at me with his wild olive eyes. For one crazy moment, I thought he was going to kiss me. Instead, he tweaked my wing playfully.

'Oh, thank God you didn't die, Charlie. Who would I have to be horrible to, and tease and pinch and play-fight with?'

'Oh, thanks very much, Puck,' I retorted with shaky sarcasm. 'Well, I'm just so glad I'm alive when I have such mean, horrible, evil –' I searched for crueller adjectives '– *ugly* friends to make me cherish my existence.'

'Ugly? Are you kidding? Did you *see* the look the space hostess was giving me . . .'

And so we left the airport together, arguing merrily.

49
Leila

I hate Christmas, Leila thought, staring out the window as snow flakes fell against the dirty blue sky. *Thank God it's over.*

She was going to a New Year's Eve party that night with Henry. Still determined to ensnare him, she had put on her favourite dress, even though it was slightly over-the-top. Ray had bought it for her in New York; it was made of crushed velvet and made her look like a slinky, feline vampire. She took a miserable sip of wine, narrowing her eyes. She opened the window a crack, feeling a blast of icy, polluted London air, smoggy with petrol fumes. She held out her palm and felt snowflakes gather there like melted tears, remembering the way Ray used to joyously catch them, as if they were falling diamonds.

She pulled away. She'd made a promise to herself and Henry that it was time to move on, take a new step. The dress was all wrong; it felt like a betrayal. This was Ray's dress; she had to change. She hurried to her wardrobe, tripping slightly on the long hem.

There was a toot below the window; it was too late, Henry was here.

Leila hastily threaded on a pair of silver hoop earrings, brushed her hair and pushed her slightly sore feet into her heels. *Oh well, here goes*, she thought. Another long evening.

Henry was gazing at his reflection in the rear-view mirror when he saw what looked like an angel of death striding down the path. He did a doubletake. Leila. She looked stunning. The front path was patchworked with ice and he saw her slide, nearly trip, grab a branch to regain her balance, and walk with slow stiffness to the car. As she slid in, he flushed, gazing at her lips, the plum-coloured lipstick lined a little outside the edges. He suffered a sudden urge to kiss her on the lips, instead of the cheek. But he squashed it. Her skin was cold from outside, as though sheened with a layer of ice.

'Happy New Year.' He pulled back.

He won't even kiss me, she registered dully. *I'm so repulsive to him he won't even kiss my lips*.

'Hi, Happy New Year. God, you need a haircut.' He was looking so horribly handsome, Leila felt she had to insult him.

'Yeah, I know,' Henry smiled sheepishly, running his fingers through his sloppy blonde fringe. 'You—' He was about to say how beautiful she looked but his voice sounded funny, as if he was a teenager again and it was breaking. Suddenly unable to look at her, he twisted back in his seat, gazed at the living room, the silhouettes of figures slumped on the sofa, the kaleidoscope square of a blaring TV set. 'Is Katie definitely not coming?' he asked randomly.

'No, she's not feeling well,' Leila lied tersely. Why did he always ask after Katie? Why not her? She flipped down the mirror, baring open her mouth like a vampire, checking her teeth for lipstick smudges. She fingered the lines

446

fanning her eyes. They seemed to be getting longer every time she looked.

A brief silence. She waited for Henry to comment on how good she looked.

'So, how was your Christmas?' Henry asked as he eased slowly down the dark, slushy streets.

'Fine. Actually – crap. My mother sent over a card from the US inviting me to share Christmas with her and Daniel, whoever he is – probably husband number seven. Anyway, it arrived the day after Boxing Day.' Leila shared his laughter, but she bit her lip remembering the gold card with its elegant swirling letters. There had been no personal message, no '*Love Mum*'. Leila was just another name on the mailing list. 'And she phoned at midnight on Christmas Day and left a drunken message on my answerphone, forgetting the time difference, asking me for advice on how to defrost a turkey. God. How could she possibly have given birth to me? How can her genes, her DNA, have any relation to mine?'

'Oh, you poor thing,' Henry reached over, squeezed her knee. *I ought to have invited her over. I wanted to be with her . . . but then again, I didn't want her to be with my family.*

'Mine was nearly as bad,' he went on, 'only in reverse – we had sixteen of us all crammed around the table at Dad's place in Hertfordshire.'

'I bet you had roast deer or something ridiculous,' Leila guessed.

'No – it was my grandparents who were ridiculous.'

'Oh, the guys from the wedding, who argue over everything?'

'Yes. This year it was about whether it's possible for humans to contract food-and-mouth and therefore whether we were likely to get it from eating lamb, at which point my mother's parents accused my father's of being so

447

bonkers anyway there wouldn't be any difference. My mother flounced out, apparently in tears. I felt so worried for her I went out on a drive to find her. I caught up with her in the local pub, where she was chatting up the barman. He's about twenty-five. I got the impression this wasn't the first chat they'd had. She looked very sheepish when she saw me, went all red, and then kept trying to impress him by talking about football. She was pretending to be a Man United supporter, but she doesn't know the first thing about it – she even said something about Posh being such a good player. He was trying not to laugh.'

'Oh dear,' Leila laughed, feeling better. It was comforting to know that somebody else had had such a dreadful time too. She suddenly felt glad she'd come.

But inside the party, however, she felt a sense of sluggish boredom again. It was the usual crowd – forty or so friends all sipping champagne and nibbling canapés from silver foil trays and sharing the same parrot-conversations: 'Wow – it's ages since I last saw you . . . God, the year's gone so fast . . . Have you heard? Amanda's had her baby . . . Yes . . . I've moved jobs, I'm in marketing now . . .'

★ She turned as her host, Kerry, proudly leaned over to click on the lights of the evergreen tree. For a moment, the fairy lights winked awake, as if setting fire to each other in a domino stream of pink, red, blue, yellow and green. A second later, they had blown dead. Kerry clucked her tongue and called for her husband in a pained voice. Leila gazed for a moment at the tree, a desolate green skeleton, and sighed, fingering a stray pine needle between her fingers.

'Even the food is the same. These sausage rolls look identical to last year's,' she said to Henry.

448

'They probably are the same – leftovers people nib-bled and then left on their plastic plates. They've probably been stuck in the freezer all year,' Henry said under his breath and Leila giggled.

Leila, having knocked back a few glasses of Christmas punch, started to feel the familiar slurry recklessness taking hold of her. She felt alarmed – she'd promised her-self to be on her best behaviour at this party. This wasn't an anonymous bar; there were too many people here that she knew. *Keep in control,* she kept telling herself as she escaped to the little downstairs toilet, grimacing as the flowery toilet roll played 'Jingle Bells' when she tugged it. She redid her suspenders with slightly shaky hands. She came out of the toilet just as a flurry of new guests arrived, shaking snow from their heads, including Amanda and Chris, a couple she'd known vaguely for years and only ever caught up with at the New Year party.

'Hi.' Leila did a double-take as Amanda, looking uncharacteristically plump in a long black coat, cuddled a white bundle to her chest. Her newborn baby.

Leila was taken aback by how different Amanda looked. Normally every year she turned up looking like a clown, her bronzed face etched with stress from years of ambi-tion, exhaustion and city living. Now she looked tired but radiant, her eyes sparkling with love as she gazed down at her baby's chubby face, his thumb tight in his mouth.

'He's so sweet,' Leila said, with an unexpected maternal tug. She thought of the baby she and Ray had been planning just before he died . . . the baby names they'd quibbled over . . .

Soon a cooing circle had gathered around a beaming Amanda and Leila drifted away. Back in the dining room, Henry was surrounded by a group of women. A teenage boy (Kerry's son, Leila assumed) was dispensing the punch, sloshing the berry-coloured liquid from a large leaf-patterned bowl with a silver ladle. When Leila came up for yet another glass, he looked impressed, a faint blush igniting his acne-splattered cheeks and spreading to the devil's peak of his Grade One hair cut. Leila, seeing his eyes on her, smiled back flirtatiously. He was probably about sixteen but in her present mood she didn't care.

Soon he was chatting her up, growing in confidence, boasting about his media degree at Leicester and the wild parties he had with his friends which were frequently broken up by the police at 2 a.m.

'Interesting,' said Leila, wondering if perhaps the flirty smile had been a mistake.

'What's, like, the most you've *ever, ever* drunk?' he asked her emphatically, as if his assessment of her entire personality would be based on her reply. 'It has to be *before* passing out; stuff your friends glug into your mouth afterwards doesn't count, nor does anything you drink after the first time you puke.'

'I don't know', Leila said irritably. 'Maybe a bottle of champagne.'

'God, is that all? Are you serious?' His face fell. 'I, like once drank *nineteen pints*.'

As he went on to describe how, if she ever ran out of drink, cough mixture mixed with water and sugar could produce an equally amazing high, Leila could stand it no longer.

'How amazing. I'm actually a literary agent, so I have little time for drinking.'

'Wow! Wow! Really! Did you, like, sell Harry Potter? No? No? (He looked a little confused when Leila explained there was more than one agent in London.) I'm writing a book. It's about this serial killer, right, who cuts people up and puts them in his fridge and then takes loads of drugs until he drives off the cliffs at Dover in a manic suicidal finish . . .'

Yeah, right, thought Leila. Out of the corner of her eyes, she searched for Henry. She wanted him to be looking at her. Seeing her laughing loudly with another man. Feeling hot with jealousy. But no, Henry was far too busy talking to some middle-aged cow in a black trouser-suit. Bastard.

Henry looked at Leila out of the corner of his eye. He was afraid to stare at her directly. Afraid he might put down his glass, stroll over, grab that stupid little tosser she was chatting up and bloody punch him. He wanted to yell: *She's mine, OK?*

But he had thought it all through over Christmas, ever since that morning she had called him up. He had spent nights blundering down labyrinths of thought. *What if we did get back together, how would it be? Does she only like me now because she can't have me? If she does like me?* And he had reached the same dead-end each time. *She needs time. She needs friendship now, not a relationship. Ray has hurt her, I've hurt her, it's too soon.*

But he was so impatient. He didn't want to be standing at a party, chatting to some ghastly braying woman, who, despite a chunky gold wedding ring, kept pretending to pick fluff off the front of his trousers. He wanted to push fast-forward, to whizz through the days, to be with her now.

Seeing the boy leave her and saunter off to the loo, Henry couldn't hold back any longer. He approached her, tapping her on the shoulder, trying not to stare at the swoop of her backless dress, the tantalising expanse of white skin.

'Hi,' he grinned awkwardly. 'How's it going with your new friend?

451

'Oh, he's fuckable, I guess. He'll do,' Leila shrugged, turning away.

'Do you think,' Henry swallowed, trying not to sound pompous, 'that perhaps you shouldn't have any more to drink?' He tried to take her cup, but Leila yanked it away angrily, keeping her fingers tightly curled around it.

Henry's mobile shrilled and he answered it. Leila watched him sullenly for a few seconds as surprise flared across his features. 'It's Jack,' he mouthed incredulously.

'Can you stop just for a second?' Jack rapped the glass again.

'Sure, honey.' The driver cut away from the traffic and pulled up on to a double-yellow line, squeezing between a motorcycle and a delivery van.

Jack was so touched by her helpfulness he wanted to kiss her. She'd picked him up from Heathrow Airport and he'd been expecting the typical grumpy sods you normally got for taxi drivers. But she was lovely – an American woman in her forties with dyed blonde hair, a hawk nose and a Ruby Wax accent. Instead of ranting on about her life story or the fascinating passengers she'd driven, she kept cheerfully bombarding Jack with questions. Been away for a break? India – funny place to go to this time of year?

Jack, who had just suffered a ten-hour flight during which (he knew he shouldn't have gone for the cheapest airline) he'd been served a dodgy curry that had had him throwing up, replied in monosyllables at first. He was shivering violently from illness and the cold, having stepped on to the plane in warm Delhi, and got off again to the icy chill of London, the grey streets mushy with snow. He was still wearing a pair of khaki trousers and a white T-shirt, so the driver let him put on her coat – a

452

black duffel with white fur lining. Finally, touched by her kindness, Jack started to open up. He told her the whole story – falling in love with Katie, his attack of commitment-phobia, his abrupt departure.

'So, are you coming back for her?' she interrogated him, like some American chatshow host yanking a confession out of a shy interviewee.

'Er . . . I think so . . .' He'd ducked his head sheepishly.

'What d'you mean, "I think so"? Fucking "think so"! You know so! Do you love her or not? Come on, you gotta be coming back for her, it can't be for the weather, let's face it.'

'Yes,' Jack laughed weakly. 'She's going to be at a New Year's party tonight. Actually . . . This is a bit cheeky . . . but I know the party is somewhere in Notting Hill and I can't quite remember where . . so if I could just borrow your mobile . . .'

'Sure!' She chucked it back at him. Jack caught it deftly and called Henry.

Now they were approaching Notting Hill and his taxi fare was already reaching ridiculous heights, but he didn't care, he made her stop so that he could dive into the newsagent's. A compulsion had grabbed him: *I have to get Katie a present*. The shop was small, the dirty linoleum scuffed with footprints. Even though it was cheap and cheerful – tacky boxes of Christmas cards with the felt-tip-pen placard, *3 for 50p*! – Jack felt quite dazzled by Western materialism. Having come from a place where beggars in rags had followed him up streets, desperate for just a few pennies, he felt as if he was in a palace filled with jewels. He fingered some threads of tinsel, saw the taxi waiting outside. He realised he was delaying. Scared of seeing her again.

Nerves, exhaustion and exhilaration were making his

stomach flutter. He kept picturing her face when he arrived at the party. What would he say? *Katie, I missed you . . . Hi, Katie, I had to come back . . .* Oh God. All so clichéd, so limp. No, he had to get her a present. Not that he had much choice – his eyes desperately scanned the boxes of Persil, cheap carrot soup, white napkins, tampons . . . Finally he fixed on Quality Street. It was better than nothing.

As he handed over his change, his fingers were shaking so much he dropped all his coins in amongst the chocolate bar display and had to fish them out. He kept saying to himself, *Oh God, please can Katie forgive me, please can she understand that I love her?*

But what if he'd blown it? What if?

He couldn't bear to think about it. Katie would forgive him, surely? She had a heart of gold – didn't she forgive everybody?

50
Katie

'I feel sick,' Katie moaned, her hands fishing inside the glass bowl of Quality Street again, rummaging through the rainbow assortments. Most of the orange and strawberry creams had gone – there were just the gold-wrapped toffee fingers and pennies which she didn't even like, but kept eating all the same.

Here she was again. Sitting with Susie in the living room, putting on a merry show for Susie's sake, pretending to enjoy the James Bond film on TV even though she'd seen it a thousand times. Every now and again, Susie would put a new outfit on her Barbie doll, like a red ra-ra skirt or a white T-shirt, and she'd hold it up and say, 'Mummy – what about this one?'

'Lovely,' Katie would smile.

When the doorbell rang insistently, she ignored it. She felt too bloated and fed up to answer it. But a few minutes later, Leila appeared. Katie was surprised – she'd only been gone a little while. Why was Leila back? Surely the party wasn't that bad?

Leila looked pregnant with gossip, news. As she sat down on the edge of the sofa, Katie wondered for a moment if she was going to announce that she and Henry had made up and got engaged or something equally sickening. Katie knew it was uncharitable but she just wasn't in the mood for someone else's good news right now.

'Jack is back. He flew in, Katie. I've come to pick you up – he just called Henry on his mobile. He's coming straight from the airport to the party.'

Although Katie didn't let a flicker of emotion show on her face, her stomach did a triple-pike backwards. Jack. Back?

'Oh. Well. That's nice, but . . .'

'Aren't you going to come?' Leila prodded her gently.

'I'm really enjoying this Bond movie, actually,' Katie lied.

'What? For the thirteen-hundredth time?'

'Look, I'm fine. OK, Leila?' Katie turned back to the TV and Leila gazed in exasperation at her profile, at her long eyelashes and turned-up nose and pursed lips. She suddenly looked oddly like her daughter in a sulk and Leila, who wasn't a patient person, said more sharply, 'But Jack is going to be there. You know – Jack. Jack. Jack?'

'Oh, whoopie-di-do,' said Katie, in such a bitter tone that Leila recoiled. She'd sensed something had been simmering between them before Jack had gone off travelling. What was going on?

'Katie, I just don't fucking get you,' Leila pressed on impatiently. Katie flinched, her fingers curled around a chocolate, the purple wrapper half-twisted in a paper corkscrew. 'You have spent the last, what, eight years lusting after Jack – it's been so obvious. And now he's finally come back for you. I mean – do you know what he said on the phone? He said to Henry, "I love you".'

'Why doesn't he go and marry Henry then?'

'Don't be silly. He said he loved *you*. He meant it. God, I was so jealous, I wasn't even going to tell you . . .'

'Wait a minute.' Katie turned, chocolate soggy in her mouth. 'Jealous? Why jealous?'

'Because.' Leila struggled uncomfortably. She looked down, playing with a stray piece of green tinsel that had fallen from its blue-tacked place on the skirting board. 'Because I do think Jack genuinely adores you, Katie. He didn't used to – but I think his love has been like, like an oak tree. It's as if he's been putting down roots and now it's only just blossomed and become apparent.' Leila stopped the analogy; she was starting to sound as if she'd had too much punch. 'Fuck it – he loves you. Just get it into your head, you moron.'

'Jealous?' Katie picked up again. 'Jealous of *me*? God, Leila. Why? What have I got that you'd want? I'm ugly, I'm fat, I'm heading for thirty, I have a daughter, which is basically a write-off as far as most men are concerned, and I'm broke. And I – I've lost someone I really love.'

'Katie, you're not ugly. Jack genuinely finds you attractive. I think he loves your personality—'

'Personality! Come on, Leila, don't insult me.'

'You didn't let me finish. I was going to say "your personality and your looks".'

'Leila, please. You have no idea. Look at you. You're gorgeous. You don't have a clue. You've spent your life being able to just look at a man and have him in the palm of your hand. And you know you are, so don't deny it.'

'I won't. I know I'm gorgeous. But what fucking good is it doing me? I'm in love with Henry and he doesn't want to go out with me. I've been married once and for the first time in years I've met someone I'd consider marrying again. And am I sitting on a sofa whingeing?

457

No. I went to the party with Henry even though it just kills me to stand there and see him so much as exchange a hello with another woman. And if I can do it, you can. So come on.'

Leila stood up. Katie gaped at her.

'Come on,' Leila said more gently, stroking her shoulder affectionately.

'I'm sorry,' said Katie, suddenly going red. 'I've been so selfish. I had no idea about you and Henry. Was it my fault? When . . .'

'We're talking about you, not me,' said Leila, pulling her hand away. She really didn't want to be reminded about Katie's involvement in ruining her relationship.

'Well, what about Susie?' Katie stammered.

'I can go over to my friend Tessa's, she wanted me over!' Susie said eagerly. She had been quietly pretending to play with her Barbie whilst listening intently to every word.

'Ah – well – OK,' Katie gave in. 'OK.'

But in the taxi, she started to regret it. The closer they came to the party, the more doubts flitted through her mind like bats. She kept fiddling with the top button of her cardigan, in and out, in and out, until the taut turquoise thread became slack and, worried that it would fall off and be lost, she had to rip it off and slip it into her pocket.

Arriving at the party, Katie immediately wanted to go. She looked a state – why hadn't Leila made her change? Women in long black dresses, glittering with jewels, gave her sneering, hawkish glances. She was wearing her oldest clothes – a pair of unironed black trousers, stained with cranberry sauce from Christmas cooking, a scarlet jumper and the ill-matching turquoise cardigan, which had actually belonged to her mother and had a hole under one arm-pit.

Katie was convinced she would see Jack at any minute, chatting up some thin blonde. And that he'd wave casually at her. Perhaps later, when he was drunk, he'd take her outside and rant about how they were meant to be together.

If he's with a girl, Katie thought savagely, as she wove shakily through the crowd, *I'm walking out right away. I won't stand here and let him see how much he has the power to hurt me. I've got my pride.*

'Katie! Oh my God!'

He caught her unawares, coming up behind her, his arms circling her waist. She turned, stunned. Jack gazed down at her. God, she looked so awful. *Did I do this to her?* He stood back, guiltily. Her skin was pasty, her hair was lank yellow seaweed, her eyes purple holes. And the expression in them was dull and lacklustre.

'Hi,' he whispered, stepping back uneasily. 'How are you?'

'Fine.' Katie slipped her hand into her pocket, fingering the turquoise button like a worry bead. 'I'm actually not staying for long – I just dropped Susie off briefly. So.'

'Katie.' Jack rubbed her shoulder. He opened his mouth and then closed it, as though he didn't know what to say.

Katie looked away. She wanted to smile at him, warm to him, but a tight snake of uncommunicated resentment coiled in the pit of her stomach. She couldn't forgive him; he'd hurt her too much over the past few weeks.

'I—' Jack began.

'So—' Katie started at the same time.

'You first,' Jack said, laughing.

She had forgotten how beautiful he looked when he

459

smiled. The way his eyes crinkled up with laughter. And the love that flashed through her at that moment only sparked her fury.

'So,' she said, 'thanks for going off to India. I liked the brief goodbye note you left. I mean, you could have tried to call, or at least spoken to me, but no, you just disappeared. But, you know, it's your life. You're a *free* man, after all. Because, God, I wouldn't dare constrict you. You can fly halfway across the planet if you so wish.'

'Katie.' Jack kept mouthing like a goldfish. 'I – I went to the airport. I asked them to take me anywhere. It was the only flight they had, but look, some special things happened out there. I – I got you some Quality Street.'

Katie didn't know whether she wanted to laugh or cry, kiss him or hit him. She'd only fucking eaten thirty-thousand of these over Christmas and there were probably numerous beautiful sculptures, silk saris or woven rugs that he could have picked up for her in India. But no – he'd got her Quality Street. It was such a Jack thing to do that she was about to giggle, to let some part of her melt, to give into him, when unfortunately fate intervened in the form of a tall girl with short blonde hair. She was wearing a ruby corset, black leather boots and a tight skirt, and she pushed past Katie, flung her arms around Jack and cried, 'Oh Jack! Long time, no see! D'you remember me? God, you're looking brown. Look at me!' She drew out her slender white wrist, holding it up against his.

Before Jack could say another word, Katie was already halfway out of the room. As she passed by a man carrying a large black sack, who was stooping down to pick up white paper plates, she chucked the Quality Street into the binliner with a satisfying thud, then hurried up the

460

stairs to find a place, anywhere, to lock herself away from Jack.

Upstairs was clearly out of bounds – the landing had been boarded off ineffectually by two elegant Edwardian chairs with bowed golden legs. She could easily have slipped around them, but in her fury she shoved one aside; it toppled over and a leg fell off. She covered her shocked mouth with her hands. Shit – what if she'd broken it? She let out a slightly wild laugh. Was Jack dancing with that blonde girl downstairs? She knelt down and tried to prop up the chair so the leg was balanced precariously underneath. She'd only pushed it gently; surely it must have been broken to begin with? Was Jack kissing that girl? Gently stroking the delta of flesh below her ear?

She heard footsteps on the stairs and backed away uneasily. Seeing a door ajar, she hurried into a bedroom – it was being used as a cloakroom, the bed strewn with coats. She stood over by the full-length mirror and caught a glimpse of her panicked expression. She heard the footsteps pause, then the thud of the chair collapsing again. A curse. An unmistakable voice.

'Jack?' she called out, without thinking.

'Katie?' he cried eagerly. She heard the squeak of a doorhandle as he went into the wrong bedroom. And then he came in and found her.

'Go away,' she said, and he stopped a few feet from her.

'Katie—'

'Go away. Please.'

'Come on, you want to speak to me.'

'No, I don't.'

'You called out, you called my name – why? Come on, Katie, we can talk this through.'

Katie sniffed. She edged further backwards, pressing her spine against the dark lacquered wardrobe, feeling

461

the cold suck of the mirror on her left side. She was suddenly horrified that she was going to cry and she lifted her hand to cover her mouth, pretending to be brushing sleep from her eye, scratching an itch on her cheek. She mustn't let him see her cry.

'Katie, I've just flown God knows how many miles, all the way from India, to speak to you – I didn't come here for the party, or the drink, or that stupid blonde girl, who, by the way, isn't even an ex, just someone I once worked with when I had a temporary job as a courier. I came over to speak to you, so at least hear me out.'

She nodded, staring at the thick peach carpet, keeping her chin set.

'Look – I love you . . . I – I'm not very good at expressing my feelings. It doesn't sound as though I mean it, but I do. I really do love you, Katie. I made a huge mistake leaving. The moment I stepped on to that plane, I felt like the biggest wanker, the biggest bastard, the most stupid idiot on earth. You know, I was sitting there, waiting for take-off, and I kept looking out of the window, hoping –' he half-laughed, desperately, '– that I'd see you running through the airport, yelling "Stop the plane", like something out of a movie.'

A tiny smile curled at her lips and Jack, heartened, found his speech stumbling on.

'But you didn't, and I found myself flying away and gazing down at England, wondering what the hell I was doing. I wanted to grab a parachute and jump out and run all the way back home to you. I was so, so – it was such a big, y'know, thing – God, sorry, I'm so inarticulate. It's just, I think it was so good, what you were offering, that I felt I didn't deserve it, and some masochistic urge in me made me screw it up. I'm really sorry, Katie, I'm so sorry.' He paused, wishing she would look at him.

462

'Jack,' she managed, and he took a cautious step forwards. She still couldn't look at him, terrified the moment she caught his eye she'd burst into tears, so she addressed her words to his boots, still dusty from Delhi. 'You know I love you, I do,' she said, quite calmly. 'But how do I know that in a week, or a month, or a year, you won't have some crisis again and change your mind? I can't have my emotions messed about like this. I can't handle it. It will drive me insane.'

'But Delhi – it was just something I had to get out of me. I won't go away again because I know how difficult Delhi was. It was as if you were there with me all the time.'

'What?'

'Well, you were in my head. Every time I visited a temple, or took a photo, I kept talking to you in my head, saying, "Hey, look at this Katie". You know. OK – maybe not, maybe I sound mad . . .'

Silence. They seemed to stand there for ages, listening to the muted party noises below.

'I can't decide now,' Katie whispered finally.

Down below, a cork exploded, whizzed into the air.

'What? What did you say?'

Silence. She shook her head slightly, unable to speak. He thought she was telling him to go. It was too much to bear.

'I broke a chair,' he said randomly. 'Outside.' He laughed. 'In the hall. I . . . hope it's not an antique.'

Silence. Then he started to cry. Katie was so touched and amazed that her chin flipped up and she stared at the tears running messily down his cheeks. She'd never seen Jack cry, not in the eight years that she'd known him. He shielded his face, started to shuffle away in embarrassment. Everything melted inside her. She knew that he was sincere. She went to him and gently pulled his hands away from his face, looping her arms around his waist. Jack pulled her in close and held on to her so tightly, she could feel his heartbeat banging like a metronome against her crushed breasts, his fingers locked against the small of her back. Then Jack felt her body shuddering and he drew back, but she ducked her head, ashamed. She nestled her cheek in the crook of his shoulder, and then finally looked at him, her blue eyes shiny with tears.

'Oh dear, now you've set me off,' she said. 'I hate people seeing me cry. D'you have a hanky?'

Jack sniffed. 'No.'

'You're useless, Jack,' she said, and he started to smile, hearing the affection in her voice. 'You come here and proposition me and you don't have a hanky for a lady's tears.'

Jack stepped forwards and lightly licked a tear away from her temple with the pointed tip of his tongue. He drew back an inch, gazing at the faint mark his saliva had left. White skin, a trickle of blue vein, a dark, damp mark. He kissed it away; her skin tasted of salt. Of Katie. Gorgeous. And then, breaking down again, he fiercely showered her forehead and hair with hundreds of kisses, drawing her in sideways, twisting her round, pulling her against him again. They stood there, their wet cheeks sliding against the other, until finally his mouth found hers. They wrapped their arms around each other, swaying, feeling forgiveness flow . . .

Downstairs, Henry couldn't stand it another minute. He broke off from his conversation, angling his empty glass and tapping it in an embarrassed gesture of retreat. He wove through the crowd, pushing past sweaty bodies and braying voices. Leila was in the corner, chatting up a man in a dove-grey suit; Henry went to her side and gently slipped his hand into hers. She flinched slightly, didn't turn round. But then he felt her squeeze his hand tightly, her nails indenting his knuckles, as if she never wanted to let go.

★
★

51
Charlie

Puck and I were most disappointed.

We had spent a frantic day gathering ingredients for the final spell. Puck had found some discarded Body Shop bottles in Leila's bedroom and we'd filled them to the brim with the highly potent love potion, which glowed a violent gold. We'd clutched them to our chests, shimmering like fireflies as we flew across Notting Hill to the New Year party.

I have to admit, fears jangled in my stomach all the way there. *What if we get it wrong yet again?* I fretted. *What if Henry wakes up and falls for the postman, or Jack wakes up and falls for a transvestite, or Katie falls for Leila and they all end up having a bisexual tryst?* The possibilities were worryingly endless.

But, arriving at the party, it appeared that our job had already been done.

We flitted from window to window, looking in, drinking in the romantic snap-shots. Leila and Henry, in the dining room, holding hands. Although they were surrounded by people, they seemed engrossed in each other. I hate to sound like some New Age wombo, but humans do have auras which shine most brightly when they're in love. Leila and Henry looked as if someone had traced a gold pen around their heads; and when I glanced down at their hands, his long fingers laced with her slim white ones, dew-drops of love sparkled in white flashes around their nails.

Upstairs, we saw Katie and Jack lying on the bed. Jack was asleep and Katie was lying watching him, nose to nose, their breaths intermingling. The headlamps from a passing car suddenly flooded a hose of yellow light over their faces which made them seem angelic in the muted light. I felt happiness welling up inside me. They just looked so right together . . .

I was about to make a gooey remark, when Puck yelled, 'Well, I'll be damned! These humans are so fucking ungrateful!'

'What! But, Puck, they look lovely.'

'We've spent, what, the last eight hours flying about like mad things, picking daisies and boiling petals and practically selling our souls in order to obtain some rare antelope hoof powder. We've stayed up in order to catch the sun's rays at exactly the right time to bless the potion. I've flown to the moon and chiselled off a piece of white cheese to grind down into moonbeam powder, and now, now, what do they do? They bloody fucking get it together without us! Couldn't they at least have waited, just a few more minutes? Would it have been too much trouble to argue just a little more? You!' He rapped on the window. 'Go on, Katie, just hit him. Whack him one! Go on, you hate him really. We'll sort it out.'

'Puck!' I burst into incredulous laughter. 'Look – it's fantastic. We should be happy. Jack's happy – our task is complete. And I think it's quite sweet that the humans have finally managed to sort themselves out on their own, don't you?'

Puck didn't. He had the sad air of a fireman who has been called to put out a fire and finds nothing but a whiff of smoke. He put down his bottle and sat dejectedly on the black plastic top, swinging his legs with a *thwack!* Seeing Katie rise and turn off the light, shutting us out, I suddenly felt disappointed too. The play had come to an end. I felt as if I wanted to shout, 'Encore,' but the humans had been unwilling actors; they'd had enough. Or perhaps it had nothing to do with the humans; I just missed the idea of running around making mischief with my darling Puck.

I sat down on my bottle next to him and a sneaky thought entered my mind: *Hey, maybe I could sprinkle a little of this love potion on Puck tonight.* But – no. Somehow it wouldn't be right. It wouldn't be real. I wanted Puck to love me for me.

Puck rolled up a leaf of icy grass and started blowing it like a pan pipe, grains spewing out in horrible squeaks.

'Puck! Please!' I groaned, curling my wings up over my pointed ears.

'It's a New Year, Charlie, this is a special rite,' said Puck, sounding a little cheered.

'What?'

'Come on!' He suddenly grabbed my hand, declaring that we had to perform the correct rites, he had read about them in *The Brahma Book of Spells*. He dragged me to the dark treehouse at the bottom of the garden. It was small and made of planks nailed messily together in a lopsided triangle, so that it seemed to be hunching its wooden shoulders against the cold. Though it was boarded-up, Puck forced me to wiggle in through a slit. Inside, I heard the click of spiders' feet as they knitted

468

webs and I shuddered, feeling cobwebs about me like silky fingers. In the corner, a bat was hanging upside down (bats are complete drunkards, they hang upside down all night to cure their hangovers), vaguely singing a slurred 'Auld Lang Syne'.

'Puck, what is this? You know I don't like spiders.'

'It has to be in a dark place,' his voice said – it was too dark to see his body, except for the gleam in his eyes and his wicked smile. 'Now – we must proceed with the rite. It's for good luck, prosperity and a happy year ahead. Close your eyes.'

I closed them. I heard a creak and shivered. I opened my eyes a crack, saw a dark hump, flipped it shut. I heard Puck whisper, 'Be silent inside,' and I let my breath soften, my thoughts slip away, until I was just transcending, floating in silence. I suddenly remembered the words of *The Brahma Book of Spells* that had been swimming in my consciousness ever since the plane crash: *Whispering your wish from the deepest silence within, where thoughts begin as seeds* . . .

I was about to make a quiet, sad wish for Puck to fall in love with me, when I felt something brush my face, my lips, and I screamed.

'It's me,' said Puck, and kissed me again.

'What's this?' I was so overwhelmed, I couldn't register. 'What about the New Year's rite?'

'Charlie – this is the New Year's rite,' he cried impatiently. 'Me! I am your New Year, and your next year, and your year after that – if you want me, that is.'

And then, seeing my gentle nod, he told me he loved me, leaned over and gave me the most tender, sweetest and loveliest kiss I have ever received in my whole life.

We flew out of the treehouse, up into the shimmering sky to just below the clouds, which were happily belching out showers of snow. Puck teasingly tugged a fluff of cloud, tipping a huge dandruff shower over me, giggling as I hit him. The clouds started getting huffy, so we flew off, laughing. I gazed down at Primrose Hill, a patchwork of green and white, the trees clothed in snow, their branches sleeved with ice. I gazed at the yellow squares of human windows; the silhouettes of people dancing, laughing, drinking, cuddling in front of the TV. And a few humans sitting on their own, staring out of windows longingly. I felt a huge bubble of universal love swelling up inside me, as if the humans were all my children, and I had a sudden ache to make every one of them as happy as Jack, to make their lives worthwhile. Maybe Puck and I could do more spells, maybe we could bring bliss to the entire world! *Well, maybe in the future*, I considered with a guilty giggle, *when Puck and I have had a little more practice.*

As we passed by the moon, I clutched Puck's hand and we smiled at each other. Sensing our love, the moon was so pleased that she let out a small laugh, causing the sky to tremble and a shooting star to spiral joyously across it . . .

52
Leila

Leila felt like screaming. There was half an hour to midnight and the dining room resembled a zoo. The noise was rising with the level of drunkenness – the punch-bowl now contained nothing more than a sticky rim – and there was a cacophony of sound, like an orchestra warming up. A man shoved past, leaving a film of his sweat on her arm, and she shuddered, revulsed. Black dots pin-pricked her eyes. Where was Henry? He'd disappeared about ten minutes ago, saying he needed air. She was about to escape when someone plonked a jazzy-coloured hat down on her head. She turned and saw the young boy she'd spoken to earlier. His eyes were bloodshot and there was a goofy, shy grin on his face.

'D'you want to go upstairs?' she suddenly blurted out desperately.

'What?' He looked terrified and then said, just as thoughtlessly, 'I'm a virgin.'

Leila couldn't help it. She laughed. His face crumpled. She felt cruel. She was laughing at herself, at her ridiculousness. She was pathetic.

She pushed quickly through the crowds, feeling her

hat sail off and get crumpled underfoot. There was a particularly inebriated bunch by the door who were dancing like mad chickens. As she passed, an arm folded around her and she found herself in a large chain of people who were all roaring a warm-up version of 'Auld Lang Syne'.

Leila joined in for a few minutes, but she couldn't get into the swing of it. A hand cramped her elbow; someone stepped on her shoe and she yelped; her hair snagged in someone else's top. Pulling away, ignoring a 'Don't be boring, come back!' shout and a hand grabbing her waist, she escaped.

As she went to the back door, she cursed as a straggle of streamers, soggy from a pool of spilt beer, clung to the heel of her shoe. She tried to scrap it off on the mat, then cursed. Shit, she was hot – her cheeks itchy, her neck red and flushed.

Outside, the air was wonderfully crisp. A thousand snow crystals glittered from the trees, as though the branches were shedding diamond blossom. The snow covered the garden like fresh linen, black footprints stamped here and there like huge cigarette stubs. The sky was cold with stars. The swing at the bottom of the garden creaked; a figure in a dark coat, no doubt passed out, was slumped on it, head bowed.

She looked up at the sky. Was there something, someone up there who was looking down and organising all this? Would her life get better, would the wheel turn and bring happiness? It's funny the cards that life deals us, she thought. So random. People die; babies are born. Some marriages fail, some marriages last, some are cut short. She liked to think that she was in control of her life, and yet she felt more helpless by the day. Losing Ray, Henry's uncertainty. She couldn't work out what was going on. When Henry had held her hand back in the party, what

472

had he meant? She felt her seduction was failing, that she was hitting her head against a brick wall. *Perhaps it's time to give up*, she considered, *love can't be forced or manipulated*. Love was perverse, unfair, undemocratic. She looked up at the sky again. There was nothing out there at all, she mused bitterly. Nothing. Just our tiny, short, useless lives.

Leila was just turning to go back inside when she heard the sound of a bird singing. The trill was celestial, like a robin singing Mozart. She turned and saw the creature bounding across the fence and smiled. The sound brought some colour of memory – of her childhood, playing in the snow with her father, innocent and free. For a moment she felt her grief slip away from her shoulders like a cloak, felt a magical rush of sparkling joy, of Happy New Year.

Suddenly, impulsively, she leapt out into the snow, enjoying the messy crunch of her footprints. She knelt down and scrunched up a snowball. Her eyes narrowed at the figure on the swing, with their back to her. It was too good to resist. With a giddy, girlish whoop, she threw it.

Unfortunately, a little too hard.

The figure on the swing started violently, letting out a bellow of pain. He twisted his head back.

'Oh God – sorry! Oh sorry!' Leila did a double take. 'Henry! Henry?' She took a few cautious steps forwards.

'What a way to be woken on New Year,' Henry grumbled blearily, brushing snow from his coat. He looked up and they stared at each other. He kept looking, muttering something about Titania. Leila wriggled uncomfortably.

'What?' Leila frowned. 'Henry, are you OK?'

'No. No, I'm not. I think you owe me a New Year's hug as an apology.' He spread his arms, slightly awkwardly.

Shyly, aware of him watching her, she trudged through

the snow and gingerly sat down beside him. As it creaked loudly, they both jumped nervously, then giggled.

'So . . .' said Henry.

'So.'

'Happy New Year.'

'Happy New Year,' Leila said unhappily. She suddenly wished she had stayed inside. She remembered the couple she had seen on walking in, dancing cheek to cheek, absorbed in their own world. She remembered how she and Ray would always spend New Year's Eve excitedly planning out their year ahead – Easter holidays in England, at that old hotel in Oxford by the crumbling church, where the graveyard was carpeted in bluebells. Boating in the summer – nights in dark cabins, sharing sweaty lovemaking, gong to sleep with the murmur of the ocean like a lullaby. Skiing at Christmas; Ray was so much better than her and he'd always laugh at the way she stumbled about, catching her when she fell . . .

She was glad she'd walked away from that boy. She just didn't feel like having yet another one-night stand tonight. She wanted something deeper. A man for all seasons.

In a moment of vulnerability, she lifted her face to look at Henry and her insides caved in. It was just something about him, the sheer *Henryness* of his face; his snub nose and sleepy eyes that turned down at the corners, his hair mussed up like a schoolboy's, the slightly sheepish, apologetic smile. She wet her lips and for one mad moment she thought he was going to kiss her. But he turned away, blinking, looking down at the snow.

Well, of course he's not going to kiss you, you stupid cow, she told herself furiously. *As he said to you the other night, you are friends.*

'You know, Leila,' Henry said. 'I've been sitting here – thinking. Thinking about . . .'

'Yes?'

'Thinking of all kinds of things, trying to get my thoughts straight, and, um, there are a lot of great things about the new year. Lots of things to look forward to.'

'What – like going back to work with a hangover? The Budget? February blues? I don't even have a holiday booked. I don't much feel like going away. Last year I ended up in Greece and it was so dull on my own.'

'No – OK – let's be more specific. It's just – you said before that you had nothing to look forward to. Well, maybe you should, you know, get more out of life. Get out more . . .'

Patronising bastard. She narrowed her eyes.

' . . . go swimming with dolphins.'

'Dolphins?' Next he'd be telling her to buy crystals.

'I mean, I could come along too. It's something that's always appealed to me.'

'I guess you could,' said Leila. Suddenly the image seemed so much more appealing – she pictured Henry splashing her in the sea, cavorting on the beach together . . .

'I guess the point I'm circling around, the point I'm trying to make – not very well, I admit – is that there are a lot of great things in life. Like Proust, and great films, and walks in the country, and chocolate – OK, no, you don't like chocolate – and me.'

'Me?'

'Not you. Me. Me, me. Well – you and me – as in – you and me.'

'You and me?' Leila smiled, lacing her arm through his, resting her head against his shoulder. 'Yeah, you're right Henry. This time last year I can't say that I had any real friends. Even Katie – there are still walls between us. I'm so glad we are friends.'

Henry turned and they caught awkwardly in a kind of half-hug. Leila's body twisted uncomfortably. She felt him drop a tender kiss on her head. *He's the big brother I never had*, she thought. She snuggled in against the fuzzy warmth of his coat. His kisses drifted over her hair like a row of falling dominoes that couldn't stop and she lifted her head and the syllable, 'Oh—' was swallowed up by Henry pushing his mouth against hers and kissing her warmly and deeply, his fingers caressing her jaw.

'Look, Henry, I can't do this.' Leila broke off in shock. 'I know it's New Year, call me a frigid cow if you like. But I can't have a one-night stand. I'm not up for it.'

'I don't want a one-night stand, I want to marry you.'

'You want to what!' Leila leapt up.

The sudden jolt was too much for the creaky old swing to bear. The rope snapped and Henry was sent tumbling into the snow.

'Oh my God!' Leila burst into hysterical laughter. *Leila, I want to marry you. Marry you? Me?* 'Henry, are you OK? Do you really want to marry me? . . . we're supposed to be *friends* . . .'

'Come down here,' Henry croaked, spreading out his arms.

'What?'

'Down here in the snow. Next to me.'

'Henry, I'm not going to lie down in the snow. It's wet, I'm cold and it's silly. And I'm wearing my favourite dress which cost several thousand dollars.'

'Please, Leila.'

Leila paused. Fuck the dress.

'Oh God. OK.'

Gingerly, she slipped down beside him, then burst into

476

laughter. They were lying in the snow. *Leila, I want to marry you.*

Henry put his arms around her, enfolding her in his coat, caressing his nose against her, so close she could see the whites of his eyes, the earnest circles of his blue pupils, feel his warm breath on her icy-dry lips.

'Leila, I mean it. I love you. Will you . . . you know . . . do what I just asked?'

'I think so.'

Henry leaned over and kissed her joyously, but an unexpected anger made her pull back. She thought of walking down that hallway again, wilting flowers in her hands, seeing Katie half-naked on top of him.

'No,' she said, forcing out the words. 'No. I can't marry you.'

'What?'

'How can you just change your mind all of a sudden? Katie one day, me the next.'

'I don't know what I saw in Katie,' Henry looked puzzled. 'I just know I've always loved you. Maybe you needed to talk about Ray too. Maybe we just weren't ready. I love you, Leila,' he said with earnest intensity. 'I love your hair and eyes and the way you pretend to be so serious and never smile when I know you're laughing inside. I love your lips and—'

'It's all about sex, isn't it? You and your dick? Nothing ever changes—' She broke off. Her brain was like a boomerang. She kept trying to force herself to spit out insults, and yet, as though programmed on a helpless loop of love, she kept looking at him and feeling her heart bursting with love, her lips aching for his . . .

'Leila – no! In the beginning, it was about sex. Yes. When I first met you, I totally idealised you. I didn't know you. I do now. I think you're – no, I won't compliment

477

you, I know how you hate men who are *nice* to you.' He smiled nervously. 'So, if I tell you I absolutely loathe you, think you're the ugliest girl I've ever met and wouldn't marry you if you were the last girl on earth . . . then will you marry me?'

'Well . . .' Leila tried to grimace but her lips turned into a hopeless smile.

'So will you?'

'Probably,' Leila snorted. She could feel love for him burning inside her, whooshing in her blood, stinging in her eyes. She was drowning in it, unable to protest any more. She leaned over and kissed him, curling her fingers into his collar. Then she felt an unexpected sob welling up inside.

'Oh Henry. You've saved me, you really have.'

'I'm always going to be here for you now,' he whispered. 'Always, Leila. For ever. I'm going to look after you, I swear.' Then he smiled, kissing away a teardrop. 'Just as long as you really do want to marry me.'

She looked into his face and saw an image of Ray, his ghostly face hanging behind Henry's features, smiling into his smile. And then Ray misted away and he was just Henry, dear Henry.

'I do,' said Leila.

'You have changed your mind three times in the last five minutes.'

'A woman can change her mind as much as she likes. A man should be a woman's slave and adore her and—' Leila shrieked as Henry's icy wet fingers slid up her dress and tickled her. 'OK! Yes! Yes! YES! I do WANT TO MARRY YOU, OK, stop, YES!'

478

53
Jack

Jack rubbed his eyes. Where was he? What was he doing here, lying on a weirdly bulky bed? Jack looked down – he was covered with coats. Blue coats, black coats, anoraks, a pink feather boa, grey mittens, scarves twisting here and there through the layers of clothing like snakes. It was as though he was lying on a huge duvet like Joseph's Technicolour Dreamcoat.

Thump-thump. Dance music pounded in the background.

A flash of fear shot through his chest. Katie had been a dream. He was still in India, in some house, in—

'You fell asleep,' a voice whispered gently. 'It must have been all that jet-lag.'

'Katie,' he gasped in relief. She was lying beside him, propped up on one elbow, her chin curled in her hand.

'Don't look so worried.' She lay back down, nestling her cheek in the pillow. 'We lay down on the bed and that was it! Still, you were only out for twenty minutes or so. I've obviously exhausted you,' she teased him gently.

'Well, it doesn't say much for me as a lover, does it?' Jack muttered, managing a nervous smile. 'Falling asleep . . . just when we've got back together . . .'

479

He felt muzzy, as though his head was filled with smashed-up bricks. He lay back on the pillow for a moment, piecing together his fragments of memory into a coherent picture. Flying home, the airport, the mad taxi ride, the blonde, the fight. Kissing Katie. *Kissing Katie.* She'd forgiven him. The relief sluiced through him like a drink of fresh water, easing the dustiness in his brain, softening the hard, cracked feeling in his head. He swivelled round to look at her as she lay there, waiting, patient now, almost dreamy, ready for him.

And that was when it happened.

God, she's gorgeous. Jack felt his heart leap. He gaped down at her hair, swirling like the sun's rays over the pillow. A single tendril curled over her cheek and he gently pushed it back behind her ear. She let out a deep sigh, parted her lips and felt his erection sharpen.

I do love her, he said to himself, his feelings finally cementing into concrete, rock-hard resolution. *It's what I've been feeling all this time, building up inside me for the past few months. I did make the right decision to come back home. I love her. Plain and simple. Love. Her.*

She looked so fantastic, lying there on the pillow, her cheek squashed against the cotton, that he just wanted to watch her for ever. They stared at each other. Pupil to pupil. Playing an old game. Neither blinking, both trembling with bitten-back smiles and desire.

He held out for three minutes; three unbearable minutes of delicious lustful agony.

Then he bent down and tenderly brushed his lips against hers. Her scarlet top had slid off-kilter, down her arm, showing a rounded shoulder, like a peach. He leaned over and gently kissed it. He wanted to kiss every part of her – skin, hair, scar, freckle and pore.

'I—' she started but he put a finger to her lips.

If they started talking, Jack feared they would lose the mood. They were awake now, but they were still hazy, dreamy, drifting at the bottom of an ocean. Words would pull them up to the surface, burst the magic bubble.

Jack knew that, yes, they'd talked a lot and still needed to talk a lot more. In fact, they needed to spend a whole bloody week talking, but later. For now, he just wanted to show Katie how much he loved her. And he wanted to show her in the way Jack communicated best.

He rolled on top of her, gazing down, trailing his fingers over her face. She looked amazed for a moment, her eyes flitting down, seeing his erection. Jack smiled, pressing slightly harder, saying, *I want you.*

For one terrible moment she frowned, and he thought, *I've lost her again. She still doesn't trust me . . .*

And then she raised her lips, just a few centimetres, and Jack felt a huge joy bubbling up inside him. He leaned down and they met in the middle, sharing a long, delicious, gorgeous kiss.

Time meandered. The party, the muffled noise, seemed faraway. Everything was just about touch.

Jack had made love to so many girls. But in the past it had always been about his pleasure. Guiding their fingers, their mouths, encouraging them, like dancing girls, to please him.

But tonight he was desperate to give pleasure to Katie. To feel her shudder beneath him. To take her to the stars.

They kissed for what seemed like hours. On and on, until their mouths were like bruised cherries, their hands roaming nervously over each other, fingers shy, like school children charting new virgin territory. Then, palms flattened, their touch became more insistent. Jack slowly slid Katie's top up, wincing as it caught around her ears. Instinctively, she crossed her arms again, shy

481

and self-conscious. Gently, he peeled them away. *You're beautiful*, he whispered in her ear, cupping her breasts in his hands like fruit. The first touch brought such a flood of unbearable desire that he had to swallow it back, hold it tight inside him, pause for a moment to catch his breath. They fumbled through more clothes, searching through mazes for the centre. Bare skin met warm skin. He kissed and tasted every pore of her, bite-groaning as if he wished he could tooth through the layers of skin and slip inside her like a sprite. He adored her. The softness of her skin. The down of hair on her thighs, brushing his cheeks. Her freckles, like a dusting of icy sugar. The voluptuousness of her flesh, like a ripe peach; juice trickled into his mouth as he drank from her, deep and hungry, as though tipping back a bottle of delicious wine, feeling her legs against his cheeks, her toes curl against his shoulder blades. He closed his eyes and felt her orgasm ripple on his tongue, the infectious rhythm dancing into his quickening heart. He felt her stretch to high-pitched tautness, then slacken, her fingers sleepy in his hair. He opened his eyes, brushed a pubic hair from his lips. She smiled at him. His eyes stung with happiness.

He pressed his fingers down her spine as she rolled on top of him, kissing him with fierce passion, her cheek grating against his stubble. *You're beautiful*, he kept telling her. Over and over and over again. But it was never enough, the words seemed tiny. He could feel his desire flooding him now, waves roaring at the gates. He rolled back on top of her, parting her thighs gently, staring down at her as he entered inch by inch, eyes locked in love.

Outside, the wind stirred the trees teasingly, licking up leaves in its mouth. An owl hooted. Clouds concealed the blushing moon. The night gathered itself up and gazed in through the window in wonder at the two lovers.

This is what making love is, he realised as he felt himself inside her, slow at first, teasing her until finally he felt everything spin into an uncontrollable climax and he pushed his lips down hard on hers and blackness whirled and stars fizzed and he heard her voice saying, *I love you, Jack*.

Afterwards they just held each other, listening to their breathing slowing down, bodies damp and warm against each other. Katie nuzzled into him luxuriously, crying quietly without him seeing; Jack kissed her gently. His eyes slid beyond her to a plane trailing across the night sky. He thought of their fight, the way he'd fled. Of India, the temple he had discovered in Delhi. His mind had been whirling with so much self-loathing, he'd felt dizzy and sick. He'd sat in the cool, egg-shaped building and it had felt like a dark womb. The faces of gods and devas had smiled at him; hands had reached out as if to soothe him. He had watched a man in yellow robes enter, curl his body into the locus position and sit with an expression of such profound calm that Jack had felt envious. He'd closed his eyes and whispered to himself; *What am I going to do? What do I really want?*

And somehow, underneath all the rubble of fear and self-doubt, he'd known deep in his heart that he wanted Katie. Pure and simple. He didn't want to travel any more; he just wanted to come home. So he'd caught a plane. And here he was. At last.

'I thought you'd never forgive me,' Jack finally whispered in her ear.

'Of course I forgive you, I love you.' Katie turned, with a smile. Outside in the party, there were the muffled cries of 'TEN . . . NINE . . . EIGHT . . . SEVEN . . .' Katie kissed him again, and Jack felt his heart thump with joy. 'Happy New Year.'

★

483

54 ★
Charlie

Well, despite finally making Jack happy, Puck and I were
still ostracised from the fairy camp. We ended up getting
arrested, shunted off for community service to the planet
Venus and paid two petals a day to sweep the semen off
the floor after the alien sex shows.

Oh, OK. I'm only joking.

Puck and I took full credit for saving the humans' love
lives. (OK, so a few spells went wrong along the way but
we weren't going to tell the other fairies that.)

We were not only pardoned, we became heroes. There
was even a ceremony where we received the Hedgehog
Cross for nobility, a little ribbon of bluebell silk. It was
funny, as Titania leaned forwards to pin on my award, she
whispered into my ear, 'I was watching you all the way,
you know. I knew you would make the journey.' And as I
looked up into her eyes, I felt choked with such an intense
love that I just wanted to surrender, to bow before her and
kiss her feet.

And, I have to say – being a superstar does improve
your love life. At the Sprite Disco, fairies fought to buy
me drinks.

'Come on, Charlie,' Puck came up and whispered in my ear. 'Let's get out of here and have some fun! Come on, CHARLIE, let's GO dance on the STARS!'

I let out a whoop of joy. He grabbed my hand and spun me up into the air. The air pressure sucked us together and, body to body, we burst upwards like a rocket, through the clouds, through the atmosphere, up, up to the glittering blackness of space.

Ever tried dancing on the stars?

It's so much fun.

'God, I haven't played this in years!' I giggled. It's very much a game fairies play when they're kids. It's a bit like your human version of 'It', only our game is played on celestial stepping-stones.

'OK!' Puck clamped his hands over his eyes. 'You've got a five-star head start, and then I'M COMING AFTER YOU!'

I leapt giddily on to a star, on to Orion's Belt, and a few seconds later I heard Puck bouncing after me. As I leapt from one star to the next, I could hear Puck laughing breathlessly and that set me off too. Soon we were lurching about like drunks. Looking back, I could see Puck gaining ground. He'd catch me soon! I turned and jumped down on to another silvery pad, Puck's hand missing me by inches.

'Ha! Missed!' I whirled round and screamed with delight.

'Just you wait, you don't stand a chance!' he yelled back.

I laughed again and a thousand laughs reverberated after me. In space, echoes are much louder; my giggles bounced off the stars and the moon, booming through the air.

Star to star. Jump, jump. I realised too late that I'd

chosen the wrong route – I was now heading for the end of Orion's Belt and the stars were growing further and further apart and the jumps were becoming more and more scary. As I hopped, I could feel my legs stretching with the strain and my stomach fluttering when I saw the long drop below.

'I'm going to get you!' Puck bounced on to the star behind me.

I turned and gazed at the star a good three-feet away, suspended in the blackness. I could do it. I squeezed my eyes shut, took a deep breath and leapt across, yelling, 'No you're not – ARGGGGH!'

The sky spun. The stars were falling away from me. In a flash I saw Puck gazing down at me from his star, his eyes round with shock. The air rushed around me and I fell, fell, fell, hurtling into nothingness. I could hear a voice in my head yelling, 'Fly, fly, fly!' but my wings were frozen in shock.

'Urgh!'

I landed with a thump on something warm and heavy. I opened my eyes and realised Puck had caught me in his arms. For a moment he gazed down at me breathlessly, with laughing eyes. Then he collapsed with the weight and we fell a few more feet on to a cloud.

'Phew!' he said.

'Argh! Are you OK!'

'I'm OK. Are you OK?'

'I think so . . .' I tried to test my limbs, but it was hard to concentrate when Puck's body was still tangled up with mine and we were lying face to face in the clouds. All alone. Our mouths inches apart. 'I think so . . .' I repeated breathlessly, feeling a gulp in my throat and a warmth spreading across my cheeks and tingling in the tips of my fingers.

486

Puck reached up and ran his fingertips along my hairline, tracing my eyebrows, circling my eyes. I smiled at him, my heart swelling with love.

'Well, I was your superhero. I saved your life, you owe me one now, Charlie,' he joked. His voice came out all thick and funny.

'Oh yeah, Puck, I'm sure Superman will be handing in his resignation.' I squealed as he tickled me indignantly.

'You ungrateful damsel in distress!'

'I'm hardly in distress, Puck, you're the one in distress.'

'Uh?'

'You. You get all shy and your voice goes weird when we're close together. It's sweet.'

Puck ducked his head boyishly and I laughed, planting a kiss on his shoulder. Then he looked up and murmured something like, 'It's because I love you so much,' but his voice was too quiet and the words rushed out in a jumble and before I could ask if it was true his lips were on mine and we were kissing. A long, slow kiss, so fabulous I felt my limbs sink into the clouds and I wanted to stay in his warmth for ever.

Hearing a faint noise in the distance, we drew back self-consciously.

'Hey, look!'

The first ray of dawn was smudging across the sky. In the distance, Aurora's Chariot sailed past, led by white horses with drumming hooves. Hidden in the clouds, we watched them blaze across the horizon like a pink comet. Puck and I turned and shared a smile, revelling in the beautiful sight.

We kissed and Puck said blurtingly, 'Charlie, we may be simple, plain old fairies who can't love properly, but I do love you.' We kissed and I said, 'Puck, you know, I love you so much I think my heart is going to break.' We kissed as the clouds lightened, staining our bodies salmon pink, and I gasped as I felt his fingers curve gently along the edge of my wings, trembling over the silver threads like a most delicate harp-player, sending thrills of delight shuddering all over me. We kissed as the clouds seemed to sigh beneath us, our toes and legs curling together, limbs moulding, lips smudging, eyes glinting red with love-lust, until I could barely tell where his body left off and mine began and I gasped, O Puck O yes stroke my wings of love I love you Puck O O O it's such a pleasure to give to you forever all my love . . .

55
Henry

Three Months Later

Regent's Park was full of fairies.

A few young girls, their hair braided with green lace like coils of seaweed, laughingly tugged each other's plaits. A girl, dressed as Titania, struggled with a blonde wig. Demetrius changed from jeans and T-shirt into an old-fashioned costume; Helena swigged back her can of Coke and walked across the empty outdoor stage, a metal semi-circle erected on the freshly cut grass.

It was Spring, and the air was laced with lilac and new blossom. The sun was setting on the mauve horizon, smoky with streaks of twilight. There was a sense of magic in the air; of summer, new growth, holidays, excitement, journeys, anticipation.

In the make-shift dressing-room in the white caravan behind the stage, Henry was being made-up. He could hardly believe it; it was finally happening. In less than an hour he would be up on stage for the opening night of the Outdoor River Theatre's production of *A Midsummer Night's Dream*. Last night he'd suffered a nightmare that the audience would be papier mâché people made from newspaper, who'd just sit there, lurid, sarcastic smiles painted across their headlined faces.

'Two friends of yours are here, Henry.' Emma, who was playing Titania, popped her head around the door, blonde wig now firmly in place. 'Jack and Katie.'

Henry hastily pulled his blue dressing gown over his camouflaged body. It flapped against his legs as he hurried out to see them. Jack and Katie did a double take when they saw him and he broke into a smile.

'God!' said Jack.

'Henry – you look – very *green*,' Katie laughed. 'Oh wow, it's so nice to see you.' She touched his cheek and leaned in to give him a warm hug, then backed off as he gently pulled away apologetically.

'Sorry – this stuff comes off,' he explained. He opened his dressing gown and gave them a peek. His pale body was streaked with make-up – jungle colours. Except for a thin green thong and the odd leaf stuck on to his muddy chest, he was gloriously naked.

'Wow, Henry, next you'll be joining the Chippendales,' said Jack, letting out a wolf whistle.

'Fuck off,' Henry laughed.

'Jack, behave.' Katie giggled again, touching Jack's arm. Jack turned and touched her arm back in mock imitation, then gave her a cuddle, lifting her an inch from the ground so that she let out a squeal. She leaned up and gently kissed his jaw.

The gesture, though tiny, went through Henry's heart like a knife. The brush of her lips. Her upturned face. The love in her eyes. God, Jack was a lucky bloke.

'Well . . . I . . . I . . .' Henry realised he'd been staring and he suddenly felt self-conscious. He scratched his head.

490

'Of course – you'd better carry on getting ready,' Katie smiled.

'Great. You're looking great – thanks for coming. Let's catch up after the show.'

'Break an elbow,' said Jack.

Back in his dressing room, Henry seated himself on a white plastic chair and allowed Mira, the make-up artist, to dip her sponge in her palette and rub colours over his face. Olive green for his forehead; black contours to hollow out his cheeks; tree-bark brown over his eyelids. Henry closed his eyes, listening to the slosh and swill of the paint, feeling his face automatically wince and blink at the metamorphic assault.

He couldn't get over Jack and Katie.

They looked so amazing together. So right. Like two spoons, peas in a pod, all the clichés. So happy. So healthy – as if their love was an energising balm. Jack was no longer his usual gritty-stubbled, greasy-haired, bug-eyed self, while Katie was all sparkly-eyed and pink-cheeked and possibly a little plumper. In the past Katie had always seemed a little self-conscious of her figure, as though she was wearing a skin which didn't quite fit. Now she looked as though she'd happily swelled into her shape, and there was something joyous about her curves – as if she was feasting on new-found happiness.

It was all just so unexpected. When Henry had seen them together at the New Year party, a lot of people had been whispering, 'About time too – after all these years!' But Henry had seen them emerge from the bedroom, hand in hand, and he'd just wanted to tear them apart, shake Katie by the shoulders and scream at her, 'Don't you realise what you're doing? Jack will just chew you up and spit you out – are you mad?' But he'd bitten his lip and kept his mouth shut. Ironically, he and Leila had

491

speculated as to how long it would last. Leila had predicted three days; Henry had given it a week, to be generous.

When Henry had heard they were still together three months later, he couldn't believe it. He'd sent the invitation to the play to *their* new place in Camden – where apparently they'd even taken out a *mortgage*. Jack was now working full-time as a photographer, satisfying his travelling thirst with brief assignments abroad. Even Dido had been returned to her beloved master, much to Susie's delight. All the same, Henry had pictured Jack turning up with a mini-harem of admirers, Katie trailing behind like a pathetic dog. Or Katie all nail-bitey and tired, clinging to Jack's arm like a child, watching him watch other girls, wondering if he was going to commit infidelity just as he wondered whether he could get away with committing infidelity.

But no. Instead Jack had kept his arm around her like a warm shawl, as if he wanted to love and protect her. And the expression on his face had been one of pride. As though he was proud to show her off to the world and say, *She's mine.*

For a moment Henry felt jealousy mixed with the warmth of respect. Jealousy because Henry had always imagined he'd be the one asking Jack to be best man at his wedding, never the other way round. Henry had thought Jack would end up as an eternal playboy, one of those jaded types who dyed their hair black, raced around in fast cars and picked up twenty-year-old girls with bottle-yellow hair and false breasts.

But today there was something different about Jack. He had the calm air of a man who had decided to stop spending his life rushing from place to place and finally stand still. He looked like a wild tiger who had been tamed. He used to resemble someone who might punch you after too many beers on a Saturday night; now he seemed the type to spend his Saturdays walking around IKEA looking for curtains. And Henry, though he hadn't liked to say anything, just in case he was wrong and put his foot in it, had spotted a glittering diamond on Katie's finger . . .

'Could you see me at IKEA, Mira?' Henry suddenly asked, sending a splash of green paint dribbling down his cheek. Mira bit her lip and tried to repair the damage.

'Eh?'

'IKEA. Could you see me, you know, shopping there for . . . whatever they sell there . . . cushions and stuff . . .'

'Er, no. Why?'

'Nothing.' Henry's face broke into a smile as she held up the mirror to enable him to survey her work. But he didn't see the Puck staring back at him, the mischievous faery with slanting eyebrows and slitty, sparkling eyes and a cruel mouth with a seductive curl. He saw what the make-up, caught in the pores and grooves of his skin, had highlighted: fans around his eyes, the grooves in his forehead, the curves in his cheeks. He was starting to look old and he suddenly felt very alone.

Please be there, Henry willed her, as he stood in the shadowy wings. A chorus girl was beside him, chewing gum like a frenetic cow, gasping in shaky breaths, muttering her lines. Henry didn't need to scan the crowds of upturned faces. He'd saved a seat for Leila in the front row. A little 'Reserved' note was flapping in the wind on the empty seat like a white flag.

'Encore!' Jack cheered, leading the standing ovation, clapping until his hands hurt. He smiled down at Katie, who grinned back at him, and they carried on clapping monotonously, staring at each other, unable to stop smiling.

The actors took their bows. As the applause rang out, Henry looked up and saw two hundred faces beaming with delight and adoration and felt that wonderful *whoosh! I did it! I was a star!*

He felt a sense of calmness, a sense of relief that made up for all the nerves of rehearsals, the days of doubting, the uncertainty of whether he was in the right play at the right time. And yet the contentment left a sense of incompleteness too. After six months of hard work, rehearsals, tears and tantrums, suddenly it was all over so quickly. And it all seemed so frustratingly . . . *insignificant,* somehow. It was a huge achievement for Henry; for the audience it was just a brief evening's entertainment. They would take a little of the magic home with them tonight but by the morning it would have trickled away, been forgotten . . .

And then he glanced across at Leila again. She had turned up at the start of Act III, mouthing, 'Sorry'. Henry's performance had changed radically – critics who had been scribbling 'and Henry Badingham gave a subdued, melancholic interpretation of Shakespeare's Puck' looked confused but concluded, 'but in the finale he came alive as Puck, gleaming with wickedness and *joie de vivre.*'

For the first time, Henry didn't give a stuff what the critics thought. It had all been a private performance for Leila. Nobody else.

As they took another bow, he gazed over the rows of heads towards the milky full moon, pregnant with promise and blessings. *Maybe this time next year Leila and I will be married.* He caught her eye again. She was smiling at him with such glowing pride. He kept looking. She kept looking. Henry blinked; Emma was tugging at his wrist, pulling him back towards the wings. He glanced back at the audience one last time, embarrassed when Emma whispered jokingly that he couldn't get enough of the fame. But he didn't care about the crowds, just about her. She was still looking, craning her neck to see over a man with a bald head.

And he knew then that everything would be all right. They would go home tonight, celebrate, spend the night in their moonlit bed, share a bottle of champagne, laugh, joke, confide. She still struggled with their relationship at times; she had asked for a two-year engagement, asked to take things slowly. But she was starting to open up to him now; her old skin of cold hardness was beginning to be shed. Every day he took a step closer to her. He was learning. Not to analyse her or put her on a pedestal, not to try to play games, but to be himself and play it cool. And yet he couldn't swallow back his rising excitement as one last look towards her sealed his fate, his future, his marriage, his children, (two, a boy and a girl) and his grandchildren (six) – that one glance on which the rest of his life pivoted. In the end, spells weren't always necessary; sometimes humans could get it right. Sometimes they could be guided by their hearts and stumble, if a little clumsily, towards The One.

Epilogue:
Charlie

★

★

The Search For A Narrator . . .

. . . I can hear the tape whirring . . . if I lean in closer I can see that the brown spools of the tape are thinning. The tape will soon be full and so my tale had better end . . .

In a way, my parting words are really my prologue. Or my acknowledgements. I think the only thing I have left to give is an explanation to our readers as to just how the book came to be published.

Basically, Puck and I decided that our adventures were tremendously entertaining and that there would be no harm in making a little money out of them. OK – we wanted to sell our story. I hate that expression because it conjures up images of footballers, the *News of the World*, and girls with plastic breasts getting wadges of cash. No, we wanted a proper narrator. After all, throughout history we have used writers to tell our tales, from W.B. Yeates to Shakespeare. It was simply a case of finding the right person for the twenty-first century – someone who would give our story a modern, upbeat feel, who would portray us as funky, sexy sprites of the night rather than fluffy old flower fairies.

Puck and I spent a long time searching for the right author. We whistled through the London Book Fair (yawn), we hung around the Groucho Club (even bigger yawn), we flipped and flicked through libraries until finally we came up with a shortlist. Now obviously we didn't just want *any* writer. We wanted an author who preferably had won at the bare minimum The Booker Prize. OK, if that was aiming a little high, we wanted a writer who was an illustrious star in the literary world. After haggling over Julian Barnes versus Michael Ondaatje, we finally decided on the most elegant and exquisite Evelyn Waugh. Until we realised he was dead. Puck suggested some guy called Nick Hornby, who apparently is doing incredibly well, but he was bound to cost a fortune and Titania had banned us from any more fiddles with the National Lottery.

And so we stooped a little lower . . . in fact a lot lower . . . and ended up with Deborah Wright.

Why her? She had little success, no reviews, no acclaim. Her only work to date had been a light-hearted romantic comedy called *Olivia's Bliss* which had a bright pink cover and some spicy sex scenes. But we figured that she must have a brain, since she'd been to Oxford and studied under the legendary Dr Stephen Gill. (Of course, we found out later, much later, that she hadn't done a great deal of work for her degree and her idea of reading *A Midsummer Night's Dream* was skimming the entire play ten minutes before her tutorial.) To be honest, she was really quite disappointing. And ugly. I mean – we were hoping for some twenty-six-year-old babe who'd look good on TV – but I guess you can't have everything. The main thing was, we felt that Deborah would tell our story as it should be told. She had no literary reputation, no acclaimed style, and would therefore have less of an inclination to lacquer over

497

our narrative with her own authorial varnish. And OK –
let's admit it. She was cheap. Very cheap.

We visited Deborah one night at her home in Surrey.
She was, unsurprisingly, a little surprised to see us. But a
few spells, a nervous breakdown and some psychiatric
treatment later, she was putty in our hands.

She didn't have much faith in us, I can tell you. She
was about to begin writing her second novel and she kept
saying, 'Look, I was actually planning to write a standard
romantic comedy . . . I don't know what my agent is going
to say, he's already talking to Random House . . .'

'Just do it,' said Puck, giving her his most alluring
smile.

She melted (yes, I'm afraid that despite being human,
even Deborah was not immune to Puck's charms). She
called up her agent, Simon Trewin, who to her amazement said the idea was 'totally fantastic' (though what he
didn't know was that we'd performed a spell involving
three dead toads the night before). He then sold the novel
to Tara Lawrence at Little, Brown (that lot took fifteen
toads in all), who, to everyone's amazement and our complete amusement, gave her a ridiculously large sum of
money for the deal. Naturally, Puck and I are taking at
least half of her royalties. So you needn't fear that the
£5.99 you've spent on this book is going to support
Deborah's penchant for ice cream, chocolate and books.
Oh no. While Deborah continues to write long, tearful
letters to her bank manager at Lloyds TSB, we're going to
be living it up with a two-month holiday on Venus in a
five-star luxury hotel . . .

And here we are. I'm sitting on a table, Deborah has
left the tape recorder running and I've dictated my little
tale in just under three hours. I know I've rambled on, but
she's going to edit it all (I'm sure this whole section will be

edited out) and fill in the human stories with her own imaginative colour. If everything goes to plan, Puck and I are going to be the most famous media couple since Posh and Becks . . .

Night is falling; I see a few stars winking up in the sky and Puck's dark-winged form flitting in to me. Ah – Puck. Every time I see him, I feel like I'm falling from that star all over again, falling into his arms, into an ocean of love . . .

The tape is running out but let's see if Puck would like to add a few words.

If we shadows have offended . . .